Praise for the novels of Chandra ~~~~~~~

"Blumberg makes the will-they-won't-they dance believable and exciting with sexy banter and plenty of humor throughout. Readers will root for this intelligent couple to get their happily ever after."
—*Publishers Weekly* on *Second Tide's the Charm*

"Chandra does what she does best in *Second Tide's the Charm*—delivering witty writing, nuanced characters, heartwarming romance, and maximum nerdiness in this absolute gem of a summer romance. Heroine Hope can't stop talking about sharks, and I can't stop talking about this book!"
—Jen Comfort, author of *Midnight Duet*

"Replete with instantly likable characters and relatable pop-culture references, Blumberg's debut is warm, engaging, and emotionally honest. Alisha and Quentin's gradual movement toward companionship hits all the right notes, and their interactions are both meaningful and fun."   —*Kirkus Reviews* on *Digging Up Love*

"The headline-making dinosaur dig offers a unique spin on the classic small-town contemporary romance, and readers will be craving treats after reading the descriptions of Alisha's baked goods. Blumberg's sweet romance offers a perfect recipe for a delectable read, combining diversity, smart characters, and a delicious love story."   —*Booklist*, starred review, on *Digging Up Love*

"Rival chefs are forced into a business partnership that sparks unlikely love in Blumberg's sweet second Taste of Love romance . . . Readers will root for this couple in both business and love."
—*Publishers Weekly* on *Stirring Up Love*

"A moving story imbued with thoughtfulness and generosity of spirit."   —*Kirkus Reviews* on *Stirring Up Love*

Also by Chandra Blumberg

Second Tide's the Charm
Digging Up Love
Stirring Up Love

Love is an Open Book

CHANDRA BLUMBERG

CANARY STREET PRESS

CANARY STREET PRESS™

Recycling programs
for this product may
not exist in your area.

ISBN-13: 978-1-335-01657-7

Love is an Open Book

Canary Street Press
22 Adelaide St. West, 41st Floor
Toronto, Ontario M5H 4E3, Canada
CanaryStPress.com

Printed in U.S.A.

For everyone who believes in the
power of happy endings.

one

Gavin

Nine Years Ago

Past midnight, and all I want to do is take off my backpack and fall into bed, but my apartment is blocked by a woman with her cheek pressed to the door, palm cupped around her ear like she's listening. The stairwell door closes behind me with a hollow thud, and the stranger jerks upright, meeting my gaze with wide eyes. She swipes her sleeve across her cheek.

Even from this distance, it's clear she's been crying. Is still crying, from the loud sniff that cuts through the silence.

"You okay?" My eyes shift from her tear-streaked face to the latched door. I moved in a month ago, at the start of the spring semester, and my roommate seems like a decent dude, but if he's abandoning crying women in the hallway at midnight—or anytime—we're going to have a problem.

Instinct propels me forward, closing the space between us to where I can talk without raising my voice, but far enough not to crowd her. "Did he lock you out?"

"Forgot something inside." Her gaze is steady, head high, though her brown eyes are blurry with unshed tears, thick lashes clumped with moisture. "I can come back later." But she glances at the door again, like she's not ready to leave without whatever she left behind.

Shifting the grocery bag to my left hand, I stick my hand in my pocket for my keys, ready to let her in, but hesitate. What if I've got it wrong? Could she be a vindictive ex trying to get revenge? Granted, Ted doesn't seem like the kind of guy to inspire violence—or passion—but you never know.

Then again, what damage could she possibly do? She's a head shorter than me, and about my age, I'm guessing. Her dark brown hair, parted at an angle, falls in a smooth curve to the collar of her puffer coat. Salt clings to the toes of her boots, probably from the sludgy sidewalks around campus. My own shoes are soaked after trudging through snowdrifts, but this stranger at my door has pushed aside my desire to hurry inside and warm up.

She's taking me in, too, not bothering to hide her evaluation. "You're Ted's new roommate?"

I nod. "And you are?"

"Ted and I . . ." She sniffs and blinks rapidly. "We, uh . . ." A tear slips down her cheek and she swipes it away with the heel of her hand, like she's frustrated with herself.

Enough of this. I hoist up the shopping bag, holding it open so she can see the paper products I picked up at the corner store. "Butts or spills?"

Her arched brows tug together in a frown, but she steps closer and peers at the paper towels and package of toilet paper.

"Butts or spills," she repeats, deadpan. Eyes lifting to mine, she gives me a wry grin. "Let me guess. Marketing major?"

Faking dejection, I sigh. "Just know that if you tell me to find a new dream, you're not the first."

She breathes out a laugh. Progress. But her nose is still running, so I raise the bag higher, prompting her to pick one.

She grabs the toilet paper. "Butts it is." Her eyes cut toward the door, a frown tightening her brows. "Assholes, more like." Tearing open the package, she takes out a roll and unwinds it, dabbing at her face.

I found my roommate through an online post and don't know him well, but I'm guessing she does. And if she says he's an asshole . . . "Want to talk about it?"

Her dark brows arrow inward. "With the stranger who caught me lurking at his door?"

"With your boyfriend's roommate." A guess, but not a stretch.

She blows her nose. "Ted's not really an asshole. We've been friends since freshman orientation. And he's not my boyfriend, either. Not anymore."

That explains the tears. "Breakups suck. How long were you together?" I go home most weekends to help out my dad with our family's tree nursery, so even though I've never met her, for all I know, they've been together awhile.

"Long enough for him to realize he chose the wrong sister."

"What?" I lose my grip on the toilet paper I was jamming back into the bag, and it bounces to the carpet by our feet.

She stoops to retrieve it. "Wish I was kidding. I told him I was falling for him, but he told me he'd made a mistake."

"Unless she's your identical twin, that's messed up." The moment the words leave my mouth, I wish I could yank them back. Humor is my coping mechanism, but I'm actually appalled on her behalf.

To my relief, she laughs, an incredulous squeak. "This isn't a romance novel."

"That happens in romance novels?"

"Mistaken identity, falling for a twin, yeah." She shrugs, like that's not a wild idea. "But in this case, he wasn't confused, just too unsure of his feelings to speak up sooner."

I can't imagine a world where someone thinks telling their

girlfriend they prefer her sister is remotely okay. "Does your sister know?"

Impossible to imagine how my brother would react if one of my exes told him she liked him instead of me, since Scott and I are pretty much opposites.

"According to him, no," she says.

"She won't go for it." Then again, what do I know? I just want to make her feel better.

Confirming my doubts, she says, "She might. He's hot, and smart."

I disagree with the last one. "He was also your boyfriend."

"My friend, first." She crumples the piece of toilet paper she'd used to wipe her tears. "Dating was a new development. And according to what he told me tonight, the worst mistake of his life."

"You're not a mistake." That's not what she said. But somehow I can tell that's how she interpreted his words.

Dating someone when you have feelings for their sibling? A mistake, for sure. But *his* mistake. One he didn't own, not if he waited to tell her until now.

Tears gleam in her eyes again, and she tips her head up, blinking toward the ceiling. A drop slides down her cheek and catches in her gold hoop earring. Another quiet sniff, like she's doing her best to hold it together, has me wrecked.

I'm sure she doesn't want a hug from a stranger, but I don't want to just leave her out here when she's having a rough time. I shrug off my coat and lay it in a folded heap on the carpet. "Want to take a minute?" I ask, wondering if she'll take me up on the offer or bolt.

She must be really wrung out, because she lowers herself down and tucks her knees to her chest. I follow suit, shifting my backpack to my lap.

"Got any food in there?" Her voice sounds steadier. Resigned, not fragile.

"Wish I did." I skipped dinner to study. "Just a project for class." I unzip my backpack and ease out the potted *Monstera deliciosa*, its deep green leaves glossy.

"Did you just casually pull a houseplant out of your bag?" She might think I'm weird, but she's grinning, tears nowhere to be seen, so I'm calling it a win.

"My lab partner didn't have room for another one at her place, so this little guy is mine now." Adopting stray plants has been a surprise bonus of studying horticulture.

"Better you than me," she says. "I can't even make bouquets last more than a day."

"Not your fault," I say. "Those are dead already."

She frowns. "Morbid."

"Just saying, have you ever owned a live plant?" She still looks skeptical, so I add, "They're easier to take care of than a pet, and they're not judgmental like cats."

"Cats are not judgmental."

"Next you'll tell me they're cuddly." The barn cats around the tree farm never let me within twenty yards of them.

"They are, and if you try to convince me plants are cuddly," she says, "I'm out."

"Cuddly, no," I admit. "But they are good listeners."

"Let me guess, you name your plants, too."

"That would be weird." I pull a face. "They pick their own names."

Shaking her head, she says, "It's nice to joke around after the day I've had."

"Who says I'm joking?"

She laughs, and I join in, feeling the tension leave my shoulders. I just listened to a voicemail from my dad, asking if I'll be able to visit on the long weekend, even though I was there last week. He's an awesome father, but he's relied on me a lot in the past few years.

"You're weird, but I like you."

"Should I be offended?" I'm not; I like her, too.

Her lips curve into a smile. "Weird is good."

"Are you lumping Ted in with us?" I drop my voice, even though there's no way he can hear us from inside the apartment, and fake a whisper. "Because he bought a doormat to put in front of the bathtub, and I think that's super weird."

"Not that kind of weird," she says, laughing. "The comfy kind."

"Weird has a feeling?"

She opens her fist, the balled-up paper unfurling in her grasp like a gardenia blossom. "Everything does, if you sit with it long enough."

If that's true, then talking with her feels like homemade lemonade on the first day of summer. Sweet and refreshing and everything you didn't know you'd been missing.

"For the record, I told him the doormat was an awful idea," she says. "But he insisted it was designed to withstand—" She starts giggling before she can finish the sentence, and I prod her with my elbow, forgetting we barely know each other like that, but she doesn't seem to mind, just holds up her hand to signal she needs a minute.

Finally, she squeaks out, "Built to handle all kinds of weather."

Now I'm shaking with laughter, too, but also horrified. "What exactly is going on in our bathroom?"

"You tell me," she says, eyes sparkling. But then she sobers up. "Not like I'll be hanging around the apartment after this. What Ted did sucks, but I think I'm most upset to lose a friend."

From where I'm sitting, he never deserved her. "Doesn't sound like he was a good friend to begin with."

"He was, though. The mistake was mixing friendship and romance." She sighs. "It's just that Ted felt safe. I never wanted to fall in love with someone who I thought could break my heart. Passion is overrated. I see it all the time, my friends falling hard and fast for someone they met in class, broken up by finals week. Even my parents. To hear them tell it, they were madly in love. Couldn't see a future without each other." She gave him a wry look. "Split up before I was born."

"My parents aren't together anymore, either." I don't bring it up much because it feels strange, like my parents' relationship status should be the last thing on the mind of a twenty-one-year-old guy. It should be, but thanks to my dad, it isn't.

The monstera's leaves brush my chin as I turn to her. "They got divorced during my senior year of high school. And seeing my dad struggle these past few years . . ." My mom seemed to rebound faster, but she moved to Madison. Made new friends.

Meanwhile Dad stayed on the farm, pouring himself into the business and not making time for himself. "He calls me whenever he's feeling down, telling me how much he wished he could've shown her sooner how he felt instead of throwing himself into work. It's a weird spot to be in, consoling him over Mom moving out. But I get it. He lost his best friend." And now he's just lost.

For a second, I wonder if I should've kept this to myself. She's dealing with her own heartbreak. But she leans into me, just enough to feel her warmth through the layers of our jackets. A soft, unyielding pressure. "That's a lot to handle," she says. "For all of you."

It has felt like a lot, even though I haven't been able to voice it. But she did. I'm grateful for that, but I'm not sure how to thank her. Instead, I say, "Anyway, sounds like you know as well as I do that love's not a sure thing, but you took a chance. That's brave."

"What part of this situation makes you think I'm brave?" Her eyes are puffy, the tip of her nose reddened. She looks vulnerable, but I have no doubt she's stronger than I am.

"You told Ted you had feelings for him. That takes guts. Meanwhile, he didn't say anything until he had to. Like a coward."

I run my hand through my hair, realizing I might've taken it too far. "Sorry, I know he's your friend."

She traces the edge of a leaf with her thumb. "He said that's why he waited so long to tell me. He didn't want to lose me as a friend."

I twist toward the door with an involuntary jerk of my head, scowling, as if my roommate can see my disapproval. "Okay, yeah, I'd definitely like to have words with him."

She laughs, the sound low and throaty, then she shifts to face me. "I have a better idea. How do you feel about a little light thievery? You could serve justice by retrieving what I left behind."

"Are we talking valuables?" I'm thinking a necklace or something.

"A book," she says. "Or it might be one day." She looks unsure of herself again. "I'm trying to write a romance novel, and I asked Ted to read it like a month ago. He hasn't gotten around to it yet, and now I don't want him to."

She put herself out there and got burned for it? I can't leave her book in Ted's clutches. "I'm going in." Passing her the plant, I say, "Hold Frank for me."

"Frank?"

I duck my head, wondering if this is the moment I go from "cool weird" to weirdo. "It's a monstera."

"Frankenstein," she says, catching the reference. "Cute."

"Hey, show some respect," I tease. "That cute plant will grow to be over ten feet tall." I stand up and dig my keys out of my pocket.

"Oh, tough guy, huh?" she asks the plant, then looks up at me. "Don't worry, I'll keep your baby plant safe while you rescue my book."

I flash her a smile, even though my guts are twisting at the thought of searching through my roommate's stuff to find her book. "I trust you."

Mia

As Ted's roommate slips inside the apartment, I realize this is probably the reason he hasn't wanted to hang out at his place this semester. No secret he's got an inferiority complex, and his roommate, I just discovered, is a very attractive dude. A cute plant daddy, in joggers and a puffer jacket he stripped off to give me a comfy place to sit. The kind of wholesome guy my single friends would be falling over each other to talk to, but the idea of another relationship churns my stomach.

Ted was the sensible choice. Sure, there weren't butterflies and our kisses left me lukewarm, but he's been a good friend these past three years. We met in a freshman mixer and hit it off. I thought dating would be like our friendship, but better.

Turns out he's been harboring feelings for my sister since they'd met while helping me move into my apartment last fall.

My legs are falling asleep, so I stretch them out in front of me, holding the potted plant on my lap. Frank, Ted's roommate called it. I know the plant's name but not his. I should probably fix that since he's currently helping to preserve my dignity. It's embarrassing to be at the mercy of a stranger, but not as embarrassing as slinking back to ask for the manuscript myself like I'd been considering doing before he showed up.

The door creaks open, and the stranger in question leans through the opening, tousled golden-brown hair highlighted against the white doorjamb. "No sign of it yet, but he's asleep, so I'm going in."

Startled, I ask, "Where?"

"His room." He darts a glance over his shoulder, like he's worried Ted will materialize behind him. Poor guy is clearly not used to sneaking around.

"You don't have to. I'll text him tomorrow and ask him to bring it to me." Even if the thought sets my skin crawling.

He shakes his head. "Don't worry, I'll find it." The door closes before I can protest again, and I'm left with the impression of his blue eyes sparking with determination.

What will happen if Ted wakes to find his roommate rifling through his stuff? Hopefully he won't catch any heat for helping me out. Or what if he does find it, but instead of coming right back out, he flips through the pages, curious. The thought of a stranger reading my words is . . . Well, exhilarating, but also fills me with the urge to change my name and move to a remote Scottish island where I'll make a new life with only seabirds for company.

I lean over and press my ear to the crack between the door and the frame, trying to hear what's going on. The door opens, and I tumble sideways, but there's a shuffle and my fall is stopped by something solid and warm. A low whisper comes from near my ear. "You really shouldn't make a habit of listening at doors."

I shift and see Ted's roommate crouched behind me, grinning, with a sheaf of paper in his hand. "You got it!"

He presses a finger to his lips, but his eyes are gleaming. He stands up and tugs the door closed gently, then collapses against it, eyes closed, hand to his heart. "Not sure I'm cut out for espionage."

"You didn't see anything weird in there, did you?"

"Nothing worse than expected." He passes me the papers. "A disturbing amount of protein bar wrappers and empty energy drinks. But this was on his desk."

The pages are pristine. No coffee rings or curled edges. "He didn't even look through it." Even though I figured as much, my heart sinks.

He drops down next to me again, long legs stretched out next to mine. "I'm not a big reader, but if a friend of mine wrote a book, I'd read it in a heartbeat." He rakes his fingers back through his hair, and I catch a crisp scent, bright and earthy, like spring. A contrast to the stuffy hallway. "Just saying."

"Can you stick around? I like the way you think." Not that I'm planning to show my writing to anyone else. Not for a while at least. Becoming an author feels like a vague dream, and I plan to earn a degree and secure a well-paying job with good benefits. Save for retirement.

"Are you just asking because you've got a friend vacancy?"

I grin at him. "You did violate your roommate agreement to steal back my book. That's ride-or-die shit."

"So, friends?" he confirms. "What's the worst that can happen?" He must realize what he said, because he pulls a face. "Before you say it, I would never hit on your sister."

I can hardly believe the turns this night has taken, and that I'm having this discussion right now. "You haven't met her." My sister isn't to blame for this mess. She's stunning, and lovely, and I've never been jealous of her and don't plan to start now.

"Don't need to," he says, and this time, his expression is earnest. Something tells me it's the truth. This is a man who doesn't hide things.

"I don't even know your name." I'm stalling; he already feels like good friend material.

"Gavin."

"Mia." I hold out my hand, sleeve brushing the fronds of the plant, and he clasps it, palm warm against mine. His hands are clean, but there's a smudge of dirt at his wrist. I get a flash of him kneeling in a garden, fingers buried in the soil, and for some reason, my cheeks heat. "Mia Brady."

His mouth quirks up and he eyes me speculatively. "Nice to meet you, Mia Brady. I can totally see that on the cover of a bestselling book."

"Says the guy who doesn't like to read." I let go of his hand and shift to sit cross-legged, facing him. "And what does that even mean, by the way? You can't dislike *all* books. There are so many genres. Thrillers, graphic novels, biographies . . . My personal favorite, romance."

"Most of the books I've read are just sad." His tone sounds dubious. "They're all about human suffering and tragedy. People die."

I remember telling my English teacher something similar. To confirm my hunch, I ask, "What books have you been reading?"

He bites his lip, a flush blooming on his cheekbones. "Lately? None. But in high school we read *The Great Gatsby. Grapes of Wrath.* That one about the guy and the fish."

"*The Old Man and the Sea*?" I ask, stifling a grin at his description.

"Yeah, I think so," he says. "So depressing."

"But okay, those were required reading. Fun novels exist."

His eyes dart to the pages in my lap, then back up, like he doesn't want to violate my privacy. "Is yours fun?"

Surreal to hear him refer to my manuscript like it's an actual novel. "That's what I'm going for. But it's hard to be objective about my own writing." Hence why I asked Ted's opinion. He's always carrying around the latest bestseller, and I figured he'd be the perfect person to give me feedback. Guess I was wrong about him in more ways than one.

"I could read it, if you want." Gavin's unexpected offer breaks through my musing.

Flustered, I lift my gaze to his face. "Let the guy who hates books read my first attempt at one?"

"Yeah. If I like it, you'll know it's great."

"Pretty sure you're not my target audience." I'm not clear on who exactly my "target audience" is, but it's been mentioned often enough on the writing blogs I've started reading that figuring it out must be important.

"You said it's fun, right? I like fun." The corners of his eyes crinkle with a smile. "But no pressure."

It doesn't feel like he's pressuring me. His interest in my story, in *me*, makes it feel like tonight is more beginning than end. The start of something. "You want me to hand over my story to someone I just met?"

"Give us a little more credit," he says. "Our friendship is sealed with breaking and entering." All sparkling blue eyes and casual eagerness, he grins at me. "Ride-or-die shit. You said it yourself."

Prompted by a rush of feeling too intense for a chance meeting in a deserted hallway, I pass him the pages. "Just don't leave me hanging for a whole semester, okay? Even if you hate it." Criticism, constructive or not, would be worlds better than getting ghosted again.

He takes the pages, but when I try to hand back the plant, he shakes his head. "Keep it."

"You're giving me Frank?" Already it's more than a plant. It's a piece of Gavin, and he's offering it to me.

There's that smile again, like he's pleased I remembered its name. "I've already got plenty of plants. You're giving me your book. Only fair you have something of mine."

"He won't last a week with me." But I can picture how cheerful it would be to wake up to the bright green leaves fanned out against the window that catches the morning sun.

"Don't underestimate yourself." He's talking about taking care of the plant, but he's right. I've been sticking with what's safe. Look where that left me.

"I'll do my best." My palms curl around the terra-cotta pot.

When I step out into the snowy night a few minutes later, I hold it against my chest, coat draped protectively over the leaves. Tonight I lost a boyfriend, but I learned a valuable lesson: Never let romance ruin a good thing. And becoming friends with Gavin feels like a very good thing.

two

Mia

My sister throws open the front door of her apartment and pulls me into a hug. "Thanks for showing up."

The silky bonnet covering Kim's curls brushes my cheek, and when she pulls away, I can't help but notice her moving-day outfit of cotton shorts and a T-shirt with the mascot of the high school where she was just hired as assistant principal is nearly identical to the writer-on-deadline style she teases me about.

We share the same brown complexion that deepens in summertime, a blend of our parents' heritage. Our mom is white, with thin, straight hair, while my sister and I inherited Dad's tight, springy curls—Kim's hair is nearly black, and mine is a warm, deep brown. Our aunt and cousins taught us how to do our hair when we were kids, and my sister has rocked a short natural style for the past few years, but I like to change things up more often.

"Yeah, well, you can repay me by being my assistant at the book convention in August. You're still free that weekend, right?" She often helps me at summer events, since until earlier this year, she was an English teacher and had summers off.

"The back-to-school picnic with parents is the following weekend, so I can definitely make it." Turning, she weaves her way through the stacks of boxes filling the hall, pausing by the arched entrance to the kitchen. "Where's Gavin?"

"Circling the block, trying to find a spot big enough to fit his pickup." I kick off my sandals. "Where are you planning to park the moving van with all the festival traffic?" Prompted by Kim's raised brows, I sigh and position my shoes neatly by the door. "Because my offer to hire professional movers still stands." Both of us are frugal, but with the huge success of my latest series-turned-hit-show, I have more than enough for a comfortable living and would much rather spend money on loved ones than myself.

It's the first time neither of our parents is around to help, since Dad recently remarried and moved to Virginia, where the woman he'd had an online-dating relationship with for several years lives. Not long after I graduated college, Mom left Chicago for a dream job. They both made career and relationship sacrifices during our childhood to stay in the city and keep our homelife stable because of shared custody, and I don't begrudge them taking their happiness where they find it now, but I do miss seeing them more often.

"Ted would hate that," she says. He claims taking favors from family leads to tension, but my theory is his conscience won't let him be beholden to me after what went down all those years ago.

"I'm not worried about what Ted would hate." I don't feel any kind of way toward Ted, not anymore, but I don't like having to take him into consideration when helping out my sister.

The front door opens behind me, and I turn to find my former friend, current brother-in-law wheeling a dolly into the condo. Sunglasses are shoved into his over-gelled crew cut, and his polo is tight enough to draw attention. If I wrote him into one of my books, readers would guess from page one that he wasn't the love interest. Too bad twenty-one-year-old me didn't get the memo.

"Good to see you, Mia," he says.

I give him our customary half hug of greeting, a gesture that used to feel second nature but has long since become cursory. Patting his shoulder, I immediately regret it when my palm comes back damp.

He plucks at his shirt with an apologetic wince. "Scorcher out there today." Another reason why Kim owes me one. Hauling around boxes in summer heat is not my idea of a good time.

Pretty sure what they're really interested in is Gavin's pickup, not my help, since Ted's friends are coming over to handle the heavy lifting. "We've boxed up most things," he says. "But Kim didn't trust me with the fragile stuff."

Lord knows it took a while for me to trust Ted with anything fragile, least of all my sister's heart. But I've been trying to see the best in him ever since their wedding six years ago when she walked down the aisle to a man who had the nerve to suggest I wear a tux and stand on the groom's side since I was always "like one of the guys" so his sister could be a bridesmaid without throwing off the numbers.

I head to the kitchen, expecting to pack up their glassware, but the cupboards are open and empty, so I'm not sure what he meant by "fragile."

Continuing past an equally cleared-out bathroom, I find Kim in the second bedroom that doubles as an office. She's sitting on a rolled-up rug, surrounded by stacks of books, and I smile. The sight brings back memories of our childhood spent reading whenever and wherever we could.

I take a paperback off the pile nearest the door. "Fragile stuff, huh?"

"Some of these have been with me since before I could read," she says, boxing up a clothbound copy of *Little Women*. The shelf behind her is filled with copies of all the books I've written, the spines uncracked. She's purchased each and every edition, from the paperbacks to hardcovers with sprayed edges.

To keep them pristine, she only reads her favorites in ebook format. I like to joke that the driving force behind her move from the classroom to an admin role was the horror of years spent witnessing high schoolers dog-ear the classics.

"You really trust me to handle these?" While Kim's collection could earn top dollar in a secondhand bookshop, my most prized books are coffee-stained and annotated, the pages splattered with water from reading by the pool, covers bent from being shoved into a carry-on after nearly missing the boarding call in airport terminals.

But I'm as careful as an archivist with other people's books, and Kim knows it. "I'll just make you give me some of your author copies if you ruin these." She pushes a full box toward me, and I grab the packing tape from her desk to seal the lid. "But I mostly wanted the company," she says. "Ted's a sweetheart, but he's almost too helpful sometimes."

That's the rub. Ted *is* a nice guy. It's why we were friends. It's why, when I told her of his betrayal and she sheepishly admitted she'd always kind of had a thing for him, I swallowed my hurt and gave my conditional blessing. I wanted her to be happy but also careful. Warned her to be braced for him to throw her aside for someone else like he did with me.

To this day, I'm grateful I didn't speak up about how hurt I was at the time. We never lost our close bond. Didn't let a guy come between us. In fact, she texted me after their first kiss, giddy with excitement, and I replied with a string of hearts. But my next text was to Gavin, asking him to meet me at the grungy college bar that offered two-dollar pitchers. Over cheap beer and a bowl of stale popcorn, I made him promise to never, ever, allow me to date a friend again.

To be clear, he'd asked. *Am I your friend?* I hesitated, just long enough to wish I could say no. Long enough for me to imagine how easily we could slip into something more, something with the potential to wreck me. To realize how much of my heart I'd already lost to this man who'd texted me a running commentary while reading my manuscript in a single weekend. Who'd carried me on his back over a slushy puddle on a freezing-cold walk to study at the library. Who'd kicked off the night with a toast to Ted's protein bars turning rancid and a second one to Frank's good health.

Looking at Gavin, golden hair mussed from the beanie he'd pulled off and shoved in his coat pocket, cheeks flushed red from the heat of a crowded bar, or maybe something else that I didn't dare dwell on, I hesitated long enough to know I had to say yes. It took all my effort to not wonder how his lips would feel on mine and instead say, *I sure hope so*, even though in that moment, I did not.

He'd raised his glass, scooting away, just a little, and said, *To friendship*. I'd clinked mine against his and swallowed down my regret. I'd made a decision to protect my heart. To make sure things stayed like this between us, more sweet than bitter. It felt like an oath, and before long, keeping it became second nature.

As for my sister, month after month, year after year, Ted showed himself to be deeply in love with her. No hint of a wandering eye. He treats Kim like the best thing to ever happen to him.

Which is why I upgraded my conditional blessing to wholehearted when they announced their engagement three years after they started dating. But my friendship with Ted never recovered. He'll always be the guy who kissed me while pining after my sister. The first guy, though not the last, who taught me romance ruins friendship.

"I'll take too nice any day." I pull another box toward me. "Do you remember the dude I went out with who insisted on not getting out of his car until I opened the door for him? Called it reverse feminism."

She makes a retching sound. "I'm so glad I never had to deal with dating apps." She darts a concerned look at me, like always when the subject of how she and Ted met comes up, and like always, I brush it off.

"It's exhausting, which is why I'm taking a break. I'm good on my own for now." Especially with a looming deadline for the biggest book of my career.

"Hardly on your own," she says, with a childish singsong lilt. "Ever think that having a best friend with movie-star good looks might be making some guys hesitate about going all in?"

We've had a version of this conversation for nearly a decade. "Any guy who's jealous of Gavin isn't worth my time."

"Agreed. But you two are so . . ." She flaps her hands, searching for the right word. "In sync."

"That's what happens when you're friends with someone so long, and exactly why no one I date should feel threatened by him. If we'd ever had feelings for each other, it would've come between us by now and he'd be long gone."

She clicks her tongue. "Do you really think that?"

"I know that." Friendships endure. Relationships are a gamble, and so far, a losing one. "Right now, dating is the last thing I need on my to-do list."

Rising, Kim says, "Dating isn't something to put on a checklist, so if you're feeling that way, it makes sense to take a break." She starts emptying the next shelf, placing books in the box at her feet. "How's the draft coming along? Wasn't sure if you'd make it today with your deadline coming up."

When I'm getting close to turning in a book, I need a lot of uninterrupted writing time. My family and friends used to try to coax me out of the writing cave, but now they know what to expect. Doesn't stop them from showing up on my doorstep when I forget to answer texts, but these days it's to bring a meal or make sure I'm remembering to hydrate.

But my deadline isn't as close as Kim thinks. I haven't mentioned that I asked my publisher for an extension. Partly because then she'd assume my schedule is open, and extra time or not, I need to focus on work. Also, I'm feeling pretty discouraged about needing to ask for one in the first place. "About as well as a book I never should've agreed to write can go."

I don't pitch a book unless I know I can execute it. But in this case, the Hollywood producers who've done an incredible job adapting my most popular series came to me with a pitch of their own that filled me with misguided belief in my ability to create chemistry between two characters whose story I abandoned years ago.

My bestselling bookish-themed contemporary romance trilogy is now a hit show, and I agreed to write a bonus book to please fans who wanted to see the best friend side characters get their own happy-ever-after.

Before the publication of the trilogy, I'd had consistent sales, but whether it was the concept or the chemistry, readers fell hard for the series centered around characters in the publishing industry. The rights sold to a big-time production company who greenlighted the project right away. Before the final episode of the second season aired last year, fans were already clamoring for a fourth season, this time featuring the lovable side characters, Sydney and Victor.

"I figured this one would be a cinch to write since you're so familiar with Sydney and Victor by now," Kim says.

I'm familiar with them all right, because what no one besides Gavin knows is they were the main characters in my first manuscript, the one I shelved after my breakup with Ted.

The front door slams and saves me from coming up with an excuse for why I'm struggling to get a handle on this book.

Gavin's deep, familiar voice calls out, "Who's hungry? I brought doughnuts."

"About time you got here," I yell back, even though I'm honestly surprised he found a parking spot this quickly.

Kim winces at my shout. "Mia." She gives me a big-sisterly glare to act right, but Gavin and I always mess around. "Tell him the plates are packed, but there are some napkins on top of the fridge."

I heave myself up off the bare floor and head out to the entry-way, where Gavin is inspecting a hole in the drywall. "Should've brought my putty knife to patch these."

"Pretty sure Ted won't appreciate you doing more than you already are."

His brows tug together. "We care what Ted thinks now?" In true best friend fashion, he holds a worse grudge than I do. He would've never brought his truck to help them move today if it weren't for me asking on Kim's behalf.

"My sister does, so I do."

"Yeah, yeah." Passing me a box of doughnuts with the logo of the shop at the end of the block, he leans in and lowers his voice. "Are we mentioning the extension?"

I blow out a breath. "I haven't yet."

"You're being proactive, Mia. Nothing more, nothing less."

"Proactively stuck." I bought myself two months of extra time—now I don't need to turn in the manuscript until late fall—but so far, breathing room hasn't equaled inspiration.

"Proactively making time for yourself to get unstuck," he says. "This book could tank, and you'd still be a huge success. Just give it time."

"Not sure time will help." But I'm not giving up. One of these days I'll find a way through. Until then I'm sticking to my schedule, even though lately I end up deleting most of what I write. "Doughnuts might, though."

Cradling the box of sugary goodness, I scoot past boxes on the way to the kitchen.

Kim comes in a moment later, no doubt lured by the sweet tooth we share. "Thanks for helping out, Gavin." Ever the polite one, she stops to hug him before descending on the doughnuts.

"No problem," he says. "But with you leaving Chicago, where will we crash after a night out?"

"What hypothetical nights out?" She takes a doughnut topped with ganache and curls of chocolate. "It's been forever since y'all went out in the city. Lately all I get from Mia are texts about what shows she's bingeing. She's spending too much time with fictional men."

"Literally my job," I tell her.

"Writing is a convenient excuse to stay at home," she says.

I thought we'd moved on from this. "She doesn't understand how much of a chore dating is," I tell Gavin, who's used to our bickering. "Pretty sure she wants me to start looking for a boyfriend again."

He pauses mid-bite, his expression going blank. Not meeting my eyes, he chews carefully, staying quiet. Probably doesn't want to get in the middle of it by siding with me.

"Maybe that's why your inspiration is lacking," Kim says, napkin held underneath her doughnut to catch the crumbs. "Getting out there might spark some ideas." That's the least logical conclusion ever.

I swallow a bite of strawberry-matcha doughnut before answering sarcastically, "Because real men are so inspirational."

"Hey," Gavin protests.

"I meant in the context of dating," I tell him. "You're exceptional." I stand on tiptoes to ruffle the hair that flops over his forehead, enjoying how his nose scrunches up.

Kim jumps on the chance to get him on her side. "Don't you think it's weird she's this meh about dating when she writes about love for a living?"

Before Gavin can answer, I say, "I'm not writing a relation-ship column or giving dating advice. I write about fictional love."

"But your books speak on a lot of real-world issues," Gavin says.

"They do, and I'm not lessening the impact of fiction." I take another bite, grateful for the sweetness of the strawberry filling to balance out this unsavory talk of love outside the pages of a book. "But my imagination works just fine. I don't need to subject myself to blind dates for source material." Yet another stereotype about writing romance that's totally false.

"Plus," a voice says from behind me, "I'm pretty sure that's unethical." Dammit, why am I cursed by Ted's terrible timing?

My sister doesn't miss a beat, though. "I'm not saying you should model the book after a real-life relationship. But a good date or two might reignite your passion to write about the magic of romance."

Ted spots the open box of doughnuts and makes a beeline for it. "You've got writer's block?" As far as I'm concerned, he lost out on the right to ask me anything about my profession when he referred to the romance genre as "fluff fiction."

With a sigh, I reply with the bare minimum. "My characters just aren't cooperating at the moment." An understatement. Pushing these fan-favorite best friend characters together feels like a doomed endeavor. All I see in their future is a broken friendship and loneliness. Real warm-and-gooey stuff.

"Does the show have a contingency plan?" Ted asks around a gruesome mouthful of red velvet fritter.

Sometimes, I cannot believe this man's nerve. "To what, move on without me if I don't deliver?" Of course they do; they're money people. But I'm not clueing him in on how I'll be cut out of the process if I can't finish the book.

Gavin casually slides the box of doughnuts toward himself as Ted reaches for another, and my brother-in-law must get the message because he says, "Not that you won't finish on time, but surely they have writers on staff—"

"Screenwriters will adapt my work, yeah," I say. They've done a phenomenal job staying true to the spirit of the books while adapting the pacing for TV. "But this is my series, and I'm not going to let someone else write the final chapter."

If my favorite two characters are getting a happy ending, I want it to be my own vision. A vision with the clarity of swamp water at the moment.

"Mia always delivers," Gavin says, with all the confidence I don't feel. Gesturing toward the hallway filled with boxes, he asks Ted, "What's going in my truck? I brought some tie-downs."

They head out, and Kim bends to put her napkin into the black trash bag on the floor. "He's a keeper."

"Good thing, since you signed on for fifty years to life," I say, grinning.

"Ted, too. But I was talking about Gavin." She lowers her voice to a conspiratorial whisper. "Dating apps aren't the only way to start a relationship, you know."

I brush crumbs from my top, ignoring her pointed look at the mess. "Let's pack up the rest of your library." I turn the faucet on to full blast and wash my hands, putting an end to the discussion.

Dating Gavin is out of the question. I wouldn't do anything to jeopardize our friendship. Romance? That would ruin everything.

three

Gavin

Mia is using my wheelbarrow as a footrest while I pull out the old brick footpath leading to my front porch. Fingers resting on her laptop keyboard, she's reclining in one of the webbed vinyl-and-aluminum lawn chairs I found in the shed after moving in, eyes hidden behind her sunglasses. She might be sleeping, but she's definitely not writing.

I drop another brick in the wheelbarrow with a clatter, and she jerks upright. Definitely sleeping. "Geez, Gavin. What the heck?"

"Just curious how your scene is going." She asked me to keep her on track today, and while I don't like how much pressure she puts on herself, I understand the need for accountability.

She tilts her sunglasses down. "About as well as your path, from the looks of things."

Almost a week has passed since we drove into the city to help her sister move out, and Mia's been holed up in her condo, writing. Between Ted insinuating the show would be fine moving on without her and Kim pressuring her to start dating again, I think she needed space to get back into what she calls a "creative mindset."

I haven't had much free time, either. Starting in late spring, business ticks up at the tree nursery and garden center where I work as manager, and I'm in the middle of several landscaping design projects. My brother and his family drive out from Colorado to spend a month with Dad on the farm every summer, and since I plan to visit at least once during their stay, I decided to use my day off to get ahead on projects at my own place. First on the list is this eyesore of a path.

The previous owners either DIY-ed or hired someone with zero experience, because the walkway is as uneven as the mogul course on the ski slope near my family's Wisconsin farm. I nearly sprained an ankle tripping over a loose brick on my way to the mailbox last week.

I've ripped out a big section of cracked bricks, leaving gouges in the exposed dirt. Resting an elbow on my grit-streaked knee, I blink against the sting of sweat and peer up at Mia. "Nothing wrong with a work in progress."

"This is more of a teardown situation," she says, glaring at her laptop. Normally when she's struggling with a plot, she talks through things with me, but she didn't say a word about the book when she arrived today. Not a good sign.

"What about your scene cards?" I lift my chin toward the stack of multicolored note cards she wedged between the chair and her thigh to keep them from blowing off in the breeze. The same cards I've seen pinned to her bulletin board and taped to her computer monitor at home.

She ruffles them with a fingertip, like she's shuffling a deck of cards. "A prop, at this point."

"Well, if you're going to nap, at least use the daybed." She talked me into installing an extra-wide porch swing, complete with soft pillows and a throw blanket. I planned on something more basic, but once Mia sent me a photo of a swing like this she'd spotted on social media, there was no going back to a run-of-the-mill design. "You're going to get heatstroke if you fall asleep in the sun."

"I was contemplating."

"Want to contemplate while you pull bricks?" She once told me walking helps jostle ideas loose. Yard work does the trick for me, but Mia grew up in apartments and doesn't see the joy in working outside.

To my surprise, she swings her legs down. "Why not?"

"You hate yard work." I wait for her to say she's joking, but she gingerly settles to her knees in the grass, eyeing the pavers like she's assessing the best approach.

"I also don't deviate from my outlines or go a full month without any salvageable words." With her bare hands, she pries at one of the bricks, fingertips scraping at the packed dirt surrounding it, and I cringe at how close she comes to scraping her knuckles.

"Maybe this is the new me," she says. "Napping. Playing in the dirt."

"I am not playing in the dirt." Sitting back on my heels, I pat my pockets for a spare set of gloves.

"There's no HOA breathing down your neck." She blows up at the curls falling in her face. "You could fill your yard with garden gnomes riding flamingos but instead you're ripping out this path on your day off." She hitches up her shoulder, trying to dislodge the strands of hair clinging to her neck without using her grimy hands.

It doesn't work, so I use my wrist to brush the curls back, doing my best not to notice the tickle of her exhale on my throat. This close, her light floral perfume mingles with the earthy scent of exposed soil, like a freshly planted garden.

I drop my hand and pull away. Just like I have for years. Just like I always will.

"Admit you love having all these projects to work on around the yard," she says.

"Of course I do." Unable to watch her struggle any longer, I pass over a trowel, which she stabs into the ground with a fierceness that has me biting back a grin. "Nothing wrong with having a hobby."

Her lips pinch together, but she doesn't respond. Whatever's on her mind, she'll share when she's ready. We work in silence, me methodically tearing out another row of bricks, Mia making up for her lack of technique with frustration-fueled determination.

"Ted was right, you know," she says after a few minutes. "The other day, he asked if production could move forward without me. They can. If I don't turn in the book on time, the screenwriters have carte blanche to write the final couple's season as they see fit."

I figured that was weighing on her mind, and no wonder. "You've never missed a deadline." But it's the wrong thing to say, because she's also never needed an extension on her other dozen books.

"I pulled out of the book fair in New York," she says, and rips out another brick, taking a chunk of grass with it. "The only signing I have this summer isn't until August. I went on a social media hiatus and my assistant helped me schedule newsletters through the end of the year before she went on vacation. For the first time in what feels like forever, I'm free to put all my energy into the writing part of my job, so why can't I get a handle on this story?"

She tosses the paver into the wheelbarrow with enough force to crack it in half.

"You've never been under this kind of pressure," I say. "Give yourself some credit."

"Maybe not, but the process is the same. Brainstorm, plot, write, repeat," she says. "But I can't deny knowing this book will end up on-screen hits different.

"Especially since I know how excited Rob and Jayla are for their season," she adds. It's no surprise she's just as concerned about the actors who play the roles of Victor and Sydney as she is about her own career.

I search my mind for something to tell her that won't invalidate her feelings. I'm in awe of her and hate seeing her lose confidence.

"Maybe I need to take a step back," she says, before I can respond. "Set it aside and come back to it with fresh eyes." She dusts off her hands, grimacing when she looks at her nails. "I could take Kim's advice and get back on the dating apps, just to shake up my routine."

"The same apps you call cesspools?" I've had some luck with dating apps, but lately I haven't felt the urge to log on. Does that have anything to do with Mia being single for going on two years? I'd like to think not, but then again, I try not to think like that at all. Too dangerous for my heart.

"The dates don't have to be good," she says, rolling right past my objection. "I just need to do something out of the ordinary. Get out of my writing cave—"

"Is that any way to talk about a place that serves ten-dollar lattes?"

"—and get some clarity. Live life, instead of writing about it," she says, ignoring my joke, so I try again.

"Sounds like a throw pillow." I make a face, trying to lighten her mood, but inside I'm shook. Since when is she feeling like this about her work? Things must really be bad.

"If only I had one to smack you with right now." Empty threats, just like her fake scowl that's already close to slipping into a smile. She talks tough, but she has the softest heart of anyone I know. The corner of my yard is overgrown because she spotted an anthill and begged me not to mow over it.

All the more reason to not let her risk her heart just to get her mind off writing. "Taking a break isn't a bad idea. You've been pushing yourself too hard." I stand up and dig my fists into my sore lower back. "Why not go on vacation?"

"By myself?" She shakes her head. "I'll just wind up spending the whole time thinking about the book, or pull out my laptop and write in circles. I need to get out of my head. Short of a year in a Parisian apartment, this is the best idea I've got." She doesn't mention it, but I picture a man with her in that scenario, maybe an artist. Serious and soulful and everything I'm not.

I shove aside the image of Mia writing at an antique desk next to balcony doors thrown open to reveal a view of the Eiffel Tower, a painter sprawled on the bed, sketching her. "You're leaving out the part where you'd be going out with strangers. Guys who don't know they're signing up to be your distraction." It's not them I'm worried about, it's Mia. But she hates the idea of anyone worrying over her.

"Who's to say I won't make a real connection?" She grabs her phone off the chair. "And I won't be leading them on. I updated my dating profile." Passing it over, she hops across the torn-up path to stand next to me, cheek pressed to my arm like she's eager to see her handiwork.

Shielding the screen from the sun with my cupped palm, I read aloud.

"'Single woman (30) seeks single man for casual date(s) which may or may not result in an exclusive relationship.'" Lowering the phone, I hook my fingertip into the nosepiece of her sunglasses and ease them down to look in her eyes. "Mia. You write books for a living, and this is the best you can do? It sounds like a contract."

"Perfect." She takes off her glasses, brown eyes aglow in the afternoon sun. "I won't have to worry about them getting the wrong idea."

"The whole thing is the wrong idea," I tell her. "It won't work." Or it will, and she'll find herself catching feelings for some weirdo who jumped at the chance for no-strings-attached court-mandated romance.

"Something's got to." Sliding the sunglasses back on, she crosses her arms, her cream linen crop top showing off the smooth, bronze skin of her belly. I pull my focus off her distracting curves and back to her predicament as she says, "At least it will get my mind off the fact that I've got nothing to show for months of work."

An idea comes to me, one foolish enough that I don't allow myself to think it over. "Does it have to be a stranger?"

"What do you mean?"

"Date me." The moment the words leave my mouth, I realize my mistake. Somehow I've gone and asked out my best friend, the woman who thinks dating is the death sentence for friendships.

"Gavin—"

"Not for real," I say, scrambling. Damn. How can I save this? "But you want to do something out of the ordinary. What could be more out of character than me and you going on a date? I could pick you up for dinner—"

"We do that a lot—"

"At a fancy restaurant." All of a sudden, I want this, very badly. "I'll bring flowers. Living ones," I add with a grin. "Open all the doors for you."

"You do that for everyone," she says.

It's how I was raised. Midwestern nice that I sometimes get teased for. "Fine, then we could go to one of those wine and painting nights or something."

"Last time we tried that, you got tipsy and accidentally drank paint water."

Let me tell you, it sobered me up fast. "The point I'm trying to make is that you can escape your routine without going out with a stranger. Us pretending to be a couple would be the furthest thing from reality."

"Fake dating is a trope," she says. "Not something people do in real life."

"A trope?" I've heard Mia talk about tropes at book signings, but I'm not one hundred percent clear on the meaning.

"A scenario common to the genre that builds anticipation. Like for fake dating, the characters might pretend to be in a relationship so their family doesn't find out they're chronically single—"

"Being single isn't a disease." Though come to think of it, my brother does seem to view it that way.

She ignores me and says, "Or they take it a step further and get engaged because a great-aunt's will stipulates the hero will lose the family farm if he's not married."

"Is this medieval Europe?"

"Yeah, it can be a hard sell in contemporary romance," she says. "The point is, it never stays fake. The characters always end up falling in love." She scrunches up her nose at the word *love* dislodging her sunglasses, which slip off her face.

Catching them, I polish the lenses on my shirt. "You and I have been friends for almost ten years, Mia. We know where we stand. A bottle of merlot and candlelight isn't going to change anything. Plus, we're not going to be in a relationship. This would just be one date—"

"You think one date with you will be enough?"

For a split second, it seems like she's implying she wouldn't be able to stop at one. Then I realize she's saying there's no way a date with me will be enough to shift her mindset.

"Maybe not, but why not try?" I hand her back the glasses. "Can't hurt."

"That's where you're wrong," she says. "It could hurt."

"Which is why your best friend is the perfect person to fake it with."

She lets out a frustrated sigh. "A friend is the last person to fake with because it never stays fake. The characters always catch feelings." She glances up sharply, but she's staring off into space, with what I recognize as the look she gets when making a plot breakthrough. Suddenly, her mouth drops open, and she grabs me by the shoulders. "That's it!" Grinning up at me, she asks, "How do people who have been friends for years have a meet-cute?"

I've read enough romance novels by now to understand the importance of a good meet-cute—the moment when the love interests interact on page for the first time. I can also see where she's going with this and find myself smiling back. "By seeing the potential for something more?"

"Exactly!" Smile wide, she says, "It would be kind of cool to get insight into what might change for my characters in that scenario." She shakes her head. "What am I saying? That's ridiculous."

"It's not," I tell her. Even though it is. A little. "I'm your friend. Who better to do something a little ridiculous with? No judgment here."

Frowning, she says, "I'm not sure . . ."

"I am." I've always been sure when it comes to Mia.

She bites her lip and her grip tightens, bunching my sleeves. "You really don't have to."

"I want to." I want to do a whole lot more than pretend. I want to close the distance between us and feel her fingers fist my shirt for a whole different reason when our mouths meet. But that's the kind of dangerous thought that would be harder to push aside if we go through with this. Can I keep my feelings in check when all the usual boundaries of friendship are gone?

Just one date. I can do that. For Mia. For myself. To prove to my stubbornly hopeful heart that she doesn't want me. Won't want me. Not now, or ever.

Doing my best to keep my voice even, I say, "Let's have some fun together. It's what we do best."

four

Mia

For the first time ever, I'm avoiding my best friend. It's been a few days since he suggested we go on a date, and I haven't been able to face him. Going out with random guys to get my mind off work was a silly idea. Going on a date with my best friend to act out a romance trope? Unthinkable. Romantic relationships come and go, but friendships are forever. Romance just complicates things.

So why did I agree to fake it with him? Desperation, plain and simple. None of the scenes I'd been writing felt right, and I wound up caving to the temptation to scroll social media, only to discover I'd been tagged in yet another post speculating about the plot for season four. Once, while tipsy, I'd nearly commented on a similar post, *Your guess is as good as mine, lol.* Luckily Gavin had intervened before I'd finished typing.

Is a pretend date with him an equally terrible idea? Probably. But I need to write this damn book, and he'd made it sound so easy.

One date. Pretend to be someone else for a night instead of stressing over deadlines and reader expectations. But I know the risks. Minimal as it seems after our years of friendship, in books, someone always catches feelings, and that would be worst-case scenario. Life isn't a romance novel. Happy-ever-after is the exception, not the rule.

So here I am, hiding out in my favorite stationery store until it's time to join Evie, my good friend and critique partner, for our weekly writing meetup. Gavin's working today and sometimes grabs lunch from the restaurant near the coffee shop, and I can't risk running into him before I've had a chance to figure out how to back out of our ridiculous deal without making things weirder than they are.

I'm not saying I single-handedly keep this store in business with impulse buys to feed my penchant for pretty office supplies, but they did recently add a shelf labeled MIA BRADY'S FAVES. Seeing my name on the display gives me a hefty dose of impostor syndrome. Doesn't stop me from choosing a geometric-patterned notebook and matching pen from the curated selection.

"Knew you'd love that set," Amari says, when I take my items to the register. Her name tag is hand-lettered in swooping calligraphy, the word *MANAGER* written beneath in neat block letters. I've got a hunch she's behind the fan account that made the viral highlight reel of scenes from the show titled "Ten Times Sydney and Victor Proved Love Exists (And They're Adorably Clueless About It)," but she's never brought it up and I don't want to make things awkward by asking.

She scans the bar code, then gasps. "Did I just ring up a notebook that's going to hold part of Victor and Sydney's story?" She clutches it to her chest, dark eyes sparkling. "Those two are the absolute swooniest. I cannot wait to see Robert Cho in the spotlight. I mean, the stolen glances from last season alone?" She drops one hand to the teak countertop for support, fanning herself with the notebook.

All signs point to her being invested enough to make that

video, and who could blame her? Robert is every bit that dreamy. The man managed to make spam calls sexy when he played a victim of identity theft in a public service announcement. Watching him unleash his trademark charm in the role of quippy best friend alongside powerhouse actress Jayla Lewis is enough to make anyone's heart race.

Amari starts to slide the notebook into a paper sack, but I say, "No need. I plan to put it straight to use." If I can write a solid meet-cute today, I'll be able to call off my date with Gavin.

Passing it over, she says, "Does it sometimes feel surreal to have Hollywood demigods bringing your characters to life?"

"Pretty sure Jayla's earned full goddess status." She's been delivering knockout performances since her early twenties and deserves a lot more recognition than she gets.

Amari's eyes practically glow. "You're on a first-name basis with her? I shouldn't be surprised. You're probably on set all the time."

Not often, but it has been pretty amazing to get a peek behind the scenes. Hard to believe that several of Hollywood's reigning stars occasionally slide into my DMs with questions and updates. I'll even get to walk the red carpet next month at the season three premiere, though the idea of seeing the cast and crew in person before I have a good handle on the final book is stressful.

Before I can answer, Amari goes off on another tangent. "Are you writing the next book with the actors in mind? I know the first book came out years ago," she says. "But seeing your vision come to life on-screen must have an impact. It's probably a lot of pressure, right?"

Pressure is an understatement. Lately I feel trapped between the fandom and my own insecurities, and this conversation is no exception. Taking my receipt, I back toward the exit, lying through my teeth. "No more so than any book. I always want to do right by my characters." The last part is true at least.

She flicks her braids over one shoulder, brows arched in surprise. "So this is business as usual? No biggie to write a book people are saying might be the breakout roles for two rising stars?" The question hangs in the air like an accusation.

Maybe it's my inner critic, but I can't help but feel like she suspects this notebook will sit unused on my shelf, like the one I bought last week and the week before. That I'll wind up drowning in a sea of blank pages because I can't bring myself to write a happy ending I don't believe in.

Back in college, when I set out to write a romance novel, I dreamed up two characters who had chemistry galore but, in the end, Sydney and Victor couldn't find a way to let go of their doubts and trust love. In the final chapter, their failed relationship sent them out of each other's lives for good.

That's why I shelved that manuscript and wrote them into my next book as side characters. Gave them their own version of happy-ever-after by shielding them from the inevitable pain of trading the solid ground of friendship for the quicksand of romance.

But now the biggest advance of my career, not to mention my personal sense of responsibility to my publisher and everyone involved in the show, is forcing me to throw caution to the wind and push these friends into each other's arms—and beds—for good this time.

"Yep. Business as usual," I say, throat dry. "Just me and the story." I shove the notebook into my tote next to my trusty character journal. Carrying around multiple notebooks at any given time isn't unusual. Doubting my ability to fill them is.

Before Amari inadvertently pokes any more holes in my deflated confidence, I wave goodbye and make a quick exit out into the warm late-morning sunshine.

Hurrying toward the café, I walk past shops, restaurants, and boutique gyms, nose wrinkling at the rotten smell of garbage as I pass an alley behind a restaurant. The odor seems out of place on this beautiful summer day, but the memory of that scent could come in handy for a future book when a down-on-her-luck bartender steps out the side door at midnight for some air and decides to chuck the eviction notice she tore off her door that morning into an open dumpster.

Cataloging my surroundings has become second nature. I've always been attuned to the world around me, particularly people, but translating my observations onto the page took a lot of purposeful effort. Now I pay attention to things like the grittiness of the sidewalk under my soles, filing the impressions in my toolbox for later when a scene might require it.

A few blocks down I pass an abandoned lot, overgrown with weeds. Despite the sketchy appearance, it's prime real estate, near the commuter line. There have been rumors of a grocery store moving in, but it's been empty for as long as I've lived in town. A shed with a splintered door hanging off its hinges sits in the far corner. Not the right vibe for my rom-coms, but the perfect setting for my friend Krish's psychological thrillers. I snap a photo and text it to him with the caption: Cover inspo?

Krish's reply comes while I'm waiting by the pickup counter at the coffee shop. We're texting back and forth about what he's been up to since the last time we connected at a book festival when a text from Gavin pops up.

Gavin: Still on for tomorrow night?

Not if today's writing session goes well. I hesitate, lip caught between my teeth. Hearing my name called for the order, I stuff my phone back in my bag without replying. Great, now I'm dodging his texts. Another consequence of messing with the equilibrium of our friendship. But all I need to do is write a dreamy meet-cute and everything can go back to normal.

The hiss of the milk steamer and clink of silverware comes into sharp focus when the steady sound of typing from Evie's side of the table stops abruptly. I look up from my laptop screen to find her watching me.

"Do you realize," she says, and I know whatever's coming next doesn't bode well for me—her head is cocked, her sleek black ponytail falling to the side, "that you've finished an entire latte without typing a single word?"

A quick glance at the dregs of foam at the bottom of my mug confirms this. We're at our favorite table in the back corner of the café. We spent the first half hour of our writing session catching up, per our usual routine. We've been cheering each other on and commiserating over the tough parts of publishing ever since we met in a local writers' group. She shared a chapter for critique, and it moved me to tears, some of which fell on the pages, smearing the ink. Embarrassed, I explained what happened, but she told me it was the best feedback she'd ever received, and we've been close ever since.

Her historical romances are sensual and angsty, and while I haven't shed any more tears *on* her work, her writing never fails to move me, and she cried tears of her own when I called to tell her the show based on my books broke viewing records in its first week.

All I ever hoped for from my career was a steady paycheck and the chance to write every day, but she always told me it was a matter of time for my stories to hit it big, and I believe the same for her. For now, she's working part-time in Admissions at the local college while releasing several books a year for a growing group of loyal readers.

I, on the other hand, have been stuck on the same book for ten months. One scene, that's all I'm asking for today. Sydney and Victor's meet-cute. The moment they realize there might be more between them than simple friendship. The hook sets up the resolution, and so far, nothing has panned out. All their motivations fall to pieces by the time I reach the midpoint, and I keep having to start over.

"I'm brainstorming," I tell her, even though all I've been doing is scrolling through my latest attempt at act one.

The first chapter shows Sydney reading submissions in her home office. She's a literary agent—the career I envisioned for my main character back when I was a college student living in sweatpants and scrunchies, dreaming of a walk-in closet with cashmere and blazers for fancy lunch meetings with editors, a brown-paper-wrapped manuscript lying on the white tablecloth.

I found out soon enough that no one mails printouts to publishers anymore and my own agent told me she wears sweatpants as much as I do, but four books in, Sydney still has a killer wardrobe.

She's humming along productively in the first scene, combing through query letters for a unique premise, when she gets a voice memo from her best friend, Victor, who hopes to one day become a sought-after narrator. He's sent her a sample for the latest audiobook he's been hired to narrate, a business manual, except he's done each sentence in an impression of a different actor. The twist is he doesn't realize he's accidentally uploaded the recording to social media as well.

The scene encompasses everything readers and viewers have loved about their friendship—Sydney even-keeled and great in a crisis, Victor enthusiastic and intuitive, the dreamer. They've supported their friends through career changes and big moves and finding love, all the while showing up for each other when plus-ones are no-shows and relationships sour. Good or bad, they'll be there for each other because there's no secret yearning wedged between them.

The opening scene is full of banter and energy, but there's no reason for their relationship to change. Unlike other characters, I can't bring myself to introduce conflict into their relationship. I don't want to shove them past the safety zone of friendship into the shaky unknown of passion.

"What's got you stuck?" Evie takes a noisy slurp of her green tea, and the middle-aged guy at the table next to us makes a big show of putting his headphones on. "Is it a sex scene?" she asks, in a louder voice, side-eyeing the grumpy man, who lets out an affronted huff.

Usually talking through plot problems is a sure way to get me unstuck, but I can't do that without explaining how personal the story feels. How every time I've tried to build a love story from a friendship, it crumbles.

Ted was the first, but there was also Stewart, an aspiring mystery author I met through social media back when I was unpublished. He cheered me on through rejections and rewrites and was there—in spirit—to celebrate my first book deal. Our friendship shifted from online to IRL when he moved to Chicago for his day job. For a year or so we met up sporadically at bookstores and author events.

Then one day he asked me out. I hadn't felt a spark but figured that might be because I'd closed myself off to the idea of friendship turning into romance. But I didn't feel any chemistry after our first kiss, or our second. The dates felt like all the other times we hung out—enjoyable, but not enough to build a future on. So I explained how highly I thought of him, but said things weren't working out. Asked if we could go back to being friends. That's when he revealed he hadn't moved to Chicago for work after all, but for me.

It felt like a betrayal. Like all along he'd been dissatisfied with what we had, only hanging out with me in the hopes of more. Maybe I overreacted, but in any case, he didn't want to "settle" for friendship. Didn't want me in his life unless there was a possibility we'd be together. When a book I was excited to launch tanked on release day, I'd scrolled to his contact, looking for someone to commiserate with, only to remember he wasn't in my phone anymore. It stung, even though years had passed.

If that ever happened with Gavin, not being able to celebrate with him after fixing a tricky plot hole, not giggling at his commentary during awards season when I host watch parties for the outfits alone, not getting a call when his dad is driving him up the wall or a client insists he move the tree he just planted in their backyard to the front because they want a sight line from their formal living room—that would wreck me.

That's why I can't go on this date with him. Not even once. Not even for pretend.

But Evie is the queen of intricate plots. Maybe she could help me find a way out of this predicament without me revealing the mess Gavin and I got ourselves into.

Trusting her not to kill me if she finds out the truth, I say, "I'm wrestling with how to get Sydney and Victor to go on a date."

"That's a tough one," she says. "What obstacle would make that a feasible choice?" Like always, she cuts to the heart of motivation, a key element of fiction structure.

But while Gavin and I have a goal—to get me past this block—I can't tell her about it. "Maybe they have to pretend."

Her eyes light up. "Oh, fake dating? Yes, please." She rubs her hands together, the silver rings on her thumb and forefinger clinking. "But they're friends. This could get messy, girl." Exactly what I'm worried about. "I *love* messy," she adds. "Readers love messy. But you've got to have rules."

She's right. If this was for my characters—and it is, sort of—then they'd need ground rules. "What about a contract? Sydney handles those for her clients all the time. I bet she could write an ironclad fake-dating agreement."

"Love that idea." Evie takes her cardigan off the back of the chair, buttoning it over her spaghetti-strap denim dress because the café is blasting the air-conditioning to compensate for the blistering temps outside. "Does the contract have a physical intimacy clause?"

The guy next to us scratches his ear, pushing one of his head-phones aside, and Evie and I share a look. Dude is definitely eavesdropping.

With a glance at him, I whisper, "Absolutely not." Gavin and I are not kissing on this fake date.

She frowns. "What if someone catches them and they have to prove they're really dating?" Oh right. She thinks we're dis-cussing fictional characters.

For a moment, I reconsider the wisdom of getting Evie's advice without divulging the truth. Throwing fictional charac-ters into mayhem makes for great books, and she doesn't know what I'm trying to figure out is how to navigate a real-life fake date. No extra mayhem required.

"They're friends," I insist. "Physical intimacy would be a bridge too far. They need to come back from this."

"Okay, but at some point—"

"They'll get there eventually." I cut her off before my brain unhelpfully supplies images of Gavin's lips pressed to mine. I've seen him kiss women, quick kisses goodbye or hello. But it's not like he's making out with his girlfriends in front of me.

Well, other than that New Year's Eve house party our last year of college. He and I were getting air on the balcony, and he'd draped his coat over my shoulders just as the countdown to mid-night began. The sliding door opened, and my then-boyfriend had stumbled out to steal a kiss. We'd only been dating for a few weeks, and it ended not long after when I found out we weren't exclusive. That night, he was drunk and sloppy, and I turned down the midnight kiss, telling him I was headed home.

Gavin had disappeared and I went in search of him to give back his coat and found him tangled up with a girl in the kitchen, his hand in her hair. I remember feeling a strange lurch in my chest, probably shock at seeing him so lost in someone else when only a few minutes ago we'd been laughing together. He'd been thoroughly engrossed in the kiss, giving her all his attention in a physical way he never had with me. That explained the twist in my gut that felt a lot like jealousy, or maybe desire.

Evie snaps her fingers in front of my face and I jerk to awareness.

"Kissing is off the table," I say, emphatic. Then, remembering to sell the idea that this is strictly for the book, I add, "For now. That needs to go in the contract."

"Why aren't you typing this?" she asks.

Good point. But right now, my computer is a reminder of how horrifically stuck I am, and looking at it might mess with my flow. I reach for the new notebook and feel a zing of triumph at putting it to good use. Opening to the first page, I write:

Rules for a (FAKE) date with my best friend

I notice Evie reading along, and rush to explain. "I'm getting in character, as Sydney." Since I often journal in my characters' point of views to get inside their heads, hopefully she accepts my explanation. Below the header, I write:

1. No kissing.

She laughs. "Can't wait to see them break that one."

"Yeah," I say weakly. "Same."

"What's the angle?" She settles back in her chair, getting into the familiar rhythm of analyzing plot stakes. "Is fake dating meant to fool colleagues or their families and friends?"

Dammit. Why hadn't I considered more people finding out? On one hand, it might be easier to fake romance on a double date with our friends Serafina and Joe. But we've known them since college—they're expecting their first child after years of trying to conceive and already asked Gavin and me to be godparents. Involving them would make things way more complicated.

Same with Gavin's family, but no worries over them finding

out—they all live out of state. His brother and sister-in-law do spend about a month at Gavin's dad's tree farm every summer with their kids, but while Wisconsin is a lot closer than Colorado, the chances of them surprising Gavin with a visit are slim.

My sister and Ted, though, they're the wild cards. I wouldn't be shocked if they somehow caught us in the act. Kim has a knack for getting in my business. When I was sixteen and I finally worked up the nerve to tell my crush I liked him as we were leaving the homecoming dance, she interrupted us by pulling up to the curb and laying on the horn.

But even if she saw me and Gavin together, what would possibly give her the wrong idea? Unless we were holding hands or something . . .

2. *No touching.*

"No *touching*?" Evie uses her hot-pink pen to cross that off. "How else will they sell it?" Her expression shifts, a gleam appearing in her golden-brown eyes. "Unless you want them to build up some serious tension that they need to work off with a sexy interlude."

My writer brain jumps to the challenge and supplies images of all the ways the characters could work off tension. I rip my mind away before visions of Gavin slip in to replace Victor in that scenario. An overactive imagination is usually a blessing in my profession, but not in this case.

"Nope, you're right." I frantically scribble through that item on the list. "An embargo on touching would only make them want to touch more." Exactly what we'd want for a romance novel, and exactly what I need to avoid with Gavin.

She narrows her eyes, and I realize how suspicious I'm acting. Not only is Evie really smart, she invents bonkers plots for a living, and I can't have her turning her powers of speculation on me.

"They're just doing it for a work thing," I say, circling back to her question about their goals. After all, this is for my work, indirectly. Quickly, I add another point to the list:

2.   Friends and family can't find out.

"It's going to be so wonderfully awkward when they get caught." Evie's gleeful words send a chill through me. Even if we manage to keep it a secret, this whole situation screams risky. Complicated, even with rules. With that in mind I write:

3.   Nothing that happens on the date is real.

Evie is biting her lip, like she's considering all the loopholes. Seeing the words inked on the page highlights the pitfalls of this plan in stark clarity. *Nothing* is real? What if we start talking about family drama, or what's going on with work? Some things will inevitably be real, and how are we supposed to decide what to believe? It's too ambiguous.

An idea begins to form. A way forward, when all I've seen for months are brick walls.

"What if it's not a date?" I roll the possibility around in my mind, seeing it take shape. My original plan, courtesy of Kim's pestering, was to shake up my routine by going on dates, but there are other ways. The same goes for my characters. If I can't maneuver Victor and Sydney on a date, can I do the next best thing and have them fake romance another way?

I realize Evie is waiting on me to elaborate and I say, "Victor wants to break out and start getting contracts for big, sweeping novels with lots of characters. He needs to be able to narrate compelling scenes that run the gamut of human emotion. Everything from grief to elation to passion."

"Okay," she says hesitantly, clearly not following.

"Even though he went to acting school and did a few commercials and small TV roles, he's rusty after years of narrating self-help books and how-to manuals."

She makes a go-on gesture. "And?"

"What if Sydney acts out some scenes with him?" I can picture it unfolding, both of them tentative at first, then getting into character the more they practice. "It would be a safe space for him to get back into the swing of portraying hard-hitting, emotional moments. Romantic ones, too," I add. "Fake dating, under the pretense of acting."

Evie is nodding along like she's starting to see my point, but like always, she doesn't let me off easy. "Why couldn't he just enroll in acting classes?"

"Because people are roasting him on social media for the celebrity impressions that were supposed to be for Sydney's ears only," I offer, seeing things fall into place. "Remixes are popping up, people commenting that he wasn't even close and not to quit his day job, that sort of thing. His confidence is at an all-time low. Sydney wants to boost his spirits and get him back on track, and this is her solution."

"You're onto something," she says. "If they're acting then they can justify whatever romantic situation comes up. Sydney won't be as worried about the potential repercussions to their friendship."

"This could work, Evie. This could be my breakthrough."

She's grinning at me. "Told you it was only a matter of time."

What would my relationship with Gavin look like, if there was no chance of getting hurt? I ignore that unhelpful train of thought.

Technically, I have the solution to my plot problems. An excuse to cancel the date. But part of me is worried I only got here because the stakes were high. Did trying to solve a real-world problem unlock a hidden well of creativity?

Role-playing. I write it down, and the word sends a delicious thrill down my spine, like sanctioned rule-breaking—pretty appealing as someone who's always played it safe. But how could Gavin and I get into character without the excuse of acting out a scene? Fake dating is a trope, but it isn't the only one. I begin to jot down ideas, pen flying across the paper. Is this risky? Yes, but I'm also feeling more inspired than I have since I signed the contract, and it's all because I agreed to date my best friend.

five

Gavin

Sitting at the bar after work on Sunday for trivia night, I slide my phone out of my pocket to check my texts again, but Mia's left me on read. That's not like her. She probably got pulled away, but it feels weirdly like I'm being ghosted. Serves me right for asking her out like that.

I had to think of a way to play it off. Maybe it's all the romance plots that Mia's talked through with me, but faking it was the first excuse that came to mind. I know she doesn't model her books off real life. It reminds me of the time a creep came up after one of her events and asked if she needed help with "research." The look she gave him was enough to have him apologizing in an instant. But did I do the same thing? God, I hope not.

She doesn't need me to fill the role of boyfriend in her life, but maybe she does need me to get past her writer's block. And we care about each other. That's what friends do, right? They step up. But I can't help but worry this impulsive move will drag us down.

This dive bar, with its ripped vinyl booths and plastic pitchers and sticky floors, feels a lot like the college bar where Mia made me promise to never let her date a friend. She made it clear that's what I was to her, and I haven't forgotten. Haven't let myself get close to that line, because I'd rather have her as a friend than not at all, and most of the time, I can convince myself I'm not interested in anything else.

But I've heard all the stories about her bad first dates, watched her try to make it work with mediocre guys. I've seen her pick herself up and try again, and I've done the same, telling myself I'll find someone who makes me feel better than she does. Hasn't happened yet.

I'm still staring at the screen as if a response will magically appear when my buddy Morris yanks my phone out of my hand. "Man, quit checking that." He slams it face down on the bar. "You're going to get us disqualified."

"No one's even looking at us," I mutter, but it doesn't matter. Even though trivia night has been taken over by a new bartender who just reads off a tablet with the enthusiasm of a substitute teacher, Morris and Riley take this seriously. They dragged me here after work a few years ago and decided I was worth keeping around for the sports questions. Sometimes one of the other guys on our crew joins us, but he likes to win, and we don't do much of that.

"Doesn't matter if he sees or not," Riley says, eyeing me from under the swoop of bangs, more auburn than red in the low light. "They'll review the security footage if someone complains."

I doubt they have cameras in here to deter theft, let alone keep trivia teams honest when the prize is a T-shirt. "Isn't that a violation of our rights?" I say, just to egg her on. Somewhere along the way, we became good friends outside of work and trivia night. In fact, I don't think trivia night is good for our friendship, if I'm being honest.

She gives me a flat stare. "Why do you keep checking it,

anyway?" Not waiting for an answer, she stuffs my phone in her purse, zipping it shut for good measure. "Did you meet someone?"

"No," I say, grateful not to have to lie.

"Is your dad pestering you?"

"No," I repeat, more annoyed this time. I love my dad, and only I get to call him a pest. Did he rely on me a lot in the years after the divorce? Yeah. But lately, I haven't heard from him much. I would worry, but he posts plenty on social media. Mostly pictures of meat he just pulled out of the smoker or baseball memes. When I checked in with him last week he was in good spirits, talking about the new contract our family's tree farm scored for a fancy mixed-use development.

"Then get your head in the game, because the next category is sports. Last time you cost us the win because you were too busy chomping down on nachos," Morris says.

They rely on me to pull my weight, but I'm mostly here for the half-price food. Not having to cook dinner on Sundays is a bigger draw than getting quizzed.

Intense teammates aside, I love my life here in the Chicago suburbs. After college, I had a job waiting for me at the tree nursery, but when the time came, I just couldn't bring myself to go back. Going to college in Illinois had given me some distance from Dad, and the idea of being his whole support system again was too much. Not to mention running the farm isn't the type of job you can clock out of at the end of the day.

The bartender reads out a question about pickleball and by some miracle I get it right. By the end of the round, we're in the lead, and Morris buys a round of beer. I'm more interested in dinner and am biting down on a brisket-topped corn chip when Riley comes back from the bathroom, scowling.

"Your phone kept going off while I was in there," she says with disgust, like it's my fault she confiscated it. "What kind of person keeps their volume on?"

The kind of guy waiting on a text, that's who. I can't remember ever feeling this nervous to get a reply from Mia; usually it's the opposite. But the texts are from my brother, not her.

Scott: Just made it to the farm.

Scott: Dad says you haven't come by in a while.

Big talk for someone who lives halfway across the country, but there's no point in arguing with my brother.

Gavin: Summer gets busy, but I'll be there for the cookout.

Dad hosts a big end-of-summer party for the employees and their families. These days it also serves as a send-off for Scott's family. He's a stay-at-home dad and ever since his wife started working remotely, they've extended their summertime trips to a month or more so the boys can spend time with our parents—especially Dad, who rarely takes time off to visit them. Mom always comes to the party in August, too, even though she lives in Madison now. Mia has joined me in the past, but this year she'll be too busy prepping for her trip to Los Angeles the following week for the season three premiere.

Scott: Let me know if you can make it out sooner. The boys are asking when they can see you.

That strikes a nerve. My nephews are awesome kids, and I fly out to Colorado to spend time with them at least once a year. But even though Dad's cooled off lately on hinting that I'd be better off at the farm, he always seems to ramp things up when I go home for a visit, and I'm torn between wanting to see everyone and not wanting to deal with the guilt trip.

Riley nudges me. "Next round is starting."

"Just a sec," I say, tapping out a reply to my brother.

"You're good." Morris leans across me to snag a chip. "The category is nature, and Riley's all over that."

"Don't pressure me, man," she says, but I tune them out to finish the text.

> **Gavin:** Why don't you bring them to the game this weekend? I can grab extra tickets.

> **Scott:** Way past their bedtime. They'd fall asleep by the third inning. What about an afternoon game in Milwaukee? Then we could have dinner at the farm.

Scott's persistent, always has been, but something feels off. I shoot off a quick text to my dad asking how he's doing, and he sends back a selfie of himself holding a platter of what I'm guessing is prime rib and a thumbs-up emoji. Nothing unusual there.

I'm about to put my phone in my pocket when I see the notification for another unread message. It's from Mia.

> **Mia:** Ready if you are. Tomorrow night?

I stare at the screen. We're really doing this?

Morris grabs my shoulder and shakes it. "Dude, we won!" He shoves a T-shirt into my hands, tonight's prize.

Riley pulls hers on over the wicking long-sleeve shirt we wear to work and climbs onto the barstool with a loud whoop, earning a round of applause from the other two teams of regulars. It's our first win in a few months, and I've got to say, it does feel good. That's the reason for the giddy feeling in my chest, not the fact that I'm going out on a date with my best friend tomorrow.

six

Mia

"We can't just go on a date," I tell Gavin. He's sitting on the other end of my sofa in jeans and a white oxford button-down, hair damp from the shower he must've taken after work, looking ready to play the part of fake boyfriend. I feel a small pang of regret that I've decided we should switch tactics.

The more I thought about the method-acting scenario, the more it seemed like a great work-around. A way to keep up my creative momentum and do something to get out of my comfort zone without risking our friendship. Straight-up fake dating—pretending to be in a relationship—could skew the boundaries of our friendship. But a spin on it might just work.

I pull a typed sheet out of the binder I'm clutching in sweaty palms, and I lay it on the coffee table. Eager to fine-tune the idea after I got home from writing at the coffee shop with Evie, I barely slept last night and spent all of today working on what might be the most outrageous plan ever. What I'm about to propose is beyond bonkers, but if there's anyone I trust enough to try this with, it's him. "At first I thought we might need a contract to lay the ground rules."

He pauses in the act of cuffing his sleeves, tanned forearms on full display. I do my best not to be distracted by the shape of muscles I've seen a thousand times when he wields hammers or carries bags of topsoil, and which have never—well, seldom, I'm only human—inspired me to imagine how they'd feel tucked under my legs, holding me tight against him.

I remind myself it's just Gavin. Good luck telling that to my nervous system, because it's still recovering from how he showed up at my door smelling all shower fresh, holding a potted plant with bright green leaves and fragrant white blossoms—a gardenia, he informed me—and my heart lit up like midsummer fireflies.

His brilliant blue eyes lock with mine. "A contract." The word rumbles out, sounding filthy and confirming I was absolutely right not to go that route.

"Just to make sure we were both on the same page," I say, grimacing at the accidental pun.

"It's a date, Mia," he says. "Not a marriage pact."

The perfect opening. "Funny you mention that," I reply, and his sandy-brown brows shoot up. I rush to explain. "A marriage pact is a trope, and I thought maybe we could explore . . . Well, not that one," I add quickly when his eyes widen. "I'm getting ahead of myself. First, you should look over the contract. It's got nothing to do with a wedding, I promise."

He grins, pushing his sleeves to his elbows and scooting toward the edge of the couch to read over the document. I maintain a death grip on the binder in my lap until he finishes the single page and looks up.

"This is very thorough." He taps his fingertips against the page, and I notice a small nick at the junction of his thumb and hand, probably from pushing the wheelbarrow around at work, picking up the slack for the new hire he told me about who didn't realize the job involved manual labor. "But is it really necessary? We've never needed any formal agreement like this to keep our, uh—" his eyes flick back to the paper where the subheading IN THE EVENT OF FEELINGS jumps out at me "—our distance."

Haven't we, though? I think about that night in the bar back in college, when I asked him to vow not to let me date friends, including him. Does he ever think of breaking it?

Instead of entertaining those dangerous thoughts, I say, "That's why I decided to scrap the idea. But I wanted you to see the potential risks before you commit."

"I'm committed already," he says, rubbing his clean-shaven jaw, tanned skin slightly rosy from the scrape of the razor.

"But if we go to a restaurant right now, nothing would be different, unless we take steps to make things different. More than just dressing up and ordering a bottle of wine," I add when he starts to protest. "Getting physical would fix that, but obviously that's out-of-bounds."

"Obviously," he says, holding my gaze in a way that makes my cheeks flush. If he were anyone else . . . Nope. I mentally shove that door closed and lean against it for good measure.

"Besides, physical chemistry alone isn't enough to build a romance on," I continue, rushing to get to my next point. "And it definitely isn't enough to make two characters who've been friends for years throw caution to the wind and try for something deeper."

He looks less than convinced. "So what do you have in mind?"

This is the moment I've been waiting for, but I feel a little queasy. "The contract was meant to illustrate all the potential loopholes of fake dating. This—" I lift up the binder "—is how we get around those."

Eyeing the binder warily, Gavin palms the back of his neck. "This looks like work. I thought you were supposed to be having fun. Getting out of your rut."

I bristle. "I'm not in a rut."

"Creatively speaking," he says. "All I'm wondering is how this—" he points to the binder, which I've affectionately titled The Love Notes "—is any different than your outlines and note cards?"

Pretty impossible to come up with a rebuttal when I used note cards to organize my thoughts, and the first tab of the binder is an outline. "Okay, yeah. I'm leaning into my strengths. But a date without ground rules is too ambiguous. I'm giving us parameters."

"This is just a bunch of date ideas?" He visibly relaxes, like the idea of planning dates with me is a relief compared to whatever else I had in mind. Surprising, but then again, he doesn't have my encyclopedia of romance knowledge to know how risky fake dates are. Good thing I'm an expert.

"Not traditional dates. Tropes. Like the marriage pact," I say, excited to have the perfect lead-in. "Remember I said we'd circle back to that."

He opens his mouth. Blinks.

"The concept, Gavin."

"So to be clear," he says, and bright spots of pink appear on his cheeks. "Getting married for non-romance reasons is or is not one of the tabs in your binder?"

"Not. And you're the one who brought it up," I add, defensive.

"Did I?" His eyes are twinkling now.

"I was just using it as a jumping-off point to introduce my plan." I wave a hand. "Forget marriage of convenience. It's not important."

"If you say 'marriage' again, I'm breaking out the shot glasses Sera and Joe brought you from their trip to Greece. We'll make it a drinking game."

It's a testament to our long-standing friendship that this suggestion doesn't earn him a glare. "My point is that tropes will give us parameters for our 'dates' that will allow us to do things outside of the norm without blurring the lines between our friendship and what's pretend."

Wordlessly, Gavin takes the binder from me and opens it on his knees. He licks his index finger and uses it to flip the page. A habit I've always found a little gross, but somehow, watching him do it, thoroughly absorbed in what I've written, it brings to mind thoughts that would definitely violate the contract, had I signed it.

His brow furrows and I glance at the page to see he's reading the description of the secret-baby trope.

"That one is only on the list for the sake of thoroughness," I explain. "Can't test it, so . . ."

"You don't want to hide a baby with me?"

"That's not what it means—"

"Our relationship started with light breaking and entering," he says. "Kidnapping would be a natural progression."

I cross my arms. "You're never going to let it go, are you?"

"That my best friend lured me into a life of crime?" His eyes are sparkling irresistibly, but I won't be lured into agreeing with him.

"You had a key," I remind him. "And to be fully accurate, we didn't know each other back then. You let a total stranger lure you into the life of crime. Shows a lack of judgment on your part, really."

"Victim blame much?"

"Now you're a victim?" I give him a skeptical look. "Thought you were the hero of that story."

"I was. Am." He sends me another irresistible grin, and for a moment I imagine what we'd be doing tonight if I hadn't met him fresh off of finding out my boyfriend was in love with my sister. Certainly not talking, not when he's sitting there looking delectable as a cologne ad. "Sorry," he says. "You were explaining how making babies will help your writer's block, which to be fair, is worth a try—"

I cut him off by closing the binder on his hand. "You don't deserve access to this information."

"C'mon, Mia. I'm kidding. I want to help. And this idea is sounding more unhinged by the moment, which is a good thing. I like seeing you daring and reckless."

Reckless? That's the opposite of what I've got planned. "The whole point of this is to keep things contained."

"Things being our feelings." His gaze is intense, voice rich, like the last bite of a caramel sundae.

"I just want to make sure we keep in mind this is an experiment for the sole purpose of determining if switching up my routine can free up my creativity."

He scratches his temple, the streaks of summer gold in his hair illuminated by the slanting evening light. "So we choose a trope at random, act it out, and see if it inspires you?"

"We could do that," I say, hedging. "Or we come up with a list, ranging from easiest to hardest to test. Hopefully we'll only have to try a few before I get into a rhythm and we can call it off."

"Okay, so if not secret baby, then what?"

"Mmm . . ." I pretend to give it thought, like I haven't spent hours ranking the tropes already. "Road trip? We could visit everyone at the farm." His brother's family is staying with his dad, and things seem to go more smoothly when I'm there as a buffer to Dennis's unsubtle hints about Gavin moving back. The two-hour drive to Wisconsin could double as a trope test.

"Been there, done that," he says. "Last time you made us listen to an audiobook instead of music."

"I was moderating a panel with the author that weekend."

"You sped it up to three times the normal rate." He fixes me with a glare. "It was like listening to caffeinated chipmunks."

I swallow a laugh, refusing to give him the satisfaction. "Enemies-to-lovers?"

"Like Tiffany and Dylan's book," he says. The feuding book-sellers in the first book of this series, who made more and more outrageous window displays in their attempts to one-up each other. I had a blast writing their story because I had no trouble encouraging them to go all-in for love, unlike Sydney and Victor, who stand to lose it all. "The scene in the back room when they were unpacking stock . . ." He trails off.

I'd forgotten that one. "You remember my books better than I do."

"Because unlike you, I'm not dreaming of new plots. I get to sit with yours for a while after I read them," he says offhandedly, like that isn't the highest compliment a writer could receive. "But we're friends. How would we act out enemies-to-lovers?"

"Remember that time we tried to build furniture together?"

He laughs. "Yeah, that would work. A little too well. I'm actually not sure our friendship could survive it." He flips the page. "Celebrity romance? Nah, that's our daily life, minus the falling-in-love part."

"You make it sound like I can't walk down the street without getting recognized."

"There was a line around the block at your last signing," he says.

"But it's not like I have to go incognito for a night out." I point at the next trope on the list. "Also, no need to do snowed-in. Remember last year in Colorado Springs?"

He flops backward. "The ratings for that vacation rental were a total scam. Four-point-nine stars my ass."

Despite myself, I chuckle. "The hot tub alone."

"Don't." He gags. "The sound of sludge churning out of those filthy jets still haunts me."

I'd flown to Colorado at the end of his trip to visit his brother last year so we could spend a long weekend in the mountains.

The vacation rental was a nightmare, but we got snowed in and had to stay the night. Needless to say, no romance ensued, but there was an epic battle with a cockroach who lived to fight another day.

He rakes a hand through his damp hair, and I catch the comforting scent of the body wash–shampoo combo he's used since college. "All of this seems a lot more complicated than going on a few dates. I've been thinking . . . The other day when you brought this up, it wasn't just for the sake of switching up your routine in hopes of getting unstuck. You planned to go on actual dates, with men you had the potential to start a relationship with. Unlike me," he adds, glancing away. "And I didn't mean to . . ." He faces me again, this time meeting my eyes. "I shouldn't have tried to convince you not to."

"I was kind of hoping you would," I tell him. "I didn't expect you to offer yourself as sacrifice, but—"

"It's not a sacrifice, Mia."

I want to believe him, but part of me feels guilty for pulling him into this. It might have been his idea, but I'm the one who can't let it go, even though I probably should. "If I'm really going through with this ridiculous scheme to get out of my head, then you're the only person I want to do it with."

After a long moment, he says, "All right. So we act out these tropes . . ." He glances at me as if to confirm he's used the word properly, and I nod. "And our goal is to help you get to the point where Syd falling in love with Victor doesn't seem farfetched?"

I know intellectually how to craft a romance plot. How to ignite chemistry and make characters fall in love. I've done it a dozen times. But knowing hasn't helped me *believe* the best friends in this book can successfully make the leap to something more. So maybe this is a tactile sort of learning. Feeling things out. There's nothing rational about it. And maybe that's what I need.

All I know is I need *something* to get past this block. Something more than long walks and new surroundings and music or silence and enough candles to set off the building's sprinkler system, nearly. I've tried all those. I've scene-charted and word-webbed and mood-boarded and still, I can't find the heart of the story.

"I know it's a weird plan, but I feel excited to write this book for the first time since I shelved it back in college. Maybe it's time to switch up my process." I write on a strict schedule. I plot the whole book before I begin, and my outlines are as detailed as many writers' first drafts.

"What's wrong with your methods?" Gavin asks.

Lots of authors I know—Evie included—pour out thousands of words before the book takes shape, and that works for them. But rather than coaxing the story out of a messy first draft, I chase down the plot, then drag it kicking and screaming back to my laptop and interrogate it before starting to write. I once used that analogy in an interview and was gently asked by my publicist to refrain from kidnapping analogies.

"I'm a plotter, but sometimes I feel like the pantsers get credit for being more artistic, even though we're all weaving a story from our imagination." Seeing his confusion, I explain, "It's a term for people who write by the seat of their pants, so to speak. They don't have to know where they're going before they begin."

"Everyone has a process. So, what if yours is less starving artist and more—"

"Formulaic?" I cringe, remembering the words of an ex-critique buddy.

He shakes his head. "Structured." He gestures toward the bookshelf that holds rows and rows of author copies. "People are obsessed with your books for a reason, Mia. Your stories are magic, and if the way you create them is a reliable process, all the better."

He's echoing my own convictions, or at least how I used to feel before I got stuck. It's comforting to have a process that allows me to produce great books. To know that readers will laugh and cry and swoon when they read a Mia Brady novel. But the flip side is, now that my method has failed, I'm doubting my abilities.

"But it's not working anymore."

"Which is why you're thinking outside the box."

"Or inside the binder." I waggle my brows at the joke, but Gavin is having none of it.

"Don't make this nerdier than it is."

"Nerdy is my wheelhouse."

"And I love that for you," he says. "But some of us have a reputation to maintain."

"As a guy who tucks in his flower beds with blankies before a frost?"

"Good landscaping isn't sexy?" He quirks a brow, leaving me momentarily speechless, then says, "And I've heard people love a man in work boots."

They do. I've written plenty of rugged heroes, and don't get me started on the way my own heart flutters at the sight, not that I'll ever admit it to Gavin. "Boots don't make a man."

"The shade you're throwing right now . . ." He shakes his head.

"Only because you implied nerdiness is unattractive."

"What?" He sounds genuinely surprised. "I said I wasn't one. Never said I didn't find it hot."

Hot. Nerds. Me? Words turn to slush in my brain, an unusual sensation. "You have a thing for nerds? How am I just now hearing of this?"

His cheekbones turn crimson. "It's not like a woman puts on glasses and—"

Pushing my glasses up, I say a tad defensively, "So all nerds need vision correction?"

"You know what I'm saying. It's not the concept of nerdiness I'm attracted to. But if a woman is really passionate about . . ." His eyes dart to the binder, and he clears his throat. "Date or not, can we continue this discussion over dinner? I'm starving."

Come to think of it, so am I. "Give me a second to change." There's a splatter of tomato soup on my shirt. All part of my plan to make sure Gavin got the message nothing between us has changed. But I draw the line at looking this sloppy in public.

I'm in the middle of swapping my stained shirt for a clean one when I hear him say, "We're going to that new place by the center for the arts."

Since I'm only wearing a bra, I poke my head back around the corner and see he's scrolling on his phone. "The one with a wine list?"

"Uh-huh."

"But that's so fancy. I'll have to put on real clothes." He looks up and seems to register for the first time that I'm not dressed. His gaze skims my neck and shoulder, catching on the crimson strap of my bra before he glances away, clearing his throat. "If I have to take notes, the least you can do is wear pants with a zipper."

"I draw the line at a zipper," I say, wondering why my skin feels suddenly flushed. "And who mentioned notes?"

"Mia, I've known you for years. Don't think for a second that I believe you're going to leave that binder behind."

Biting my lip, I duck back inside my room, unable to shake the image of how Gavin's eyes darkened when he caught sight of me, his gaze on my bare skin almost tactile, like the slow tug of satin. Suddenly my unfinished manuscript is the last thing on my mind, and isn't that the point of all this?

I slip on a gauzy sundress I bought on a recent procrastination shopping spree, fluff my curls, swipe on some lip gloss, and at the last second, take off my glasses. I usually wear contacts on dates, and even though this isn't a date . . . Stepping back out into the living room, I find Gavin by the door, spinning his keys on his finger. If I didn't know better, I'd say he was nervous.

I turn for him to zip my dress, and he obliges, fingertips warm.

"Thought you said no zippers." This close, his words land like rose petals on the sensitive skin of my nape. Instinctually I turn toward him, but he takes a step back.

"Figured I could make an exception." I actually like getting dressed up, but standing here next to him in heels and a dress makes this feel disconcertingly like a real first date.

I slide my fingers into the cutaway at my rib cage, loosening the fit, and his eyes dip for a moment, dark blond lashes lowered. Just as quickly, he pulls the door open, beckoning me through. "We've got a reservation."

He wasn't exaggerating—he really is committed. And even though this might be the most farfetched thing I've ever done, so am I.

seven

Gavin

We're seated on the rooftop terrace and Mia is squinting at me from across the candlelit table. It could be that she forgot to put in her contacts, but I have the sinking feeling it's professional curiosity, which in her case means analyzing people's motivations.

My reasons for going along with this scheme aren't as altruistic as I made them out to be. This might be my only chance to find out if we could ever be more than friends. But things are already slipping off course. Instead of the romantic dinner I envisioned, I showed up to find Mia in a stained T-shirt, armed with a binder full of ways for us to avoid falling in love.

Seems like overkill, but then again, she has every right to guard her heart. I just wish she didn't put me on the list of people who might break it. I'm not sold on the idea that experimenting with romance tropes makes more sense than fake dates, but hopefully I'll be able to think more clearly once I've eaten something.

Hunger aside, Mia's scrutiny is making me feel queasy. Resisting the urge to unbutton my collar, I ask, "Everything okay?"

Her eyes rake over me, like she's taking in my gelled hair and dressed-up appearance. "Just wondering what entity body-snatched my friend," she says. For a split second I wonder if the romantic setting and sunset have worked transformational magic and erased the best-friend filter from over my face. But then she adds, "You made a reservation."

"It was supposed to be a date." Fake or not, I wanted tonight to be special.

"It's just surprising." She shakes out the cloth napkin and lays it on her lap. "You never make reservations when we go out."

"Because it's not like that between us."

"Like what?"

I let out an exasperated huff. "You know what."

How can she be surprised that I act differently around women I'm dating? Then again, I guess there's a difference between knowing and experiencing, because damn, when she came out of her room earlier, all long, bare legs and bouncy curls, it was impossible not to want her to be mine.

Years of knowing she was off-limits should've cured me, but all it took was one moment of experiencing what things could be like if we were together to make me crave more.

She sits back, putting distance between us. "It was thought-ful, that's all. Thank you."

Before I can reply, the server walks up with a basket of breadsticks and scoots the binder aside to make room. Eyeing the glittery stickers on the cover, she says, "Big test tomorrow?"

"You could say that." Tonight feels like a test of its own, a pop quiz I wasn't prepared for.

The server must be thinking of her tip because she doesn't ask any more questions, just recites the seasonal menu. When she's gone, Mia says, "We don't have to go over this right now." She tucks her hair behind her ears and the silvery strands of her long earrings catch the light, guiding my eye along the curve of her neck. "We could just have, like, a normal conversation."

"Pretty sure we've never had one of those." I grin. "Hit me with your best alphabetized mayhem." Grabbing a breadstick, I flip open the binder.

"Be careful," she says. "I don't want crumbs on the pages."

"On second thought . . ." I pluck the wine list off the table and pass it over. "Pick a wine first. I have a feeling I'm going to need alcohol to get through this."

"Now look who's supporting drinking while studying," she says in a *gotcha* tone. Mia once brought champagne to a study session in college, and I haven't let her live it down. Clearly, she's been primed for a chance to get back at me.

"Last I checked, this isn't finals week." A bunch of us met up at our friend's apartment to study. Most of us were supposed to bring snacks, but Mia was a barista at the time, so she got put in charge of drinks. Pretty sure everyone assumed she'd bring leftover brewed coffee from the early shift.

She sets down the menu, rattling the cutlery. "That wasn't my fault, and you know it. Delia called it a study 'party' and asked me to bring drinks. I brought drinks."

"Alcoholic ones." I can't hold back a chuckle at the memory of her pulling champagne bottles out of her backpack. "We met up at ten a.m. to study and you brought booze."

"Stuff to make mimosas," she says, as if that makes it better. "That's a perfectly reasonable brunch beverage."

The fact that she still gets riled up over something that happened years ago is pretty cute. "I did ace my soil science final."

With a groan, she lifts the menu again, hiding the smile I saw slip onto her face. While she looks over the selection, I flip through the pages explaining different tropes. Some are familiar from attending her bookstore events and watching her interviews, but a lot of them are new.

One trope in particular catches my eye. "Cinnamon roll hero?" Referring to characters as pastries isn't really that outlandish compared to some stuff I've heard discussed at her panels over the years. "Not to be confused with the closely related glazed doughnut hero."

"You joke," she says. "But I could totally see that term taking off."

I'm almost afraid to ask. "What would that even mean?"

"Well, a cinnamon roll hero is the opposite of an alpha male. He's sweet and thoughtful, totally gooey."

Thinking aloud, I say, "Glazed doughnuts are deep-fried and decadent. Would a hero like that shower his love interest with gifts and romantic gestures?"

She frowns thoughtfully, then shakes her head. "Glazed doughnuts are indulgent, don't get me wrong. But they're not over-the-top. They don't have tons of frills like sprinkles and filling, but they're reliable. You can always count on them for a sweet pick-me-up. A glazed doughnut is never going to let you down."

Her eyes soften as she says this, and I catch a glimpse of the same expression I saw for a moment back at her condo. Something new in the way she looks at me.

But then her phone dings loudly from her purse. She pulls it out and frowns at the screen. "Shoot. I keep forgetting to confirm which panels I'm speaking on for the book convention next month. Do you mind if I answer this email real quick?"

Neither of us ever bothers with the no-phones-at-dinner etiquette, but maybe it's because I put effort into making tonight out of the ordinary that answering a work email right now feels like she's purposely trying to lessen the impact of the candlelit atmosphere and rooftop view.

While I wait for her to finish, I check my phone. There's a voicemail from my dad, and for a moment, I fear the worst. The morning after trivia night, Scott's texts pressuring me to visit the farmhouse got in my head and I called Dad to check in, but he didn't answer. But the voicemail is just him apologizing for being out of cell range on the back acreage and letting me know everyone's doing well.

I'm about to put away my phone when the screen lights up with a call from my friend Joe. In my rush to reject it, I accidentally answer. "Hey," I say quietly. "Can't talk right now."

Mia glances up and I mouth the word *Sorry*, but she waves a hand, distracted.

Meanwhile, Joe says, "Our softball team needs another player for tonight's game. You in?"

"Nah, not this time." Half the people on his rec league have kids and can't make it to every game, so I fill in when I have the time.

"I can pick you up. What else you got going on?" His voice is loud amid the hushed conversation around us, and I lower the volume, cupping my hand over the phone.

"I'm on a date, man." A flicker of movement catches my eye, and I look over to find Mia frantically shaking her head, eyes wide. Oh shit.

Joe pounces on my accidental confession. "A date? With who?"

Pulling at my collar, I say, "Not that kind of a date." True, at least. "I'm just hanging out with—" A kick to my shin cuts me off short. Not hard but strong enough to make me realize mentioning Mia would raise all sorts of questions.

"Are you making up excuses because you're still mad we put you in right field last game?" Joe asks.

"That wasn't cool," I say, momentarily distracted. "I'm the best fielder that team has and you know it." Out of the corner of my eye, I catch Mia's death glare and cut the argument short. "Give me a call next time you need an extra player and I'll prove it."

"Okay, but I expect to hear all about your date when I see you next."

"Not a date." I pinch the bridge of my nose.

"Then I want to hear about this woman you're keeping things casual with," he says. "Don't make me have Sera ask Mia. You know she'll get it out of her."

Shit. That would ruin everything. "Sera has enough on her mind." She's been putting in a lot of hours in preparation for taking time off when the baby comes.

"Exactly. She needs a distraction from the stress of getting ready for the little one. She'd jump at the chance."

The threat fills me with dread. I finally manage to get him off the phone with promises to explain at the Brewers baseball game this weekend. I'm nervous to see what Mia will say, but she just shakes her head.

"See? That's why a date was a bad idea," she says. "Pretending to be a couple would get us in trouble." She must not have heard Joe's threat to get Sera involved, or she wouldn't be so chill. "Hence, the binder." She hoists it up with a *ta-da* smile, and I can't help but grin back.

"Are you sure trope tests will be any better?" I thought Mia was exaggerating the risks, but after that phone call, I see her point. I've never had to hide anything from Joe, but if it's a question of telling him the truth or protecting Mia, there's no contest.

"Yes, because the situations aren't inherently romantic." She scrunches up her nose. "Not all of them at least. Anyway, we have rules. We won't be acting like a couple out in public, or fooling our friends and family."

Mia and her rules. "And if you change your mind, you'll tell me." I'm not asking, but she answers anyway.

"Always."

I blow out a shaky breath. "So we're doing it. Until you're ready to call it quits."

"Or you are." She issues it like a challenge, but if she thinks I'm scared of intimacy with her, she's very much mistaken.

The appetizers arrive and we both dig in like we're grateful for the chance to not talk for a moment. Once the food has hit my bloodstream, I hail a passing server. "Excuse me. Do you have a pen we could borrow?"

With a skeptical glance between me and Mia—dressed up, with emptied wineglasses—and the binder, he shrugs and hands me one from his apron. Uncapping it, I flip to the list of tropes. "You're the expert. What trope should we start with?"

"I was thinking workplace romance."

"You want to come spend a day with me at Hill and Dale?" That actually sounds fun, and I'm sure the owners would go along with it. "We could tell Faye that you're shadowing me for book research."

"Ha, no. It's supposed to be ninety degrees this week." Mia's preferred summer involves moving from air-conditioning to the pool, not working in the hot sun, which is why I know she must've been at her wit's end to help me pull up paving stones. "I was thinking you could bring your landscaping design work to my place," she says.

"You write when I'm around a lot. How would this be any different?" I point to the trope definition and read aloud. "'Concern that a breakup would make the workplace awkward.' You work alone, so if we metaphorically broke up, no harm done."

She jumps in. "At the core, an office romance is simply about characters who work together falling in love."

"Which we aren't going to do." I raise my brows, daring her to object, and when she doesn't, my heart falls, even though I should know better by now. "So I think we need to raise the stakes a little." She was adamant that a romantic evening wouldn't change how we saw each other. How is working side by side in her home office any different?

"Can we at least try it my way first?" There's a note of desperation in her voice and I get the feeling that even though she seemed confident about the plan, she doesn't trust it enough to let go.

But she's supposed to be getting some distance from her work and this would be the exact opposite. I glance down at the page, looking for a way to change her mind.

I read the next bullet point: "'Possibility for coworkers to discover the relationship.' No coworkers at your condo, unless you count Frank." The plant I gave her the night we met not only survived but has grown to towering proportions. She often jokes Frank's size is the reason she chose a loft. "And let's face it, he wouldn't take his chaperoning duties seriously because he knows you'd never fall for me."

"Give yourself some credit," she says, index finger tracing a slow circle around the rim of her wineglass. "You think it's never crossed my mind since we made that pact?"

Maybe it's the wine on a mostly empty stomach, but I can't let that slip by. "That's news to me." When? And why didn't she make a move?

"There's one thing all my exes have in common," she says, in what feels like a total change of subject. But her next words make it clear. "We're not in each other's lives at all."

It's true, for her. All of her ex-boyfriends have disappeared from her life, or she from theirs. But I went to my first girlfriend's wedding last year. And I've stayed in touch with my college girlfriend, the one I broke up with a few months before I met Mia. She's a doctor now, out in Maryland. I dated one of the bartenders I met at trivia night for a few months, and we chat whenever we run into each other. We're not the best of friends, but we're not strangers, either.

Mia speaks again, cutting short my thoughts. "Friendships last. But relationships . . ." She pauses. Maybe the alcohol has loosened her tongue, too, or maybe this fake date is changing how we see each other, after all. "With relationships, who knows? Could be the best thing that ever happened to you or your biggest regret." She meets my gaze, dark eyes serious, like she needs me to understand. "When it comes to you, that's not a risk I'm willing to take."

I get it. Love isn't a sure thing. We've both seen it crumble and break. But the one thing I am sure of is Mia. If she wants to stick with the routine but pretend things have changed, then I'll enter that fantasy with her.

eight

Gavin

Mia was onto something with this trope test. I underestimated how different it would feel to sit next to her knowing we're supposed to be acting like characters in an office romance.

She cleared off the end of her desk for me to set up my laptop. Afternoon light is streaking through the windows, illuminating floor-to-ceiling shelves accessible by a library ladder I installed for her last year. The corkboard on the wall across from her desk is tacked with slips of paper and photos and sticky notes.

I went straight to bed after our non-date last night and awoke to a text from Joe that was just three question marks. I put him off by reminding him we'll have time to talk at the game this weekend. Might've made it harder on myself since my brother will be there, too, but at least I gave myself time to think of a good explanation. But it was an important reminder of why we need to keep this a secret. I can only hope he hasn't already told Sera I'm seeing someone.

Ironically, even though the surroundings are familiar, I am seeing Mia in a new light. Or rather, I'm allowing myself to think of her in the way I've always suppressed, because I'm supposed to be acting like her lovesick colleague. That must be why I'm captivated by the furrow in her brow as she types, the way she nibbles her thumbnail before returning to the keyboard.

But she doesn't seem affected. No furtive glances or evidence of the temptation to cross the best-friend line that she mentioned last night. Driven by an urge to see if this made-up scenario is getting to her, I ask, "Is this working?"

She pulls her attention from the monitor, eyes unfocused behind her glasses, like her mind was elsewhere, and I feel bad for speaking up. "Is what working?"

"This?" I twirl an orange pen in the air, the one I nabbed from the jar to doodle with. "Are you getting—" I shift, trying to get comfortable in the space-age chair she insisted I sit in "—inspired?"

"It's been five minutes."

"Is that all?"

She leans across the desk and taps an oversize hourglass I hadn't noticed. "Yep."

"Wait, where have you been hiding that?" I make grabby hands.

She snatches it out of reach. "It's not a toy, it's a tool." I can't hold back a smirk, and she rolls her eyes, knowing me too well. "That's what she said. Yeah, yeah."

"You walked right into it."

"I'm a romance author. Innuendo is part of the job. What's your excuse?"

"My best friend is a romance author?"

She grins. "Fair enough. But stop distracting me."

"Shutting up now." But it's so quiet that I swear I can hear the sand shifting through the hourglass.

I'm more sure than ever that Mia picked workplace romance because it's the easiest way to claim she's doing something outside the box while sticking to her usual routine.

One thing is for sure: Even though I'm on edge about how to act, this does feel less risky than last night when there was that flicker of curiosity in her eyes. Like if we tested the only-one-bed trope, no one would sleep on the floor. I can imagine waking up next to her, gorgeously disheveled in the only open room of a fully booked hotel. Seeing an awareness dawn in her eyes, then a rush of desire as she nestled closer and . . .

Yeah, something's got to give. Normally I do my best not to pester Mia when she's writing. But she didn't invite me here to behave like I typically would. The vibe in here is all work and no play, and based on everything we discussed last night, it's my mission to change that. I resettle myself, trying to find a position that isn't pure agony since this is the most uncomfortable piece of furniture I've ever sat on, and I'm struck with an idea.

Biting back a childish grin, I email her a formal complaint about the chair, then open my design software and get to work, laying out a plan for a job I recently contracted, two acres surrounding a renovated mid-century home. I'm dying to revive the pear grove on one corner of the property and tone down the maximalist landscaping at the front of the house.

After working for almost an hour, I check my email. Ha. Mia replied to my complaint. I glance over at her, but she's typing away, curls brushed back into a bun that gives her a no-nonsense appearance. Paired with her striped button-down, she's going for an all-business approach. Now I feel kinda bad for sending the prank email.

RE: Can't work in these conditions

Greetings Mr. Lane,
    The team has reviewed your complaint, and while we take all concerns seriously, we take issue with you singling out Mia Brady as "the evil mastermind" behind your discomfort. Not only is Mia our most dedicated

employee, you've been assigned her preferred form of seating. It is not, as you so erroneously stated, an "alien captain's chair."

I highlight *erroneously* to check the definition and snort. Erroneously my ass.

> Your seat is an ergonomic, cushioned marvel of engineering (see link to the product description and note the five-star rating). You should count yourself lucky to rest your butt in such luxury.

"Pretty sure talking about your colleague's butt in the workplace is frowned upon," I say.

She keeps her eyes on the screen, but the corner of her mouth lifts in a grin. "We have great lawyers. I'm not worried."

Oh, that's how she wants to play it. "Fine. We'll see how you do when complaints start stacking up." From what I've read, a lot of office-romance novels are basically a long string of HR violations.

Typing furiously, I write a reply and send it to her. Two minutes later there's a response in my inbox.

RE: Workplace-appropriate behavior

Hello again,

With all due respect, Mr. Lane, we're wondering how you have the time to file multiple formal complaints during business hours. While we failed to use the proper anatomical term for your gluteal region, we believe you understood our meaning. Your posterior is blessed to be sitting in Mia's chair of choice, and she's quite frankly an angel for bestowing it upon you.

P.S. Furnish your own chair if you're going to be such a crybaby.

I let out a laugh. "You've resorted to name-calling?"

"Better than wasting time with falsified claims." Her posture is rigid, shoulders back, as if she's getting into the character of the prim-and-not-at-all-proper boss. It shouldn't be sexy, and it's not, of course. Nothing about her precise words and hint of wickedness is at all arousing.

I shift in my seat, and my focus gets yanked from how closely we're toeing the line between joking and flirting to how massively terrible this chair is. "I meant every word. Feels like I'm being eaten by a Venus flytrap."

The corner of her mouth twitches, but she keeps her expression neutral. "It's firm, to establish good posture."

"It's a torture device."

"Ungrateful." She's smiling now.

"Unethical."

She laughs. "I really didn't mean to punish you." Her expression turns apologetic. "I thought you'd like it."

"I don't hate it." I'm not talking about the chair. I'm talking about having this side of Mia—flirty, teasing—directed at me for the first time. "But yeah, it is pretty bad," I say, covering my slip. "Want to switch?"

"Won't help. This one's the same."

I'm shocked she owns two of these monstrosities. "You keep a backup?"

"I ordered an extra one for you," she mumbles. "When you agreed to this, I figured the least I could do was make sure you were comfortable."

"You bought me a desk chair?" That's pretty damn sweet.

"Yeah, but you hate it." She looks dejected, and I instantly want to fix it.

"Okay, yeah, I do. But you spent hundreds of dollars on this?" I clicked through the link—it retails for over five hundred dollars. And she must've assembled it, too. "You didn't have to do that."

"You're doing this for me."

"Hanging out with you for the afternoon isn't a hardship."

"It's not just hanging out with me, though, is it?" She holds my gaze, long enough that warmth blooms in my chest. I'm an expert at pushing it aside, but lately my feelings for her are resistant to pruning, like a weed, and just as unwelcome.

"Since we haven't discussed what exactly we're doing here, it kind of is."

"Good point. We need roles to play," she says, and her cheeks flush a deep rose color.

An answering heat rises to my own face, which is ridiculous. It's not like I'm a stranger to role-play, just the idea of doing it with Mia. To pull my mind from tempting images, I say, "Makes sense. We're acting out workplace romance, so we should get into character." I go to lean back, but the chair has me in a vise grip, posture like a supervillain. "Why am I here working in your office?"

"Backstory. Hmm." She drums her fingers on the desk, slipping into what I recognize as brainstorming mode. "You work remotely, but your roommate is your ex-girlfriend who's trying to become a yoga influencer, and she says your loud typing ruins her flow."

I'm nodding along. "So I've been working in the coffee shop, and we got to chatting about how expensive their cold brew is when you can just—"

"Make it at home," she says, lighting up. "And then we got to arguing over whose cold-brewing method was superior—"

"Mine. I use dry ice."

"I tell you that's ridiculous, which it is by the way. Dry ice?" She raises her brows but keeps rolling with the idea. "And how you should try mine instead, but we both have projects to finish, so we sample each other's coffee while working late into the night . . ."

That catches my attention. "That took a steamy turn."

"It's kind of what I do best," she says, with obvious pride, but then she deflates. "Except this isn't a book. We're sitting here in my office in the middle of the day and physical stuff is off the table, so really, this is pointless."

I hate seeing the defeat in her eyes. For this to be a success, she needs to let me in. Even though she's never seen me as anything more than a friend, I can't help but remember what she said last night. That maybe, I might have a chance.

"Nothing's going to happen," I venture, testing the waters. "But we can pretend, right?"

Her eyes shoot to mine, dark and curious. "Pretend how?"

"However far we want to." The words slip out. "I mean, getting physical is out of the question. Per the contract."

"One you never signed," she says.

"Neither did you," I remind her, steering my mind away from that potential loophole. "But I was thinking more along the lines of flirting. Fake flirting," I clarify.

"What's the difference?"

"Intent. If I flirt with you today, it will be to help you forget about your book."

"And if you flirted with me for real?" She's holding herself very still, only her gaze roving over my face, and I realize I'm barely breathing, muscles taut.

"If I flirted with you for real, it would be to get closer to you. To see what makes Mia let go." I shouldn't be saying this; I've never even let myself think it. "If I flirted with you, it would be to tease out the hidden parts of you, the ones you hold back."

Her lips part, eyes wide, and for a moment, I wonder if I've pushed it too far. But there's more than surprise in her gaze . . . interest, maybe? Curiosity, for sure. Seeing it has me tipping toward her, my normal resolve to resist the attraction frayed to a thread.

She swallows, and my gaze dips to the kissable peek of skin at her open collar. "Flirt away, then. I can handle it." She sweeps a casual hand toward her stomach. "No butterflies in sight."

I jerk my eyes back up to hers, and see a flicker I long to ignite. "No?" I lean forward, elbows resting on my knees, watching her. "Because I think you like being teased."

"Excuse me?" Her voice is breathy, and my pulse kicks up. She's definitely affected.

"You like a guy to mess around with you. You always go out with serious guys in real life, but in your books, the heroines always fall for the guys who get a rise out of them."

"That's fiction."

"Or it's you holding yourself back from men who you might fall for." I've seen her around guys she likes, and ones she doesn't. And I know just how much she likes someone that can make her laugh, pull her out of her routine. It's just too bad I can never be that guy. "You pursue men who are nothing like your friends—"

"Nothing like *you*, you mean?" She crosses her arms, settling back, and I get the sense she's faking being unaffected, and it only fuels my desire to get past her walls.

"All I'm saying is maybe you're scared of how good things could be between us."

"And how is that, exactly?"

The wise thing to do would be to back off. But it feels like a challenge. Like she thinks I haven't been paying attention all these years.

"Can't say for sure, but I have a few guesses." A bluff. I've never allowed my mind to wander in that direction. Kept it reined in. But now it's easy to go there, to let my mind slip through the padlocked gate of desire.

She swallows, her throat working, and my own pulse kicks up. "Guess away." She's joining me in this game. And it is a game, I remind myself. An experiment for her work. Not personal. Not *real*, even though my pounding pulse says otherwise.

What would Mia like? She's someone who gives freely of herself. Her time. Her energy. Aware, sensitive. Receptive. "You're used to taking the lead, controlling how much you feel. Holding yourself back. I'd like to see you come undone. To take you past the point of holding back, to watch you get swept away."

Her mouth is parted, pink tongue visible between her lips, and I speak the next words on instinct alone. "I'd start with slow kisses, deep ones." I can't tear my eyes away from her. "Drawing out the moment until you couldn't take it anymore. You'd want me to rush things, prove nothing could make you lose your grip, but I'd take my time. Savor you with lingering kisses, and you'd surprise yourself with how much you wanted more."

She lets out a shuddering breath. "You think I'd be surprised by how I'd respond to you?"

For a moment I'm speechless, knocked off-balance by her directness. Even more so when she unfolds her legs and leans in, matching my pose. "You don't think I'd be ready for all of that and more? That I've been craving the freedom to cross that line?" Her lips curve upward. "The only surprising thing is you thinking I haven't already imagined how good you'd taste."

Our knuckles are brushing, our faces inches away, and the only thing keeping words from becoming reality is years of habit. Years of reminding myself there are good reasons we don't touch, good reasons we don't give voice to thoughts like these. Reasons that have fully fled my mind at this point, but muscle memory keeps me still, keeps my distance. The intensity in her gaze sparks something in my chest, but I learned to ignore those bursts of attraction.

Which is good, because a moment later Mia pulls back, a smug grin on her face. "Is that what you had in mind? Because we might want to tone it down if we don't want our hypothetical colleagues to catch on."

She was pretending. Of course she was. Pulling from her creative well and years of writing love stories. Or maybe, like me, she was finally letting go.

nine

Mia

The cursor blinks on a blank page. Forty-five minutes since I awkwardly segued us back into normalcy—three flips of the hourglass—and my replies to Gavin's emails are the sum total of my word count for the day.

I haven't managed to write a single word since our attempt at role-playing. Seeing that side of Gavin gave me the irresistible urge to explore, like a book left open on a table. He's terrible at bluffing—when we play cards with Joe and Sera, I always know when he has a bad hand—and I didn't expect him to be so good at pretending to flirt. Except it didn't feel like pretend. It felt effortless. Real. Which is why I never should've agreed to blur the lines with him.

Nearly ten years of friendship and he was able to fake flirt his way under my skin in less than ten minutes. In my defense, he's heard me moan about countless bad first dates and helped me cope with all my breakups. He's like an inside agent, using my deepest desires against me, or in this case, *for* me. Because what he was saying really worked for me.

Surprising, since office romance didn't work out too well when I tried it in real life. After breaking up with Ted, I had a couple years of false starts. Disappointing first dates and short relationships where things didn't click. I was working at a small accounting firm and hit it off with a coworker. After a tax season of long hours and late-night fast-food runs, we mutually agreed to take things further. About a month into dating him, I mentioned maybe it was time to bring up our relationship at work and stop pretending we were just friends. His response? *Aren't we?* Things at the office were a lot less fun after that.

It was years ago, and I'd forgotten all about stolen watercooler glances until Gavin started talking about how he'd act if he were interested in me. And for a long, forbidden moment, I'd wished it was our friendship that had slipped into something more, instead of the other men who'd left me unsatisfied.

We came close, once before. A guy I'd gone out with a few times got us tickets to a musical I'd been dying to see, then ghosted me a week before the show. Gavin surprised me with great seats to make up for it. At intermission we saw the jerk I'd been dating, holding hands with another woman. Gavin had looped an arm around my shoulders as the lights dimmed and made a joke about a rebound being the best way to get over someone. *As your friend*, he said, low into my ear as the orchestra swelled, *I'd be willing to fill that role.*

But we agreed to always be the reason the other smiled, and no one smiles after their heart is broken. *I'd never break your heart*, he'd said, and I'd answered, *I know.* But then reminded him if we fell in love, things wouldn't be so simple.

Yet in my attempt to avoid the complications of fake dating, I've landed us in a situation that's the farthest thing from uncomplicated. I can't help stealing glances at him, as if a few words could shift him from my lovable best friend into . . . what? A boyfriend? That would be a step backward, based on my own experience.

He's frowning slightly at the screen, lips pursed . . . and why am I looking at his mouth? I yank my gaze away and open the file containing Victor's character journal. The truth is, writing those tongue-in-cheek responses to Gavin's chair complaints was the most fun I've had at my desk in months. Acting out workplace romance brought the third book in the series to mind, a romance between Sydney's friend, an editor, and a publicist he works with. I reenvision a pivotal scene in that novel from Victor's perspective.

I already know him inside and out. He and Sydney have been secondary characters for the entire series. Best friends, ready to step in with one-liners and last-minute rides to the airport. They're woven into the heart of the books, the thread that connects everyone's stories.

Their bond is unbreakable, and some readers argue it's the strongest relationship of all. But it's not love. Or at least not the romantic kind. Not yet.

Authors are warned never to write ourselves into our characters. To keep a healthy distance. But I couldn't help pouring myself into these two. Gave them soft hearts easily bruised, and an unshakable trust in each other. Told myself it was fine because I'd never have to delve into what was keeping them from a happy-ever-after.

That's why, when the producers approached me about a fourth book, my knee-jerk reaction was to say no. But the more I thought about it, the more I wanted that for them. I love the idea of the cheerleaders, the goofballs, the friends always ready with quiet support or vocal encouragement, getting dragged onto center stage to discover what's keeping them apart isn't worth holding on to.

But because I went and made these characters so much like me, that's pretty impossible. My own parents' love story didn't even last until the birth of their second child. Them not being together wasn't a tragedy so much as a fact I saw echoed in countless other lives—sometimes love works out, and a lot of times it fails miserably.

I believe happy endings exist in real life, but they're not guaranteed. I like knowing the end before I begin. I even flip to the last page of love triangle romance novels to make sure I don't root for the wrong person. I want to give readers that same certainty with Sydney and Victor, but first I need to convince myself.

Seeing the scene from his friends' love story play out through Victor's eyes, I realize his focus isn't on the drama unfolding, but on Sydney. Writing this into my manuscript would be a flashback, filling in the gaps of why he's ready for something more. Mind outpacing my typing, I enter that blissful place where I'm swept away in writing, and when I look up, the late-afternoon sun is filtering through the branches outside the window, my back aches, and Gavin is gone.

I pull my phone out of the desk drawer and see a text.

Gavin: Are there mandated breaks in this workplace? Getting coffee. Don't tell those nightmare HR people.

Smiling, I text a thumbs-up and ask if he can grab me a bagel or something from the pastry case, then open the internet browser. I've just typed "cost to rent out a theater" for a possible grand gesture into the search bar when Gavin walks in with an iced coffee and a quiche. "What're you working on?"

"Research." For once it's true and not a pointless rabbit hole I've gone down to avoid writing. "You got here fast."

He leans against the desk. "I was already almost back when you texted. You were lost in your work, huh?" He motions to the website. "Makes sense."

I give him a little shove. Regret it the instant my fingers connect with his thigh, his muscles hard beneath the thin fabric of his shorts. "I *was* writing, actually. I didn't even hear you go."

"Didn't want to interrupt but I texted the heads-up since I know you keep your phone on silent. Wouldn't want you accusing me of clocking out early without notifying management." His grin is infectious, with no sign of the earlier intensity, and I should be happy we're back to normal. *Am* happy. Of course I am.

"They've been breathing down my neck." With a surreptitious glance over my shoulder, I drop my voice into a stage whisper. "Something about visiting NSFW sites while logged into the company Wi-Fi."

He shakes his head. "Overlords." He takes a glug of my coffee, and I commandeer it before he drinks it all.

"Did you finish up your designs?"

"Got to a good stopping point, and I couldn't do another minute in that sorry excuse for a chair. Let me try yours."

"It's the same model." I've tried out a lot of desk chairs over the years and finally settled on a gaming chair. Between that and my ergonomic keyboard and vertical mouse, I'm able to battle the joint pain brought on by long hours of typing.

He makes a shooing motion, and I give in. It'd be good to stretch my legs anyway. But he yelps when he plops down, back arching like he's been stung. "Shit, this one feels even worse somehow. No wonder you haven't been getting anything done."

"It's not the chair, it's the story."

"Fifty-fifty." He uses my mouse to open a new tab in the browser window.

"Dig into a writer's search history and the results are on you."

"Don't tease me with a good time."

This man. I hold back a smile, barely. "Why are you so nosy?"

"Says the woman who eavesdrops on conversations and uses them as inspiration."

"That happened once." The corner of his mouth hitches, and I cave in a heartbeat. "Twice, whatever."

"Not that you need to borrow from real life." He lifts the candle on my desk to his nose and breathes in, chest rising. "You're always coming up with new plots."

Imagination has never been my problem. "It's not the lack of ideas that's tripping me up, it's the heart of the story." I bite into the quiche and my stomach rumbles in response. Didn't even realize I was hungry until now. "I don't know why I can't convince myself these characters would take the leap into something more."

No push seems strong enough to overcome the risk of losing their friendship. That's why faking it is so appealing. They can end the scene they're acting out and go back to the same low-stakes friendship.

Instead of answering, Gavin types *leap* into the search bar, as if that will help.

"Problem solved," I say, sarcasm less effective with a mouthful of buttery crust.

Ignoring me, he clicks on a video of bungee jumping. "What about this? We take a literal leap to inspire your characters' metaphorical one?"

I don't bother to answer. I don't mind heights; I do mind trusting my life to a glorified rubber band.

He swings toward me, his legs brushing mine through my linen pants. A meaningless touch I normally wouldn't notice. But all this talk of sparks and chemistry has me wanting him to do it again, deliberately this time. To see if his touch would have the same effect as his words.

But he's chattering away like nothing's changed. ". . . The thrill pushes them to live life without regrets."

"Bungee jumping would be the regret. If I lived that long."

He grins, a flash of white teeth. "You're not making this easy on me."

"Oh, I wasn't aware you were writing the book." The words

come out snippy, though it's myself I'm frustrated with, and his smile dims.

"Sorry. I'm not doing this right—"

Does he really think he's the problem? "Gavin, it's got nothing to do with you. I'm supposed to be taking a break from writing, but I came up with a work-around just to try to hit my word count. You gave up your day off for this, and I know you'd rather be fiddling around in the garden than pretending to flirt with me."

"I signed up to flirt with you. That's been the highlight of my day."

I thought we'd dropped the pretense of role-playing. Was that Gavin talking, or the smitten coworker he was pretending to be?

"Also, what I do in my yard isn't fiddling. One wrong snip with the pruning shears and . . ." He draws a finger across his throat.

"A perfectly good rosebud loses its life?"

"Number one cause of accidental death among roses. Reckless pruning is no joke." He gives me a lopsided grin. "Unlike your complete disregard for workplace ethics."

"Those emails were the most productive part of my day." Even though I did some good character work, I need to be checking off scenes by now. "You were right. I need to get away from this book, mentally and physically."

He not-at-all-subtly inclines his head toward the screen, where the bungee jumping video is paused.

"Technically speaking, that would work," I admit. "But less peril, please."

His eyes light up. Swiveling back to the desk, he navigates to an ominous-looking website.

I squint at the header. "An escape room?"

"Faye's been asking me to schedule an escape room for team building, but I've never tried one. It would be good to experience it before I take the group there." The owners of the garden center place a high priority on a quality work environment, and this wouldn't be the first team-building event Gavin's led. "No time to stress over the plot if you're working to beat the clock, right?"

I highly doubt figuring out puzzles will be enough to free up my creativity, but the whole point is to get out of my routine. I can't keep staring at my laptop, willing words to appear. "An escape room it is."

Forced proximity always was a favorite trope of mine. Maybe spending an afternoon locked up with Gavin will shift my focus enough to get clarity. Either way, we're keeping this experiment between us and there will be no need to flirt. All that's required for this trope test is two people stuck together. What could be simpler?

ten

Gavin

I pull a paving stone off the bed of the truck and stack it atop the others in my driveway. It's Saturday afternoon and Scott and I are headed into Chicago for the Brewers-Cubs game today, but before he gets here, I need to unload these bricks and grab a shower. My gloves are gritty, shirt damp with sweat, but I'm grateful for the physical exertion to keep my racing thoughts at bay.

Flirting with Mia the other day felt so real. To stop myself from replaying the memory of her leaning close, lips parted and gaze sultry, I stopped by the garden center this morning and bought a load of paving stones, even though I took the day off for the game.

The task should keep me occupied, but my mind keeps returning to Mia's declaration—*"The only surprising thing is you thinking I haven't already imagined how good you'd taste."* Was she just playing a role, or was there truth in her words? Either way, her confession sent me into a tailspin of desire that left me delirious enough to volunteer to be locked into a confined space.

Three hundred square feet. That's the size of the escape room. I'm not sure which I'm more worried about, the tiny space we'll be stuck in or acting like I didn't mean every word I said.

I slide another paver off the bed of my truck and catch sight of my brother's car pulling up to the curb.

He steps out, wearing a jersey, sandy-blond hair ruffled by the breeze, and scans the torn-up yard. "Thought we could get to Wrigleyville early and grab a drink before the game, but I guess not."

"Next train into the city isn't for another hour, but help yourself to a beer. Won't take me long to finish."

He shakes his head, already unbuckling his watch, the pale skin beneath the band a contrast to his sunburned arms. He's probably spent the past week outside chasing after Paxton and Brett. "What, and get grief for standing around watching you work?"

I grin at him. "How are Amber and the boys?"

"Good," he says, climbing up onto the truck bed. "I feel bad leaving her with the kids all weekend, but she practically shooed me out the door."

"Dad's there to help." And I know for a fact his wife doesn't mind, especially since Scott and I don't get to see each other often anymore. She thanked me once for pushing my brother to get out of the house and have fun. Parenting two young kids turned him into a hermit for a while.

"Speaking of Dad . . ." Scott says, with a casualness that has me on high alert. "Have you talked lately?"

"Not since last week." Once again, I get the sensation something's up. But every time I've called recently, my dad seemed to be doing great. Would he hide something serious from me? "What's wrong?" All sorts of scenarios fly through my mind, none of them good.

"Nothing."

"It's not nothing if you're asking."

"He says it's not my place to tell you, but I think you should know." His mouth pulls to the side. "They're selling the farm."

It takes a second for his words to sink in. Mom started teaching college courses after the divorce, but she still has a hand in operating the business side of the tree farm. "What about the house?" They built it together, on ten acres of land that has since expanded to more than fifty.

"That, too. Dad's moving."

I shield my eyes with a gloved hand, wondering if he's messing with me. "Where?"

He dodges my glance. "There are some nice town houses near us. He wants to be close to the grandkids again."

Dad's moving to Colorado and didn't bother to mention it? "He wouldn't just give up on the business. He's barely sixty."

"Not like he hasn't had offers," Scott says. "He could've retired a few years ago."

I can't imagine Dad not running the tree farm. He's poured himself into that place, heart and soul, my whole life. "Never mentioned wanting to."

"Not to you."

That stings. Dad and I are close. Have been ever since my parents' divorce. Mom moved to Madison, and I stayed at the farm. Didn't want to leave my friends, the house I grew up in. The land.

Scott seems to notice my sense of betrayal and hops down from the truck, tailgate hinges squeaking in protest. "Mom and I wanted to tell you, but he asked us to keep it to ourselves until he could talk to you in person. He didn't want to pressure you."

"Into what?" I ask, dreading the answer.

"Taking over. What else?"

"C'mon. He doesn't expect that of me." But he has in the past. Why wouldn't it come into play now, if what Scott's saying is true?

"Maybe not, but he should," Scott says. My father never

understood my decision to make a life in Illinois, but he's come to terms with it, mostly. Scott hasn't. "You run the garden center, and Faye and her husband, Dale, aren't even family."

They've become like a second family, but that isn't what keeps me there. "Run it, don't own it. I get to clock out at the end of the day and not worry about keeping the lights on." Working alongside Dad would've consumed my time. After college, I was tired of being his confidant. Tired of him pouring all the regret he harbored into the farm instead of rebuilding his life.

Scott squints against the midday sun, like he's trying to figure me out, and for once, I wish he'd really listen. "I love the work," I tell him. "But Dad's whole life is the farm."

"Not anymore," he says.

"He's got a buyer?"

He pulls the last paving stone off the truck. "Don't think he's in a rush. But he's taking steps." Slyly, he says, "He'd let you have the land for cheap."

I've known that since he tearfully hugged me at graduation and told me he always knew I'd be the one to take over. Right before I told him I'd taken a job near Chicago.

"He deserves what it's worth." I pull the tarp off the truck bed, brick dust catching the wind, then roll it up and head toward the backyard, ready to put an end to this conversation.

Catching up, Scott says, "Shit, Gavin. Why'd you get your horticulture degree if not to run the nursery someday?" Here we are again. As if I haven't explained myself often enough. How I want to work to live, not live to work.

But a lot of that stemmed from knowing I'd be the one Dad leaned on, his excuse to keep hiding from life. Awful as it sounds, without him, running the farm might not be so bad. "You don't want it, either," I tell him.

"I'm not the one working at a garden center." Scott never liked outdoorsy stuff. He had his share of chores, same as me, but whenever he could he'd take a shift at the register or filing receipts. "And our life is in Denver now. We can't uproot the kids."

"I'd never expect you to. But my life is here. And I don't want to pull up my own roots any more than you do."

He glances around. "You've got what, a quarter acre? The shed alone takes up half your backyard." It might not look like much, but I own a home in a town I love. "One of Dad's seedling greenhouses is bigger than your whole property," he adds. "Think what you could do with all that land."

"Grow trees," I say dully. Sell them to subdivisions and commercial developments. Dad does most of his business with developers, and I can't get excited about the cookie-cutter plots. I like to get to know the clients I work with and tailor the designs to their property.

"And the gardens back home? You're fine letting those go to a stranger?" He knows I can never stay out of the gardens when I visit. Always advising Dad on what fertilizer to use and when to divide the hostas. But it hasn't been home for a long time. Not for Mom or Scott, either. And soon, it seems, not for Dad.

"I have my own gardens." They're not as showstopping as the ones at our childhood home, but it's only a matter of time. "To be honest, I'll miss the cabin the most." My dad and uncle built it on the small lake on the east end of the farm back when I was a little kid. Mia's even used it as a writing retreat a handful of times.

"You sound entitled."

"I think I am entitled to choose to do what I want with my own life," I say. "We both got a lucky draw. I'm not denying that." Our parents made enough money to send us to college, and if I'd needed one, I had a job waiting for me. It isn't a privilege I take lightly, but I've absolved myself from letting it dictate my actions. "But I'm not obligated to take on a life someone else built for themselves. It was Dad's dream, not mine. He obviously agrees, since he's not the one here asking me to give this all up."

"I just think you're taking the easy route."

I turn to face him in the shadow of the shed. "Easy? You think my decision to stay in Illinois and work at a garden center is easy to explain at every family occasion? You think I enjoy opening up LANE TREE FARM shirts for my birthday each year and hearing the same jokes about how they're supposed to be for employees only? You think it's easy to know I've let Dad down, but knowing if I do what he wants, I'd be letting down myself?"

Scott sniffs, shoving his hands in his pockets. "I didn't mean it that way. But what's really keeping you here?"

"Besides a good job, my house, and my friends?"

"By friends, you mean Mia?"

Knew that one was coming. "She's one of them." I step inside the cedar-scented dimness of the shed, searching for an open shelf to store the tarp. "Also, my buddies from work, and Serafina and Joe, you know, the parents of my future godchild?" Joe's in full dad mode already and recently texted me asking if their houseplants were toxic, even though the baby's not born yet, let alone crawling.

Scott shifts a flowerpot to make room on one of the shelves. "So if Mia wasn't in the picture . . ."

I want to protest that staying close to my best friend would affect my decision even if I didn't have romantic feelings for her, but that would mean admitting he's partially right. "This isn't about her." I shove the tarp onto the shelf, and brush past him, back out into the open air.

"You've been friends since college and you're both single more often than not," he says, trailing after me. "Has nothing really ever happened between you two?"

"Nope." Not until this summer. But that's all pretend. "You

can't seem to wrap your head around it, but I'm happy here," I tell him. "Happy with the way things are." Mostly.

"Enough to give up any chance of moving back?"

I hesitate. Am I willing to lose somewhere that was a part of me for so long, just because I don't want it right now?

Scott shuts the door with a smug smile. "I'll tell Dad you're thinking about it."

I *am* thinking about it, that's the trouble. I can't *stop* thinking about it, not when Scott takes one look at the contents of my fridge and says he'd rather pay stadium prices than drink the beer I have on hand. Not even Joe catching a fly ball and giving it to the kid a few rows below us is enough to get my mind off my responsibility to take over the family business.

All I can think is, *am* I ungrateful?

I picture Dad's face when I told him I was doing an internship at a home-improvement chain the summer before I graduated, instead of coming back home to work like I usually did. I think about how I've tried so many times to explain the farm isn't just good memories, it's sad ones, too. About how maybe I've tricked myself and it's not really that I want to be here, but that I don't want to be *there*.

Maybe it is an act of rebellion, or entitlement, or a stubborn desire to not end up like him. Dad spent years living with regret and I don't want that for myself. I've never told Mia about my feelings because I don't want to risk losing her. But if my dad is trying, after nearly fifteen years, to move on with his life, then maybe I should rethink things.

Because that look in Mia's eyes yesterday . . . It wasn't apathy, or disinterest. It was desire. The same desire that flared in my own chest, despite years of pushing it aside.

I guess my brother is right. There's more to consider than where I make my home. There's whether I'm going to end up stuck, just like Dad, dreaming of a someday that's out of reach. I need to decide whether what's between Mia and me will always be enough. Whether trying for more is worth the risk. And this experiment is the perfect way to find out.

Scott had it backward. I'm staying for me, but if I move, it would be because I need to let her go.

We make it to the bottom of the third inning before Joe stretches and says, "Hey, I'm going to grab some nachos. Want anything from concessions?"

Scott, who already inhaled a Chicago-style hot dog and a pretzel and is happily drinking a beer, shakes his head. I do, too, but Joe shoots me a look. "Don't you owe me one?"

I catch his eye and realize he wants an explanation about my supposed date. Knowing he won't let it go, I sigh and scoot my way along the crowded aisle after him, since Scott catching wind of anything Mia-related is the last thing I want.

Once we're in line, Joe turns to me, dark brown eyes alight with interest. "All right, you've kept me hanging all week. Who is she?"

I already went through all the possibilities—telling him a version of the truth or making something up—and haven't settled on a decision.

Hands in my pockets, I shrug. "I was trying something new. Didn't work out."

"What, like a blind date?"

My boss tried to set me up with her niece once. Not going that route again. "Something like that."

Joe frowns in sympathy, which makes me feel like shit for not being honest. "What went wrong?"

"We want different things." A cheer goes up from the stadium and we turn to see the Cubs have scored another run. We both curse under our breath; Joe's a White Sox fan and rooting for the Brewers like me and Scott.

The people ahead of us step up to order, and he says, "Sorry to hear it, but I'm glad you're putting yourself out there."

I frown. "What's that supposed to mean?"

"You haven't dated anyone lately. Not since Mia ended things with her last boyfriend."

"Yeah, I have." There was the disastrous blind date, and Morris set me up with someone. We went out a few times, but it was clear she was just trying to make him jealous.

"No one long-term." He looks over at me, expression serious. "I was starting to think you were staying single for a reason."

It only takes a second for me to connect the dots. "You think I'm staying single for Mia?" If he's noticed something, does that mean she has, too?

He lifts a shoulder. "I've never seen you look at any of your girlfriends the way you look at her."

"Because I haven't met the right person."

"Maybe you have," he says.

I drop my eyes to the floor, popcorn crunching under my shoes as people jostle into line behind us. "She doesn't want that." He knows all about Mia's policy on dating friends.

"She *didn't* want that," he says. "People change. She's been single for what, almost two years?" Another cheer, but neither of us bothers to check the scoreboard. "Hell of a long time, man."

"You think she's . . ." I don't trust myself to say the words aloud.

"Holding out for you?" He shifts to make way for a passing group of teenagers. "Don't know, man. But wouldn't now be the perfect time to find out?"

The next cashier opens up, sparing me from having to answer. We place our orders and stand off to the side of the counter, waiting.

"Did you know Sera and I have been attending relationship retreats?" Joe raises his voice to be heard over the pulsing beat of a player's walk-up song. "We started a few months ago, to make sure we're in the habit of making time for each other when the baby comes."

Grateful he's left off badgering me about Mia, I say, "Good for you. Is it helpful?"

He nods. "Especially for communication. One thing I realized is how often I would choose to stay quiet about something, rather than risk messing with the status quo. But when I told her, I found out Sera wanted me to speak up. She'd been waiting for it."

By now I can tell what he's getting at. "I can't just ask Mia out." Except I did, kind of, and it got twisted into faking things. None of which I can get Joe's advice on, and that sucks.

He picks up our beers and hands me one. "Why not?"

"Because it's not that simple. Think how awkward it would be for you and Sera if we broke up." Not to mention how hard it would be to tell Mia I wanted to stop pretending, or that I never was in the first place.

"The alternative is one or both of you finds a partner and you drift apart." He takes a long drink of his brimming cup, and I follow suit, not wanting to end up with beer spilled down my front on the way back to our seats. "Either way," he continues, "this doesn't end up with you staying best friends for life."

"That's the old bullshit of men and women can't be friends."

He shakes his head. "You can't stay friends with someone you're in love with. Not forever."

My first impulse is to deny it. "I've been Mia's friend for almost a decade."

Joe stays quiet, and I think maybe I've finally won the argument, but then realize I've denied the wrong part. I said I could stay friends with Mia, not that I don't love her.

Because I do.

eleven

Mia

Are you free for a chat later today regarding season 4?

I stare at the email from my agent. My editor is cc'd. Turns out there is something more stressful than an unwritten book and a looming deadline, and it's an unwritten book, a looming deadline, and an unexpected mid-week call about said book.

After replying yes, I'm faced with the daunting task of focusing on writing while I wait for the call. To make matters worse, whenever I sit at my desk, I think about Gavin scooting his chair closer and his words, low and intentional . . . *You'd surprise yourself with how much you wanted more.*

His words unspooled possibilities in my mind, yearnings buried beneath fear and doubt. But even if I did want to explore the shift in my feelings toward Gavin—and I'm not sure I do—that's not going to get this book written. Days of uninterrupted writing time stretch between now and the forced proximity test, and I need to make the most of them. Deliberately turning away from the extra chair I seriously need to think about reselling, I open my manuscript.

I realized during my last writing session that Victor might have had feelings for Sydney all along. But what about her? Is she clueless, scared, or ambivalent? Desperate to cling to friendship in the face of the unknown, or simply too happy with what they have to want more?

My mind is full, but the page in front of me is blank. It feels like a judgment on my abilities as a storyteller. Normally a few days without writing leaves me cranky and annoyed. Lately, trying to write feels the same. My inspiration has tucked its tail and run, like love is a big scary thing. I wonder whether it's Sydney and Victor's story I'm more worried about or my own.

Too distracted to finish the scene where Victor almost ruins everything by sending Sydney a bunch of in-character texts that get read by one of their friends, I search for appetizer ideas to bring to Sera and Joe's baby shower next month, only to get a flurry of texts on the group chat that result in a decision to pivot to catering. Faced with proof my procrastination was doubly useless, I return my attention to the manuscript, trying not to feel defeated.

One scene at a time. But in the midst of writing a funny moment where Sydney scrambles to delete the incriminating texts, my own phone chimes. I should've put it on Do Not Disturb, but it's too late.

Evie: I'm dying to know how the method acting scenes are going. Send pages if you have them! No pressure. But you told me to ask. So a little pressure. Like a nudge, not the crushing weight of society's expectations.

I grin. Evie's texts read like her novels, off-the-wall in a charming way.

Evie: Also, I have a few chapters to send you, but I feel bad because lately you've been reading all my stuff without reciprocity.

Mia: Send away! Giving you feedback makes me feel productive.

My phone trills again, this time with an alert. Time for the video call. I carry my laptop out to the window seat and settle back against the plush cushions, hoping the comfortable surroundings will help me relax.

I log on and both my agent's and editor's faces appear onscreen. "Hello," they say in near unison, and I know instantly it can't be good news.

"Hi, Saheli." My agent's Pomeranian jumps into her lap, and she ruffles his ears. I wave at my editor. Her gray pixie cut is tousled and her fiery orange lipstick is on point. "How's it going, Claire?" She's smiling, but her posture is stiff, like she's perched on the edge of her seat.

"First off, don't worry," she says. Guess that confirms it. "But we do have some less-than-ideal news."

"Bad news?"

"Definitely not bad," Saheli jumps in, always diplomatic. "Difficult."

I wager a guess, wanting to get it over with. "They're scrapping the fourth season?" I hate how hopeful I sound, but I'm dying to be let off the hook.

"That would be bad news." Saheli's black brows tug together in a frown. "You know I'd never sugarcoat things." Face framed by a wavy bob, she meets my eyes, and I brace myself. "They're moving up the filming date by six months."

Before I can react, Claire says, "Apparently, Robert has a conflict with the next film in his espionage series."

"What does that mean for me?"

Saheli nudges her dog gently away from the teacup he's sniff-ing. "They need the story sooner than expected, in order to have time to adapt it."

"Or else . . ." I prompt.

"Or else they'll be within their rights to create their own series finale."

The implication hits home. Exactly the outcome Ted asked me about a few weeks ago. "So my extension—"

"Sorry, this isn't coming from us," Claire says, meaning the publisher. "The studio is forcing our hand, but if you want this to be *your* story, then you've got to finish sooner."

"How much sooner?"

"End of August." That's the same week I fly out for the premiere of season three in LA. "We can push the manuscript through copyedits, but they need something readable by mid-September."

"A month?" My voice startles a pigeon who'd landed on the ledge outside the window. "That's sooner than my original deadline." So long, extension.

"Five weeks," Saheli says, like that's much better.

"Five weeks to write a whole entire book?"

"You haven't started?" Claire's head tilts, green eyes sharp behind her bold red glasses.

Oops. "No, I have. Of course I have."

Saheli's expression is full of concern. "Mia, how bad is it?"

I can't bring myself to divulge the whole truth. "It's bad enough that I can't make any promises."

"How much time do you need?"

Three to six years? A lifetime? An eternity?

I'm quiet for so long that Claire leans forward, close enough for me to see the smudges on her lenses. "If you don't think you can deliver, the show's writers know the characters—"

"I don't want that." The screenwriters adapted my previous three books and stayed true to the bones of the stories. I even got to weigh in on some of their stylistic choices, which is kind of unheard of. But the idea of them crafting Victor and Sydney's story from start to finish? The two characters most precious to my heart? I can't let that happen. "Tell me you didn't imply I'm leaning that way," I say to my editor.

"I would never," she says. "This is your story. But it's also Hollywood, and they have their own rules. If you don't produce the manuscript on time, they'll make sure someone else delivers the story."

"I just feel a lot of pressure to do right by them. Not just the characters, but the actors, too. This is their time to shine." There's no question of recasting at this point. To most people's minds, Jayla and Robert *are* Sydney and Victor. "This is different than all my other books, and now I'm expected to rush it?"

"You're a fast writer. How far along are you?" Claire adjusts her caftan casually, but her brow tightens in a way that suggests she's nervous about my reply.

I usually produce about three thousand words a day. More than some writers I know, far less than others. Everyone has their own pace, but mine is quick and steady. Right now I've got the opening chapters. Less than a typical week's worth of work.

"I'm not going to lie. It's not coming easy."

"Want to talk about why?"

Avoiding the weight of her speculation, I track the progress of a squirrel navigating the leafy branch outside. "I don't know that there's anything to talk about. I just can't find the glue to make their relationship stick. That's why I asked for more time." Humiliation, wasted.

"And I hate rescinding the extension, but this is out of my hands," Claire says.

Saheli's dog jumps down from her lap, and she leans on the desk, deep brown eyes sympathetic, but wary, as if she's more worried than she lets on. "From what I've heard, Roan Watkins asked for Robert personally." The acclaimed director is synonymous with box office success. "Robert wants to stick with the show, but he made it clear the film will take precedence."

I don't blame him. A spy thriller with the legendary Roan Watkins could be a career maker. But the timing is immense pressure. Maybe I should bow out. But that would mean letting someone else have the final say on the fate of my two favorite characters. Stories are remembered for how they end, and I want the last word.

"I'll make it work."

"Knew you would." Claire smiles warmly. "I know it must be throwing off your creative process to have so many people involved. Do your best to tune them out."

Saheli nods in agreement. "It's your story, Mia. Tell it."

My story. That's the problem. It's too close to me, or at least the me I was before I realized friendship is no basis for romance. But at the end of the day, it's not actually my story. It's Sydney and Victor's. And I don't need to convince myself their happy ending is real, I just need to convince readers.

Five weeks to get this done, minus an afternoon in an escape room. But it's for the good of the story, I tell myself. Anything to justify my sudden craving for time alone with Gavin where the usual rules of friendship don't apply.

twelve

Gavin

I'm no writer, but an escape room seems like a pretty good metaphor for how I feel after spending the entire game last Saturday trapped between a brother who wants me to move and a friend pushing me to *make* a move. The pressure is building, and I'm pretty sure an hour trapped in a confined space is only going to make things worse. On top of that, every time I'm around Mia lately, my feelings get harder to ignore.

I had trouble sleeping all week, imagining her getting married and starting a life somewhere else. Or settling down with someone local only to watch our friendship get eroded by the trajectory of family life, growing apart until I only hear about her through social media or mutual friends. No more late-night doughnut excursions or advice on what to wear to a wedding when the invitation mentions "cocktail hour trampolining."

Would it be better to take the proactive step and move back to Wisconsin? Put some distance between us before my heart gets more tangled up with hers? Normally I would've texted Mia for advice the moment Scott left, but my feelings about Dad's decision are tied up in my feelings for her, all of it a confusing mess.

Ditching these trope tests would be easier. We could go back to the way things were, and maybe my feelings would fade. But this was my idea, and Mia's counting on me. I'll just have to think of a way to figure out what's real and what's pretend.

According to the notes in the binder, the forced-proximity trope is when the main characters are stuck together in a situation, and the enforced time together changes their perspective or pushes their restraint to the breaking point.

It's the last scenario that worries me. I can't let my heart get confused, but then again, we're only testing the trope for an hour—less, if we solve the clues quickly. Nothing like the weeks or months from the examples Mia outlined. My good intentions have survived years already. An hour should be a piece of cake.

The mall is pretty much deserted. Our first stop was the food court, where most of the tables were empty. Snacks in hand, we walk past vacant stores plastered with advertisements for local businesses and an eerily silent carousel. Mia stops to peer into a closed-up kids' play area and I drift over next to her and say, "This is depressing."

"So depressing," she agrees. "It was bad before the movie theater closed but—" she nods at the deflated bouncy castles in the dark space behind the metal gate "—this is downright grim."

I take a sip of my smoothie. "At least the food court is open." I ordered the largest size, hoping it would settle my nerves, but my stomach is in knots, and I can barely swallow down the tangy blend of mango and banana.

"For who, though?" Mia takes a bite from the cinnamon-sugar pretzel I bought her. She was going to pass it up because it was overpriced. Even with the successful turn of her career, she doesn't like spending money on frivolous things, other than office supplies. Buying her the pretzel was a small gesture, but I love any chance to treat her.

"Good question." I glance around the empty concourse. "Any

chance you want to switch genres to horror? This would make an epic zombie showdown setting."

She visibly shudders, turning away from the abandoned store. "There are all sorts of paranormal romances. But you know how I feel about creepy stuff."

The same way I feel about small spaces. The idea of being trapped in a confined space makes my skin crawl. Good thing the escape room is all for show. I double-checked the website, just to be sure. "Fun fact, we won't actually be locked in the room today," I tell Mia, mostly to reassure myself.

"Can you imagine the liability?" She plucks off a piece of sugar-dusted pretzel. "Might make it more exciting, though."

Not for me. We don't have many secrets between us, but pride has kept me from revealing how much I used to dread taking the elevator whenever I visited her high-rise apartment building in the city. But since the last trope test was a bust, I'm willing to endure an hour of confinement if it means helping Mia get past her creative block.

By my side, she pauses to check the mall directory, munching as she scans the listings. "Here it is." She points out the spot, then seems to notice her finger is covered in sugar. Making a face, she asks, "Got a napkin?"

I shake my head, so she slips her finger into her mouth. Helpless to look away, I watch her suck the sugar off. Today her lips are the deep red of a ripe apple, and her confession replays on a loop. *The only surprising thing is you thinking I haven't already imagined how good you'd taste.* Now I'm the one imagining her mouth on mine, sugary sweet, chased with the bite of cinnamon. Backing her against the map, hands pinned above her head, the teasing scrape of teeth on tender skin . . .

She slides her finger out of her mouth with an audible *pop* and I force my gaze away, whole body ablaze. My best friend is more off-limits than ever thanks to the no-touching rule of these trope tests. Why has my brain decided right now is the time to fixate on how sexy she is?

I've always been attracted to her. The night we met, I wrestled with the temptation to tell her that if *I* was lucky enough to go out with someone as gorgeous and smart and clever as her, I'd never waste a second wanting anyone else. But I've never allowed myself to dwell on it. Not until this past week, when she's all I can seem to think about.

I've kept my feelings for her in check all these years, even though she's as beautiful in sweatpants as she is in the ball gowns she's worn to premieres. But all evidence points to her not being attracted to me in the slightest.

There were times, early on, that I thought she might be ready to forget the pact we'd made to stay friends. But then she'd start dating a guy from class or show me the profile of someone she thought would make a great match for me, and I figured it was all in my head. Now I'm not so sure—

"Gavin?"

I blink, and she's looking up at me with concern, like I missed a question. "You've been kind of off today. We don't need to go through with this if you're having second thoughts."

Oh, I'm definitely having *thoughts*. But not about the escape room. Not anymore. Desire for the woman standing in front of me has pushed all my worries to a far corner of my mind.

Well, most of them. "Are you?" I don't want to pressure her into anything she's not comfortable with, especially given my more-than-friendly thoughts. "Last week you thought this whole idea was nonsense."

Her mouth tugs into a straight line. "Last week I thought I had months to finish the book."

"Don't you?"

"Turns out working with Hollywood is more complex, as if the last few years haven't taught me that." She explains that the lead actor for the season has a filming conflict, and the big-budget franchise film he was cast in won out over reprising his role in a streaming rom-com series. "I get it," she says. "Rob's just doing what he needs to for his career."

Not for the first time, I'm floored that she's on a nickname basis with movie star Robert Cho. But I don't love how his priorities are complicating things for her. "Can't they just push the season's release date?"

She makes a face, mouth scrunched, a sugar crystal clinging to the corner of her lips, and I bite my tongue against the urge to brush it away with my thumb, or better yet—

"A delay might result in the series being canceled." Her all-business tone should banish thoughts of kissing her, but it's the opposite. She's a powerhouse and hearing her casually talk about "the industry" is super sexy. "Hollywood is fickle like that. If the show's final installment is a disaster, I don't want it to be my fault."

"Robert Cho's schedule isn't your responsibility," I say, with a sense of surrealism that we're even having this conversation.

"But it won't be an issue if I meet the original deadline. Like I have for every other book." The ferocity in her voice makes it clear how much she wants to conquer this story.

"Then you're sure you want to spend the afternoon solving puzzles and not writing?"

"Sitting around rewriting the same scenes isn't helping," she says. "At least today I'm following through on my goal of branching out. Maybe that will translate to a breakthrough."

"In that case, let's do this." I head off in the direction she showed, swallowing down my unease with another gulp of smoothie. We discover the escape room has taken over the lower level of what used to be a department store. The clerk at the sign-in desk frowns when I show her the ticket confirmation on my phone.

"Huh, we just got a group set up in the abandoned library room. Our booking system must've had an error."

"Bummer," Mia says. "Literary clues were my best hope of beating the clock."

We both check the laminated poster on the counter showing the other options.

"Gallery Ghosting doesn't sound so bad." Mia reads the description aloud. "'Get locked in an art collector's private vault and search for the combination to set yourself free using clues in the sculptures and paintings.'"

Locked in a vault? Hell no. That might be my number one fear.

"Sorry, we actually had to shut that one down." The clerk looks apologetic. "Group of college kids defaced all the paintings." She points to the last option. *Cavern Cave-In: Search for clues with the help of a headlamp in a rubble-filled cave.* Hello, nightmares. "I think you'll love it," she assures us. "It's the one that feels the most real."

Just what I want to hear when my plan is to remind myself this is all fake and I'm not about to be trapped underground with no way out.

Mia bites her lip. "We could just come back another day when the library room is available." But I can tell she's thinking of the ticking clock on a deadline that's coming a lot sooner than she expected.

"A cave sounds cool," I hear myself saying. As in, bone-chilling. But either way, I'm signing up to be trapped. Does the theme really matter? I grit my teeth through signing a waiver, being briefed on how to use the walkie-talkies, and getting strapped into climbing gear.

"For authenticity's sake," says another escape room employee who introduced himself as the game manager.

Inauthentic would suit me just fine, but I remind myself that no matter how real it feels, we'll just be wandering around what used to be a Sears department store.

"Don't turn on the lights on your helmets until the countdown ends," the game manager says, looking comfortingly ordinary in a polo and khakis.

"Let me guess, authenticity?" I try and fail to keep the sarcasm out of my voice.

He shakes his head. "In this case, it's to make it harder for you to find the first clue." He asks us to test our headlamps and we obediently flick the switch on and off twice. "Great, you're good to go."

The door marked CAVE ENTRANCE SHAFT opens to reveal a path sloping into darkness. Reminding myself this is just a mall, I picture wide aisles between rows of appliances and TVs. He tells us to stand against the wall, which is textured like rock.

"See you on the other side." Shutting the door, he says, "Or not," with a laugh that's probably part of the gig but feels way too genuine.

We're plunged into darkness, and I can see now why he told us to stand with our backs to the wall. Or rather, can't see. It's pitch black and without the wall behind me, I'd feel totally disoriented. "Remember what I said about horror movies?"

Next to me, Mia's fumbling. "Just turn on your headlamp."

"Trying." My fingers are shaking, and I'm not sure I really want light, after all. She might notice how embarrassingly freaked-out I am.

Her headlamp clicks on, illuminating the clammy gray-brown passageway. The light emphasizes how dark the rest of the space is, and I realize I forgot to ask the dimensions of this escape room. Before I can spiral about the lack of space, Mia steps in front of me and rises on her tiptoes, hand on my shoulder for balance.

Is she about to kiss me? On instinct, I bend my head and . . . she reaches up to click my headlamp on. Embarrassed, I'm glad she turns away quickly so she won't catch sight of my blush.

She stays close, searching the area near us. Logically, I know we're in a man-made room, but with the low ceiling and small passageway, my brain is warning me that crushing tons of earth are above us. Propelled by the urge to get out of here as fast as possible without making a fool of myself, I head down the path, which angles sharply, hiding the rest of the room from view.

"I've never been in a real cave," Mia says, right on my heels. "We should stop by the one on the way to your dad's house sometime."

"I went once, as a kid."

"And?"

"I didn't like it." An understatement. "My dad ended up asking the tour guide to take me out early. They had to radio up to someone at the entrance to come get us while Mom finished the tour with Scott."

"That happened when Kim took me to see my first horror movie in theaters," Mia says, no trace of judgment. "Except she had to leave with me and didn't let me live it down." Her voice reaches me, warm. "We didn't have to do the cave challenge."

"This isn't real," I say as much to myself as her. Besides, any enclosed space sucks. I'm not used to holding back with her, but this particular fear has always seemed juvenile. I don't have an explanation for it, and I thought I'd grow out of it.

"Okay, then let's start cracking codes."

"I don't see any." The passageway has opened up into a room and stalactites—or maybe stalagmites—jut up from the floor and drip from the ceiling.

Mia bends and crawls underneath an overhang. "There's something in here."

I squat down to see and she pushes a battered container out of the spot.

"Are we supposed to be moving stuff around?"

"How else will we open it?" She's already flipping it over, looking for clues. "Can you check the other side of the room to see if there's anything else we can use?"

"Like an emergency exit?" I aim for a jokey tone but it comes out tense.

Hand on the case, she scowls up at me. "We're supposed to be working together to solve this."

"Sorry, I did want to do this with you." I can either keep my pride or tell her the truth so she doesn't think I'm a total jerk. "Being trapped in here is just stressing me the hell out."

"Seriously?"

I kneel down on the uneven floor. "I'm pretty claustrophobic."

"Since when?"

"Since always, I guess. But that visit to the cave was the first time I remember the fear pressing in. I knew we were fine, but my brain wouldn't accept it." Even now, I'm fighting off the choked sensation of not having enough air. "That's why I avoid elevators whenever I can."

"I always thought you were showing off your fitness."

I manage a laugh. "I don't even go to the gym."

"Yeah, but you're always hauling around those big bags of dirt and stuff. You've got the muscles to show for it." She frowns. "That's a bad thing?"

"Inconvenient." Her voice is low, hoarse. Like she's thirsty all of a sudden. "Don't act like you don't realize the impression you have on women."

Women? Yes. Mia in particular? No. But maybe it hasn't been as easy for her to keep her distance as I thought. I've caught her looking sometimes. A quick dart of her eyes from under lowered lashes when we're at the lake. Things like that. But just now the sweep of her eyes didn't feel like an objective observer.

Before I can process what that might mean, she says, "I wish you would've told me." For a numb second, I assume she's talking about my feelings for her.

"What would you have said?" I wait, breathless.

"I already felt bad about roping you into these trope tests, and here you are, stuck in here for my sake."

Reality sends me back to my senses. She's talking about my fear, not my clueless heart. "I didn't tell you because it's not the biggest deal. Not like I have some childhood wound to blame it on. I just don't like small spaces."

She squeezes my shoulder. "Your fears don't need a deep-rooted issue to be valid." That's the thing about Mia. She knows me and accepts me without making me feel the need to justify things. When I talk to my dad or Scott, I feel like I need to prepare a case beforehand. "You can tell me anything," she says.

That reminds me there is something I haven't brought up, and telling her will be better than blurting out how much I want to be with her. "My dad's retiring." Her fingers go still on the padlock. "Following Scott and Amber to Colorado."

Her head whips around. "When did he tell you?"

Shielding my face from the light, I say, "He didn't. Scott did."

She clicks off her headlamp, face slipping into shadow. "Did you call him?"

I shake my head, the helmet rattling, and I unsnap the chin strap, setting it by my knee where it casts a glow on the stalagmites. "Not yet." Part of me is upset he didn't tell me himself, but I think it's his way of not pressuring me. "Scott thinks I should take over for him."

Mia doesn't say anything for a moment, which isn't typical for her.

"What do you think?" I'm desperate to know how she'd feel if I left.

"It's not for me to say." Her tone is cautious, and I turn to face her.

"Since when do you not have an opinion?"

"This is big, Gavin. I don't want to influence you either way."

"What else are friends for?"

"Listening," she says. "Giving you a nudge if you're on the wrong path."

"Or telling me which is the right one." I need her to say she wants me here.

She sighs and tugs her knees to her chest. "That I can't do. It would be a big change, but who's to say it's not a good one?"

Who's to say? I'd give anything to hear her say I shouldn't go. "You wouldn't mind me moving to Wisconsin?"

"It's not the other side of the world," she says. "We visit often in the summer anyway."

"It's not the same."

"For you and me, no." She sounds matter-of-fact, like the distance wouldn't bother her at all, and it's a kick in the gut. "Why haven't you spoken to your dad about it?"

"Because I don't have an answer."

"He's not the one asking you to take over, though."

"That's the other thing. It bothers me he didn't tell me himself." I shift, trying to get comfortable on the weirdly rubbery floor, and settle for resting my back against the wall. Mia follows suit, our legs stretched out in front of us, side by side. It's nice to sit with her like this. No pretense. Just us.

Even though everything might be changing, I'm grateful for this moment. "He must've been considering it for months, if not years, but he never said a thing. I thought he'd work until he couldn't. At least another decade."

She nudges my shin with her foot. "You should ask him why."

"Back to giving out advice?"

She grins, and my heart catches in my throat. I love that smile. "When the right choice is obvious, yeah." Her expression shifts from teasing to solemn. "I know he relied on you too much in the past. Maybe he's realized it, and that's why he's been more distant."

"Or he's decided to depend on Scott instead."

"Would that be so bad?"

"No, but it doesn't feel great to be left out. I want him to open up to Scott. It's good his circle is expanding. But I still want to be in it."

"Easy choice, then." She crosses her legs, and I do my best not to notice how we're connected now, her bare knee resting against my thigh. "Call him. You don't need to decide now."

She's given no clue on how she feels about the situation, and I know it's on purpose. She doesn't want to sway me. Maybe it's asking too much to expect her to weigh in on something this life-changing. But I can't help but remember when I showed her the listing for my house. How excited she'd been I was settling down close to Chicago. How she'd fallen in love with this town and a year later, bought a condo a few blocks away.

But we're in our thirties now. Most of our friends are married and building a home together, and maybe Mia's not so concerned about where I fit into that next step. Maybe it would be better for her if I wasn't there to complicate things. Or maybe—probably—I'm just overthinking it and I should take her advice and call Dad before I waste any more time worrying.

"We'll have to find our way out first," I say. "Can't believe they confiscated our phones."

"No service a mile underground anyway," she says, slipping back into character. She turns her headlamp on, and I grab my helmet and rise to my feet. "You good to keep going?"

Surprisingly, I'm doing okay. Maybe the conversation distracted me. "Less than twenty minutes to solve this." A red countdown timer is set into one of the boulders. "I don't want to quit."

With one last searching look, she nods her head. "All right. I'm going to work on this puzzle if you want to investigate the rest of the space."

The room branches off into three passageways, but one is blocked by a pile of boulders. I pick one of the remaining paths at random but immediately regret my choice. The path narrows as I ascend, the ceiling height dropping. I take deep breaths and focus on searching for clues.

"Gavin!" Mia's voice, panicky.

"Found something?" I call out, happy to have an excuse to abandon the narrow path.

"My headlamp went out. I can't see a thing."

"Coming." But when I rush out of the tunnel, bent low to avoid whacking my head on the roof, I collide with her. She must've been moving fast, and the force of impact sends me stumbling back, my foot slipping on the uneven floor. I land on my ass with a hard thud. Mia crashes down on top of me and my back hits the floor. My helmet connects with the ground with a loud crack, and I let out a startled yelp.

"Oh shit, Gavin!" She struggles up onto her knees, straddling me. Her thighs settle on either side of my hips and she tips forward, eyes wide with concern. "Your head."

My head's not the part of my anatomy I'm concerned about. With deft movements, she unbuckles my chin strap, apparently unaware that she's sitting on my lap. "Are you okay?"

I mumble something that doesn't satisfy her, because she picks up the helmet and holds it with the light aimed directly into my face. That pulls my attention from the spot where our bodies are connected, and I hold up my arm to shield my eyes. "What are you doing?"

"Checking for a concussion."

"How?"

"Looking at your pupils." She tries to pull my arm down, but I squeeze my eyes shut, concentrating on anything but the warmth of her weight on me.

"I was wearing a helmet."

"Just let me check." Knowing better than to argue with Mia on a mission, I let my arm fall. She must've expected more resistance because she comes down with it, pinning my wrist above my head. The helmet clatters to the ground and the light goes off.

I can't see anything, but Mia's breath comes light and quick against my face, stirring the air near my lips. Close. So close.

Her fingers are still locked around my wrist, hips notched against mine. Unable to stay still any longer, I take a reflexive inhale, catching the light floral scent of her perfume.

I'm surprised by how delicate she feels against me. Mia never shies away from a challenge. She's self-assured and gives as good as she gets when we joke around. I guess that's why I'm startled by the softness of her, even as she's pinning me in place, locked between her legs. It takes all my self-control not to move, even though I should stand up and get back to the challenge. Laugh this off and never think of it again.

But I'm ensnared by years of pent-up yearning, barely breathing for fear of breaking the spell, held captive by the woman who's had my heart since the day we met. Captured, and loving every forbidden second.

Mia hasn't moved, either, but her fingers are trembling, cool and fine-boned around the tender skin of my wrist. "I got scared." Her words are barely audible above my pounding heart. "The game master probably saw me run like a coward."

"He can't see us now." Can't hear us, either. They said the cameras are just for monitoring our progress in case we need assistance. With the lights out, we're on our own. My free hand comes to her hip, anchoring her. Just for comfort, I tell myself. "Still scared?"

"Not anymore." She dips her head and says low, against my ear, "Never when I'm with you." The promise in her words tugs at the cord of my resolve. My fingers tighten on her thigh reflexively, and she lets out a little gasp against my ear.

The walkie-talkie at my hip crackles to life and Mia jerks upward. She fumbles by my waist for the radio, but I grab it first out of desperation. If her hands wander much more down there, we're going to have a situation.

She must realize this because she scrambles to her feet and I scoot backward against the wall, flicking the button with a shaky thumb. "All good here." Damn, I sound breathless. "Just lost the light for a second."

"Gotcha. Let me help you out." Suddenly the cave brightens with lights inset into the brown rock walls. Without the eerie effect of the headlamps bouncing off the walls, it's kind of cozy in here. Or at least not awful. It's also embarrassingly obvious everything is man-made. Papier-mâché stalagmites and a camouflaged speaker that must be piping in the dripping sounds.

Mia, however, looks like she survived a real-life cave-in. One strap of her sleeveless top is hanging off her shoulder, and her helmet is askew.

"You two set to continue?"

She vigorously shakes her head, dislodging the helmet even more. I click the button. "Uh, no," I answer, for both our sakes. "We're gonna cut out early."

"You don't want to finish?" Based on our recent predicament, it's impossible not to read into those words.

"No, I think we're good, not, um—" I dart my eyes toward Mia "—not finishing."

She lets out a tiny huff of laughter and I feel a sudden burst of affection for her, stronger than ever. These little moments of connection mean everything. The kind of moments that would happen a lot less with hours of distance between us.

The game master is explaining how to get to the exit, but now that I know we aren't stuck here, all I want is to stay here with Mia. Confess that I'm a goner for her.

But she's beckoning me down the passageway I skipped, which opens up into a room with an underground lake made of blue resin. There's a door inset in the wall and she pushes it open, smiling at me as cool air wafts in.

We made it to the end, but somehow it feels like we're just getting started.

thirteen

Mia

Gavin and I burst out of the door like we really did just escape from the center of the earth. They weren't kidding about authenticity. The game master presses flyers into our hands and asks us to leave a review, but mine would be along the lines of: *Headlamp malfunctioned, resulting in almost kissing the friend I swore never to get involved with.* Two and a half stars rounded up for realism. Because things almost got very real in that cave, and I'm not sure what to do about it.

"New guideline for these tests," I announce, when we're finally out of the fake spelunking gear and back in the mall. My heart is still racing from the moments I spent on top of Gavin. Oh lord, *on top of him.* "We don't do anything that makes us uncomfortable."

He runs a hand over his golden-brown hair, tidying the strands that were rumpled by the helmet. "I thought getting out of your comfort zone was the whole point of this."

"*My* comfort zone," I correct. "Not yours. You don't need to be knight-in-shining-armoring scary situations for my sake."

He smirks. Smolders, really. Is this a new thing or a lingering effect of our unintended embrace? "Trust a romance author to turn *knight in shining armor* into a verb."

"That's what you got from what I said?"

"You're right." He stops, leaning against one of the pillars, hands in his pockets. A romance hero move if I ever saw one, and to my dismay, it sends my heart fluttering. "I should've told you that I don't like small spaces. But that goes both ways. Are you scared of the dark?" His blue eyes have turned watchful, intense.

I cross my arms, defense against his casually attentive pose and his handsome face and the disarming way he never seems to get enough of knowing me. "A little."

"You never mentioned it."

"I thought we were going to be in a Victorian library, not a cave. And it's super embarrassing to be a grown woman who sleeps with the light on." I was hoping to gloss over it, but no such luck.

His brow furrows. "Every night?"

"Only a little light."

"Like a night-light?"

I shrug, twitchy. "A small lamp."

He's eyeing me contemplatively, like he's taking in this new information and comparing it with what he knows about me. "How small?"

"About this tall." I make a space with my hands.

"Like a desk lamp?"

"Yeah, a bedside lamp."

He's still got that look of deep focus, and I can tell he's not judging me, he's intent on discovering me. It gives me a thrill to be the object of his concentration, like we're learning each other for the first time. "You sleep with an actual lamp on. Every night." It's a statement, but I feel compelled to answer him.

"Only when I'm alone." I don't want him to think I'm forcing my boyfriends to adopt my weird habits. "I'm not scared with someone else around."

"But you haven't had a boyfriend since . . ." He trails off.

"Yeah, since the series premiered." Two years ago. Saying it aloud is more embarrassing than running from the dark like a child, but Gavin knows what happened with every guy I've gone out with since then. Either they acted threatened by my small measure of fame, or I didn't fit their idea of a romance novelist—I'm a regular girl who likes staying in and bingeing shows.

"I get it. You've had a lot on your plate."

"It's not like I'm undatable."

"Mia." The rumble of his voice stills me. "I know." His gaze sinks into my skin like summer heat. "I'm just picturing you turning on a full-fledged lamp to chase away the shadows and I . . ." He runs a hand through his hair, mussing it all over again. "Sometimes I don't know what to do with you."

That makes two of us. I almost kissed him, and now I'm trying to fit my feelings for him back into the friendship box, but the lid won't close. Or maybe what I feel for him is too big to be contained. "Anyway, you can't judge, since you didn't tell me your fear, either." I go on the offensive, but he doesn't bite.

With a hitch of his shoulders, he says, "I wanted to do this with you."

"You mean *for* me."

He steps forward until the toes of his sneakers brush against my sandals. "No more of that." The words are a growl, a rasp of delicious friction. I forget to breathe as his fingertip slides along my jaw—soft, slow—then gently hooks under my chin and tips up my face. "You're not the only one who wants this, Mia."

His eyes hold mine, blue rimmed with gray, and a millisecond later, drop to my mouth. He's going to kiss me. He *wants* to kiss me. And I want it so badly that I freeze, as if a single movement would shatter the moment. My whole being is fixated on one request. *Kiss me.*

He doesn't.

With a deep inhale—and oh, I feel the tension in him, tightly leashed—he drops his hand. The bop of pop music and the squeak of shoppers' shoes filters in where a moment ago only the sounds of our intermingled breathing reached my ears. We're in the middle of a mall in the afternoon. This is my friend Gavin. And I've never wanted to kiss anyone more.

I wanted him to press his lips against mine with an ache that's throbbing in my chest, even though nothing about this setting is romantic. Nothing about this moment is right. Not the fluorescent lighting or the fact that he might be moving and leaving me behind. Nothing else matters but the person standing in front of me. Maybe my other relationships haven't worked out because he's what I've been looking for all along.

That thought jolts me out of my lust-induced haze, propels me backward, putting more distance between us. "So you're saying I shouldn't doubt your commitment again?" It's meant to be a joke, but I wince at the weight of the word *commitment*. Commitments can be broken.

"Never." Instead of letting the moment pass, he catches it, holds on to this new thread of connection between us. "I'm in this with you until you tell me we're done."

I believe him, but I suspect I'll never be done. Not with him.

Word Count Goal: 85,000
Current Word Count: 24,901
Backspace, backspace. 24,899.

Fictionally, I'm back on track. My real life is in shambles—rogue feelings for a bestie who might be moving hours away and a deadline that's now only four weeks away, but hey, at least my muse has returned.

Maybe I'm writing to escape. That's how I got my start, after all. Bored with classes that left no room for imagination. Needing a place to let my mind play. Maybe in the last few years, between the success of my career and all my close friendships, I'd stopped feeling like I was missing something.

But when I found out Gavin might be leaving, the illusion that we'd keep up this perfect existence was shattered. What better way to forget that looming possibility than burying myself in the book where I can write the ending and make sure it's happy.

The past three days I haven't left my condo. I've survived on a bag of stale popcorn and the raisins and peanuts leftover in a package of trail mix after scavenging the M&M's. Twice I've fallen asleep with my face on the keyboard.

Victor and Sydney are starting to notice each other in ways they never have. The fall of his hair over his forehead has her heart aflutter; the way she commits to the scenes has him wondering if there's more to this than acting. Now my dilemma isn't getting them to notice each other, but to make them do something about it.

Every time they're done acting, they go back to their old routines. I could send them on vacation, but this isn't a destination romance. What readers and the show's fans alike love about Victor and Sydney is their easygoing bond, the cozy familiarity of evenings on the couch and favorite booths at restaurants.

Their relationship isn't far-off travels and a whirlwind fling. It's nights in and GIF-filled text conversations. How will they ever hurry up and kiss already when she opens her texts and finds a picture of him flexing by the pool with a temporary tattoo of a grinning starfish that he got at his niece's birthday party along with the text, Next tattoo, or nah?

Even the goofy photo has Sydney swooning, which is a testament to exactly how far gone she is. I'm typing Sydney's thoughts about Victor's toned chest and a peek of nipple when something solid nudges my shoulder. Since Frank is the only other living thing in here and he's not capable of sentient motion, I nearly jump out of my skin.

"Nipples, huh?" Not something. Some*one*. My sister.

Heart racing, I don't dignify her with a response. Mostly because I'm breathless from the scare. Sneaking up on me while I'm deep in the writing zone has been one of her favorite pastimes since we were kids. She has a key, and this isn't the first time she's barged in unannounced.

She bends down to get a better look at the screen. Her short curls are glossy, and I catch the hint of lime from the leave-in she got me hooked on. "About time our girl Syd finally woke up to the hotness that is Victor Lark."

If Sydney's anything like me, she probably wishes she could go back to blissful ignorance of his sex appeal. "Yeah, she's noticing, but instead of doing something about it, all she's done so far is wax eloquent—internally—about how attractive he is."

Kim sets down the bags she brought and takes a seat on the chaise lounge I found at an antique shop with Sera. It's the perfect spot to collapse in a dramatic swoon when I receive bad publishing news. Nothing hurts as much when you pretend you're on a fainting couch in a regency romance, poised to reprimand a handsome rogue who dares assume you need rescuing.

My sister shifts around, crossing and uncrossing her legs like she's trying to find a comfortable position, and if she hadn't stopped by unannounced, I'd tell her it works best if you embrace your inner duchess. "Can't you just make them kiss?"

I refrain from rolling my eyes because she loves to claim that being the older sister means she's more mature. "They're not Barbie and Ken. I can't just smush their faces together without good reason."

"The pleasure of kissing is reason in itself."

"In real life, maybe. But without motivation, the characters will ring hollow," I reply.

She frowns. "Might help if you took my advice and left the house once in a while."

"For your information, I tried that." My claim is less effective considering I'm dressed in a mismatched lounge set and there are no less than six half-finished beverages of varying alcohol and caffeine content on the coffee table.

Kim must interpret this evidence of my writing binge incorrectly—in her defense, wallowing and deadline mode look very similar—because she gives me a pitying look that I'm sure is meant to appear empathetic. "Did you get ghosted? Or go on an awful date?"

The image of Gavin, sleeves cuffed, grinning at me across a candlelit table, beckons, but I slam the memory shut. I won't be able to prove I've been following her advice without mentioning him, and I won't be able to mention him without her jumping to conclusions. Conclusions I've been trying not to jump to myself after what happened between us at the mall. The tender way he touched me, eyes full of longing . . .

"I absolutely cannot focus on a relationship right now." I grab two of the water glasses off the table and water the gardenia with one, then pour the other into Frank's pot. The monstera's uppermost leaves are taller than I am. Poor thing has witnessed me try and fail at keeping many of his plant brethren alive over the years before I gave up and realized Frank is special, immune to my utter lack of a green thumb. Secretly, I think it's because Gavin raised him to start, but I'm not about to tell him because it would go straight to his head.

"Why do you make relationships sound so stressful?" my sister asks.

For me, they have been, but it's not just that. "I have a book to finish and a lot of people counting on me." I can't help but picture the cast and crew I've met while visiting the set. I want to live up to their faith in me. "But I did try some new things. Got out of my comfort zone, and it's working." To a point.

"So I was half right?" Kim will take that win and run with it.

"Half wrong." I gesture at the in-progress scene on my laptop. "I need more than just interest and attraction."

"True. But for years you've been saying there's no way to invent chemistry between these two." She gives up on sitting normally and reclines on the bolster. "Sounds like a good start at least."

"But according to my schedule, I'm supposed to be nearly done with the first draft, and I've barely made it into act two," I say. "Last week, I found out my deadline is firm because Rob's filming some blockbuster movie next summer, and even though the characters are finally starting to feel each other, I'm worried I can't make them fall in love."

Confessing this erases all the good vibes of my momentum, or maybe my rising sense of overwhelm is a side effect of sitting in the same spot all day. Either way, I sink down onto the living room rug and let gravity take hold until I'm flat on my back, staring at the ceiling.

Kim's face appears, blocking out the skylight. "Now might be a good time to mention I brought cake?"

The knot in my chest eases a notch. "Wouldn't hurt."

She disappears from view. "Okay, but you're gonna have to get up off the floor. No feeding the ants on my watch."

"I do not have ants."

"Not yet," she says, singsong.

I stay put for another ten seconds out of an urge to prove my independence, realize that's the definition of *childish*, and am taking out silverware by the time my sister's washed her hands.

I grab two plates and a serving knife, which she takes from me, cutting two huge slices from the Bundt cake. "Have you eaten?" she asks.

"I'm about to." I use my fork to carve off a bite.

"Fruit. Vegetables. Protein?"

"Bar," I reply around a mouthful of delectable cake.

She slides my plate out of reach. "I brought real food, too, let's start there."

"Dessert first," I argue, and she gives up, mostly because my slice of cake has already been reduced to crumbs.

"Tell me what the cool single people are doing these days." Since Kim hasn't been single since college, she always says she feels out of the loop. "Did you sign up for one of those groups where you go on excursions?"

That's what she would do in my position. She was president of at least half a dozen clubs during high school and college, and head of countless committees at the schools where she taught. She's been training for a leadership role since middle school, and I bet she won't stay assistant principal for long.

"Nothing that fancy." Hoping to distract her, I root around in the bags and pull out a bunch of carrots with the greens attached, like she bought them at a farmers market, which is probably the case.

She starts taking spices out of my cupboard, most of which are probably expired. "Got a big pot?"

I squat down and pull out the Dutch oven I bought last year on impulse. Gavin and I had been trying to one-up each other with elaborate descriptions of eye colors like in romance novels, one of my favorite elements of the genre. He'd pointed at the pot and asked me to describe it. *The shade of waves darkened by an oncoming storm*, I'd quipped, but the color appealed to me, and I wound up buying it.

I've only used the pot a handful of times, and it isn't until I set it on the stove that I realize the slate-blue glaze is a near-perfect match for Gavin's eyes. Great, I've officially lost my head over him and we haven't even kissed. *Won't* kiss. I click on the burner with unsteady hands.

Oblivious to my worries, Kim says, "There's a pottery studio near our new house that offers classes, and I was thinking of going." She sets a cutting board on the wide marble island. "You could join me if you're tired of doing excursions on your own."

"That's sweet of you, but I'm not doing it on my own." Too late, I catch on to her tactic. But before she can ask who I've been going out with, my phone vibrates.

Grateful for the intrusion, I waste no time in picking it up, expecting yet another text from Sera's family about the baby shower we're throwing—they've totally hijacked the planning but it's probably for the best with how much of the book I've yet to finish—but instead of a question about table linens, I see two new texts from Gavin.

Gavin: I've got the perfect way to test fish-out-of-water.

Gavin: You, me, and a landscaping crew.

Biting back a smile, I tap out a response.

Mia: Sounds more like the title of a why-choose romance.

Gavin: That wasn't on the trope list. Should I look it up?

Mia: We both know you're going to anyway.

"Thought you didn't have time for dating." Kim looks up from chopping an onion. "That's the goofy grin that comes from reading a crush's text."

"I am not crushing." Another buzz from my phone, and I bite my lip at the GIF Gavin's sent of a guy looking shell-shocked.

Gavin: Definitely not what I had in mind. I convinced a bunch of coworkers to join me for the annual community restoration project. We're cleaning up a lot on Fifth Street this Friday and Saturday. Wanna join?

He sends a screenshot of the Annual Community Give-Back Weekend website.

My sister pulls the phone from my hands and frowns at the texts. "Just Gavin?" She shakes her head and mumbles, "I thought you were actually putting yourself out there . . ." She trails off, scrolling up through the messages, and a nefarious gleam lights her eyes. "He's the one you've been going out with, isn't he?"

"Yes, but it's not like that."

She lets out a whoop and starts dancing.

"You're being ridiculous."

"You—" she amps up the moves that make it clear she hasn't set foot in a club in ten years "—need to tell me everything."

That's asking a lot. I'm not even sure what we've gotten ourselves into. "Best I can do is the broad strokes."

"Mia." She draws out my name like when we were kids and she was trying to get me to do something scary, like the ropes course at summer camp, and I can't hold back a smile.

"It's a long story. Don't you have unpacking to get back to?"

Her grin is the opposite of reassuring. "Painters are at the house, and I brought the fixings for braised beef ragu. I've got all day."

This wasn't a drop-in visit. It was a planned invasion, and I fell for it. But maybe it will be good to get her perspective on our wild scheme.

Three hours later we sit down to eat. My contribution to the meal was setting the table and putting the zinnias Kim brought into an oversize coffee mug I got at a friend's book launch party that says, NOT ALL HEROES WEAR CAPES. MINE WEAR KILTS.

Kim, on the other hand, transformed a garden's worth of produce and an honest-to-goodness butcher-paper-wrapped cut of meat into the delicious sauce she's ladling over pappardelle noodles. "Since when do writers method act?"

I break off a piece of the crusty bread she brought, warm from the oven. "It's just to get out of my routine." I explained the trope tests as briefly as possible, and after dodging a few nosy questions, managed to distract her by asking about her new job and sitting through a few episodes of her favorite reality show that I usually refuse to watch.

But I should've known she wouldn't leave the topic alone. "Why Gavin?"

That's the angle she's stuck on. "We trust each other. And I don't have to worry about navigating dates with strangers."

She settles back, twirling noodles on her fork. "And he doesn't mind joining you in these experiments?"

"He suggested it."

"Is he single?"

"Of course." The rapid-fire questions are making me defensive. "I'd never do this with him if he . . ."

She raises her brows in a *gotcha* expression, but I shake my head.

"It's not like that." Except now I'm thinking of how close we came to kissing. Twice.

"It's kind of like that," she says, as if she can read my mind.

I spear a piece of meat with my fork, not wanting to admit she's right. "Kim, I'm telling you. There's nothing going on between me and Gavin. This is me doing something out of character for the sake of my inspiration. Nothing more."

Her expression turns thoughtful. "What do you plan to wear this weekend?"

The question catches me off guard. "Hadn't thought about it. Whatever people wear to do yard work, I guess."

"Aka, nothing in your closet."

Jeans are my mortal enemy, and my only pair of sneakers is white. "I'll figure something out."

She shakes her head. "Hurry and eat. It's makeover time."

My sister passes a pair of jeans through the cracked door of the fitting room. Reluctantly, I take them. "Any of these would work." Nonetheless, I yank on yet another pair of pants, hoping that we'll hit on one that doesn't make me feel like I've gone cold turkey on comfort.

I catch sight of myself in the mirror and wow, maybe there's something to be said for denim and strategically placed pockets. I open the door and strike a dramatic pose.

"How do you feel?" Kim asks.

I tamp down a smile. Never thought I'd feel this bubbly while trying on jeans and cargo pants. Almost like I'm getting ready for a date. "Like I'm ready to show some rosebushes who's boss."

"Think they'll trust you with pruning shears?"

I rub my hands together. "A girl can try."

She spins her finger and reluctantly I turn in a circle. Okay, these do accentuate the curves of my butt and thighs, but the point is not to look cute. I'm only doing this to fit in.

"You need a hat," Kim says.

I shut the door before she can voice any more opinions. "I look terrible in hats."

"You look adorable in them." Her voice carries through the angled slats of the door, and I'm sure everyone in the fitting room can hear us. "Remember those Easter bonnets Mom used to make us wear?"

"I try not to," I reply, and she laughs. "Also, kid in church is not the look I'm going for." Too late, I realize my mistake. "In the sense that no grown woman wants to be infantilized." I pull open the door again, dressed in my own clothes. "Not because this is a date."

She steps inside and helps sort the pile of discarded clothes.

"Sure is a lot of hoops to jump through when you could just admit you like the guy."

"Of course I like Gavin." Shaking out a pair of jeans, I fold them neatly. "I love him."

I catch sight of Kim's wide eyes in the trio of lighted mirrors, but shake my head, forestalling her reaction. "I love him as a friend. He's one of the most important people in my life and falling for him wouldn't just be messy. It would be a huge mistake."

"Why?"

Sometimes my sister's cluelessness about how things shook down with Ted baffles me. He went from being a good friend to someone I had to keep at arm's length so things wouldn't be weird between me and my sister. But I'm complicit in her lack of awareness since I downplayed things, and now it's far too late to bring up.

"I'm not denying I haven't ever thought about it." Obviously Gavin is hot, I'm not blind. I'm also smart enough to know that my attraction for him would probably equal good chemistry. "But it's not the dating that would be the problem. It's that when it inevitably ended, we couldn't go back to what we have."

"Who says it would end?" Kim's always had a rosy view of love, like everything will work out how it's supposed to. For her, it has. Our parents haven't given up on love, either. Dad is on his second marriage, and our mom recently started dating again after her four-year relationship ended. But I'm not comfortable with the margin of error. Life isn't a romance novel, and I'm not willing to gamble Gavin if happy-ever-after isn't guaranteed.

"What Gavin and I have is special. I'm not risking him over a fling."

"You've been afraid to go for things ever since we were kids," she says. "You didn't quit your accounting job until your first book hit the bestseller list, and even then, you gave two weeks' notice."

"That's called being conscientious, not cowardly." I was brave enough to tell Ted how I felt about him. Brave enough to tell Stewart we didn't want the same things. Brave enough to keep dating until recently, even though it's always ended in failure.

"I just hate to see you settle for being content instead of going after something better."

"Why would I, when what I have is enough?"

"Is it?" Kim searches my face, like she's looking for a sign that I'm truly happy before she'll let it go.

A simple question, and a few weeks ago I would've said yes. That was before I let myself imagine more. *You're not the only one that wants this.* But are either of us brave enough to make the move?

fourteen

Gavin

Did I almost kiss Mia after fleeing the escape room like our actual lives depended on it? Yes. But in my defense, she almost kissed me first.

Or at least I think she did. The lights were out, but the darkness only heightened my other senses. Days later and I can still feel the grind of her hips against mine, the way her lips were a whisper from my mouth. How the smallest movement from either of us would've sent us past every boundary we've put up . . .

I deliberately push away the thought. I won't relive the moment. Won't think of how she pinned my wrist in her grasp, taking charge in a way I hadn't known I needed, letting me cede control.

The awful thing is how badly I wanted us to careen over the edge. The rules are clear. Flirting and teasing are part of the setup. But a kiss would end this. Pretty sure there's no way Mia would continue if we crossed that line, and she needs this. Not for inspiration—I don't believe for a second that she truly needs my help with that—but to shake off the demons telling her this story can't have a happy-ever-after.

We might've already come too close, because I haven't seen her since. She texted to let me know she's focusing on work this week, which makes total sense with the deadline moved up and the pressure she's under. I just hope the escape room disaster didn't make things worse.

In the meantime, I've got issues of my own to deal with. I can't wrap my head around the fact that my dad is selling the farm. I almost convinced myself Scott made the whole thing up, but when I finally call Dad on my lunch break Wednesday, he confirms it.

"Can't be too surprising." His voice comes through strong and clear on speaker. I'm resting in the shade of a sturdy red maple by the curb. I gave Morris some cash and told him lunch for the crew was on me, hoping to buy myself a few minutes alone for this conversation. "I've loosened the reins on the farm a lot in the last year," Dad says. "Remember my vacation last fall?"

He went to visit my uncle's family up in Door County. "Big difference between vacation and retirement." I don't want to talk him out of it, but I can't see him being happy without work.

"That's what I'm counting on," he says. "I'm ready for a change."

"And you're moving to Colorado?" That might be the most shocking part. Dad's Midwestern roots go back generations.

"For now." He sounds less certain. "Scott's got an extra room and I can help out with the boys if he ends up going back to work." I try and fail to picture my dad trading in twelve-hour days outdoors for shuttling around my nephews in the family van. "But long-term, I'm still figuring things out."

"You don't mind someone else taking over the farm?"

"Someone was always going to take over for me eventually. For a while I thought it would be you." *Hoped* it would be me is more accurate. "Have you changed your mind?"

"I'm happy here." The answer comes automatically.

There's a pause, and I can picture him stepping into the shade of the Christmas tree barn, empty for the season but with a piney scent that lingers year-round. "That why you stopped coming out?"

The question I've been dreading. "I've been putting in work around the house. Fixing it up. You know how it is."

"Not really," he says. "You haven't talked about it much."

I thought he might not want updates, since I was making a life here, not at the farm. "You could come out sometime, if you want." I haven't invited him, afraid he'd turn me down. "Since apparently you have all this free time," I say, keeping my tone light.

To my surprise, he says, "Sure. After Scott and Amber go back home. Send me some dates."

Never in my life did I think I'd hear Dad say that. Mom managed the family calendar. He was always focused on running the farm. "You won't be busy with getting stuff in order for the sale?"

"No big rush. I've been meeting with consultants. Won't bore you with the details. But my guess is things will move fast, so I'm holding off till fall." The rumble of a tractor fills the background, and he says louder, "I wanted to discuss all this with you in person. But Scott says you won't make it out before the barbecue?"

With Mia's deadline moved up, I'm leaving my weekends free for trope tests. "Probably not."

"All right, well if you find yourself with a free day, come on out. Brett learned how to cast, and he's been out to the lake every morning, catching us supper."

I smile at the thought of my nephew turning into a master fisherman. "Bet he's proud. Tell him I'll show him the best spots when I get there."

The mention of the lake reminds me of what I stand to lose when Dad sells. No more nights at the cabin and fall bonfires.

No more hiking in the snow to find the biggest balsam fir for Mia, one that makes Frank look like a seedling. Mom will still be close by, and I'll see Dad when I fly out to visit Scott's family, but we won't have our central hub without the farm. Am I ready to sacrifice my life here to keep it?

Riley pulls up behind the trailer of equipment parked on the street and she and Morris climb out, followed by a few of the summer hires, college kids home for break. Riley passes me a gyro and when I ask Morris for change, he pulls out empty pockets. Typical.

"So we finally get to meet the famous Mia Brady on Friday," Riley says around a mouthful of pita. "Or did she get second thoughts about pulling weeds for charity?"

"She's coming." Unless she's thought better of it.

"I hear season four is filming soon," Riley says. "Think I can get the inside scoop?"

My stomach twists. I should've thought twice before inviting her to hang out with someone who's super into the show. "Don't bring it up, okay?"

Morris glances up from tying his boot, sunburned face shiny with sweat. "Why not?"

I wrack my brain for a good excuse that doesn't involve her writer's block. "Because she wants to fit in. Be one of the crew. She's never done anything like this before."

"Want us to go easy on her?"

"No." Mia would hate being coddled. "I mean, yes. Don't throw her in the deep end. But don't assume she can't handle something. Just act normal."

"Right," he says, dragging out the word.

"And don't grill her about the show."

"You're acting weird." Riley stuffs her trash in the paper sack. "Is something going on between you two?"

If only. "Nope." I tug my hat down and call out to the group scattered on the grass. "Ten minutes, everyone. Let's finish up so we can head back." Taking a big bite of my gyro, I turn my back on Morris and Riley before they can ask anything else about Mia, the book, or the tightrope we're walking.

A couple days later, on Friday morning, I'm idling at the curb by Mia's building to pick her up for the Community Give-Back event. These experiments are her way of containing the situation, but I'm dying to see what happens if we forget about the rules. Would she flirt with me if it wasn't just a box to tick?

We agreed no touching for the trope tests, but she wasn't in any hurry to get off of me when she toppled into me in the escape room. What if Joe is right and she's been waiting for me to make a move? I won't be able to test that theory with all my coworkers around, and I wish I'd thought of a more romantic trope for today. But when I got the sign-up email, it struck me as the perfect way for Mia to try fish-out-of-water.

There will be too many eyes on us for real or fake flirting, but I hope today helps Mia get a break from agonizing over the book. I want her to remember that she's more than her career. She's an accomplished author and that won't change. But she's also an amazing person and a great friend, even though calling her a "friend" feels like too small a word for how I feel about her, like a root-bound plant that's outgrown its pot.

Emerging from her building, she climbs into my truck and pulls her oversize sunglasses down over her eyes, then powers the seat into full recline as if evading paparazzi, looking every bit the famous author she is, even though it's just daylight she's hiding from. I'm so amused by her grumpy, pre-coffee persona that it takes me a second to notice her outfit.

She's wearing a baggy T-shirt, a decent choice given the heat, though long sleeves would protect her arms from scratches. What catches my eye are the nylon shorts paired with crew socks and hiking boots. The rounded swoop of her thighs does something to me that's not platonic in the least, and the long expanse of bronze legs between the hem of her shorts and white socks has me more distracted than a woman's body has in, well, forever.

Since the farthest Mia ever hikes is from her house to the coffee shop, I'm guessing she bought the boots especially for today. I forgot to mention that the crew usually wears pants and long sleeves, and don't have the heart to tell her now, since she's clearly put a lot of thought into looking the part.

"I can't believe I thought this was a good idea." She hoists herself up on an elbow to take a sip out of her giant travel mug before settling back with a groan. "It's way too early to be awake."

"Even for a good cause?"

"Only for a good cause."

I ease back onto the busy street, full of commuters in a rush to get to the train station or headed toward the freeway into the city. "How late were you up writing?"

"Two a.m.," she says. "The story is actually going somewhere. I sent Evie the latest chapters."

Normally she sends pages to me, too, but I ignore the pang of jealousy. I can't give her anything close to Evie's professional level of critique, and she probably doesn't want the pressure of extra eyes on it yet. "Since you've found your rhythm, we could've called off this trope test."

"I might've found my groove, but I'm not going to mess with the process. You don't shave your beard in the middle of the World Series."

Can't argue with baseball logic. "I'm happy you're coming along today, experiment or not."

"My lack of gardening skills might make me a liability."

"Experience doesn't matter," I assure her. "Each year we get volunteers of all ages and abilities. Don't worry, we're not going to give you a chainsaw and aim you at the nearest tree."

"That would make a good scene for a rom-com," she says. "Or a gruesome thriller, depending on which way you spin it."

Her imagination is equal parts cool and terrifying. "Glad we're going for the romance vibe. I don't need to worry about you mistaking my arm for a tree limb."

She laughs. "Speaking of romance . . ." Out of the corner of my eye, I notice she's toying with the hem of her shorts nervously. With effort, I refocus on the road. "There are going to be people around today. Let's just stick to being ourselves. Role-play will just make things trickier and I'm already out of my element."

"Fine by me. I'm going to have my hands full already keeping you away from the power tools." I'm glad we're shedding the games. If Mia reacts to me today, I won't have to second-guess it. "You cool with a stop at my work? I need to pick up a few things before we meet the crew at the site."

"Sounds good, but can we grab some food?"

"Got it covered." I turn into the parking lot of our favorite breakfast spot.

"My hero," she says airily. Ha. The heroes she writes wouldn't need a trope test to push them to make a move. Then again, none of them have to worry about losing their best friend if they do.

I head inside but the order isn't ready. By the time I get back to the idling truck, Mia's dozing, mouth slack, sunglasses askew. Adorable. For once, I don't block the surge of affection, and my breath catches with a hitch of relief, like the cool burst of lake water on bare skin at the height of summer.

But our pledge to not screw things up with romance hangs over my head, like always, compounded by the confines of the trope test. I turn off the A/C and power down the windows to distract myself, letting in the comforting scents of sod and mulch from the freshly landscaped median.

While I navigate the familiar route to work, it's easy to feel like this is a typical day. But the moment we're in my office, everything changes.

Mia flops into my desk chair and spins in circles, gripping the armrests. "Maybe I had it wrong. Your office is ripe for a workplace romance."

She's got a look in her eye that tells me she's up to something. "What do you mean?" I grab a clipboard and thread a pencil through the top.

"Your desk is all tidy and organized. Practically begging you to sweep everything to the floor and do decidedly un-HR-approved things to me."

My mind goes there in an instant. Mia on the desk, me between her legs, slipping my hand under the flimsy hem of those shorts . . .

I glance at the closed door, a full body flush taking over. "What about getting caught?"

"That would only heighten the tension," she says. "At some point our desires would reach the breaking point." She says this in a matter-of-fact way that shouldn't have my mind racing after possibilities.

"We'd have to be quick." And I'd want to take my time, knowing this might be our only chance.

"It would be messy." Her words are a promise. "Spilled coffee, ink stains. Might even break your keyboard."

"I've been wanting to replace it anyway." My thighs bump the desk. Somehow I've moved closer, drawn by her voice.

She hasn't moved, though. She's holding herself very precisely. Both hands on the armrests of the swivel chair, fingers curled tight, posture rigid. But her legs are splayed, lips parted. Almost controlled, but not quite.

And there it is again, the reckless urge to shatter her poise, pull her down with me to the place where desire clashes with duty in tantalizing friction.

"With you on top of it, you think I'd worry about the state of my desk for even a second?" Hell no. "You'd command every ounce of my attention."

There. Subtle, but unmistakable. The moment she lets go, her gaze dips in a hungry sweep along my lips, neck, down my chest, making my abs clench, and the desk is low enough that—

The door swings open. I startle at the noise and my elbow bangs against the computer monitor, which topples over and knocks my employee of the month plaque to the floor, like a Rube Goldberg machine gone haywire.

My boss stands in the doorway, surveying the chaos. "Thought you were volunteering today." Her gaze lands on Mia, who froze the moment the door opened. "Mia Brady." The name is infused with all the warmth of an aunt greeting a long-lost niece she hasn't seen in years. "You're even prettier than your author photo."

Mia sits up straighter. "Um, thank you."

Stooping to retrieve the framed award, I tell her, "This is my boss Faye."

"One of them," she says with a grin. "My husband's a late riser. Never makes it in until afternoon." She puts her hands on her khaki-clad hips. "Come to think of it, why are you here this morning? Aren't you supposed to be meeting the crew at that vacant lot on Fifth Street?"

"Just picking up some supplies."

"Well, get on with it. Don't want people thinking our employees are slackers." She winks at Mia.

"I'll make sure he doesn't shirk his duties."

Faye laughs. "Wait until I tell the book club you stopped by. We've got tickets to that convention in Chicago in a couple weeks and you're the first booth we plan to stop at."

"Awesome," Mia says. "I'll be sure to put together some extra goodies for your group. How many are there?"

"Well, aren't you sweet," Faye says. "There's ten of us, counting my husband." They tried to get me to join but I draw the line at reading steamy books with my bosses. "Gavin, you ought to give her a quick tour since she's here."

"I thought you wanted us to hurry."

She waves this off. "It'll be another hour before they're organized enough to get started." Turning to Mia, she says, "Help
yourself to a free plant or two. Have Gavin show you the azaleas.
You got a garden?"

I chuckle and usher Mia out. "It's too early for your badgering, Faye."

She huffs good-naturedly. "You'd better have made coffee,
with that sass."

"There's a pot brewing, and I put a fresh carton of half-and-
half in the fridge." I push the exterior door open before she
bombards us with any more questions. Like what exactly we
were doing in the office before she arrived. Because I'm pretty
sure the answer is verbal foreplay, and we're not even in character
today.

A quick tour turns into me troubleshooting the sprinkler system. Always something to fix around here. Cold water dripping
between my fingers, I stand up after turning on the tap and find
Mia lowering a tomato plant to the concrete floor. "What are
you doing?"

In answer, she hops up on the table, scooching her butt
around in a way that makes the wooden platform wobble. I
take ahold of the edge to steady it, and my thumb inadvertently
brushes the silky skin of her thigh.

I adjust my grip, but don't let go. Only because Faye would
kill me if Mia took a tumble on my watch.

"Testing for stability." She glances down at my hand but
doesn't move away. "How much weight do you think these tables can hold?"

"Seriously, Mia?" My voice is gruff, frustrated at how easily
I'm able to imagine the scene.

"Can't pass up an opportunity for research." She shimmies

around in an alarmingly rhythmic way, and I do let go then, palming the back of my neck.

"Is your research always so . . . physical?" I've sure as hell never seen her do anything like that for research.

She slides down. "Never, actually. I don't know what's gotten into me." She sends me a coy look over her shoulder and it hits me that she's doing this on purpose. Flirting, toeing the line we've drawn. Maybe she's more curious about this new electricity between us than she lets on.

Whatever it is, the same feeling has me by the throat, pinned under a mixture of pleasure and the very real knowledge we're headed down a path we've vowed never to venture onto.

Maybe all this time spent learning about her process has kicked my own imagination into high gear. "If you're looking for romantic spots, I can do way better than a wobbly potting table."

The humid warmth of the greenhouse sinks into my skin. Condensation slips down the fogged panes of glass in long, lazy drips. The tang of soil reaches my nostrils, the hum of a box fan muted by the thick air. I inhale a breath of what feels like pure oxygen, which must explain the heady feeling when I look down at Mia by my side.

"Gotta admit, I never got it until now." She bends to sniff the delicate petals of a violet. "But I can see the vision of a greenhouse hookup."

"Oh, so is that a microtrope? Greenhouse sex?"

She grins at me over her shoulder. "Looks like someone did the assigned reading."

"When have I ever not read something you recommended?"

"You're a really cool guy, you know that, right?"

I shrug. "A decent one."

"Never met a better one." She says it so casually, but the compliment shimmers in the stillness, iridescent as a butterfly's wing.

I'm not sure what to say, or if I can even speak, because if that's true, then what really is holding us back?

"I can see why you like working here," she says, interrupting my thoughts. "It's calming, and the view . . ." She turns in a slow circle, taking in the rows of lush plants.

"Hard to beat," I agree, watching her. "And Faye and Dale are like family." Morris and Riley, too, though I'd never admit it. "Can't imagine working somewhere else."

"Not even your family's farm?"

Wondered when she'd bring it up. "I called my dad. He really is selling. He planned to tell me on my next visit and Scott wasn't supposed to say anything."

She gives me a rueful smile. "Sounds like your brother."

"Never doing as he's told? Yeah." I push my sleeves up to my elbows to combat the humid warmth. "I feel like there are things Dad's not saying, but I get the sense that he hasn't given up on the idea of me taking over."

"I'd miss you," she says. "You didn't ask but—"

"I didn't ask because I was afraid you'd say it was no big deal."

"It would be a huge deal." Her gaze dips, lashes skimming her cheeks. "I'd be happy for you, but I'm not going to lie, adjusting to life without you around would suck." She comes right out and says it without holding back this time, and I'm so grateful to hear it. "But you have to promise you won't stay for me."

"You'd have nothing to do with it." I make a show of looking around. "Mia who? Never heard of her."

She laughs, wandering down one of the aisles before resting against another potting bench. "This place feels safe, like a haven. That's where Sydney and Victor are in the plot, and I'm struggling to yank them into the next step."

They were the first characters I ever got invested in when I read the book she sent me to rescue on the night we met. "You never planned for them to stay friends." A truth only I know.

Publicly, Mia invented the friends-only backstory because after what happened with Ted, she abandoned their story, convinced friendship isn't a solid foundation for love.

"As friends, they get a happy-ever-after. Add romance and it becomes volatile." She bends to sniff a bright red geranium. "Their love shifts from being the anchoring point to just another element of chaos. Unpredictable."

"Change isn't always bad. Without change, seeds are just un-realized potential."

"Don't you dare make a plant metaphor."

I laugh, playing along. "Let your characters bloom, Mia."

She claps her hands over her ears.

In the mood to be a pest, I stand in front of her, grinning at her show of not listening. "All you need to do is plant the seed, and let nature take its course."

"That wasn't half bad." She lowers her hands, which were clearly not doing a good job of shutting out my words. "Clunky, but the spirit was there."

I put a hand to my heart. "Hurts that you doubted me. From what I hear, anyone can write a novel, not like it's hard." At one of Mia's signings, a reader came up and told her that. She didn't miss a beat. Just signed her name and told them she'd be first in line to buy their book when the time came.

"If I had a dime for every time I heard that . . ." She shakes her head. "It's half true. Everyone has a story to tell. But easy? Hardest thing I've ever done, every time." She picks up a fallen moss rose, spinning it between her fingers. "Will I be a fraud if I give them a happy-ever-after I don't believe in?"

Looks like she hasn't been able to leave Sydney and Victor behind today. "You don't believe in it now, but could you get to that place?" I need to hear her answer, for us. "After all," I say, when the silence stretches too long. "Feelings . . ." I pause at her warning look, but can't resist. "Grow."

"That was a bridge too far," she says, grinning nonetheless.

"But it's true. Love doesn't always follow a neat and tidy three-act structure. Maybe Victor and Sydney weren't ready that first time around. Maybe they needed four books to figure out their love is deeper than friendship."

She looks up at me. "You know what? Maybe they did." Her skin glistens with moisture, like dewdrops on petals, heart-stoppingly beautiful. I know she's not talking about us. She can't be. But tendrils of hope twine around my heart.

What I feel has nothing to do with the setting. It's not the tranquil, rhythmic drip of water off the leaves, or the sweet fragrance of growing things that's making my breath come shallow. I felt the same way in the gritty darkness of the cave and the too-bright concourse of the mall. She tugged at my heart when she was slouching, adorably groggy, in my passenger seat. Stirred my blood when she was keyed up and breathless in my office.

This tender new thing between us isn't a result of atmosphere or circumstance. It's her, opening up in a way I never saw coming. *Unexpected.* This woman I've known for years still manages to surprise me.

We're not touching, but I feel her in every part of me. Lately our hangouts have an agenda and rules. Gone are the casual hugs hello, the brush of our legs when we're watching a movie on her couch. Maybe that's why I feel starved for her.

My control feels fragile, like a vase of the finest crystal, ready to shatter at the least bit of rough handling. But there are no vases here. Only the foundation of sturdy pots and soil and roots and the promise of good things to come.

I take a step toward her, another . . . she reaches for me . . . And suddenly we are touching, for real, not the fantasy we created with our words.

Her hands are on my waist and my hips are slotted between her thighs in a perfect fit that only heightens my desire. The wanting is almost too good, the ache igniting an intense craving in me, echoed by the dig of Mia's fingertips, the hitch in her breath when I skim my fingers under the hem of her shorts, the way she pulls me against her, hard, our bodies notched together with a force that knocks the air from my lungs.

"Mia." I bend my head to kiss her, when the potting bench begins to rattle.

For a moment, it's just another sensation, but then diesel fumes hit my nostrils. Someone started up the tractor.

I pull away faster than I would've thought possible a moment ago. "Better grab the tools and head out before Faye comes looking."

"Can't have that." Mia looks as dazed as I feel but I resist the urge to reach for her hand. Touching her again could be catastrophic.

Her voice reaches me as I open the latch on the toolshed. "She'd miss you, too," Mia says. "So would Dale. They'd understand. But you're someone people want to keep around. Whatever you decide, don't forget that."

She doesn't know everything Scott told me. How he assumed the life I'd built here was easy to turn my back on. How he made me feel like my friendships were nothing compared to marriage and kids, and it was time to grow up and build a real life.

I haven't let on how uncertain I've been feeling. Wondering whether what's next looks nothing like I'd imagined. But Mia knew anyway because she's not some casual friend. She's my roots. Instead of picturing our relationship as a seedling breaking through the soil, fresh and new, suddenly I imagine a full-grown tree, lush and vibrant, uprooted by the storm of our shifting feelings. Change can be a beginning, but it can also be the end of something beautiful.

fifteen

Mia

I've always been a firm believer that gardening is overrated. Who wants to spend their Sunday sweating in the dirt when they could be washing down waffles with a mimosa on a patio or curled up indoors with a good book by a bay window over-looking said garden?

Not that I don't appreciate the beauty of gardens, but I never saw the appeal of doing it myself. Turns out it's even worse than I feared. Not only is this a ton of work, but it's painful, too.

I bend to grab a branch to haul away and am rewarded by the jab of a thistle hidden in the tangle. Shaking my stinging hand, I glance around to see if anyone noticed, but the other volunteers are all busy with their own tasks, laughing and making small talk like this is a walk in the park.

A future park, maybe, but right now the vacant lot is a mess. I'm glad it's being cleaned up, but less glad that I'm the one who signed up to do it. I send a silent apology to all my characters who I put through fish-out-of-water situations.

I knew I would be outside my depth physically but figured this would be better than a trope that put me in over my head emotionally. Big miscalculation. Technically, we're encouraged to take breaks whenever we feel the need, according to the person who checked me in. But my competitive streak has me wanting to keep up with all the other volunteers.

Gavin got pulled away the moment we arrived, and since we were late, I jumped in with a group who was pulling weeds. I immediately got scolded by one of the older volunteers for not yanking out the roots—I wasn't given a tutorial, but she acted like it was common sense—and after ten minutes of struggling to dig out the root of a single giant weed and breaking two nails, I slunk away when no one was looking and joined the people hauling branches to the curb.

My arms are stinging from the prickly bushes, but I've done my best to keep up, which means no chance to join in the conversation around me. My throat is dry, and I regret leaving my tumbler in Gavin's truck. I noticed water bottles in the tent during sign-in, but I'm trying to brave it out until lunchtime.

In front of me, a guy is struggling to drag a huge branch, and I jog over to help. He smiles his thanks and together we haul it across the lot. But when we set it down, a twig catches in my hair. I twist my head, trying to get loose, and reach around, feeling blindly for the spot that's snared. My head is tilted upward, and I squint against the sting of the bright midday sun.

The guy must not have noticed my plight because no offer of assistance comes. Just as well. I'd rather not have any witnesses to this embarrassing moment. I bend my knees, hoping to create slack, but the twig yanks at my roots. "Ow!"

"Here, let me," an unfamiliar voice says. I'm not in the position to be picky over my rescuer, so I hold still, thankful for the help. "You're Mia, right?"

Oh no. Please tell me this isn't a fan. I don't get recognized often but it would be just my luck to have it happen when I'm at the mercy of a nefarious twig. A rosy-cheeked face appears in front of me, framed by flyaway tendrils of light red hair. "I'm Riley by the way. Gavin and I work together."

Ah, so that's how she knows me. "The trivia queen," I say, and smile.

She gives a little laugh. "Doesn't say much considering the level of competition, but I'll take it." Another small tug, and she drops her hand, stepping back. "You're free."

"Thanks." I pat my scalp to ease the pain and try not to think of how my hair must look. Should've worn a scarf. Yet another misstep.

Riley is giving me an appraising look, hands on her broad hips. "Wanna stick with me for a while?"

I give her a grateful nod. At least she knows what she's doing.

Heading off toward the tent, she gestures for me to follow. "First stop, water."

I take it back. Gardening has one redeeming quality. The sheer physical effort involved makes dwelling on emotional stress impossible. Normally I would be questioning what the heck I was thinking when I flirted with Gavin earlier—without even the excuse of a trope test to fall back on—but struggling to keep up with Riley and the others has taken all my focus.

Anytime I feel worry creeping up over how I'm going to resolve things now that Sydney and Victor are a couple or shame blossoming for how I flirted with Gavin less than an hour after calling a time-out on the trope tests, I just yank out another weed. Riley showed me the bin of gloves set aside for volunteers and gave me a special shovel that makes it a lot easier.

At home, my mind would be spinning over the way Gavin's touch affected me, but out here I've been too busy to even keep track of where he's at.

Digging in the dirt is cathartic, and I'm actually enjoying myself right now, in spite of my sweaty face and grime-caked knees. I definitely regret changing out of my new jeans when

I saw the forecast, but the upside is feeling the slight relief of the breeze on my bare legs.

The other thing making this work tolerable is Riley. Gavin's been pulled away by one person after another since we arrived, but she's kept me entertained with gossip and snippets about her life. I have the sneaking suspicion she's my self-appointed babysitter, but the steady flow of conversation is another thing taking my mind off the twenty bazillion lines Gavin and I crossed this morning.

Riley does in fact have a chainsaw, and looked incredibly badass using it, protective goggles and all, but she's finished cutting down what I expertly identify as a tree-bush hybrid, and we're hauling the branches to a giant pile by the curb.

"Did you respond?" I've only known her for a couple hours, but already I'm fully invested in the latest escapade of her entitled sister-in-law, who apparently counts the presents at birthday parties and sent a strongly worded text to the family group about how her beloved child got one less present than his cousin in the same calendar year.

Riley flashes me a grin. Her freckled cheeks are flushed, septum piercing twinkling in the bright sun. "I asked if she'd accounted the local sales tax increase that went into effect on May first."

"Wait, what tax increase?"

"The one she probably wasted at least twenty minutes googling before she realized I made it up."

I snort out a laugh. "Your poor parents, having to deal with that kind of pettiness."

"Oh, don't worry. They can hold their own. My mom told her maybe the other one got lost in the mail, along with her own birthday present from my sister-in-law."

Dropping the branch, I try not to wince at the ache in my palms. "Remind me not to cross any of you."

Without making a big deal of it, Riley tosses the limb farther up onto the pile. "It's our way of letting her know we're not going to let this kind of stuff slide. But I don't mind too much because her antics make for the best stories." Her pale green eyes are glinting with mischief, and I recognize the joy she gets from storytelling. Exactly how I've always felt, until this book.

Ironic that the story that started it all might be my undoing. I won't let it be without a fight. That's why I'm here in the scorching sun, sweaty and dirt-streaked and entirely out of my element. I'll do whatever it takes to get into the writing mindset.

The cotton gloves aren't much protection and my hands feel raw from the rough bark, but I turn to go fetch another load and nearly bump into Gavin. It's the first time we've run into each other since we arrived, and I'm struck again by how good he looks in the lightweight long-sleeve tee and dirt-scuffed jeans.

"When was your last water break?" he asks.

Riley steps up alongside me. "Ever the foreman, huh? We're not even on the clock, and you're checking up on us?"

He shakes his head, mouth in a firm line, but she cuts him off. "To answer your question, we stopped for water ten minutes ago."

Ignoring this, he frowns at my hands. "Where'd you get those gloves?"

"They're handing them out at the sign-in table." I tug one off, wanting to get some fresh air on my hot skin.

"Let me see," he says. He catches my wrist in his hand, gently, but the touch sparks sensations I've spent the morning burying. Turning my palm upward, he lifts his sunglasses to get a better look, but I yank my arm away, feeling like a new recruit and stubbornly wanting to earn my keep, even though we're all volunteers.

"I'm fine." I lace my fingers behind my back, gritting my teeth against the sting of tender skin.

To my surprise, he tugs at the fingers of his leather glove, one by one, then takes it off and hands it to me.

I pass it right back. "I don't want your sweaty glove."

"It will protect you better than those cheap fabric ones they bought in bulk for the volunteers."

"Then it's hardly fair that I get a better deal."

He rolls his eyes. It's pretty cute, to be honest. "I don't have enough for everyone. Not that anyone else would want to wear my gloves."

"We have that in common, then, because no way am I putting my fingers in those sweat-soaked gloves. Is leather even washable?"

He glares at me, blue eyes icy, but finally relents and walks off toward the tree line at the back of the property, shaking his head.

Riley lets out a quiet huff of laughter, and I turn toward her. "Would you have worn them?"

She shrugs. "Bodily fluids don't really give me the ick. Now, don't get me started on the texture of mushy grapes. But sweat? I wouldn't be in the right profession if I minded a little perspiration. We should probably grab a sandwich, though, or we'll be left with tuna salad."

At the tent, she gets pulled into conversation by another volunteer, and I grab a sandwich and chips and eat in the shade with a few others, then toss out my trash. Realizing I misplaced my gloves, I go to fetch a new pair.

A shadow falls over me. I look up to find Gavin standing there with his arms full of what looks like laundry. "What's all that?"

"The proper attire." His gaze sweeps down my front, lingering on my bare legs in a way that reminds me of how his fingers skated over my thighs in the greenhouse. "Nothing we can do about your legs unless—"

"I'm not wearing your pants. Or any of your other clothes, for that matter." I squat down and tug a box toward me from under the table. Aha. I pull out a pair of cotton gloves triumphantly. He takes them and tosses them back in.

Handing me the pair from atop the pile he's holding, he says, "I keep extras in my truck." Next, he sets a sun hat on my head, disentangling the string from around my ears. "It's hard to make these look fashionable, but you're totally pulling it off." One corner of his mouth twitches.

"Hilarious. Are you happy now?"

He shakes his head and holds out the last item of clothing. A long-sleeve T-shirt.

"It's ninety degrees. I'm not wearing that."

"Barely eighty, and I would've offered it to you before but . . ."

"But you thought I'd be stubborn as always?"

A half grin appears, crinkling his eyes. "That, and I didn't want to rain on your parade. You clearly put so much thought into your outfit." He glances at my boots, and his lips turn down in a slight grimace.

"What's wrong with these?"

"Nothing. But did you break them in?"

"I planned to. I was going to walk to the coffee shop in them the other day but I got caught up writing." Suddenly this all feels so silly. Me, here, when I'd be better off donating like I've done every other year. If this is how fish-out-of-water feels, it's freaking embarrassing, not romantic.

Gavin steps closer, close enough for me to feel his heat, except this time I'm not concerned about sweat, because my senses are full of *him*—the midday sun glinting off his golden-brown hair, the smattering of freckles joined by flecks of potting soil along his cheekbones. His lips, a rosy shade of pink, shoulders filling out his own shirt in a way I do my best not to notice, but when I drop my eyes, it's not much help. His work boots are plenty broken in, the leather scuffed, laces worn.

"You don't have to get everything right the first time." He's talking about today, but all I can think of is the book, the only manuscript I've left unfinished.

"Being sweet isn't going to get me to put on another layer. It's like a hundred degrees out here." The forecast said low eighties, but then again, I'm used to enjoying hot summer days from the brisk air-conditioning of the great indoors.

"Sweet? Me?" I'm not used to the way his cocky smile is making my heart flutter—normally it would just give me the urge to double down in our debate. "Would someone sweet commit breaking and entering on behalf of a total stranger?"

"Yes, you goofball," I tell him. "That's pretty much the definition of a sweetheart." He's the kind of man who donates to every GoFundMe that pops up on his feed without doing hours of research like me, who calls all his friends and relatives on their birthdays, even if they haven't seen each other in years. He's not trying to rub it in that I'm making newbie mistakes. He's just looking out for me, like he always does.

It feels strangely intimate to slip on his gloves, flexing my fingers and trying not to think about the imprint of his fingertips on mine. But I draw the line at taking his shirt. I'm sweating already; adding another layer would do me in.

"You're not covered up, either." I gesture at his bare forearms—tan, toned, and dusted with golden hair that just looks more ruggedly attractive thanks to a sheen of sweat.

He yanks down the sleeves bunched at his elbows, a reverse of all the times I've written a hero undoing his cuffs, and yet the result is the same. The brusque gesture, full of restrained strength, has me imagining how much I'd like to use his sturdy arms as leverage to rise on my tiptoes and kiss him, just once, so I can get it off my mind.

Instead, I yank off my hat, shake the wrinkled shirt out with a quick snap, and tug it over my head. The sleeves dangle over my hands outrageously, and Gavin laughs, not bothering to smother it.

I stretch out my arms to demonstrate how huge it is on me. My fingertips are barely visible. "Happy?"

"Incredibly." He catches hold and cuffs the sleeves in two deft rolls. I could do it myself, but being fussed over is doing a lot to ease the sting of how awkward this afternoon has felt.

"Thank you, I guess." I scrunch my face into a grumpy expression, fighting a smile.

His dimple makes another appearance. "You're welcome, I guess."

We're back to yanking weeds, this time tackling the giant patch at the back of the lot. The stems are covered in prickers, and I have to admit Gavin was right. With my hands and arms covered, I'm itchy, but at least I haven't gotten any more scratches. Another one of Gavin's coworkers, Morris, is helping, too.

He lifts his ball cap to run a bandanna over his head, the sheen of sweat on his scalp visible through his buzz cut. "If you think Riley's family chat is bonkers, you should see mine. Nothing but hamster photos. Let me tell you, waking up to a rodent's face is not my idea of a good time. Got so fed up that I set up a social media account for the damn hamster just so my brother would quit spamming us."

I grab hold of a weed near the base. "Does he have many followers?"

"Thousands," he says. "But he didn't at first, so I gave him a pity follow. Now my algorithm is screwed and my feed is nothing but pet videos."

"Big softy," Riley says, and reaches over to rub his head, which sends a shower of dirt along his shoulders, and he sputters as clumps fall over his face.

Gavin trundles by, pushing a wheelbarrow. On his way past, he shakes his head at their antics. "It's not always like this."

"Usually he joins in," Morris says. "But he's on his best behavior for you."

"Gavin's never been on good behavior around me." I glance over, sure he'll agree, but he's already out of earshot. A group of people spreading mulch beckon him over, and he pulls a box cutter from his back pocket, then stoops to slice open a bag of mulch with decisive strokes that accentuate his biceps in a way that has me taking a swig from my water bottle.

I wipe my mouth with the back of my hand. "What I mean is, we've known each other forever. We don't worry about impressing each other."

Morris and Riley share an unreadable look. "Does Gavin ever come to your book signings?" Morris asks.

"Whenever they're local, yeah."

"And do you want things to go well when he's there, or is it business as usual?"

"I get a little self-conscious," I say. "But that's not his fault. He's super supportive."

"Okay," he says. "But think of it this way. This is his chance to show he's good at what he does. Since you two are close, your approval would mean even more."

"I hang out with him while he works in his yard all the time."

"Yeah, but that's different." Morris brushes his hands on his baggy jeans. "Here, he's not just working for himself. He's a project manager. He's running things, people look to him for leadership and expertise."

I glance toward where I saw him last and see he barely made it halfway to the road before he got waylaid by two men with pickaxes. He lifts the clipboard he brought off the pile of dirt in the wheelbarrow and flips to a new page, scribbles something on it with a pencil.

I think back on all the times I teased him for playing in the dirt. I love getting a rise out of him, but I know how it feels to have people judge you for your profession—plenty of trolls talking about how romance is cliché and worse. Landscaping isn't a profession that gets a lot of love, either, but making the world more beautiful is important work.

As someone whose genre gets ridiculed for being silly and pointless when it's anything but, I should've known better than to tease him. I finally grasp what Morris is getting at. It's not about impressing one another, it's about validation.

I've been focused on how I could make it through fish-out-of-water with my dignity intact, but Gavin is in his element. I've entered his world, and this is my chance to show him it matters, like he's always done for me.

sixteen

Gavin

I'm having trouble keeping my eyes off Mia working alongside the crew. She's basically been left to her own devices since we arrived, even though I planned to stick by her side. She's never done this sort of work, but I got pulled away the moment I got out of my truck, and every time I'm on my way to check in with her, someone else finds me.

I didn't even get a chance to join her for lunch, but that hasn't stopped me from keeping an eye on her. She's held her own in every task, keeping up with Riley, who's the toughest worker on our crew. But for some reason, I'm suddenly feeling protective. Maybe even territorial.

Morris's laughter drifts toward me and I look over and see the two of them taking a water break on a boulder in the shade. As always, his shirt strains to contain his pecs and biceps—the man is built like a pro wrestler—and I try not to grit my teeth at how close they're sitting. Not much space on the rock, I tell myself. But when she gets up and heads in my direction, I'm embarrassingly happy.

I pull a roll of sod off the pile in an attempt to look busy. "You want to call it a day?" I ask when she walks up. "I know this isn't your thing."

"Nah." She leans against the open tailgate. "It's growing on me. No pun intended."

"Really?" I don't mean to sound incredulous, but this is the same person who I caught watering her monstera with day-old coffee.

But she nods, pushing off her hat so it hangs by the string, treating me to a view of her brown eyes, framed by dark lashes. "When we showed up, this lot looked like you'd get tetanus just from setting foot inside." She lifts her chin toward the tangle of car parts and rusty barbed wire protruding from the top of a dumpster.

At the thought of barbed wire, I can't help risking a glance down at her legs. Her shins are glistening with a sheen of sweat, knees smudged with dirt. Normally I'd justify it by telling myself I'm only looking to check for injuries. It's my job to make sure no accidents happen on the job. Not that I'm not concerned. I am, because even though she's strong and capable, she's new at all this and she's barely sat down all day.

But even after I assure myself there's no telltale welts from poison ivy or scratches from bristly yew branches, my eyes linger on her skin, cataloging the shapely curve of her thighs. And after how close we came to kissing this morning, it feels like there's no point in denying it: I'm totally checking out my best friend.

"Now this lot looks ready for a game of kickball," Mia says, pulling my attention back to the conversation.

"I thought recess was your least favorite part of school."

"Just because I resented the rule about no reading at recess doesn't mean I'm not fully in support of giving the neighborhood kids more space to play," she says. "It's impressive what we've managed to accomplish in less than a day."

"You've all done such good work, but I haven't been able to pitch in as much as I'd like. Had to keep putting out fires." It comes out like a humblebrag, but I mean it. I'd rather be getting my hands dirty, but people keep coming to me for guidance.

"That's why it looks so good. You've had a hand in every-thing."

Her unexpected praise means the world. "Only because I have the experience. It's no big deal."

"You're kind of a rock star at this, Gavin Lane." She hops up on the tailgate, swinging her legs, and I lean against it, trying to seem casual even though my heart is racing at being close to her. "I know I joke around a lot about how lame gardening is," she says. "I go on about how it's an old man's hobby, and how anyone with a life would never waste their time puttering in the garden . . ."

I glance over and see she's grinning wide. She was exagger-ating to get a reaction out of me. "But seriously, you're making our town more beautiful, every day. All I need to do is look around to see that. And I'm proud of you, even if I do tease you for knowing the scientific name of every green thing imagin-able."

"Hey, being able to identify any tree is cool."

"In a nerdy sort of way," she teases.

"Says the woman who once created a flowchart of the dif-ferent Darcys."

"That was a service to humankind," she says. "You might not be running a whole tree farm, but you're doing important work right here. I hope your family sees that."

Whether they do or not, she sees, and that matters more. Hearing her say it is exactly the kind of reassurance I craved after weeks spent worrying about my future. "Does that mean I can bring you another plant to keep Frank company?"

She laughs. "Between him and the gardenia, I'm already pushing my luck." Her eyes go soft, looking out over the freshly cleared lot. "But I have a new appreciation for what you do all day when I'm wrestling with plots and characters."

"Mostly wrestling trees and bags of mulch."

"And loving it."

"And loving it," I agree, straightening up and hoisting a roll of sod onto my shoulder, eager to finish up so we can get to the part of the day where it's just the two of us in my truck.

"Is that my cue to get back to work?"

"Come find me when you've had enough. Another hour at the most." I put on my best stern foreman face. "Don't be a hero, Brady."

"How can I when you've got that role covered?" she teases, and I duck my head, glad I can blame my flushed cheeks on the heat. This woman has my heart on a string and doesn't even know it.

The shadows are lengthening, and I should call it a day, but Mia seems so happy. Relaxed, too, with no trace of the desperation that's clung to her lately.

Hard to believe gardening is what put a smile on her face. She's not used to manual labor, and I know from personal experience how many blisters she'll have by the end of this, even with the thick gloves I lent her, but she insisted on doing the same work as everyone else and seems to be having a great time.

"Going to quit lazing around and actually help us?" Normally the ribbing would come from Morris or Riley, but this time it's Mia. Grinning widely, she taps her smartwatch. "Time is money, boss."

Riley laughs, and I glare at her. "Barely a day and you've already turned her against me?"

"You've done that yourself, bringing her along. She told me she's never even weeded a garden, and she's out here digging out tree stumps."

"She's not supposed to be doing that sort of thing." I take

hold of the thick trunk of the sapling with a decisive grip, arching my brows meaningfully at Mia. "She's supposed to be pruning the bushes or spreading mulch. Not," I say, bumping her shoulder with mine, "planting trees."

Mia pushes right back, hip-checking me, and heat radiates through the thin fabric of her shorts.

I straighten the trunk, and use my boot to scrape loose dirt back into the hole. Morris empties a wheelbarrow full of dirt near us and Riley fills the hole with a shovel. Normally I'd be proud of the seamless way the crew works together, but lately it reminds me how hard it would be to leave them. Either way, I'm letting someone down.

Another group is planting trees on the far side of the lot, and Morris and Mia head off to get mulch. She climbs up into the pickup, waving him off as he extends a hand, even though she's a bit wobbly.

"She'll be sore tomorrow," Riley says, watching Mia drag a bag of mulch toward the tailgate. "Heck, I'm going to be sore tomorrow. This is a big job."

"Should we call it early?"

Riley snaps her gaze toward me. "Your friend seems like she can hold her own."

"She can. I just didn't expect her to jump in feetfirst. I didn't invite her here to wear herself out."

Riley watches me with perceptive green eyes. "Yeah, you said that." She looks back over toward the truck where Morris is pointing out the different kinds of mulch. Knowing Mia, she asked for the details, storing them for use in a future book. Morris scoops up some cedar mulch and drops it into her upturned palm, bending close to tell her something.

I tear my eyes away and find Riley watching me. "You two never . . ." She trails off, but there's a question there, and I shake my head so forcefully that my sunglasses slip.

"Never. It's not like that with Mia."

"Okay," she says. "But is it like that with you?"

Lately? More than ever. "Mia doesn't date friends."

"No one goes out looking to date their friends, Gav." Riley is the only one who calls me that, just to get under my skin. "From what I remember about your and Mia's origin story, life friend-zoned you from day one."

"What are you, a boomer with that shit? Friend zoning is not a thing."

"It is for you." She smirks.

"No, it's not. This is how things have always been between us." I'm not about to bring up the pact we made back in college. Riley would be all over that, and I know it seems silly, but for years it felt like the foundation of our friendship. I'm worried removing it will topple everything.

"You and I are friends, but you've never pried your sweaty gloves off your own hands to save me from blisters." Her voice is low, but I dart a glance toward the truck, in case they heard, but they're off-loading mulch, Morris's steel-toed boots making a racket on the truck bed. "That's like the landscaping equivalent of a penguin giving their mate a pebble," she says.

"You've lost me." I'm guessing it's something she learned from all the nature documentaries she watches. She loves to rattle off random facts. Morris doesn't mind because she nails all the nature questions at trivia nights.

"Probably because you haven't been able to tear your eyes off her all day," she counters.

Like clockwork, my gaze swings back toward Mia. I wish I could say I was making sure she hadn't overheard us, but the truth is Riley's right. My gaze keeps finding Mia, and not just to check on her. I turn away, embarrassed Riley noticed. "I'm just worried about the heat. It's a lot, even for us, and we're used to it."

"There's no shame in crushing on a friend, dude."

Oh, but when it comes to Mia, there absolutely is. I press my lips together. "Seriously, Riley. It's never been like that with us." I've never let my feelings get this far. Not until I faced the reality of losing her and realized this might be our only chance to explore something more.

Riley casts a thoughtful glance at the truck, and this time, when my eyes inevitably follow, Mia is looking right at me. "You sure about that?" Riley asks, and a few weeks ago, I would've said yes.

But now I'm not sure of much of anything. *Chaos*, that's what Mia called falling in love. Uncertainty. But what this feels like is anticipation, like the thrill of shaking a birthday present. The hope that what comes next will be everything you've been wishing for, even if you've been too scared to ask.

seventeen

Mia

"I've never been so exhausted in my life." I stretch as far as the cab of Gavin's truck will allow, trying to ease the ache in my muscles. My toes feel pulverized from the stiff boots and my arches are cramped. I would've already taken them off if I wasn't certain my feet stink, clammy in the thick socks I wore.

Unable to summon the energy to lift my head, I roll my neck sideways to eye Gavin, fully upright and unbelievably alert in the driver's seat. His gray T-shirt is rumpled, forearms streaked with dirt, but he looks unaffected by the day. Like he could go home and casually build a pergola, which is literally his plan for the evening.

"How do you do this day after day?" My words come out as a pathetic croak, and he darts a quick glance toward me. He returns his eyes to the road, but at the next stop sign, he hands me my insulated tumbler from the cupholder without the slightest wobble of his grip.

I, however, have to cradle the bottle to my chest with my forearm, not trusting my raw hands to hold on.

Watching me fumble with the straw, he asks, "Is it that bad?" His voice is gruff, and embarrassment swells over me.

Defensive, I hold out my hand as evidence that it is, in fact, that bad. I've been scared to look closely at my palms since I took off my gloves, but it must not look great, because Gavin swears under his breath.

"Shit, Mia." He flicks on his turn signal, eyes on the rearview, and swerves over to the curb, coming to an abrupt halt. "You said your hands felt fine."

"I didn't want to hear 'I told you so,' or act like a big baby."

"A big baby?" He gently loosens the cup from my grip, and now his hand is trembling, so maybe his muscles aren't invincible, after all. But instead of lowering it back into the cupholder, he shifts in his seat, worn jeans sliding on the smooth leather. Gripping the straw between his fingers, he guides it to my lips.

"Drink." One word, said in a gravelly tone I hardly recognize as belonging to my chill friend. It's a tone that feels like fire injected into my bones, yet it roots me to the spot, unable to do anything other than open my mouth and obey.

The water is cool against my throat, soothing yet another ache, and I suck down a long gulp, releasing the straw with a gasp.

"Thank you," I say, and this time it's less of a croak than a whisper.

He glares at me. "You're thanking me, after I let you—" His voice cracks, and he darts another glance to my hands. "Mia, your hands." He puts the tumbler back in the cupholder, bumbling it this time, but when he reaches for my upturned hands, the tremor is gone.

He slides his fingertips under my knuckles, cradling my hands with a gentleness totally at odds with the forceful way he handled the tools earlier. He holds my hands with all the tenderness I've seen him use to plant petunias in a window box. He *tsks* as he takes in the raw edges of the fresh blisters, grimy with dirt that worked its way through the heavy-duty gloves.

"Mia," he says again, and this time I recognize it's concern roughening his voice, not frustration.

"It's not that big a deal. I've been meaning to try out a new dictation app for writing anyway," I say, only half joking. Despite a sore back and what feels like a pulled tricep—or what I assume is my tricep based on how I've been describing heroes' musculature for years—I enjoyed myself. A few blisters seem insignificant.

"I'm not worried about your job, Mia," Gavin says. But before I can bristle at his words, and explain how my writing is so much more than just a job for me, he adds, "I'm worried about you." He tips his forehead against mine, and at first I think it's just an accident, that the confines of the truck cab and his height don't mix, but when I shift to give him room, he doesn't pull away.

With my face upturned, our mouths are perilously close together. He exhales, the barest brush of air across my parted lips. I hold myself still, so still, even though all of me is aching to kiss him. Yes, he's my best friend, but also a man I want so much right now that I crush my lower lip between my teeth to regain control.

He lets out a soft groan, audible only because of our nearness, and I look up to find his eyes trained on my mouth, darkened to the deep blue of twilight with something that looks dangerously like need, the moment charged with the kind of desire usually reserved for my characters around the 50 percent mark.

But Gavin and I were never supposed to reach this point together. We were supposed to bear witness to each other's happy-ever-after, not be the cause of it. But endings are the last thing on my mind right now. All I know is I cannot go another day without kissing this man.

Exhaustion takes a back seat to desire, leaving me dizzy, only able to form a single coherent thought: Yes. Yes to the question he hasn't asked. Yes to a touch that should be denied. Yes, and soon.

His eyes lift to my own and recognition flickers in their depths. We may not know this side of each other—the longing, hungry side—but we've spent nearly a decade reading each other. Whatever he sees on the open pages of my face is clear enough for him to gently set my hands in my lap, and position his own at ten and two on the steering wheel, and inhale so forcefully that I unconsciously mirror him, before he shifts the truck into gear and pulls back out onto the road, making a tight U-turn to head back toward town, determination in the tightening of his jaw.

Gavin jogs out of the pharmacy with an overstuffed plastic bag. He slides into the driver's seat, leaning over to set the bag in the back of the cab, and his shirt hikes up with the motion, revealing a peek of very toned abs.

To distract myself, I ask, "What did you do, rob the place?"

"Trust me, you're going to want everything in there." He throws the truck into Reverse.

"If there's a bottle of wine in there, then you're right."

He lets out a soft laugh and pulls out of the parking lot. "Didn't bother. I know that's one emergency supply you do keep on hand."

When we reach my building and I try to get out, I encounter the first obstacle. Between my noodle arms and blistered hands, I can barely undo my seat belt.

Gavin jogs around to my door, pulling it open. "Need a hand?"

I open my mouth to say no, but honestly, I'm not sure. "Up until today, the closest I'd gotten to planting a tree was an annual donation to that charity you told me about." I finally manage to unsnap my buckle and twist in the seat, ready to climb down from the cab that suddenly feels very far from the ground. "So forgive me if I'm a little tire—" The last word gets clipped into a yelp as my knees give way and I topple off the running board.

Except I don't. Closing my eyes against the inevitable crack of my knees hitting the sidewalk, I find myself enveloped in something warm and sturdy and distinctly masculine. Gavin's arms.

But this isn't the kind of friendly hug we usually share. He's wrapped me up in an all-out embrace, saving me from a fall like some swooning debutante. Except I'm not at my first ball, overwhelmed with nerves. I'm in front of my condo in the arms of my best friend, who is most definitely not a romance hero.

It's always seemed humiliating to be carried like this, and that's why I've never submitted my characters to the indignity, despite my own secret soft spot for the getting-swept-off-your-feet trope. But in Gavin's embrace, all I feel is tenderness.

"You can put me down now." The words are muffled against his shoulder, and I inhale the earthy notes of mulch and topsoil and the citrus aroma of the heavy-duty soap he uses after work, a mix of scents that's uniquely Gavin.

"Not sure that's a good plan." His voice is a low rumble I could lose myself in.

I lift my head enough to meet his eyes and my stomach flutters. "What's your endgame? Because I'm not letting you haul me up two flights of stairs."

"There's an elevator."

"After what you told me about your claustrophobia? No way."

He lowers me to the seat but stays close, filling the open door with his frame. "You were a huge help today. The least I can do is make sure you don't face-plant on the sidewalk."

"I really did have fun." I'm doing my best to ignore the casual way he's leaning, forearm on the upper edge of the doorframe, T-shirt bunched at his biceps. To distract myself from how utterly kissable he looks, I say, "So what if my hands are a mess and I've got aches in muscles I didn't know I owned?"

He groans, looking pained, but the way it shoots straight to my core is pure pleasure.

I clear my throat. "Today was honestly the best thing to take my mind off, well, everything." The deadline, the dread I'll wind up failing my readers, the impostor syndrome. "Trope tests aside, it's been good for me to try new things. Get out of my routines. But you might be right about me being a fall hazard. Just help me down and I'll make it from there."

"I've got a better idea." He reaches into the back seat to pull out the first aid supplies. Once he's slid the handles of the bag over his wrist in a gesture I recognize from my all-in-one-trip groceries habit, he turns his back to me.

It's the same back I rubbed sunscreen on during countless weekends at the lake. The same back he carried me on when I made the poor choice to wear strappy stilettos out to college bars in slushy winter weather. The same broad, strong back I did my best not to ogle this afternoon, unsuccessful in my attempts for the first time in years.

Yeah, Gavin is hot, but up until now I've been able to acknowledge his good looks in an objective way, not this recent and very pressing urge to take him home and kiss him senseless.

Except, when he leans back, nestled between my thighs, and says, "Climb on," kissing him senseless is the least of what I want to do to him. "Seriously, Gavin, I can walk up a flight of stairs."

"Do you *want* to walk up a flight of stairs?"

"Currently, no. But I also don't want to make you haul me up the stairs like a sack of potatoes."

"It's no problem, Mia." When I don't budge, he cocks his head. "Did it look like I had trouble hauling stuff around today?"

That earns him an eye roll. "You are not seriously using this as an opportunity to flex."

"I mean . . ." He draws his arms in front of himself, bending them in a way that makes his biceps pop. He's messing around, but there's nothing funny about the way the sleeves of his shirt mold to his muscles, or how a slant of sunlight turns the light dusting of hair on his forearms into spun gold.

"You're not the only one who moved dirt around today." I

lift both arms in what I assume is a classic weight lifter pose. To sell it, I contort my face into my best tough girl expression.

He lets out a laugh and reaches out to clasp my upper arm. "Where've you been hiding these guns?" My pulse skyrockets at the casual touch and I lower my arms, blushing.

"Never underestimate someone who can type seventy words a minute."

He smiles. "Won't happen again. How're your legs, though?" For half a heartbeat, I imagine he's going to give my thighs the same treatment with a playful squeeze, and I honestly think I'd lose consciousness on the spot, so ridiculously keyed up as I am. But instead, he lifts his chin over his shoulder at my building. "You can walk if you want, but if you let me carry you, I promise not to hold it against you."

It's too impossible to resist. "That's what he said."

He rolls his eyes heavenward. "This is what I get for trying to be a gentleman."

"Trying? You're a gentleman through and through. You don't have a rakish bone in your body."

"Rakish?" he says. "Is that some sort of insult based on my profession?"

"Oh my gosh, no." I really need to get him some historical romances. "Rakes are the devilish heroes in regency romance. An old-school bad boy type. Readers go wild for them."

"Not surprised. No one wants the nice guy."

"I do." I'm so used to debating tropes and archetypes in interviews and panel discussions that it takes me a moment to realize we're not talking about book boyfriends, and I've just said I'm into sweet guys like him. So be it. I am. "It's a lie that nice guys finish last. Give me a guy willing to embark on a life of crime for a wronged woman over the bad boy any day."

"I wish you'd stop referring to our first meeting as a crime scene."

I shrug. "Call it how I see it."

"Also, isn't stealing the definition of being a bad boy?"

"You were taking back what was mine. Robin Hood stuff."

"I'll take that." He grins. "Now will you quit being stubborn?"

"If you really don't mind." I scoot to the edge of the seat, legs splayed, and Gavin bites his lip.

He turns with a brusque motion and steps close again, bending so I can climb on. I drape my arms around his neck, and he scoops under my thighs, hauling me up, and oh geez, I didn't think this through. Now I'm plastered to his back, fully touching him from chin to inner thighs, and I'm pretty sure my body couldn't care less whether this man is a friend or foe.

He kicks the truck door closed and I let out a squeak, clutching him hard with my thighs. The moment my legs press into the firm ridges of his obliques, he lets out a muffled groan, the sound reverberating through my chest. "Sorry," I tell him.

"Don't be. It helps if you hold on." The words sound ridiculously dirty out of context, and since I make a living out of innuendo, my mind inevitably goes there in a heartbeat. And when he shifts his grip, tightening his fingers on the backs of my thighs, I pinch my eyes closed and focus on cataloging every aching part of my body, which unfortunately is a very short list at this point. One singular part of me is aching, and it's not my hands.

We make it inside, and Gavin's barely out of breath. Never again will I underestimate yard work as cardio. I'm more winded than he is just from the effort of not focusing on how much of our bodies were connected.

I expect him to set me down once we're inside, but he carries me all the way to the chaise lounge. Maybe he sensed I was tired enough to collapse by the door and use my entryway rug as a mattress.

"Consider your bid for Rake of the Year denied." He's kneeling by my side, which only enhances the knight-in-shining-armor act he's got going on. Except it's not an act. Over the years, he's found ways to take care of me every time I've been sick, dropping off chicken noodle soup at my doorstep when I'm contagious, keeping me company when I'm not. "You haven't even tried to flirt with me for your troubles."

"Haven't I?" His eyes flicker to mine, haloed by lashes tipped with gold. Is he remembering the greenhouse? Or our conversation in his office? Or how we flirted during the workplace romance trope test, mere feet from where we are now? The implication that none of it was fake for him leaves me breathless.

When I don't answer, he returns to tending to my hand. "How'd you get so good at that?" I ask, trying not to stare at the peek of his tongue at the corner of his mouth as he dabs ointment into my cuts. "You chickened out of biology because the labs involved dissection."

He grimaces, brow creasing. "Not wanting to slice flesh is different than bandaging a wound."

"Ew, don't say 'slice flesh' when you're dealing with my cuts." I pull back my hand involuntarily, and he lets go, shifting back on his heels. There's a small tear in the knee of his jeans that wasn't there earlier, evidence of how different his days are to mine—dealing with weather and physical exertion and people, so many people.

"I don't know how you do it," I say, voicing my thoughts. My job isn't easy, but it suits me, the solitary nature of it, working on my own schedule.

He rips open a packet of gauze, forearms flexing, and, geez, the man has had arms since we met. What's gotten into me?

"I've had my share of blisters," he says, mistaking my comment to be about the bandaging. He holds up his palm as evidence, but all I see is healthy skin, calloused near the base of his fingers. "Dad taught me and Scott how to care for them. They'll need air to heal, but for tonight, you should protect them."

He unspools gauze as he says this, placing a pad against my

skin, and I let out a hiss. He glances up, treating me to a flash of his blue eyes, gone aquamarine with the light streaming in through the bay window. "Sorry." He bends and presses a featherlight kiss to the inside of my wrist.

So quick, so natural, that it takes me a moment to register what just happened. Gavin's lips touched my skin. He. *Kissed*. Me. On my wrist, nowhere scandalous, but there's a reason my collection of historical romances is dog-eared, the pages falling open to the best spots. There's something about a chaste kiss that's anything but.

His head snaps up like he's realized his mistake. "Damn, Mia. I shouldn't have . . ." In one telltale instant, his eyes drop to my lips. "I'm sorry."

"Don't be." I lean over and kiss him.

His mouth is soft under mine, yielding, and his fingers tighten on my wrist, drawing me closer, obliterating any doubt I had about whether he wanted this. His lips part, treating me to a delicious swipe of his tongue. Maybe kissing him after years of keeping our distance should be strange or outrageous but all I feel is good. So good that I'm mad at us for not trying this sooner. For being so worried about what we'd lose that we never realized what we were missing out on.

But all coherent thoughts are wiped from my brain when he deepens the kiss, lips sliding against mine. With him on his knees, me on one elbow, we're on the same level, both surrendering to a desire we've decided to stop denying. I never dared dream of this, yet the need for his touch is all-consuming.

Why did we ever spend a single moment not doing exactly this? Gavin must be having similar thoughts, because his other hand finds its way to my shoulder, my waist, my hip, tracing my body in a way that feels like an awakening.

Maybe it should feel out of place to be kissing him, but it feels like we're right where we're supposed to be. We're not testing the limits because who we are to each other has expanded.

This kiss doesn't cross any lines, because the lines we'd drawn in the past don't apply. They were for someone else, an old version of Mia and Gavin, not the people we've become, the relationship we've developed over the years.

Right now, I'm not worried over the end of our story, I'm just enjoying the pure bliss of his mouth on mine, a gentle pressure that slips into something hungrier, his breath catching when my hand skims his arm, fingers tightening of their own accord, and I let out a yelp as my raw skin connects with his shirt.

He pulls away, eyes wide. Then he glances down at my open palm and worry knits his brow. "Are you all right?"

I nod, trying not to wince. He must notice, because he sits back on his heels, running a hand through his hair. "I should head out so you can rest."

Resting is out of the question, but I nod, feeling suddenly shy, though my brain hasn't caught up to the enormity of the moment. He rises to his feet, stuffing the scraps of trash in the bag. "Can I get you food or anything?" he asks, bringing over my tumbler.

I shake my head, embarrassed by how much I've already let him take care of me.

"All right," he says, seeming to be at a loss. "Call if you need anything."

"Should I tell them I won't be volunteering tomorrow?" I signed up to volunteer two days in a row, but with my hands like this, I can't imagine making it through a second day.

He shakes his head, not meeting my eyes. "I'll do it. Take it easy."

And with that, he lets himself out, locking the door with the spare key I gave him. No mention of the kiss we shared, and I'm sure all he wants to do is forget it ever happened. Too bad that will be impossible.

eighteen

Gavin

Leaving Mia after our kiss was pure self-preservation. I couldn't bear hearing that it was a mistake. I was afraid she'd play it off as nothing or ask me to pretend it never happened and I can't. Not yet, at least.

So I didn't stay long enough to hear her regrets, and all I can hope is I haven't ruined things. The threat of losing her was the entire reason I never asked her out back in college, bottling up my feelings until I thought they'd ceased to exist. But the trope tests loosened the lid and our kiss knocked the jar open and out came every pent-up desire.

I turned off my phone, scared of getting a text making it clear our friendship was over, even though in a way, I want it to be over, traded in for whatever comes next. But if it's the choice of going back to what we had or losing her, I choose friendship any day. What scares me is knowing I might have cost myself that choice.

Desperate to find an outlet for my jumbled feelings, I set to work on the pergola. By the time I installed the last of the rafters it was well past dusk, but my body was still humming from kissing Mia and sleep still didn't come easy.

With my phone off, I overslept the next morning and had to rush out to the site, glad for a busy day of volunteering to keep my mind off the way I obliterated any doubts Mia might have about my feelings. But she kissed me, too. Passionately, like she wanted nothing more. Has she changed her mind about us? Or was this just the consequence she warned me about—fake dating getting in her head and creating emotions that aren't real?

She might not ever want to see me again, upset we ended up where we swore we wouldn't . . . lost in each other. But when I hustle up to the crew, Mia is there, handing out doughnuts, laughing with Riley. Seeing her here where I least expected, sparkly and radiant, my heart twists.

Walking over, I shove my hands in my pockets to keep from wrapping my arms around her waist, not knowing how to play this, but certain we haven't made the jump to PDA, whatever her thoughts are on last night's events. "Didn't think I'd see you here today."

She looks up at me with a shy smile that sends my stomach flip-flopping. Our eyes meet, hers a rich oak brown in the sunlight, and something tender takes root in my chest. It's the look she gives me when we're sharing a secret, and my heart starts beating again for the first time since I left her place.

"Figured since I couldn't make it out for day two, I could at least bring breakfast," she says. Her bandages are gone, and she's holding the box of doughnuts gingerly, but I resist the urge to check her palms. "Probably more useful than me working anyway."

"Please, you were a natural," Riley says. She swipes the apple fritter I had my eye on and takes a big bite. "And you even made it here before Gavin. Late night?" she asks me, brows raised.

I can only imagine what I look like, wrecked after a night of no sleep and hoarding thoughts of Mia's lips on mine, knowing I might never get the chance to kiss her again.

"Speaking of late, where's Morris?" I say, to change the topic. His name was on the volunteer sign-up for both days, but he's nowhere to be seen, which is surprising given I'm pretty sure he could smell fresh doughnuts from a mile away.

Riley finishes chewing and says, "At the other lot. They were doing a shed teardown and asked for his help."

"Yeah, that's where he found the kittens," Mia says.

"The what?"

"Kittens," she repeats. "Did your phone die or something? He found a mother cat and her kittens at the other lot. You should see the pics. Adorable." Mia is clearly thrilled about this, but my brain has snagged on a detail, and it's not kittens.

"Morris texted you?" I drag my phone from my pocket, powering it on.

"He said he couldn't get ahold of you."

"He has your number?" I'm not jealous, I'm just . . . intrigued.

She frowns. "We all exchanged numbers yesterday. I told him and Riley I wanted to take them out for drinks for putting up with me."

"Putting up with you . . ." I pinch my forehead. "You did more than your share of work yesterday."

"Like I keep telling her," Riley interjects.

"Yeah, yeah," Mia says, like she doesn't believe us but is willing to play along. "But kittens. Focus, Gavin." She reaches down to unzip the belt bag slung over her chest, pinching the tab between thumb and forefinger. She bites her lip to hold off a wince, and without thinking, I step closer.

"Let me." But in my eagerness to spare her discomfort, I didn't factor in the placement of the bag. Right in the middle of her chest, which is currently only covered by a thin tank top. Well, and her bra, of course. Though . . . is she wearing a bra?

Whether or not Mia is wearing a bra isn't something I ever let myself dwell on, and picturing the possibilities now . . . The timing is inconvenient, to say the least. I yank my hand back. "Sorry. I was just . . . Sorry."

I can feel Riley smirking, but don't dare give her the satisfaction of looking her way.

Meanwhile, Mia has gotten her phone out and shifts closer to show me the screen. On it is a scrawny calico cat with three fluffy kittens nestled alongside her on what looks like a ripped couch cushion with stuffing bursting out of it.

"Morris wanted me to show you. Apparently he thinks I can do a better job than he could of convincing you to keep them."

"He wants *me* to take them?"

"Well, my place doesn't allow pets. And Morris says when he was six he killed a goldfish. Accidentally," she hurries to add. "He overfed it. But he's worried he doesn't have what it takes to adopt kittens. I told him maybe that's something he needs to explore with a therapist, because it's been over twenty years—"

"These were all texts?" I shouldn't be gritting my teeth, but geez, how much have they been talking? It's barely 9:00 a.m.

"I called him on the way over." She tilts her head, eyes narrowed. "Oh my gosh, are you jealous?"

"Of Morris?" My voice lifts an octave, and she breaks out in an incredulous smile.

"You think he's angling for best friend position?"

Morris is most definitely not angling for a friend position, best or otherwise, but the fact that Mia's thoughts have turned in that direction is both reassuring and unsettling. Reassuring that she isn't interested in dating Morris, but also, we kissed last night. That's more than friends to me, but maybe Mia's thinking of a friends-with-benefits situation. Or a forget-it-ever-happened sort of plan.

My heart sinks. Maybe I should've stuck around last night, after all, and talked through things. Can't very well have a conversation now with Riley right here. I do my best to laugh it off. "I know for a fact he would never put on a sheet mask for movie night, so I'm not worried."

Mia's smile dips, her expression guarded. "About last night—"

My phone rings, and I check it and find *Morris the Great* displayed on the screen, along with a winking selfie, complete with duck lips. That's what I get for leaving my phone in the truck while we're working. I slam my thumb onto the accept call button. "I am not adopting a family of cats."

I walk up my driveway two hours later with a box full of cats. After a harrowing trip to the vet, where my eyes glazed over from the amount of information thrown at me and the size of the bill, which Mia insisted on splitting, I'm on autopilot. She came back to help me get them settled, claiming she feels partially responsible since she bullied me into adopting them. When she notices I'm headed toward the side of the house, she steps in front of the gate.

"Where are you going?" The suspicious tilt of her head makes me think she's not planning to lend a hand unlatching it.

"To the shed."

"The potting shed?"

I raise my brows and shoulders, like, *obviously.*

She crosses her arms. "No."

"They were found in a shed," I remind her. "It'll feel like home."

"It's not climate-controlled."

"They're animals. They don't need air-conditioning."

"*Domesticated* animals," she says. "Humans took away their ability to survive when we invited them into our homes."

There's a lot to unpack there. "Um—"

"Shut up, you know what I mean. They're teeny widdle babies." She shifts into a cutesy tone, making kissy lips and bending over the box. The mama cat hisses and swipes bared claws at Mia's nose.

Biting back a smile, I say, "Domesticated, huh?"

"She's defending her young." I'm not at all surprised she's sticking up for the cat, though she does take a few steps back. I lower the box a smidge, in case the mama decides I'm a threat, too. But her movement disturbed the kittens into a bout of mewling, and she sets to licking their fur to calm them. "And it's not about her manners," Mia says. "It's about keeping everyone safe."

It's adorable how she uses the term *everyone* as if the fate of a litter of kittens affects global welfare. "What about predators?" she asks.

That touches a nerve. "No coyote is getting in my shed." I rebuilt it myself last summer.

"Raccoons can open doors."

Do raccoons eat kittens? I'd better add that to my list of questions to google later. "Pretty sure you're thinking of the velociraptors from *Jurassic Park*." I can't help but goad her, even though I'm starting to agree with her. I glance down into the box at the tiny furballs clustered around their mom. Ferocious as she is, all of them seem pretty vulnerable at the moment.

Ignoring my joke about the raptors, Mia says, "It's supposed to storm, and they could get spooked. What if she abandons them? You want to hand-feed three kittens around the clock?"

I was nearly convinced by the temperature argument, but this is enough to put to rest any hopes I had of keeping my house cat hair–free. We all make our way to the porch, and Mia swings the door open in a proprietary way that makes my heart do a happy swoop, and announces in a singsong voice, "Welcome home, babies!"

We spend the next five minutes arguing about where to put them. Mia wants them in my room, but I don't like the idea of being watched while I sleep. The main living area seems too wide-open for them to adapt to all at once. We settle on the laundry room, which is actually the coziest room in the house.

I remodeled it first, using it to teach myself drywall installation. Mia helped me pick out curtains, which will be useful to dim the room if the kittens need rest.

"Plus," she says, cooing over the kittens from a safe distance, "running the washer and the dryer will acclimate them to the sounds of the house. Sera was telling me it's good for babies to get used to a little noise."

My head is spinning. Somehow it feels like we skipped over dating and went straight to playing house. No offense to the cat family but I regret running away last night, and all I want is time alone with Mia. "Pretty sure cats are different than humans."

"Both are mammals."

"Okay, but . . ." I trail off, not sure of how to argue with that. "I feel like I'm in way over my head." My parents vetoed pets because they said running a business was hard enough without adding animals to the mix. Other than the semiferal barn cats that had free rein of the property, I have zero experience with pets. "I don't know how to raise one cat, let alone a whole litter."

"We're not going to raise them, that's the mama cat's job," she says. "We're just babysitting." The *we* part of that sentence cheers me up a little, but I'm still not loving the thought of taking care of pets on top of everything else going on.

"Okay, but for how long?" I drop my voice to a whisper out of respect for the kittens, who've fallen asleep curled next to their mother. "How soon can we put them up for adoption?" I'm pretty sure that's one of the answers the vet covered, but I was so overwhelmed by all the information, I can't remember.

But Mia took notes, and the way she sticks her tongue in her cheek, avoiding my eyes, is answer enough. "About a month."

A whole month of caring for four unexpected pets while navigating the trope tests, if we're even doing those, and figuring out what to do about my dad's retirement. Overwhelmed, I sink down to the floor, my back against the washer. Mia joins me, groaning with the effort, and I wince in secondhand pain, knowing full well how sore her muscles must be. She leans on my shoulder for support, and the press of her fingertips reminds me of everything that happened between us last night.

By the time she's settled against the dryer next to me, I'm buzzing with the need to pull her close, in a way I never would've allowed myself to dream of until this summer. But with an entire cat family a few feet away acting as witnesses, thoughts are about all I can hope for.

Cold air blasts from a floor vent, and I make a mental note to get a few blankets for the kittens. Do they need a bed? A litter box is top of the list. My head begins to swim from preemptive exhaustion, and I let my eyes fall closed. Mia nudges me.

"Hey, I can help. It shouldn't be too hard."

I open my eyes enough to see her concerned face, surrounded by springy curls. "No way. You need to be writing."

"What if I stayed here?"

I make a solid effort not to read into that. "Stayed over?"

"Just to help keep an eye on them while you're at work. It might even be good for me to write in new surroundings. Getting out of my office where I was blocked for so long might be just what I need."

"During the day, you mean."

"Of course. I'd never . . ." She looks down at her hands in her lap. "That would be presumptuous. And you'll be here to watch them at night. No reason for me to stay over."

No need, but I wouldn't say no reason. "I think we should talk about last night."

Her brown eyes meet mine, not startled, but wary. "It's okay. I get it."

"Get what?"

"It was a mistake." She looks down at her hands, clasped in her lap. "We were exhausted, and you'd bandaged me. It's a classic caretaking scene. Nothing more."

"Are you trying to say we kissed because I put a Band-Aid on your blisters?"

"Well, it was more of a—" she makes a vague wrapping gesture "—bandage. Very gallant. Romance-novel worthy."

I'm even more confused now. "And you think I kissed you because that moment was . . ." I search for the right word, but they all feel wrong. "Sexy, or something? You were hurt." Nothing sexy about seeing her in pain.

"Not sexy. Intimate. The kiss was just a result of that unexpected intimacy." She enunciates each word, as if she's been rehearsing.

My stomach lurches. "Do you regret it?"

"Don't you?" She's not looking at me, and I realize I've played this all wrong.

"Not at all."

Her eyes fly to mine. "You left. I figured that meant it was a mistake."

"No. Oh, Mia." I shift toward her, wanting to reach out, but not sure yet. "I was just scared. We promised never to do anything like that, and I thought I might've ruined everything."

"You didn't." She looks over at me with those deep brown eyes. "But I don't know where to go from here. All I know is I want to do it again."

Her confession unlocks everything holding me back and I lean over and kiss her, unable to resist another moment. The touch of her lips sends tingles up my spine. This is what I've been searching for. I don't have a name for it, but I've found it here, with her. A loud yowl cuts through the pulse thundering in my ears and we break apart.

Mama Cat is glaring at us, tail twitching with animosity.

"She's probably starving," Mia says.

"Or feral."

She laughs, which earns her a glare from Mama Cat. We've yet to name the kittens, but I have a feeling the mom's nickname will stick. Letting go of my hand, Mia eases herself up off the floor.

I'm distracted by the way the fabric of her shorts clings to her legs as she stands but then it dawns on me that she's standing so slowly because she's sore, and I scramble up to offer a hand. "Where are we going?"

"To get supplies." She grins mischievously. "Looks like we're pet parents."

By the time we buy supplies and swing by Mia's house for her laptop, it's lunchtime, and I promised the crew I'd be back on-site in the afternoon. We check in on the cats and set up their room, then I make us sandwiches while she spreads out her stuff at the kitchen island. My phone lights up with a text and I dart a nervous glance her way when I see who it is, but she's busy setting her stuff up.

Joe: Sera told me her cousin is single and coming to the baby shower. Interested?

Gavin: Baby showers aren't for hookups.

Joe: You don't do hookups. I'm just talking about a conversation. Sera could give her your number.

Gavin: You're doing this on purpose.

Joe: Obviously. Have you talked to Mia yet?

"Who are you texting?" Mia asks, and I slam my finger on the screen shutoff button.

"Just Joe." I wish I could tell him what's really going on, and that I don't need the nudge. But what *is* going on?

"What did you tell him after he called during our date?" Mia's flipping through a book on cat care that she insisted on picking up, showing every indication of being distracted, but I know better. "I thought he might sense something fishy, but Sera never brought it up."

Probably because Joe didn't want to tell his wife he suspects his best friend of being in love with her best friend. "He didn't guess it was you."

But he wanted me to ask you out, I don't add. Too early to talk about what we'll tell our friends, even though I'm ready to be honest with her and them and everyone about how I feel about her.

She seems to accept this, or maybe is too preoccupied to push the issue, and opens her laptop. I finish making lunch and set a plate next to her, but she's typing, fully absorbed in her work, and doesn't notice. I can't help pausing to admire her. Her posture is relaxed, but her brow is furrowed, lips moving, like she's thinking aloud, under her breath.

"You're low-key a genius." The thought makes its way into words. "You know that, right?"

She looks up and blinks at me from behind her glasses. "For suggesting we stop at a bookstore before the pet shop?"

I shake my head. "No, that was a waste of time," I say, just to get a rise out of her, and she scowls adorably. She wanted to get pet care books, but I lobbied for looking things up on the internet. The stack of books by her laptop shows who won that argument. I bought the latest in an espionage thriller series I love, so I guess we both got a win.

"But you create stories for a living. Actual books. More than one. More than ten. That's wild, Mia. Sometimes I forget for a minute how amazing you are. And then you're sitting here in my kitchen and I'm like, damn. What did I do to deserve this woman in my life?"

"You make things grow, for one thing." She smiles over at me. "Not that you have to do anything to earn my friendship," she says, and part of me latches on to that word and fantasizes about hurling it out the window, but she's still talking, and I refocus. "You plant living things and nurture them. You might think it's easy, or simple or whatever, but I know better. I've single-handedly been responsible for the demise of enough plants that they probably pass down myths about me to their grandchildren. I'm an urban legend to them, whereas you're like the plant god."

I can't help laughing. "I dunno. I've pruned enough branches to be a vengeful deity. And what about Frank? You've helped him grow."

"Frank's an anomaly. But I'm glad he's still around. Glad I met you that night." Her grin turns mischievous. "Even if it was the start of your descent into a life of crime."

"Rescuing your book was worth it."

"Just a manuscript."

"Back then. Now it's going to be a novel *and* a show."

"Maybe. Hollywood is never a sure thing, and I still have to finish the thing." She turns back to her laptop, and I take that as my cue to finish tending to the cats. Setting up a litter box and dealing with the disgusting slop of canned cat food wasn't in my plans, today or ever, but watching the mama cat take small, precise bites of food while her kittens are curled up in the fleecy bed is kind of worth it.

When I return to the kitchen, Mia doesn't look up. The sandwich is untouched, but I know she'll be grateful for it later. Not wanting to disturb her focus, I let myself out. For the first time since I moved in, I won't be coming home to an empty house, and the fact that it's Mia who I'll be coming home to makes it all the sweeter. It also makes my decision to stay or take over for my dad even more complicated.

nineteen

Mia

Blinking, I take off my glasses and rub my eyes. I check the time—no wonder I'm stiff, I've been writing for over three hours. It's hard to believe how much has happened in twenty-four hours. I woke up today unable to focus on the book, worried kissing Gavin had ruined everything. Now we're co-parenting kittens and I'm counting down the minutes until he comes home and kisses me again.

This morning, I had every intention of forgetting about the kiss. Gavin clearly wanted to. With the memory of him fleeing the scene replaying in my mind, all signs pointed to us making a huge mistake. If I hadn't been so physically exhausted, I never would've fallen asleep, but when I woke up to no texts checking in like he normally would, I honestly thought I'd lost him, and the only thing I could think to do was avoid him as long as possible.

That turned out to be all of half an hour because when I checked my phone after showering, I found three unread messages, but not from the person I was desperate to hear from. Morris texted asking me to convince Gavin to take the kittens, and who can say no to kittens? So I bought breakfast for the crew, bracing myself to play things off like kissing Gavin hadn't rocked my whole world. I kept it up all day, reminding myself how important it was to stick to friendship.

But none of my old excuses held weight against the reality of how good it felt to kiss him. It's like that was the one thing missing from our relationship, and finding out he was right there with me, not wanting to forget it but wanting to dive into this newfound twist, was the sweetest relief. But everything feels so tenuous and new. The foundations of our friendship are shaken, and I'm worried that without the excuse of the trope tests, all this will crumble.

I don't want to lose the magic we've just found. If I'm honest, I used looking after the kittens as an excuse not to go back to normal right away, to stay here in this place for a little longer where Gavin and I aren't just friends. I should go check on them, but before I do, I take my phone off Do Not Disturb and see a string of texts from Evie. She must've read the chapters I sent her.

Evie: Omg, this is so good.

Evie: Sydney and Victor, who would've thought? Aside from the legion of fans clamoring for this book. Honestly, I wasn't seeing it. But that scene in his friend's closed-up mechanic shop where she was pretending to be a stranded motorist? Pure fire. I'm officially team friends-to-lovers.

Evie: Send me more when you have it. Or now. Now is good.

I stand and stretch, my palms sore, but better than yesterday. I took a picture of my bandaged hands to send Kim last night for sympathy before realizing texting her might be a slippery slope to revealing I kissed the man I've told her for years will never be more than a friend, which I absolutely wasn't ready for. But the photo is still on my phone, and on impulse, I send it to Evie along with the caption: The things we do for our craft.

My phone immediately buzzes with a call from her. "Writing is not a contact sport," she says when I answer. "What really happened?"

"I volunteered for a community lot cleanup day and let's just say my soft hands were not prepared."

"Another procrastination attempt?" We've both gone to great lengths to avoid tricky projects, including, in her case, drafting an entire novella instead of the book she was meant to finish.

"No, uh . . ." What will I tell her? The truth, I decide. I can't bear to open up to Kim about what happened. She'll be way too dramatic. But I need to debrief with someone before Gavin gets back. "You know how I was brainstorming with you about the method-acting scenes?"

"Yes," she says warily.

"That wasn't for the book, exactly." I lay it all out, from the low-stakes office romance attempt to the way I kissed my best friend of nearly a decade and adopted cats with him the next day.

"Let me get this straight," Evie says when I'm finished. "Despite his own fears, this man saved you from an escape-room blackout, nearly compromised you in a greenhouse, tended your injuries, ravished you on a fainting couch, and rescued kittens for you? I'd be moving in with him, too."

I laugh at her assessment. "It's just temporary, during the day, until we know it's okay to leave the kittens."

"Stop. You're in it now. May as well send me a save the date."

"We're just friends." The old line comes out by habit.

"Friends with benefits."

I don't like the sound of that. I've never done casual relationships, and this is Gavin. Our friendship is already deeper than any romantic relationship I've had. All the reasons why we've never crossed this line come rushing back with a vengeance and

I swivel around to slide off the stool. "I'm worried things will never be the same."

"They won't be," she says, and my stomach clenches. "Relationships change for a lot of reasons, and that's not always a bad thing. But you two do need to talk and at least you have practice, being friends and all."

We do. We've worked through our share of miscommunications and disagreements. We've shared advice and offered support. But we've never discussed how to move forward after making out.

"Mia, you there?"

"I'm here." I peek inside the laundry room and see the kittens have been exploring. The gray one, Ash, is batting at the sleeve of Gavin's hoodie that's draped over the edge of a laundry basket. "Just checking on the cats."

"Avoiding the topic at hand."

"Which is supposed to be my manuscript."

She blows out her breath. "From what you sent, you're on the right track. But you've been running yourself into the ground for this book. Remember that you're more than your career. How you spend your time is worth it for its own sake, not just as fodder for your creative well. Enjoy yourself and stop worrying over how everything will work out in the end."

"Says the woman who just turned in a manuscript."

"No better feeling," she says, and laughs. "But I mean it. You deserve to have a little fun. Hell, a lot of fun. But be careful with those hands."

"It looks worse than it is. Typing is no big deal. Getting dressed on the other hand . . ."

"And that's why you have a sexy new roommate," she says. "Okay, bye!"

The call ends before I can reply, and I'm left shaking my head. Evie is the kind of person most people picture when they think of a romance author. Witty, poised, quick with a comeback. The truth is she's no more brazen in her love life than I am, but she talks a good game. Right now I could use some of that artificial confidence because I'm guessing Gavin will be home soon, and I'm not sure how to act when he walks in.

Should I order dinner for us? He might be bringing food. Filled with nerves, even though this is Gavin we're talking about, and we've spent countless evenings together, I lift my phone to ask him and see that Sera's texted a bunch of question marks, and below that, a link to a celebrity news site. Dread in my stomach, I click on it.

Booked in Love actor Robert Cho set to star in upcoming Roan Watkins film. What does this mean for the future of everyone's favorite BFFs? We foresee a bad breakup, and they haven't even gone on a single date.

I stop reading, sick to my stomach. Another text comes through.

Sera: Did you know about this? Please tell me they aren't canceling your contract.

Mia: Yes, I knew. No, nothing is changing as long as I turn the book in on time. If not, the studio gets carte blanche on how Victor and Sydney's story ends.

Sera: No offense, but I don't trust them. I want a Mia Brady love story or nothing at all. How's the book coming?

Mia: Much better, but a long way to go.

Sera: I'm going to tell my mom to take you off the text chain for our baby shower. I don't want you to have any distractions.

Mia: Don't be silly. They aren't letting me do anything anyway, and it's entertaining.

Sera: Says you. Meanwhile I'm over here trying to convince them that if anyone tries to play that game where they measure my belly with string, I'm disowning them.

I bite back a laugh at the thought. I have no doubt Sera would do it, too.

Mia: Don't worry. If I see anyone try to smuggle string into the party, I'll have Gavin play bouncer and kick them out. He's surprisingly strong.

I added that last part because I'd been thinking about how he'd carried me up two flights of stairs after a long day's work like it was nothing, but now Sera might ask a follow-up. Knee bouncing nervously, I wait for a text with a pair of eyes to come through. Or a snide, *Oh, and how would you know?* But no new texts appear. I should feel relieved, but nerves well up, along with a heaping dose of reality.

How long can we walk this tightrope? Sooner or later our friends will suspect. Joe might already. And if things go wrong, what then? We'd have to arrange separate times to hang out with them. Or would Sera and Joe choose sides? The combination of work stress and personal stress sends me diving back into my manuscript, dinner uncertainty forgotten, ready to find reprieve in the fictional world where things follow a comfortingly familiar structure, and third-act breakups never last.

twenty

Gavin

Things run late at the Fifth Street project, and then I have to stop in at work and take care of a few tasks our summer employees aren't trained on. Mia hasn't answered my texts about what she wanted for dinner, so I figure she's caught up in her writing. I tell myself all is well between us, even though we haven't really talked through things. By the time I make it back to the house, it's late evening.

Not sure what sort of food she'd be craving, I bring home burritos and a giant salad for us to share. But when I walk through the door, the house is dark and quiet. I lean back out and yep, her car is parked on the street. Still here, then.

I set the food on the counter and check the living room. Mia is perched on the arm of the couch, laptop on her knees, face lit by the screen's glow. For a moment I watch her, fingers flying over the keyboard like a honeybee in the garden, then stopping, hovering, a hummingbird in mid-flight. Her brows are furrowed, lip caught between her teeth. I don't know what I look like when I work, but Mia is poetry.

A quiet meow draws me away and I chuckle at a tawny paw swiping under the laundry room door. Cedar, we named him, on the way home from the pet store. Mia says picking names exhausts her and let me do it, then declared it perfection that I named them all after trees. I'm trying not to play favorites, but Cedar's playful personality already has a hold on me. I take care of the cats quietly, not wanting to disturb Mia. Soon we'll give them free roam of the house, but not before making sure everything is kitten-proofed.

Once they've been tended to, I head back to the kitchen, torn between leaving Mia in peace and offering dinner. If there's one thing I can be sure of, it's that she loves writing snacks. I once listened to a podcast where the interviewer asked her if she ever snacked while she wrote, and Mia laughed and listed about fifteen different foods. It was no surprise to me because I've been supplying her midnight snacks since junior year of college.

But the takeout I've brought home won't be easy to eat while she's typing, so I pop the salad in the fridge and raid the pantry and fridge to make a plate for her. Salty kettle-cooked potato chips, cheese curds we picked up at the farmers market—Mia had never tasted one till she visited Wisconsin with me, and now she's hooked—raspberries from the bushes I planted last year, then a few more when I can't resist popping some in my mouth. A homemade chocolate chip cookie from the tin Faye sent home with me earlier this week.

Figuring I have all the bases covered—salty, sweet, cheese—I take the plate to the living room, where Mia is sitting, her back propped up against the wall. My plan is to leave the food and go, counting on her absorption in her writing, but the scene must not have been working, because she looks up the moment I enter the room.

I hold up the plate as reason for interrupting her, suddenly unsure of myself despite this being my own home.

"Did you just get back?" Her gaze lands on the plate. "Sorry, I planned to text to see if you wanted me to order food, but . . ."

"It's okay. I'm glad you're in the zone."

"Did you cook for me?"

"I assembled some food." I glance down at the mishmash. "Does that count?"

"You're talking to the woman who once ate nothing but frozen dinners and raisins for a week while on deadline."

I make a face, coming to sit on the couch cushion next to her. "You never told me about the raisins."

"Some things are too shameful to share." She plucks a raspberry off the plate, the fruit dainty in her fingers. I allow my eyes to linger on her as she savors the tart berry.

"You're never embarrassing."

Her eyes sparkle with mischief. "Even when I'm eating handfuls of raisins at two a.m. in the glow of my laptop screen like a gremlin?"

I laugh at the image. "Okay, maybe then."

She digs her toes into my hip. "Meanie."

I press a kiss onto her knee, without thinking. Her skin is smooth and cool under my lips, and I raise my eyes to hers, half afraid I've overstepped, consumed with thoughts of where I want to kiss her next. Her eyes are wide, but she doesn't pull away. I do, but not far, my lips a whisper away from the rounded curve of her knee. My fingers skate up her calf, and her eyes drop, watching me touch her. The glow from her laptop shows her lips plump and parted, and I sink my teeth into my bottom lip.

So beautiful. I've always known Mia was gorgeous, but I never allowed myself to dwell on her allure, to let my gaze roam, drinking in her sexiness.

"Gavin," she says, and I stop. Let go, but when I meet her eyes, she's smiling. "Did you come in here to feed me or seduce me?"

"Is there a difference?"

She laughs. Setting her laptop aside, she scoots down to sit in the crevasse of the couch, all curled up, and brings the plate of food to her bent knees. She bites into a potato chip, then catches me looking. "What?" A small shower of crumbs falls from her lips, and I grin.

"Just thinking how lucky I am to come home to you." It's bliss to have her tucked against me in the twilight.

She stops chewing. Swallows. "It's not weird to have me here?"

"Does it seem weird?" I hope desperately that the answer is no.

She licks a crumb from her lips, watching me with her dark eyes. "It seems perfect."

Happiness pulses through me at her declaration. Honest and open, just like the friend I've come to love. The lover I didn't dare hope for. Channeling my willpower not to pull her into my arms, plate of food be damned, I ask, "Are you finished eating?"

She tugs the dish closer to her, protective. "Why?"

"Because I'd really like to kiss you again."

"Why didn't you lead with that?"

"Because food is always your top priority."

"Only because kissing you has never been an option." Before I can register the implications of her confession, she swipes her thumb at the corner of her mouth, catching a crumb and licking it off with a quick swipe of her tongue.

Rising, she sets the plate on the side table and moves over me, one knee on either side of my thighs, caging me in. The corners of her mouth lift in a coy smile. "Kissing you *is* an option, right?"

She's teasing me now, hovering over my lap, hands on my shoulders, her face inches from mine. We've joked around for years, but this kind of teasing is new.

"Kissing is one option, yeah." My voice is a rasp.

Her lips lift, curving in the moonlight. She's enjoying this as much as I am, the years of banter slipping to something deeper, edgier. Then she kisses me, and the tether holding back my emotions snaps with sweet relief. It's only been mere hours since we kissed, but already I'm starved for her. Mouths parted, both greedy, we give ourselves up to each other, to this very new and welcome twist in our relationship.

Kissing Mia is all the joy of spending time with her, heightened. Pleasure magnified. It's dizzying, the way her tongue swoops against mine.

"Gavin," she breathes. "You've been holding out on me."

Holding out *for* her, more like. All my past relationships pale in comparison to this. But I don't voice the thought. Don't want to give too much away, even though I can't deny I'd give her everything, if only she asked. Instead, I press kisses to her lips, her neck, the soft notch of skin at her throat. Friendship is the last thing on my mind.

twenty-one

Mia

I slide my laptop off the end table a few hours later. Sitting back on my heels, I cast a glance toward Gavin, dozing on the couch. Will the clack of the keys wake him? He's a light sleeper. I discovered that one night at the cabin when the writing bug hit and he came out of his room for water, roused by the sound of me typing at the tiny kitchen table.

I don't want to disturb him, but inspiration is knocking, spurred on by worries over the article Sera sent. The hooting of an owl pulls my attention to the sliding door to the backyard. My eyes are adjusted enough to see the gray-dark shape of the shed. Carefully tugging the blanket off the edge of the couch, I wrap it around my shoulders and ease out the back door. The grass is cool and damp under my bare feet, but the air is warm with a gentle breeze, like the night is breathing deep in slumber.

Notebook and pen clutched to my chest, I make my way across the lawn, ignoring the shadows. It's not just that I'm afraid of the dark, it's the unknown I don't like. Without light, it's impossible to see what lurks in corners or what's ahead. But

I'm spurred on by purpose, and once I step inside the shed, I reach for the lantern Gavin keeps on the shelf by the door.

Instead of hanging it from the hook on the ceiling, I carry it with me to the back wall, where bags of soil are stacked in a neat heap. Hoping he won't mind me disturbing the order of his sanctum, I set my stuff down and use both hands to pull a bag from atop the stack. My sore muscles protest and the bag hits the ground with a muffled *whomp*. I dart a glance back at the house, as if Gavin could've heard from across the yard. But the windows stay dark and I relax.

Snuggled in the blanket, I settle in. The faint scent of moss and crumbled leaves permeates the small space. It smells like Gavin. Earthy and welcoming. Our relationship has shifted into something beyond friendship, and maybe I should be more worried about the ramifications. But it's still night. This feels like stolen time. A liminal space.

The wonder of kissing him felt like joy unleashed, and I keep the feeling with me as I begin to write. I've reached the middle of the manuscript. Sydney and Victor are together, no more faking it. They've had "the talk" about their relationship and no longer need to hide behind the excuse of method acting. Things in their careers are going well, too. Confidence restored, he sends in samples for several high-profile books, and one of her clients just sold a book for seven figures at auction.

I want to let them linger here. Soon, I'll have to ramp up the tension en route to the big confrontation that will force them to fight for their happy-ever-after. I'll have to pull them apart enough to see how much they yearn to be together, despite the cost.

For now, I want them to enjoy their happiness, dawdle with breakfast in bed and tender kisses. But my characters have other ideas. Maybe because this is my thirteenth novel, and the arc of the story is part of me now. The characters rush out into the world before I can stop them. They're naive, and excited, ready to live their new reality as a couple, sure of their love. They started as friends, after all. They know how to coexist in the world, how to weather fights, and how to make each other happy.

So they go to an author event at Tiffany and Dylan's bookstore. The former rivals from book one are now co-owners of a thriving bookshop. Sydney and Victor show up for the book signing together like they often do. Except this time, they're holding hands. My fingers fly over the keyboard, but not fast enough to capture the image that plays out in my mind in real time.

What they don't know is Dylan planned to propose, and the bookshop is full of friends and family. The shock of seeing Victor and Sydney together throws a wrench in his careful plans and things go topsy-turvy. Tiffany leaves and he chases after her. Meanwhile, their friends and family have questions. So many questions, overlapping, tumbling over each other, a stream of well-meaning worry and advice that forces the new couple apart, to opposite ends of the room.

It's an interrogation, their loved ones poking and prodding for the roots of the relationship, for the reason for the change, and all of their questions are too much, too heavy, too soon. That's what Victor asks when they're finally alone again. *Is this too soon?* And at the same time, Sydney wonders if it's far too late. If they were meant to be, wouldn't they have been? Wouldn't this move into something deeper have happened years ago?

The tap of keys is loud in the nighttime stillness, my own worries bleeding into the story. It's inevitable for some of the author to escape onto the page. I see myself reflected a little in every narrative, but none of the stories are my life. They're a composite of my dreams and wonderings and musings. They aren't my essence. They're made-up. They're entertainment. Fiction.

But I started this book before I learned to draw a line between myself and my characters, when I poured my whole self out on the page without keeping anything back. That's why this manuscript, the first of my stories, never worked.

I thought I could disentangle the pieces of the story from myself. I thought I was good enough to reopen the pages and remove all my fears and insecurities, replacing them with ones true to my characters, but I can't. Or I haven't yet, at least.

This isn't what I had planned for their conflict, but the easy way they fell into a relationship left them overconfident, and now all I see for them is a fumbling breakup. Drifting apart. They've crossed the threshold into something more than friends and there's no going back, but I can't see a way forward. Frustrated, I close my laptop and gingerly pick up the lantern with fingertips, blistered palm stinging with the effort of typing.

No longer brave enough to cross the darkened yard without light, I bring it with me, fumbling with the door, my demons at my back. No matter how far I've come, I still can't conquer this first attempt. My worries have resurfaced in the dark, and not just for the manuscript. Everything is wonderful here, in our bubble. But our relationship could have ripple effects on our friendships. In our families. And Gavin might be moving. A long-distance friendship is hard enough.

I rush inside, no longer worried about waking him. All of a sudden, I want him here with me to chase away the doubts.

But he's not on the couch any longer. I shut off the lantern, comforted by the homey nighttime sounds: the soft rustling of the cat family and the hum of the refrigerator. Light warms the hallway, and I round the corner to find the laundry room door ajar, Gavin bare chested, seated cross-legged on the ground, mewling kittens crawling over his jean-clad lap.

He picks up the tuxedo kitten, Juniper, holding him up to his chin, and looks up at me with no trace of the worry curled around my insides like a stubborn case of food poisoning. "Writing?"

I nod, and he settles back against the wall, kitten to his chest. It's irresistible, and I join him, the worn denim of his jeans soft and reassuring against my bare knee. "I didn't mean to wake you."

"I wasn't sleeping," he says, surprising me. "Too busy being grateful. I knew you needed space to write."

I lean over and lift the gray kitten he named Ash. Her springy ribs expand under my fingers, purring starting up like a motor. "Sometimes when I get in a good flow, I wake up with ideas and want to write them down right away."

The mama cat is watching us with half-lidded eyes, feigning boredom, though I can't help but feel like she's fully invested in our conversation, making sure she's entrusted her babies to people with their shit together. Last year, I would've said yes. I felt capable, in control. But I've careened into my thirties off-balance and unprepared. Trying to live up to the weight of other people's expectations.

"So you're not freaking out?"

I huff out a rueful chuckle. "Oh no, I am absolutely freaking out." Though with him next to me and the purring kitten in my lap, the panic I'd succumbed to outside is nowhere in sight.

He tugs me against him, wrapping one arm around my shoulders. "Me, too."

"Well, that's helpful."

His chest shakes in a quiet laugh. "We're friends for a reason, Mia." I stiffen at the implication that's all we are to each other, but he squeezes my arm. "Because we think alike. I think that's not the same with all couples. They care about each other, they're passionate about the same things, have similar goals or visions for the future, but their personalities are opposites. But we have similar tastes, and we worry about the same things."

"Like whether we've totally ruined things?"

"We couldn't," he says with certainty. "What's between us is stronger than that." His tone leaves no room for dissent, and I don't want to argue, because I believe him.

What I don't know is where to go from here. Work to re-turn to what we had? Or push past it into a different kind of relationship, one that might not last? My questions tumble out. "What if it's too late? If we were destined for anything more than friendship, wouldn't this have happened years ago?"

"When? The day we met you'd just suffered a breakup," he says. "My dad was constantly calling me, giving me the worst advice about love." *Never marry your best friend*, his dad used to say, fresh off of losing his mom. "We weren't in the right place."

I stroke between the kitten's soft ears. "Are we now?" He might be moving. My next book is in shambles.

"Do you want to stay just friends? Because we can do that. Forget this ever happened. If you can do that, if you want to, I will." Juniper meows, and he sets him gently in the cat bed.

"I'm not sure I can," I admit. "I never wanted to kiss you, because I worried once we crossed this line, we could never go back. But now I can't imagine not wanting this."

"Wanting what?" he asks, and I know he wants to define this shift in the relationship. "If all you're looking for is friends with benefits, I don't think I could. Not with anyone, but especially not with you."

I don't want that, either, but putting a name on it, breaking that last barrier between who we've been to each other and something more, will signal the end of our friendship.

"What if it's just . . . us?" I gather my courage and twist around to meet his gaze, and Ash scrambles from my lap. We're on the precipice of more, or less, or nothing at all. And that last possibility is the one that has me holding back. "What if we don't put a label on it yet? We could just do this, be this, for each other."

"Friends?"

"More," I promise. "I don't want to deny this is different. But we can take it slow, right?"

"Slow, and exclusive?"

"Of course. Geez, Gavin, this is me you're talking about. I've had, like, three long-term boyfriends." And I'm worried if I call him one, then when he decides he's ready for someone more fun, more flirty, more romantic, we can't go back to friends. I need that escape hatch.

I need ambiguity, the ability to chalk this up to a sensitive time for both of us. A mistake, but not a friendship-ending one. "I just don't want to move too fast," I say. "Or make it into, like, a big deal."

"You've always been a big deal to me." He pulls me close again, which gives me the most absurd butterflies. "I get that this is new and totally not how our relationship has been like, but you're right. We're still us. We trust each other. If it takes some time to trust this, I get that."

"And by 'this' you mean . . ." I trail off, tentative again, wanting him to fill in the blanks. To say aloud what I'm scared to. I know it's cowardly, to not say it first. To be afraid to name the big feelings, the huge, overwhelming desire to claim him. I'm a hypocrite, but the idea of saying it aloud, of being rejected, again, is too much to overcome.

"More than friends," he says, and leans in to kiss me.

For now, that's more than enough.

twenty-two

Gavin

This breakfast with Mia is going to be nothing like other meals we've shared together. Even the mornings we've spent at the cabin, we were joined by friends, or my sister-in-law and nephews, my brother and I trying to one-up each other with dad jokes and Mia proclaiming such a feat was impossible.

There was never just us, not at the coffee shop where we have our orders memorized and eat at tables surrounded by people on their computers, or at our usual brunch spot, Mia bleary-eyed at the early wake-up, the bustle of the weekend rush filling the air.

We've never woken up together, her lips looking impossibly plush, face pressed to my pillow. I've never seen her from this angle—the dip of her neck where it meets her shoulder, tender and exposed, the curve of her cheek as she turns to look at me.

I couldn't resist kissing her again, lingering in bed until the sun rose high enough to reach the photo of us at Scott's wedding on my dresser, a beam of light slanting across our smiling faces. My last girlfriend told me it was weird to have a picture of Mia in here, facing my bed. She made it sound illicit, but the truth is, Mia is with me wherever I go. She's been in my heart since that night we met in a dingy hallway, her heartbroken and me already halfway in love.

The photo stayed; that girlfriend is long gone. And maybe that should've been a sign that what I've felt for Mia is stronger than what I've felt for anyone else. Except, last night I tried to tell her, and she rebuffed me, like one of the kittens batting at a string, claws sheathed, no malice, but her insistence we not define the shift in our relationship stung. Her kisses soothed it away, as she led me back to the bedroom, but now, even though she's here, even though she wants this, part of me can't help but wonder if she wants all of me, like I've wanted her, since forever.

Finally, my noisy grumbling stomach has her climbing out of bed, laughing at the sheet tangled around her legs. She ignores my promises that food can wait and tugs me down the hallway, leaning into the laundry room to check on the kittens, balls of fur nestled in next to their mom, who understandably looks like she could sleep for a week.

Today is my day off and technically I can sleep in, too. Yet another perk of being an employee for a small establishment like Hill and Dale is the ability to set my own hours, something I'd never be able to do as owner of the tree nursery. Up until recently, Dad hadn't taken a full day off in my life, and that could never be me. I decided early on I wanted to work to live, not the inverse.

Mia is like my dad. Dedicated. Passionate about what she does. But also, like my dad, I worry she's headed toward burnout, or maybe she's already there. It's half of why I agreed to the trope scheme. Because it sounded like a way for Mia to let loose a little. Never thought it would end with her bare-legged in my kitchen, humming as she takes out a carton of orange juice.

I step up behind her, wrapping her in my arms, and press a kiss behind her ear.

"What are you doing?" she asks, leaning into me.

"Kissing you." And then I do just that, sliding my hand up

to pull her hair aside, pressing my lips to her neck, the juncture of her shoulder. She spins to face me, and I take the juice from her, set it . . . somewhere. I'm not concerned with anything much besides her. Her back is to the open refrigerator door, the cool air vapor around us.

My thumb cups her jaw and I slot my mouth against hers. Our kiss is sweet and slow, a discovery. Awareness spreads through me, of how good it is between us, how we fit, effortlessly, not just in friendship, but in this kiss.

Desire for her flares bright, a match sparking into flame when she moans, parting her mouth. I slide my hands under her thighs and lift her, kicking the fridge door closed as I turn and set her on the counter. She's smiling, perfect lips curved in invitation, and I decide just friends is never going to be good enough again.

"Please tell me you have something other than gruel." She's called oatmeal "gruel" ever since our college days, when she insisted on sitting at least a table away in the cafeteria anytime I served myself oatmeal from the breakfast bar. Which, since I was on a four-year-long mission to grow man-size muscles, was pretty often.

She still teases me for the amount of eggs and oats I consumed during my college years, second only to wings and cheap lager. I make a show of taking out both steel-cut and rolled oats but really I'm scanning the pantry for Mia-approved options because the last thing I want to do is venture out for breakfast. Normally I'd love to hit up one of our favorite spots, but normally I wouldn't have her all to myself, sitting at my dining table looking like a whole meal herself.

She clears her throat, and I realize I've turned from the pantry to stare at her. Instead of scolding me, she holds my gaze, pursing her lips to blow on her coffee.

"Geez, Mia . . . I thought you wanted to eat."

A smirk curves her lips, and I bite my lip, hard. She's shown me herself with the filter off, undiluted, and I want to drink her in.

I cross the room and bend to kiss her. She palms the back of my neck, arching upward. We're in tune, her touch perfectly calibrated to set me on fire. Her fingers are on my chest when the doorbell rings. We spring apart, the chair tipping, and I make a wild grab for the back of it and catch Mia mid-fall. An impatient knock sets off a chorus of meows from the laundry room, and Mia's laugh tickles my skin.

"This funny to you, Brady?"

Another knock sounds, and her eyes flicker up, wide, as if she's just realized what we're doing, and where. She ducks under my arm and sprints for my room. Grateful I installed blinds last month, I rush to the laundry room and grab a shirt at random from the hamper, ignoring the questioning blinks of the cat family, whose curiosity looks more accusatory than normal. I shut the door on Mama Cat's feline judgment, then open the front door and catch Morris in the act of ringing the bell a third time.

He gives me a slow once-over. "Catching you at a bad time?"

"What makes you say that?"

"You're wearing a polo with sweatpants."

I glance down and—shit. He's right. "Laundry day."

He laughs. "Okay, we'll go with that. Is she still here? Should I come back later?"

"Why are you here anyway, at . . ." I lean back to look at the microwave clock. Almost ten? Damn, I can't remember the last time I slept past eight.

"Did you or did you not extort me for free manual labor when you agreed to take the cats?"

I swallow, trying to recall anything before last night. Everything else outside Mia and me seems hazy, unreal.

Morris blinks at me. "Have you been drinking?"

"No, I just—" The can of wood stain by the porch railing catches my eye and I remember. "The pergola."

"Yep," he confirms, still eyeing me suspiciously. "Though why I agreed to spend my Sunday staining your pergola when it's clearly not a priority for you is beyond me."

"Sorry, man. It's just these kittens—"

His face brightens. "How are those little fuzzballs? Can I see them?" He makes a move to get past me, but I step to the side, resting my forearm on the doorjamb.

"Not right now, they're, uh . . . sleeping."

"Cats sleep all day, man," he says.

"But kittens need their rest."

He peers around me. "You *do* have a woman in there, don't you?"

"No." I send silent vibes for Mia to stay put but have no doubt she will. She didn't even want to discuss the change in our relationship with me. I'm sure the last thing she wants is Morris finding out. "But we should get started. The day will heat up fast. Let me change and I'll meet you out back."

He narrows his eyes, then shrugs. "Whatever. But I'm not leaving without seeing those kittens. I gotta make sure you're doing right by them."

"Chill. I spent half of yesterday getting them settled in." Once he heads around the house toward the deck, I close the door and jog-step to the bedroom, but Mia's not there. I hear voices in the backyard and peek through the blinds. I can't believe what I'm seeing. Mia is coming out of the garden shed, fully clothed in her shorts from yesterday and what I recognize as one of my T-shirts, knotted at her waist, waving a gloved hand at Morris. What she's telling him, I have no idea, but damn if I'm not once again impressed by her.

Here I was fumbling, and all the while Mia was executing a plan. Thinking on her feet in a way that astounds me but also unnerves me. Does she care that much about Morris drawing conclusions? Then again, it's none of his business. I push the clench of worry aside, riffling through my drawer for an old shirt and pair of gym shorts. It would've been awkward for him to walk in on our cozy breakfast, even if she was my girlfriend. Right?

Tugging the shirt over my disheveled hair, I catch a glimpse of myself in the mirror. I look frantic, stressed, the exact opposite of Mia's calm demeanor. I need to get it together, to prove I can support her in this. That she can trust me, like always. And then I need to convince her we can make a go of this, for real.

When I come outside, Mia is in the middle of telling Morris she'd just arrived to help with the staining, too.

"And this dude had the nerve to come to the door half dressed," she says, shaking her head like she can't believe my flakiness. She's putting on a show to deflect his attention from the two of us, but it stings a little, the memories of all the other times she's gotten frustrated at my forgetfulness. Once again, the way details slip my mind almost got us in trouble.

"You're telling me you guys have been friends since college and you've never seen Gavin shirtless?"

She laughs. "Are you kidding? More times than I can count. We used to go to the beach in Chicago most summer week-ends. But I wasn't expecting to be confronted by his bare chest this early in the morning." She slants me a small smile, and I see the truth in it. Truth and more than a little lingering lust. Her appreciative look eases the sting of the teasing, and I jump in.

"Don't go getting any ideas, Morris." I gesture at his shirt. "If you don't want that ruined, I've got an old shirt you can borrow, but this is not a clothing-optional activity."

"Bummer," he says, shifting his gaze toward where Mia is se-lecting a paintbrush from the box she brought out of the shed.

Part of me wants to tell him to cut it out, but he's not being creepy about it. If Mia and I were just friends, I would do my best not to get in the way of something developing between them, like I always have with other men she's been interested in. And she doesn't want me to act differently around her in public, that much was clear from our 3:00 a.m. conversation, even if nothing else is.

So I grit my teeth and try not to stomp on the way to the shed to grab the extra cans of wood stain.

"You've got to make long strokes with the brush," Morris says. He drags the bristles along the plank above his head, shirt hitching up with the motion to reveal a swath of ripped abs. Unlike me, he does more than just garden for a workout, and it shows.

He's been playing teacher for the past half hour, and I'm honestly not sure if he's doing it to screw with my head or because he's genuinely into her. Given the way he's asked her about a million questions about herself, I'm going with the latter.

My mind goes to the list of tropes in the binder. *Jealous love interest.* That one was near the bottom of the list, one Mia said readers love or hate. I don't want to be that guy, the one feeling possessive, or jealous of anyone who so much as looks at the lady he likes. But I can't deny that Mia not wanting to define our relationship makes me feel unsure of where we stand.

Morris is a good-looking guy, if you're into the bearded, burly lumberjack type, which pretty much everyone is, judging by how often he ends up with someone's number at the bar without even asking. And the times when he chooses to put on the charm, like now? Riley once told him it was like looking into the sun during an eclipse: stunning, disorienting, but so worth the experience.

While I disagree about blindness being an acceptable side effect, Riley wasn't wrong about his ability to be charming. Mia has turned the tables, showing him how to blend the extra stain, and he's watching her closely, laughing at himself when he fails to replicate her even strokes.

I know it's just Mia being herself. The kind of person who gets along with everyone—well, anyone who's not an outright jerk. But she's keeping herself distant from me, trying not to tip Morris off to what's going on, and I miss our usual closeness.

Normally we'd be joking around, teasing each other about our technique. She'd threaten to sign her name somewhere, and I'd dare her to do it, knowing she couldn't handle the imperfection of it. But today I feel like I have to be on my best behavior, weighing every word for innuendo, when we usually try to outdo each other in that area.

But after another hour, I can't take it any longer. I need a break from playing pretend, like we're even less than friends. This is the most I've had to put on an act since we agreed to the experiment, and we're not even testing a trope right now.

"Anyone want a drink?" I set down my paintbrush and motion toward the house.

"I could use one," Mia says. "I'll get them. I need to use the bathroom anyway."

"I don't mind," I say, but she's already headed inside, probably hoping for a break from the heat. Morris climbs off the ladder and joins me in the shade.

"You sure you two aren't a thing?" Morris uses his forearm to wipe sweat off his brow. "Because if not, then I need to seriously up my game."

"Just because she's not into you doesn't mean she's into me," I say. "It is possible for a woman to resist your charm."

"Normally I'd disagree with you, but I pulled out all the stops, and she all but fell off the ladder watching you."

It's ridiculous how happy hearing that makes me, even after what we did last night. "I didn't notice her looking."

"That's because you've been in a mood all morning. It's just like the other day. She checked you out more times than I can count. Riley and I did a tally afterward—"

"You what?"

He holds up his hands. "Relax, man. It was cute. She clearly thought she was being low-key about it, but she's obviously into you. Why else would she show up at your house to stain your deck in ninety-degree weather?"

I want to tell him that I know she's into me, because she made it very clear last night, more than once. But part of me wonders whether the magic of last night will fade with the day, extinguished by the reality of waking up together.

Mia steps back out onto the patio, a six-pack of New Glarus beer in hand, and her eyes slide to mine, like it's just the two of us out here. That's when I decide I'm done hiding how I feel.

twenty-three

Mia

I step into the shade, fanning myself. It's blazing out here, but the real reason my skin prickles with warmth is from Gavin's heated glances, the way his eyes linger on mine before sweeping away, like a stolen touch.

Who is this man, and what has he done with my best friend?

Last night was not at all friendly. It was hot and sexy and more intense than I ever could've expected. But then Morris showed up and Gavin acted so closed off that I wondered if he regretted it. If seeing me in normal Mia mode, hanging out with him and the guys—er, guy—had him wondering why he'd ever seen me as something more.

Up until a few minutes ago, he'd been quiet and standoffish, which I attributed to Morris's surprise visit. A visit that turned out not to be all that unexpected, but I'm used to things like this slipping Gavin's mind. Half the time he swipes away calendar notifications without reading them or doesn't bother to enter stuff in the first place. It's one of the ways we complement each other, me with my lists and him with his tendency to take life as it comes.

I doubt Gavin thought Morris coming by to help him stain the pergola warranted a calendar entry. He probably figured he'd be spending his day off working back here anyway and Morris could show up whenever. He'd never have guessed I'd spend the night and wake up in his bed.

My cheeks heat, despite the shade. What's happening between us is moving way faster than any of my previous relationships. I met my last boyfriend's entire family before I even saw his place. And yet I spent the night with Gavin twenty-four hours after our first kiss. Then again, I haven't just met his family, I'm close with them. We've known each other nearly a decade. Knowing each other this way, though, is different.

When he raises the beer to his lips, I can't help but remember the press of those lips on my own skin. When he swipes his forearm across his brow with a tantalizing flash of biceps, I remember being lifted off my feet, how powerful I felt in surrender to him.

He catches me staring and the corner of his mouth tilts in a grin that sends heat simmering under my skin. Sometime between me going in to grab drinks and coming back out, he's flipped a switch.

"Need a break?" He steps up next to me, sharing the sliver of shade, and I swallow hard, startled by how physical my want is. I'm used to wanting his attention, his companionship, but this tangible longing is entirely new.

Or is it? My mind flashes back to the early days of our friendship. The sidelong glances I found myself returning. The growing desire that was half the reason I felt the need to make a pledge to stick to friendship. Why form a pact if there was no danger of falling for him?

"You could take a breather inside," he says when I don't answer right away. An innocent offer, but I remember exactly what we did inside last night on the couch. His bed.

"No, I'm good. We can finish." He smiles at my unintentional innuendo and I decide to play along. "Might be better to wait till Morris leaves."

Hand on the support beam, he leans in, close enough that I have to look up to meet his eyes. "You could always fake a swoon. It's superhot out here." His eyes do a slow sweep of my body and, yeah, it's a line, but the low tenor of his voice has me biting my lip.

Morris drops his brush with a clatter, and I realize Gavin and I have just been standing here. Gazing at each other. I move back out into the sunlight, and when I brush past his shoulder, he turns his head, tracking my movement. It's hot. I don't know how else to say it. He follows me with his eyes, and I feel myself swinging my hips, bending at the waist to pick up my brush, swiping the excess on the rim of the can. Once, twice.

Is he watching? I peek over my shoulder, and yeah. He's watching.

I'm surprised at how good it feels. Getting checked out is nothing new. Not like I'm fending off men right and left, but when we go out, guys buy me drinks, ask for my number. But there's a different kind of desire in Gavin's eyes. Like he wants all of me.

But with Morris here we're both on our best behavior. If anything, not being able to do what I want to right now—which is to invite Gavin to the writing nook I made in the shed last night—is making me want him even more. Forget the fact that we might be headed down a road to ruin. If ruin looks like my best friend in a paint-flecked T-shirt, the sun glinting off his golden-brown hair and highlighting the sweep of his forearms as he climbs the ladder, then give me a first-class ticket.

The ladder wobbles and Morris glances over at Gavin. "Steady."

"I got him." Without thinking, I step over and take hold of the ladder with both hands, my cheek near Gavin's hip.

He hesitates on the next rung and looks down to check in with me. "Want to switch places?"

"Nah, I'll let you do the hard part," I say. Joking with him is easy, until he breaks out in another wide smile. How is it that I've been clueless to how sexy his smiles are? Wide and daring, an invitation.

"Unless you don't trust me," I add, grinning up at him. "Would you rather I let Morris take over for me?"

"He wouldn't rather," Morris calls from over on the other side of the deck where he's staining the support beam. Maybe I should be concerned that he's onto us, but at the moment there's not much room in my brain for anything but Gavin.

He dips his brush into the stain, then works it into the corners of the crossbeam. "Thanks for helping out with this," he says. "If you've got other plans—"

"You know full well I can't leave until this is finished. It would be like quitting on a power-washing video when they're halfway done." I shudder.

"Can't have that." He doesn't look at me, but I can hear the smile in his tone.

"You joke, but leaving things unfinished is my literal nightmare."

"Good thing for you—" he brushes the stain on in even strokes "—I always—" the bristles of the brush slide along the wood, slow and rhythmic "—finish what I start."

Between the skillful way he works and the innuendo in his words, I'm pretty sure my bosom is heaving like a heroine on a vintage stepback cover. I'm even more certain that, dangerous or not, I want to keep this thing going with Gavin. We might be headed for disaster, but I'm too caught up in the bliss of experiencing him this way to worry about the future.

Morris goes inside for a another drink, and I rise on my tiptoes to say, "Are you flirting with me?"

"Mia." He sets down the paintbrush and gives me another one of those searing looks, eyes brilliant blue. "I've been flirting with you all summer."

"I'm not talking about the trope tests," I say. "I meant for real."

"I never had to fake it," he says. In that moment I realize, neither have I.

Morris left not long after that, and we didn't waste any time. I showed Gavin my improvised writing spot in the shed, and he showed me how possible it would be for me to forget we'd left the pergola half finished.

The man kisses like pleasing me is his job. By the time we stumbled back out, what felt like hours later, we were both starving. Gavin's pantry wasn't up to the task, even though I ate all that was left of a package of fudge stripe cookies while he tended to the cats.

We wound up at our favorite burger spot. We've come here countless times, but never while holding hands, with the trail of kisses he left on my neck a recent memory.

The moment the server leaves with our drink order, I blurt out, "Is this our first date?"

His brows go up. "You're asking me?"

"Who else would I ask?"

"I'm trying to follow your lead here," he says.

Sweet of him, but also unhelpful. The server comes back with the lemonade I ordered and Gavin's water. "On second thought," I say, smiling apologetically. "Could I please get a cup of coffee? No cream or sugar."

He nods and takes our orders, which we rattle off by heart.

"Tired all of a sudden?" Gavin asks, once the waiter has left.

After being up half the night, absolutely. But I also need to be alert for this conversation. "We have a lot to work out," I say. "We're here, like always. But we came together." I point at him just as he opens his mouth.

"That's what she sai—"

"Now is not the time, Gavin."

He rolls his lips together against an errant smile and folds his hands on the table. "What qualifies as a date?"

I should know this. I write fictional dates for a living. "Romantic interest."

"Check." No hesitation. His eyes hold mine, clear blue in the afternoon light slanting through the shades.

I swallow, trying to keep my galloping pulse in check. Are we really doing this? "Attraction." The word comes out surprisingly steady.

"Check." Gavin's voice is pitched low, but I hear him loud and clear.

"A desire to get to know the other person better, in order to determine compatibility."

"I think we checked that one off years ago."

We're compatible, no doubt. Our tastes. How we spend our spare time. Our interests.

Physically, though, that's new. A flush creeps up my neck. I bite my lip, embarrassed, for the first time in as long as I can remember, in front of him.

"We can always revisit physical compatibility." His eyes drop to my lips, and the next time he speaks, his voice is rough. "If you want."

"Might have to, in the interest of thoroughness."

The waiter sets my coffee down, and I lean back, realizing the table has been cutting into my ribs with how far I'd leaned across in order to get closer to Gavin. The restaurant is nearly empty, midday, and we're *that* couple.

Holy crap, did I just call us a couple?

I take a scalding slurp of coffee and let the burn chase away the butterflies. "I'm worried we're rushing into this."

"We've known each other since college, Mia."

My hands are shaky, and I don't understand how he's so calm

about all this. "Don't you think we should consider the ramifications of taking this step?"

He sits back, head cocked. "You mean, what happens if I
decide to take over for Dad?"

Caught up in the whirlwind of the past few days, I'd managed to banish thoughts of him leaving, but they come roar-
ing back with a vengeance. Contemplating a relationship when
we don't even know what our friendship will look like in six
months seems like madness.

But if we were together, Gavin moving would almost be
easier than if we were friends. No need to make up excuses to
visit each other, or worry about overstaying our welcome . . .
And somehow I've invented a reality where dating Gavin makes
sense, is plausible, even. Could it be that after all these years,
dating would be easier?

But that possibility doesn't take into account the potential of
a breakup and all the messy hurt feelings that go along with it.

"Trying this out is one thing. But what happens if it ends?"
It's embarrassing how easy it is to remember the shame of telling
my sister's now-husband that I had feelings for him. Gavin and I
are at the beginning, yet already my heart breaks at the thought
of him trading me in for someone he loves more. Am I so afraid
of heartbreak that I'm scared to let myself love?

"I can't promise it will work, and I know you don't expect me to." Gavin's voice is rough, but this time it's gruff with
emotion. "But if things don't work out between us, there is
no world where I would stop being in your life. Not unless
you didn't want me in it. There is nothing that could happen
between us where I wouldn't want to complain about relief
pitchers with you or vent about Morris's latest antics. I think
it's pretty clear that I want more. But I will never settle for less,
not for as long as you want my friendship."

"Always." A lot is uncertain right now. Whether I'll finish

this book in time, what's next for my career, what my relationship with Gavin will look like in the future. But one thing I
know is I want him in my life. "I'm just worried we're rushing
things." I keep thinking of the scene that hijacked my plot last
night: Sydney and Victor's friends and family asking them questions they weren't prepared to answer.

"This isn't a book, Mia," he says. "We don't have to worry
about the right pacing. We can just do what feels right for us.
There are no rules."

I like rules, though. Organized outlines and scene progres-
sions. But one thing I've learned from writing romance is that
happiness is never achieved without taking risks and going for
what you want. And what I want is a real date with Gavin.

Hands wrapped around the coffee mug, I ask, "What would
you do if you were here on a date?"

"I never bring dates here. This is our spot," he says, eyes
never leaving mine. "But if this were a real date, with you, I'd
want to get closer."

I want that, too, the ache to be near him surprising only in
that it's not all that unexpected. I'm used to wanting him close,
even if craving his touch is new. But it feels right. It feels good,
to want him this way.

Before I can second-guess the urge, I scoot over to make
room. He grins and stands up, then slides in next to me.

"Is this okay?" He grazes a finger over my knuckles.

"Mmm-hmm." I feel like I can't see him, though, so I make
use of what little space I have and shift to face him, pulling my
leg up on the booth, wedging myself between the table and the
wall and Gavin. My shin is pressed along his thigh. It's familiar
and comfortable but somehow brand-new. "Different."

"But good?" He lays his arm along the top of the booth,
fingertips brushing my shoulder.

"Very good."

"I know you're worried about how all this will work," he says, sweeping his thumb along my collarbone. "I get that things are different. But, Mia, I like you so much."

He leans in and presses a kiss to my lips, like he can't help himself. And neither can I. I wrap my fingers around the smooth swell of his biceps, anchoring him, or maybe me, because this kiss is unspooling me. Taking me away to an alternate reality where we're not Mia and Gavin, just friends, but Mia and Gavin, in love.

Love. The forbidden word slips into my consciousness like a whisper. It's how I've felt about him for years, but deeper, or maybe higher, like the pinnacle of a coaster when your stomach is in your throat but the safety bar is keeping you grounded. Elation, and safety, too.

This isn't just anyone, it's my best friend, and I can trust him. His mouth on mine is sweet, hungry. My fingers can't help but trace his stubbled jaw, grip the trimmed hair at his nape. His mouth coaxes mine open, asking for more, and I give it, sweeping my tongue against his. Kissing him doesn't feel like a risk. It feels like everything finally makes sense.

The bell above the door chimes, startling us apart, but his eyes hold mine, irises swallowed up by his pupils, like he's taking me in. Sunlight from the wall of windows falls on his hair, highlighting the range of hues from cedar to pine, and nestles in the hollow of his throat, illuminating his hammering pulse.

I'm breathing too fast, too hard for such a brief touch. But every time our lips meet, it feels like something I've waited my whole life for.

And if I'm certain of anything, it's that after today, friendship will never be enough. But if this doesn't work out, it will have to be.

My phone buzzes in my purse, and when I pull it out, I see Serafina's calling. I mute it, looking over my shoulder by reflex. We're overdue to hang out, but between work and her preparation for the new baby, we haven't found a time to catch up, which means she doesn't have a clue what's going on here.

"Aren't you going to answer?" he asks.

"What if she hears you?"

"She'll think we're hanging out." He shrugs, not seeing the issue.

"Yeah, but we're *hanging out*." I take a deep breath, trying to explain. "This is a big deal. I know your nephews' birthdays, for goodness' sake."

His lips curve in a confused grin. "How is that relevant?"

"How is it not?" I wave my arms, flailing metaphorically and physically. "We're wrapped up in each other's lives, Gavin. We're *friends*." The word comes out pained, and I rush to explain. "We know everything about each other. You were there when I came out of anesthesia for my wisdom teeth surgery."

His smile dips, like he's catching on, and not liking the implication. "That means we can't be more?"

"No. It means we're way past the first date here." And the thought of Sera finding out, or any of our friends and family, means more potential fallout if this ends.

He nods, his expression thoughtful. "About that . . . There's somewhere I'd like to take you."

Which is how I find myself agreeing to go on a real date with Gavin, the exact thing I hoped to avoid at the start of all this. But this time, there's no pretending our feelings are fake. I like him and he likes me, and if the date ends in disaster, we won't be able to find refuge in each other like we normally do.

Who we are to each other has already changed, and I'm not sure I'm ready.

twenty-four

Gavin

The arboretum is one of my favorite places—a college buddy of mine works here and I visit at least once a season. I feel like I can breathe with the wide-open spaces and shady groves. I'm fully aware I should be driving the other direction tonight, toward the farm and the hard conversations I've been avoiding, but I can't help wanting to stay in this bubble a little longer.

Mia seems sure that others finding out about us will complicate things, and while I disagree in general, I do hate the thought of Scott thinking he was right and that Mia is all that's keeping me here.

Still, it was hard to keep quiet about what happened between us at work all week when I wanted so badly to share the news with Riley, who kept looking at me like she wanted to say something but was holding back, and Morris, who I'm 90 percent sure has already told her his suspicions after spending Sunday staining the pergola with us.

But coming home to Mia every evening has made up for the secrecy. She's stayed at my house every day to watch the kittens, and most nights. Sometimes she works until I'm long asleep, nudging me awake after I've dozed off on the couch or rising in the middle of the night to write with a shift of the mattress that has me instantly awake but pretending otherwise, not wanting to disrupt the rhythm she's found.

With only three weeks left until she turns in the book, the last thing I want is to be a distraction, but these past few days have been some of the best of my life, and I don't want to think of what will happen if she decides she never wants to make this trial run the real thing.

Tonight feels like a big step and I'm excited to bring her to the arboretum. I haven't come here for a date since a disastrous night out with my then-girlfriend who made it clear I was a walking cliché. Even though I know Mia would never tease me for loving it here, I hesitated to invite her, because I wasn't sure she'd enjoy it. But I wanted to bring her somewhere we've never made memories as friends so we could start fresh as a couple, and the timing is perfect because tonight the arboretum is hosting a sip-and-savor night with food trucks and tastings from local wineries. Mia will never have a bad time if good food is involved.

The drive over was quieter than normal, since I was filled with first-date jitters, a weird sensation around the woman who's been my friend for years. But things feel so different now, even though—or maybe especially because—I woke up in her arms this morning.

She's never been a fan of bouquets, so I snipped a few sprigs of lavender from my garden and tucked them into the string knotted around a charcuterie box I picked up for the road. The flowers are in her hair now, the stems tucked into the braids she knotted into a low bun. She's gorgeous as ever, and I have to remind myself not to stare.

We order kebabs and spring rolls to share and eat on high-top tables near the arboretum entrance, then take our wine on a stroll along the garden paths, before I lead her out onto one of the many woodland trails.

"Where are you at in the book?" Conversation is an uphill battle tonight since I'm weighing all my words, not wanting to get it wrong, but I know she's thinking about the story from the far-off look in her eyes. She gets that way when her characters push to the forefront of her thoughts.

"Ugh, now is where things start to fall apart. Tensions are high, and not in a good way. I just want to protect them from what's coming next."

"So do it." Sounds great to me.

She shakes her head. "It's important to put their relationship to the test. But right now I'm not in the mood for that."

A smile tugs at my cheeks, and she glances my way with a cute grin. "Quit looking so smug. Or don't actually, because it's sexy."

Mia just called me sexy. I think my brain might have short-circuited, but I'm okay with it.

But she still has that faraway look. "I just feel like I've stop-started this project so many times, I don't know which way is up." On impulse I stop and gather her into my arms, aware we're in the middle of the path, but not caring much.

"You'll find a way to make it work," I say, holding her close. "You always have. And even if you don't, you're still incredible. One tough book isn't going to define you."

She wraps her arms around me, cheek pressed to my chest. "How do you always know the right things to say?"

"Remember that next time you come at me for my take on socks with sandals."

She pulls away, eyes narrowed. "Sometimes a girl needs to run to the mailbox. Besides, you've got a lot of opinions on footwear for someone who didn't understand why I needed a pedicure before the last premiere."

"You weren't planning to wear sandals with your gown," I protest.

"Slingbacks," she says, as if that explains anything.

We start strolling again, the sun fading as fireflies start to flicker in the shadows.

"This place is enchanting." She squeezes my hand. "You've been keeping it a secret." Her face is silhouetted against the evening sky, impossible to read.

"How did you know?"

"You haven't looked at the map once, and this place is huge, yet you led me straight to this beautiful spot," she says. We're standing in front of a pond bordered with towering oaks, water lilies dotting the gleaming surface.

I take a sip of wine, embarrassed she caught on, but not surprised. "I brought Megan here once. Remember her?" Mia nods. We'd been dating for about six months, a long time for me. "She teased me about how cliché it was. 'What a shock,' she said, 'the tree guy thinking a forest would be romantic.'"

"'The tree guy'?" Mia looks affronted on my behalf.

"I'm paraphrasing. But yeah. The only thing she was really interested in was the hedge maze. I figured it would be fine since it's open overhead. It wasn't." Even though I knew there was a way out, my mind refused to accept that. "After the first few turns, I told her she could go on without me but I had to head out. Explained how enclosed spaces were difficult for me."

"That must've been hard to admit, considering you didn't even tell me." There's no hint of accusation in her voice, just sympathy.

"It was, yeah. But she laughed it off. Said it would be good to face my fears. And maybe it would've been, but I didn't want to." Not with her.

"For what it's worth," Mia says, "I think human mazes are sadistic. Are we hamsters, or what?"

Grinning at her, I say, "To be fair, that's also your stance on treadmills."

"Rightly so." She shakes her head. "I liked Megan, but it sounds like she showed her true colors."

We follow the gravel path around the pond, watching a heron land in the shallows. "Since we're sharing secrets," Mia says, "I've been thinking about why I decided not to date friends. It wasn't just because I was scared of losing them. It was because when I got rejected, I'd rather have been able to tell myself it was because they didn't know the real me."

Swinging our joined hands between us, she adds, "Guess it's too late for us on that."

I'm about to reassure her that she doesn't have to worry about that with me when the bushes next to us start to rustle. I step in front of Mia, wondering whether a deer is about to leap out. Whatever it is, it's bigger than a squirrel or raccoon.

"Uncle Gavin!" The shout comes a split second before my nephew catapults into my leg. A second later his brother tumbles out of the bush in a shower of leaves.

"Boo, scared ya!" Paxton announces.

I look around for their parents and sure enough, here come Scott and Amber on the path behind us. There's no way they could've missed seeing Mia and me holding hands, but she lets go anyway, and I gulp down my disappointment.

Stooping, I let both my nephews give me a quick hug, then they're off again, picking up rocks to throw in the water. Standing, I smile at my brother and sister-in-law. "Hey, Scott, Amber."

Scott's sandy brows lift, and he says to his wife, "Hon, you remember Mia. Gavin's friend from college."

Amber gives him a puzzled look. "Of course." She goes in for a hug, but a shriek comes from off to our right and I turn to find Brett and Paxton tumbling in a wrestling match.

"Oh gosh," Amber says, and jogs toward them. "Boys, cut it out!"

They break apart as she gets closer, and I turn my attention back toward my brother. "What brings you all the way out here?" The arboretum is a good three hours away from the farm.

"We're spending a few days in the city," Scott says. "Met up with one of Amber's friends and her family. Thought this would be a fun outing for the kids."

"A wine tasting?" I don't mean to sound sarcastic, but I'm shocked to see them here, of all places. Especially when I haven't spoken to him since the baseball game.

He points back toward the front. "They have a children's garden. We didn't realize there'd be a special event."

Amber comes back, a little breathless, my nephews trailing behind. "Sorry. The boys had cotton candy and shared a cupcake. They're wired." Her phone chimes and she checks it. "My friend's kids finally made it to the front of the face-painting line," she says. "We'd better go, but we'll catch up next week, yes?" The end-of-summer barbecue. Hard to believe it's already August. "Great to see you, Mia. Can't wait for your latest. Victor and Sydney are my favorites."

Out of the corner of my eye, I notice Mia stiffen, but she pastes on a big smile. "Thanks, Amber."

Scott waves, his expression neutral, but I can see the wheels turning. "See you at the cookout."

The boys are already off and running, and they hurry to catch up.

Watching them go, Mia frowns. "What's going on with you and Scott?"

"Besides that he's pissed I don't want to take over for Dad?"

"But he barely spoke to me. What do I have to do with it?" Her eyes widen. "He thinks I'm pushing you to stay, doesn't he?"

I shake my head, though she's not far off.

"Then what? Because 'Gavin's friend from college'?" She

makes air quotes. "I see them every summer. I've done virtual author visits with Amber's book club."

"I know. He's . . ." I didn't want to tell her this. "He doesn't think you're trying to get me to stay. But he does think you're the reason I don't want to leave."

Understanding dawns on her face. "So he thinks something's going on between us, and running into us like this justifies all his assumptions." Her fingers are pressed to her temples, like she's warding off a headache. "If he thinks I'm the reason you're turning down the farm, he'll resent me forever."

"So what?"

"So what?" Her brows go up, and so does her pitch. "That's your brother. And you think he won't mention this to your dad? Can't you see how I would be the bad guy? How would they ever be okay with our relationship if they thought I'd kept you from taking over the farm?"

Dad would never, but Scott . . . "I thought we weren't thinking about the future."

"Of course I am," she says. "I just didn't want to put a label on this too early." Her lips press into a thin line, and she looks off in the direction Scott's family left, brows furrowed.

"What if I do end up taking over the farm?" I haven't considered it. Not truly. But would I do it to keep the heat off Mia? Maybe.

"Then I'd worry you did it for me, just so they couldn't accuse me of keeping you from it."

"So there's no way to win." I blow out a breath, wondering how we've gone from the perfect evening to this. Except I know how. If I'd been honest with Scott and Dad about my reasons for staying away, none of this would've fallen out on Mia.

She runs a hand over her head, dislodging the sprigs of lavender. "I don't know, Gavin."

"It's just Scott. He'll come around."

She lets out a breath. "I told you this would be messy."

"But maybe me moving would be like adopting the kittens." She looks at me questioningly, and I explain, "I didn't want to bring them home, but I don't regret it. Maybe it would be the same with taking over for Dad. Not exactly what I planned, but good."

She looks unconvinced. "Good enough?"

Everywhere I turn, it's the same question. I thought I had the answer. Then I got a taste of life with Mia, and I know for certain I can never settle for second best again.

twenty-five

Mia

Sera and Joe's backyard is decked out in shades of green, with sage lanterns in the trees and mint-green tablecloths topped by fern centerpieces. I wish I could say I had a hand in how beautifully the decor turned out, but after Sera found out about my new deadline, she forbade me from coming early to set up.

After our interrupted arboretum date, things were tense, and Gavin dropped me off at home. I can't believe I thought that being in a relationship would make the question of him moving simpler. Scott's reaction to seeing us just proves I was right to keep this between us.

Unable to sleep, I ended up writing most of the night. Between Evie's nudging and the existential dread of not finishing in time, I've managed to make it to the third act of the book. But Gavin called me at 6:00 a.m., frantic because Ash was missing. I came over to help look and we found her sleeping in his open sock drawer. One thing led to another, and I discovered that even if things are more complicated this way, making up is a lot more fun. I barely made it back to my condo in time to get ready for the baby shower.

We decided to arrive separately to avoid clueing our friends in to what's going on between us. Well, I decided and convinced Gavin. He thought not driving together would lead to more questions. But Sera's aunt greeted me at the door and slyly reminded me I could've brought a plus-one before directing me through to the yard, proving I was right and people would've jumped to conclusions if I'd shown up with Gavin.

Sera wraps me in an enormous hug the moment I step outside, her round belly still small beneath her flowy maxi dress. She wanted to wait until later in the pregnancy to have a baby shower, but her doctor mentioned the possibility of bed rest, so we're having it now, when she's in the second trimester.

And by *we* I mean her sisters, aunts, and mother, who took over the planning, leaving me to do the text message equivalent of smile and nod. The only suggestion of mine that won out was to request guests bring a signed picture book instead of cards.

"I'll warn you," she says, arm linked through mine as she leads me through round tables decked out with woodland centerpieces. "My aunts were in charge of the games, and they're planning to throw down. I hope you're prepared for things to get fierce."

She hardly looks ready for battle in a floral dress with a sweetheart neckline, her honey-blond tresses flowing loose down her back, but when it comes to Sera, looks can be deceiving. She's a lawyer and was winning disagreements with our landlord back in college long before she passed the bar.

My last baby shower was at the age of eight, and all I remember was sherbet punch and blowing bubbles, but I'm always up for a friendly competition. "Bring it on. Should I go easy on them?"

"Ha." She lets out a humorless laugh. "Don't, or they won't respect you."

"No mercy, got it." This is going to be more fun than I expected. Also, it will be easier to hide what's going on between Gavin and me with everyone riled up over party games.

Joe is by the beverage table, looking handsome as ever in a loose short-sleeve button-down and khakis, chatting with a handful of guys. I recognize his two brothers, but the rest are strangers, and Sera introduces us.

"Where's Gavin?" Joe asks, once the others have stepped away to chat with other guests.

"On his way, I'm sure." I'm actually not sure, since I tore myself away from him hours later than planned and went back to my place to do my hair and makeup in record time.

"Figured you'd ride together since it's such a drive," Sera says. They live closer to the city than us, about a half hour away.

"Nothing like the trip out to Wisconsin, though," Joe says. "Can't believe Gavin's thinking of ditching us." He pauses, brown eyes wide. "Please tell me you already knew."

I brush off his concern. "It would be a big change, that's for sure." An understatement, but I'm trying to play it cool. "Then again, things are already changing." I lift my chin toward Sera's rounded belly. "You're about to be parents."

She eyes me with concern, like she's not buying my nonchalance. "But this baby is all happy news. Gavin leaving would be bittersweet, especially for you."

I don't bother to play dumb. Girlfriend or not, out of the three of us I'm the closest to Gavin. More so than even Joe, though Gavin stood up at their wedding. We used to joke about what cut of gown he'd look best in as my man of honor, but now the thought of him giving me away to another man feels utterly wrong, like a misprinted page in a book, the text flipped upside down. "I'd hate to see him go, but I want him to be happy."

"Always seemed happy where he's at," Joe says. "Especially lately. Didn't even have a comeback when I messed with him about the Brewers' losing streak the other day. I asked if he'd met someone new, but he denied it."

"Because I haven't." Gavin walks up, his denial the perfect cover because it's true; we've known each other forever. "Nice to know you'd be spilling the news if I had, though." He grins and pulls Joe into a handshake-hug and I catch the scent of the woodsy cologne that lingers on his pillow.

He's dressed for the outdoor party in chambray shorts and a short-sleeve button-down that hugs his frame. I left his house not long ago, but the sight of him, all big smiles and casual hotness, has me flipping through my mental list of excuses in case we get a chance to duck out early.

Joe laughs. "You know I can't keep a secret to save my life. Besides, anything you tell me, Mia already heard yesterday," he says, and I don't bother denying it. "She's a closed book when it comes to talking about your love life, though." He takes a sip of his fizzy drink, eyes on Gavin.

Is it my imagination, or does a look pass between the two of them? To get Joe off the trail, I ask, "Is that a virgin paloma?" Last week, the group text was a flurry of nonalcoholic drink ideas, and I can't remember what they settled on.

"A sparkling peach-ginger mocktail," Sera says. "If I can't drink, nobody's drinking."

"Makes sense to me." Gavin picks up a crystal glass and ladles punch into it. Renting tableware was Sera's mom's idea. At least she footed the bill. "So what happens at these things?" he asks. "I've got to admit, it's my first baby shower."

"We've been to our share since starting parenthood classes," Sera says. "But the main thing you should know, like I was telling Mia, is my family doesn't play around when it comes to games."

Gavin pauses, glass halfway to his lips. "Isn't that the point of games?"

Sera and I share a look that says *easy target*. "I know who I don't want on my team," I tell her with an exaggerated tilt of my head in his direction. He may be handsome and the best friend a girl could ask for, but he's one of those annoying everyone's-a-winner types and I play to win.

"Oh, come on." He turns to Joe. "Guess that leaves us."

"Why not?" Joe lifts his chin to where the older women are hovering near the hors d'oeuvres, with hair-sprayed pixie cuts and lacquered bobs, deceptively innocuous in their linen pant-suits and A-line dresses. "I don't stand a chance against those ladies anyway."

Turns out I didn't get to be Sera's teammate. The women in her family insisted she pair up with her husband, claiming it wasn't right she be with anyone else, but I think the truth is they know he's the weaker link and they want an easy path to victory.

I contemplated asking one of her cousins to team up with me, but figured Gavin might give me an edge since we know each other so well.

"No way Team Baby is losing this round." Sera points at us. "Team Besties is going down."

Gavin cringes, like he has every time she's called us that, and I bite back a giggle. He's so cute when he's affronted. The name is awful, but I'm enjoying his reaction too much to mind.

"We'll see about that," I call. We're three games in and so far, the matriarchs are dominating the competition, as expected. They matched the most baby socks in a minute—ten more pairs than any other team—and in a purse-and-pocket-emptying game, which seemed to be rigged in their favor, they won with a grand total of ninety items between them, not counting indi-vidual sticks of gum.

Next up is Cram the Stroller, devised by one of Sera's friends who's the mother of a toddler. The goal is to fill a stroller with as much baby gear as possible before the timer beeps.

Three games deep into this tournament, and the chalkboard bracket is taunting us youngsters. "Ready to take them down?" I ask my partner, who's currently on his third mocktail. I don't blame him, it's hot out here despite the shade from a tall maple, and that's not even counting the level of the competition.

He sets down his drink. "'Them' being a grandmother and Joe's great-aunt?"

"Never underestimate a matriarch," I tell him.

"You're going down, Grandma," Sera shouts, gathering her hair into a ponytail, and I raise my brows at Gavin. He holds up his hands in a gesture of surrender.

Joe is eyeing his wife with mingled admiration and fear. She notices him watching and blows him a kiss. My gaze connects with Gavin's and we both roll our eyes, but the truth is I'm a bit jealous of their sanctioned displays of affection. Maybe I was wrong to keep our relationship under wraps.

Sera's aunt whistles for everyone's attention and I shake out my shoulders, bouncing on my toes. Sera follows suit, stretching her arms overhead and cracking her knuckles, even though she's perched on an upholstered dining chair someone brought out from the house.

In unison, we settle forward, me in the crouched stance of a sprinter at the starting line, Sera sliding to the edge of her seat, ready for action.

"These two," Joe says to Gavin.

"I know, right?" He shakes his head.

"Shh," Sera says, at the same time as I flap my hand in his direction. "You're going to make us miss the countdown."

"Heaven forbid we get a late start," Joe mumbles, and Sera gives him a quelling look.

"Get ready," she says. "This challenge is all you." Her doctor wants her to stay off her feet as much as possible.

"Take it easy," he says, and kisses her on the forehead. "I got this." He lowers into an exaggerated lunge that has the younger members of their families giggling.

That gives me an idea, and I grab Gavin's hand, rising on tiptoe to whisper in his ear. This close, I notice a nick on his jaw from shaving—he had to get ready in a hurry—and barely catch myself before I press a kiss to the spot. Team Besties is not going to use a party celebrating our friends' long-awaited baby to reveal the change in our relationship status.

Just as I finish telling him my plan, Sera's mom shouts, "Three, two, one, GO!"

I bend and grab a toy at random, tossing it into the stroller, but instead of helping, Gavin jogs over to the group of kids watching us make fools of ourselves. A moment later he comes back with two children who start throwing stuff into our stroller.

Joe glances over and does a double take. "Hey, what are you doing?"

"There's no rule about how many people per team," I call out, not pausing in my efforts.

The kids stick their tongues out at him. "Better hurry, Uncle Joe."

"This is my baby shower, traitors," Sera says, but she's grinning.

Joe pauses, mouth downturned in an exaggerated pout. "Just yours?"

"Ours, babe." She leans over and pecks him on the cheek. "Now hurry. Don't let those cheaters win!"

The guests have caught on to what we're doing, some cheering us on, others recruiting kids to join them. Soon it's a free-for-all, with kids and adults alike rushing over to help their favorite team until everyone but Sera is in on the game.

In his rush to throw a sippy cup into the stroller, Gavin bumps me with his elbow, and I nudge him back playfully. "Same team, remember?"

"Always." He grins at me, face flushed from exertion, eyes bright. His hair is mussed and dark with sweat at the temples, the wheat-brown strands practically begging for me to run my fingers through them and smooth them down. He's glowing, all exuberance and cheer, and all I want to do is kiss him, claim him. Stop pretending I want anything less than all of him.

But this is Sera and Joe's day, and the last thing I want to do is take the spotlight off of them and the baby they've waited so long for. So, sacrificing my yellow sundress in the name of victory, I kneel down in the grass to grab the small items that have gotten shoved under the stroller—a granola bar, a diaper, bottles, and pacifiers—and toss the whole armful into the stroller a split second before Sera's mom shouts, "That's time, everyone!"

I'm panting, and next to me, Gavin lets out a breathless laugh. The kids are holding on to the teetering pile of stuff to keep it from tumbling. But when they catch Sera's menacing glare, they let go and a plastic xylophone tumbles to the ground.

Losing an item may have cost us the game, but I can't bring myself to care, because Gavin pulls me into a tight hug. I savor what to everyone else is just friends celebrating but to us is a stolen embrace, his heartbeat thudding against mine, the muscles of his back warm with exertion under my splayed hands. My cheek is against his chest and my heart is whispering, *Mine*.

The guests have all left and it's just the four of us. Sera's seat of honor has been swapped for a gifted rocking chair, her feet propped up on the matching stool. Joe's dad brought it over in his truck, fully assembled, and she used it as a throne while they opened gifts. "You're going to have to carry me in the house along with this chair," she says to her husband. "Who would've thought a baby shower could wear me out?"

"Maybe it was all the yelling," Gavin says in an undertone. We're taking care of the cornhole game set up near the back fence.

I shush him, but he grins. "What? Give her a headset and she'd be good to go on the NFL sidelines."

He's not wrong. Her family's competitive streak definitely didn't skip a generation. "She'd probably take that as a compliment," I say, smiling at him.

"Aw, look at you two," Sera calls. "Couple goals, for real."

I freeze, hoping I heard wrong.

"Don't look so panicked." Sera shares an unreadable glance

with Joe. "What I mean is you're so in tune with each other. Making small talk back there like it's only the two of you in the world."

My cheeks heat. We were just messing around. Is that how it's always looked when we're together?

"Except they never bicker." Joe grins devilishly at his wife.

"And what, we do?" Sera asks, sitting up straighter.

"We argue plenty, but about silly stuff," I tell them, wanting to stifle the impending argument. Bickering is how Joe and Sera flirt, a rivals-to-lovers couple if I ever saw one. "Like whether streaming or cable is superior."

"The problem is too many choices," Gavin says. "Impossible to decide what to watch with all the options."

I put my hands on my hips. "We could if you'd agree watching people buy houses is not entertainment."

"Look what you did." Joe gestures toward us.

"I think it's adorable," Sera says. "Like an old married couple." She sits up quickly, then winces, hand to her belly. "Oh my gosh, babe. They should take our spot."

I don't like the sound of that. At all. What's she talking about?

Joe frowns. "At the couples retreat? It's only for people in relationships."

A couples retreat? That's a big hell no. It would technically work to test the relationship-in-trouble trope, but we agreed we wouldn't involve anyone else in our charade. And now that it's not a charade, attempting something like a couples retreat would put our relationship under a microscope we aren't ready for. My mind flips to the scene I wrote where Victor and Sydney's relationship gets put to the test. That didn't end well.

But Sera's not deterred by Joe's hesitance. "Not like they have to be married, or even dating. What are the organizers going to do? Ask how often they sleep together? Pretty sure a lot of the couples are there because they stopped having sex in the first place." Before I can counter this dubious logic, Sera tells us, "We already did the first three weekends. I have to sit the final one out because it's a day of outdoor activities. You guys should take our spot."

"Maybe if I wasn't on deadline." Lies. Under no circumstances, busy or not, would I participate in a couples retreat with Gavin when we're not even technically dating.

"That's perfect. You could count it as book research."

"The book is friends-to-lovers meets fake dating, not relationship-in-trouble. Sydney is acting out scenes to help Victor tune up his acting skills."

Gavin looks up sharply from gathering the scattered bean-bags, and I realize I haven't shared the premise with him yet. Mostly because I don't want him to see the similarities between their situation and ours.

She smiles. "Even better. What if they decide to up the stakes and see if they're good enough to convince the other couples they're dating?"

It's hard to argue with a pregnant woman, especially one who debates for a living. And that's how we find ourselves agreeing to one final trope test.

It's also no easy feat to stomp toward my car with the ten pounds of leftover party food that Sera foisted on me, but I attempt it. Gavin is a few steps behind, carrying his own culinary loot.

I balance the containers on my hip, fumbling for my keys. "You could've said something back there."

"Like what? We agreed not to tell anyone we were together."

"That's why you should have protested."

He shrugs. "Thought you might want to use it as another trope test."

"We're supposed to be done with those."

"Yeah, well, that was the perfect moment to tell them the truth about us, and you denied it."

I look up from digging for my keys in my purse and notice

his jaw is tight. "I couldn't tell them without checking with you first."

"I made it clear where I stand," he says. "I don't want to fake it."

"We weren't faking it today. We just weren't being super obvious."

He gives me a dubious look. "But when she straight-up called us a couple, you shot her down."

"Looks like I was right to do so. They foisted couples therapy on us while under the impression we're just friends. Can you imagine their reaction if they found out we were dating?"

"Um, be happy for us?" He shrugs. "Maybe this is them matchmaking. If they knew we were together, they'd have no reason to force it on us."

"Okay, I see your logic," I admit. "But I still don't think it was the right time."

"Springing it on them during the baby shower probably wouldn't have been in good taste," he admits, leaning against the cab of his truck.

"You're saying I was right?"

"Mostly, yeah," he says, and smiles.

"You're pretty good at this boyfriend stuff."

"I've had a lot of time to prepare. Almost ten years."

"So friendship was just the warm-up?" I raise my brows, challenging him. I went through that with Stewart, who only wanted to be friends because he thought it would lead to more.

Gavin shakes his head. "Friendship with you was everything. But this?" His eyes darken with intensity, the leafy branches overhead casting dappled shadows on his face. "This is the kind of thing I only ever expected to read about in your books. You make me feel greedy, Mia."

I know the feeling. "Your place or mine?" We've spent the afternoon pretending to be just friends, but now it's just us, and I don't intend to hold back. Not ever again.

twenty-six

Mia

The third act. That's all that stands between me and finishing the book. Lots of readers hate this part. Some even skip it. Sometimes it's a breakup, sometimes not. Either way, the characters are headed to their lowest point. This is where I got stuck last time, unable to pull Sydney and Victor together again after pushing them apart. But now I have years of experience putting characters to the test and letting them prove they've learned how to love and be loved.

For the first time, I see what these best friends gain by embracing love, not just what they stand to lose. Even though I've been a little distracted—okay, a lot distracted—by Gavin and the kittens, I'm midway through writing it and ready to give the best friends their own happy-ever-after, but first I need to get through this weekend—the book convention on Friday and Saturday, then the couples retreat on Sunday. After that, I have two weeks to buckle down and finish the book.

The first day of the signing is Friday, only two days from now, and I'll be checking into the hotel tomorrow afternoon to get settled, but I haven't gone over the talking points, picked out outfits, or crated up any of my swag. Totally unlike me, but since "me" is currently sitting on my desk, making out with Gavin, it's not the biggest shock.

I'm supposed to be sorting through stock, but he came over with pizza and kissing him turned out to be a lot more appealing than packing. The truth is I've been procrastinating on preparing for weeks because I'm nervous for the inevitable questions about the unfinished book. It's just another stress on the growing list: a moved-up deadline, the possibility Gavin will be moving, and the change in our relationship.

Up until recently, our friendship was something I took for granted, something steady and reliable. Part of me misses that surety, but the other part of me is very much enjoying this current stage of our friendship.

On the desk, my phone vibrates, and I pull back with a groan. Dizzily, I check the text.

Kim: Hey, do you still need me to be your assistant for the book con?

I frown at the screen. She wouldn't be asking unless something's come up, but I absolutely do need help. The con is a huge event, and there's no way I can manage on my own. Up until recently, she was my assistant at most big events, especially in the summer. Then she got busy with her second master's degree program, and I hired Lydia, who also assists with shipping, my newsletter, and administrative tasks. But she's spending the summer in Europe.

"Everything okay?" Gavin's cheeks are flushed, eyes bright, and I want nothing more than to go on kissing him.

"Kim was supposed to be my assistant at the book con this weekend, but I don't think she can make it, after all." Sure enough, another text appears letting me know they had to reschedule a back-to-school picnic. "I'm sure Evie wouldn't mind filling in, but she's signing this weekend, too, and there's no way I can go it alone."

"Take me."

I eye him. "You've got better things to do with your weekend. And no offense—" I slide off the desk and press a quick kiss to his lips "—time management is not your forte."

"Why does that matter?"

"Because one of the things my assistant does is keep me on schedule." I put the lid on a plastic bin full of books. "I'm on two panels, and with the long lines, it'll be easy for me to lose track of time."

"So I'll set a timer." He starts to sit in my chair but thinks better of it, leaning against the desk instead. "I'm used to running full shifts at work."

"Your employees have nothing on eager fans who've waited in line for hours." Meeting readers in person is my favorite non-writing aspect of my job, but it's also overwhelming and draining at times.

"Try me." He kisses me again, on my neck this time, his hand straying to my waist.

It's tempting, but he's already done so much for me this summer. "You'd be stuck inside all day," I murmur, eyes falling closed. "Pretty much your least favorite."

"Being around you is my favorite." His thumb traces the skin above my waistband, and it's hard not to melt into him.

"You won't be saying that when you're juggling Post-it notes and the map of the convention hall."

"If you can plant trees for me, I can get out of my comfort zone for you."

"Is this your attempt at fish-out-of-water?"

He shakes his head, stubble grazing my cheek. "I never needed an excuse to be near you." His blue eyes connect with mine. "But I'm guessing none of this at the booth?" He smirks, but his eyes are serious.

That breaks through the haze. I want to keep things between us a little longer, but I feel bad asking him to pretend again. "Let's get through this weekend, and I'll finish my draft, then once it's turned in, we can tell everyone that . . ." At a loss, I look to him. How will we frame it?

"That we're not just friends anymore," he says, like it's that simple. And maybe, hopefully, it is.

"We're out of sticky notes." Gavin squats down next to where I'm seated at the signing table so I can hear him in the crowded convention hall. The two-day event kicked off this morning and will wrap up on Saturday evening, but I checked in to the hotel last night to get settled in. Gavin had to open the garden center this morning then took the rest of the day off to help.

He dressed up for the occasion in a button-down shirt and gray chinos paired with low-top Chucks. With his glossy hair freshly trimmed, and the sleeves he's rolled up to his elbows not doing a thing to disguise his muscles, he looks more than cover-model worthy.

But I need to focus on the issue at hand, not ogle my former friend. We pass out sticky notes for readers to write their names on while they're waiting in line, and the last thing I want to do is misspell someone's name.

"There are more in the clear storage bin," I say through a smile, cheeks stiff after a couple hours of this, then finish my signature and slide the book back toward a beaming reader. So far, I've been able to deflect questions about the next book, and I hold out hope that today will go off without a hitch.

"I checked there, and there aren't any. Not in the crates, either," he adds.

I'm sure there are, because I checked everything off on my laminated packing list. But I'm too distracted to tell him where to look.

"Meghan with an *h*," the woman in front of me says, lifting her badge with her pronouns and first name in front of me. But it's too late, I've already written *Megan*. "Don't worry about it," she says, waving me off, but I'm not about to let her cart around a book personalized with the wrong spelling.

"Gavin, can you pass me another copy of *Rosette*?" This is the last one we had on the table.

"Uh, and that would be where?" He's glancing around, hands in his pockets, as if the book will appear out of thin air. My assistant would know exactly where to look, my sister, too, because she would've taken notes when I explained everything in painstaking detail. Gavin had just tapped his temple and told me he'd remember.

Except now he doesn't, and since he's the one who brought in most of the supplies while I set up, neither do I. "Um, in whatever box the rest of the series is in."

"It's fine," the woman repeats, with a nervous glance at the winding line.

"No, really, I insist." I swivel on my folding chair, the metal digging into my seat bones after two hours of signing, and see Gavin digging in a bin of what's clearly just bookmarks and stickers. "Never mind." The words come out terse, and I paste on a smile. "I'll find it."

I start rummaging through the storage bins. Gavin stacked them in orderly rows, but the problem is, it looks like he put the books on the bottom. "Why'd you arrange them this way?" I mutter, hoping only he can hear me with all the ambient noise in the convention center.

"Heaviest things go on the bottom. That's Warehousing 101."

"Except we're not in a warehouse." I lift off the top box, and he goes to grab the second, our arms bumping. But this time it feels less like chemistry and more like we're out of sync.

"Maybe a neighboring table has some sticky notes. Do you mind asking?" I make sure to keep my tone level. None of this is his fault, and he's doing me a huge favor.

"No problem." He bends in and drops his voice. "You're doing great. Everyone's here for you, and they don't mind a wait." With that, he's hurrying off, and I feel my shoulders relax. We're still us, Gavin and Mia. We have each other's backs, and he believes in me, even when I'm stressed and cranky.

With a deep breath, I open the next bin, and to my relief, it's the right one. I redo the inscription for Meghan, adding a personal note and a few extra pieces of swag.

When Gavin returns fifteen minutes later, his hair is mussed and his badge is askew, but he brandishes the sticky notes overhead like a victorious hero. "Mission accomplished," he says above the din, and the whole line of people clap, with more than a few appreciative glances thrown his way.

"That's some real romance-hero stuff," the woman in front of me jokes, and I nod, hoping my smile doesn't look as smitten as the warm feeling in my chest.

"They're just friends, Emma." Another woman steps up next to her, and I recognize her in an instant. Gavin's boss. This must be a member of the book club she was talking about.

"Just friends, huh?" the first woman says. "Now I see why you saved Victor and Sydney's book for last." She gives me a knowing look, but Faye nudges her.

"Hush, you," Faye says.

My hands grow cold. I open the book and swipe my Sharpie in quick strokes, then thank her and pass back the book.

"Sorry." She casts a glance at the line behind her and drops her voice. "I probably shouldn't have gone there. Too many romance novels, I guess."

"No such thing," I answer on autopilot, but the words come out as a rough croak. I hate the reminder of how close our story is to the one I can't envision a happy ending for.

I glance toward Gavin, worried about his reaction, but he's caught up in conversation with Faye and a man I'm assuming is her husband. After a brief conversation, they head off and he leans across the table and passes me a water bottle. "How am I doing, boss?"

"I told you not to call me that."

"Ma'am?" he jokes, and a titter of laughs comes from the line. "Ms. Brady?"

I roll my eyes, and take a sip of the water, then slide the next book toward me. He goes back to the line, joking with people as he passes out Post-it notes and digs extra pens out of his back pocket. His pants are snug, and my eyes snag on his round butt for a moment before dragging back to the task at hand. It's the kind of appreciative look I've avoided for so long that even a split second of lingering feels illicit.

My pulse ratchets up, thinking of the quick kiss we shared in the hallway, too short but enough to have my skin tingling at the memory even now.

The line at my booth is thinning, and I notice other authors in knots, talking or stretching. When Gavin's done passing out notes, I ask, "Time check?"

His face falls when he looks at his smartwatch. "Oh shit. It's three thirty."

"Two thirty, you mean?" I look around frantically for my phone, as if confirming the time myself will make things better.

He shakes his head, looking miserable.

"I've got to go." I shove back from the table, rattling the mugs filled with branded pens.

"But I've been waiting half an hour," someone says.

"Sorry, I'm late for a panel." Half an hour late, to be precise. And it's across the convention center, which adds another five minutes.

"Do you mind giving everyone swag?" I ask Gavin, shoving my arms into the sleeves of my blazer. "You can offer signed bookplates if they can't make it back later."

"Signed bookplates?" Gavin's face is the picture of confusion, and I realize he might not even know what a bookplate is, let alone where I store them.

Not his fault, not his fault, I repeat to myself, teeth gritted. After all, if he asked me to find mulch at his store, I wouldn't even know if I was looking for piles of it or bags, let alone what variety.

I bite my lip, torn between fixing the situation here and rushing to my panel, but Gavin's face transforms into determination, and he puts a hand on my shoulder. "Don't worry, I've got this handled."

I don't need to ask him if he's sure, because I'm sure of him. Even if he forgot to remind me of the time or memorize where all my swag is. He's here to support me, like he always has, and no matter how late I am for a work event, knowing he's on my side makes everything okay.

Everything is not okay. My bladder is fit to burst, courtesy of the water I've been chugging all day to keep from losing my voice and the coffee I drank to make up for lack of sleep. Sitting down, it had been fine, but now I'm really wishing I had stopped to use the bathroom. Thanks to a wrong turn and an out-of-service escalator, it's been ten minutes by the time I hurry in through the backstage entrance, sweaty and disheveled, momentarily blinded by the stage lighting, and take the last remaining open seat on the panel.

In the center of the row. With a full water glass, taunting my near-to-bursting bladder.

It seems odd that this is the only seat left. I expected to slide into the last seat at the end of the row, as unobtrusive as possible for someone at the front of a packed auditorium. But events since the success of the TV adaptation have been wild. I attribute the placement of my chair to the upcoming season premiere.

There's a lull in conversation as I slide into the chair, and I lean toward the microphone. "Sorry, lost track of time," I say, which is true, but also sounds like this wasn't a priority, which it really was. The problem is, so was engaging with readers at the table. I want to do everything to the highest level and lately feel like I'm falling behind.

"But I'm so glad to see everyone!" I give a wave, discreetly crossing my legs.

All the other authors on the panel are staring at me, and that's when I realize I don't recognize any of them. I was supposed to be speaking alongside a couple of my friends and two debut authors who I haven't met but am familiar with on social media.

I turn in my seat to check the projector behind us and have a jump scare. An eerie cemetery scene is displayed in lurid tones. Overlaid is the cover of *New York Times* bestselling author Marshall Anthony's latest book, and standing beneath it with a laser pointer is the renowned author himself, whose vacated seat I'm guessing I just took.

I lift the mic in front of me and say, "Somehow I don't think y'all are here for the panel on Euphemisms and the Rise of Chili Pepper Ratings."

This garners a few titters from the audience, but this clearly isn't my crowd. "My mistake. Happy sleuthing!" I stand and give a small bow, letting out a squeak when the motion exerts even more pressure on my aggrieved bladder. I all but run from the auditorium in a haze of embarrassment and collide with Gavin right outside the door.

"I was coming to get you," he says, catching me with both hands on my arms. "They switched rooms for your panel."

"Yeah, well, it's a little late." I huff out the words, uncomfortable and cranky. "I just crashed Marshall Anthony's panel."

"Marshall who?" Gavin still isn't a big reader and mostly sticks to recommendations from me, so I'm not surprised he doesn't recognize the name.

"He's been writing bestsellers since before we were born, and I just waltzed in and took his seat."

"Like, wrestled him out of it?" A corner of his mouth twitches, but at my glare, he wisely sobers up.

"He wasn't in it, obviously. He was presenting and I created a commotion in the middle of it."

"So what? It was a mistake."

"I don't make mistakes." I realize how that sounds and try again. "I don't make mistakes at events." I plan ahead and memorize the schedule and familiarize myself with fellow panelists' work. I prepare, but this time, I was too busy wallowing in writer's block and then too wrapped up in the glow of things with Gavin to get ready.

"You missed one panel." He rubs his hands up and down my arms soothingly, but his casual dismissal is getting on my nerves.

"This is my career we're talking about, not just a job."

"What's that supposed to mean?"

"That you wouldn't understand. You say all the time that the garden center is just where you work, not your whole life."

"That doesn't mean it doesn't matter." He lets go, crossing his arms. "You think I'd turn down working for my family for just any job? Hill and Dale is my second home. But you're right, it isn't my whole identity, because I recognize that I need a life outside of it. Balance."

"You think I don't have balance?"

His brows pinch together. "You were considering dating again just because you were blocked. That's pretty extreme. I know you're a creative person, and your life is always going to be wrapped up in your work, but at the end of the day, you're more than what you produce."

He's not saying anything I don't know, but it's the last thing I need to hear right now. I thought I'd been doing a good job of maintaining balance considering that I'm behind on the biggest book of my career and my least complicated relationship has transformed into the messiest one.

I tug at my lanyard, feeling like today is spiraling out of control. "At this moment, today, work is all I need to focus on. I shouldn't have pulled you into this."

His nostrils flare, and he opens his mouth, then shuts it, like he's decided against a retort. "How are you going to get everything packed up by yourself?"

"I'll figure something out."

"Mia—"

"We promised not to make things complicated. To do that I need some separation between work and . . ."

"Us?" He nods once. "Got it."

He doesn't get it, though. He thinks it's him I'm mad at, but it's myself, for breaking my rule. For letting myself start to fall for him, knowing it could ruin everything. But I let him walk away, watching him thread his way through the crowd until he's gone and I'm left wondering if this is how I lose him.

Evie ends up helping me close down the booth, and I go back to my empty hotel suite and tell myself writing a new chapter is a better use of my time than worrying over what's happening with me and Gavin, even though nothing feels like the right choice. I finally crawl into bed in time to get a few hours of sleep and make it through a morning of signing before exhaustion and emotional overwhelm catches up with me and I call Kim. She shows up forty minutes later, armed with a whipped-cream-bedecked latte and dressed in a shirt with a photo of stern Mr. Darcy.

"My hero," I tell both her and the shirt, and take a hefty gulp of the caffeinated sugar. "Thank you for rescuing me from my poor life choices."

Obviously pleased at this show of humble sisterly gratitude, she says, "This is a walk in the park compared to yesterday.

Dealing with anxious freshman parents out in the summer heat? We are not hosting a picnic next year. The gym might be old but at least it has A/C."

She's already organizing the books and pens I've jumbled in my attempts to keep up. "You've got an hour until your next panel. Go find some food."

"I'll eat afterward."

"Your eyes are glazed. You need to step away for a second." She stops what she's doing to give me a hug. "Don't think I'll let you off without the full details of why I'm filling in for the man you adopted kittens with."

"We're not keeping them."

The look she gives tells me that's not the point. "Go eat, I've got this covered."

When I come back with a falafel pita and a jumbo order of fries, she's flipping through one of my older books. "I don't know how you do it. Writing my thesis just about killed me."

"Says the woman in charge of two thousand adolescents."

"Not yet." She blows out a breath. "But I've got to admit, I'm nervous."

"You're going to be the best assistant principal that high school has ever seen." I hold out the fries and she takes one. "I'd be scared to step out of line with you in charge."

She takes another fry, then steals my napkin. "You've always been scared to step out of line," she says. "Which is why I still can't believe you hatched this wild scheme with Gavin." She grabs for another fry but I hold them out of reach. No way she's getting more fries after that rundown. "Are you two done pretending you need tropes in order to get cozy?"

My lips twist at the aptness of her words. "The tropes were a way for me to get out of my head, not get with Gavin."

"I almost believe you," she says. "But the delivery could use a little work."

"I'm not going to discuss this when we're about to be swarmed by readers."

"How about I guess, and you tell me if I'm right?" Without waiting for my reply, she says, "You decided to act out only-one-bed, except no one slept on the floor."

I merely blink.

"A nod or shake of the head will suffice."

"Not when you're being nosy."

She snags a fry while my guard is down. "You decided to do it once, just to get it out of your systems, but fell madly in love."

"Why do all of these tropes involve sex? Do you really think we'd need games to get into bed with each other?" Not the right answer, though by the way her eyes simultaneously light up and narrow, in a villainous glow, I realize it's exactly the tell she was hoping for.

She grabs my wrist, tugging me into the corner of the booth, as if that will put us in a bubble of silence, even though I can see the next stall over through the gap in the fabric. "Are you and Gavin hooking up?"

I balk at hearing her describe it that way. "It's not like that."

"Like what?"

"Like a random fling." I knew this interrogation was coming and planned to downplay everything. Chalk it up to proximity and stress. But it's not. It's real and deep and already I'm worrying about how it will end.

Her arms are around me in a flash. "Oh, Mia, I know. I just got excited because you two are perfect for each other and I've been waiting, keeping my mouth shut for—"

"Don't do that, either." I pull away. "Don't get all over-excited. We're very much in the figuring-out stage. We had a big argument yesterday, and that almost never happens."

"About what?" She finally drops her voice to a whisper, though there's really no need. The hall is loud enough that readers and I have basically been shouting to each other across the table to be heard.

"It's a long story, but he might be leaving to take over for his dad, and I think the stress of everything got overwhelming in the moment. But instead of pulling us together like it usually does, it pushed us apart. What if that's because we're—" I lower my voice to a whisper "—together?"

Kim grins. "You make it sound like a bad word. What if the issue isn't how your relationship has changed, but that you refuse to acknowledge it? If you were committed to dating, wouldn't that be one less stress?"

"Maybe, but it would also take away the possibility for us to treat this like it never happened."

"Mia, come on. That was never a real possibility."

She's right, and my stomach churns at the thought. Like it or not, Gavin and I have crossed the point of no return.

"And in the end," she says, "you two are grown adults. What's the worst that could happen, you break up?"

"Yes, and then I lose one of my best friends."

"Or you acknowledge this wasn't the right move and go back to the way things were. You don't have to pretend it never happened if you can move past it."

Maybe that's the escape hatch I've been looking for. My chance to stop overthinking things. If this doesn't work out, there's no reason we have to lose each other. Friendship is still an option. But for that to work, I'll need to keep my heart in check.

The rest of the con passes with only the slightest of hitches—a question on the panel about how long it took me to finish writing this book, to which I replied honestly, "I haven't." But I was able to join in the laughter that followed because the end is finally in sight.

I don't have time to check my phone until Kim and I finish dinner with some author friends of mine and I'm in an Uber back to the hotel after saying goodbye to my sister outside the restaurant. My heart falls when I see I've missed several texts and a call.

Gavin: I'm sorry about yesterday.

Gavin: Can we talk?

A voicemail notification pops up, and I tap it, heart fluttering with nerves.

"Hey, Mia. I feel like this might be the first time I've left one of these in forever. Are we still on for couples therapy? Because I think we might need it." A chuckle. *"Seriously, though. I hate fighting, and I understand that you're under a lot of pressure. I didn't mean to make light of it. That's it, I guess. See you tomorrow, I hope. And, Mia, I really am sorry."*

I call him back, but it goes to voicemail—not surprising since it's almost 11:00 p.m. I text him back: Me too. Stressed and shouldn't have snapped at you. Can't wait for tomorrow. My thumb hovers over the heart emoji that I've used a million times with him but feels like a declaration now. A declaration I'd rather make face-to-face than over text.

I was scared to admit it, but friendship doesn't feel right anymore. People always say therapy is a safe space. I think that's exactly what I need. A safe place to show Gavin that I'm willing to take a chance on love.

twenty-seven

Gavin

I'm waiting alone for the relationship workshop to start on Sunday afternoon, trying not to feel like I stand out as the only single person among couples who all seem to know each other from previous sessions. The convention wrapped up last night and Mia promised she'd be here, but my stomach is in knots. We're both under a lot of stress, and instead of letting me support her, she pushed me away for the first time ever. I can't help but feel it's because we're in a weird in-between place. Not quite friends, not quite dating.

This couples retreat feels like the final hurdle to clear. Get through this and then we can tell our friends and family about our relationship when the time is right. Except I don't know if we're being real about our relationship or faking friendship today. Mia is coming here straight from the convention, and didn't answer when I called her back after seeing her missed call from last night, so I figured she was busy packing and checking out of the hotel.

The excursion is at a park near the river, and most of the people are gathered under one of the picnic shelters, snacking and chatting, but I'm too nervous to eat. The email Sera forwarded said we're supposed to "Dress to Get Wet," and when I see the pile of inflatable tubes, I'm glad I wore my swimsuit instead of shorts. Hovering near the edge of the group, I finally catch sight of Mia. Her face breaks into a huge grin when we lock eyes, and something in my chest shifts and settles into place.

She's dressed in a belly-baring tank top and windbreaker shorts. The light colors pop against her glowing skin, and when she throws her arms around me in a tight hug, I have to tamp down the reflex to press my lips to hers. But she surprises me by rising on tiptoes and kissing me.

"I'm so sorry, Gavin," she says when she pulls away. "I let stupid stuff crowd out what matters and—" She tenses, lets go, and stares.

The move is so abrupt that I follow her line of sight and— No way. Her sister and Ted are making their way over from the parking lot. Kim says something to him and angles off toward the park building marked *Restrooms*. "Did you know they'd be here?"

"Kim never mentioned it," Mia says under her breath, stepping behind me like I'll be able to hide her. She peeks out and whispers, "But why would she? Not like she thought it would be something I'd want to sign up for."

"We didn't sign up," I whisper out of the side of my mouth, keeping my focus ahead. "Sera and Joe set us up. We don't have to go through with it." How are we supposed to act? I have a feeling she might've told her sister about the trope tests, but does Kim know what's really going on between us? Before I can ask, Ted's voice rings out.

"Gavin?" My eyes pinch shut. Freaking Ted.

With a deep breath, I open my eyes again, ready to ask what Mia wants to do, but she's gone. Headed over toward her sister. Ted pulls me in for a handshake-hug. "Dude, you're the last person I expected to see here. I didn't realize you even had a girlfriend."

I have no idea what to say. The moment he sees Mia, he's going to draw conclusions, and I doubt this is how she wants her family to find out about us. Then again, maybe this is the perfect way to break the news. Instead of an awkward conversation, they'll see us together and guess the truth.

I need to talk to her alone, but it's too late. Ted's already caught sight of her. "Hey, isn't that Mia? What are the chances . . ." He turns back toward me, awareness dawning in his expression. "Hang on. You and Mia?" He jostles me good-naturedly. "No shit, man. How long has this been a thing?"

I look toward her, willing her to give me a sign of how she wants me to play this, but she's absorbed in conversation with her sister, their heads bent together, telling her . . . What? That we're here for book research? "Um," I say, stalling. "It's not what you think."

"You two came to this thing as friends?" He's squinting at me like that's suspicious, because it is. But it's what we agreed to back at Joe and Sera's place. Just friends. Book research. The final trope test. *Relationship-in-trouble*. Except the relationship *is* the trouble.

"Friends of ours gifted the experience. Mia came to research a plot idea."

"Seriously? And you're her what, guinea pig?"

I flinch at the word. "I'm here to support her. She couldn't very well come alone."

"Guess you're right," he says. "But isn't that a little weird? I know you two are close, but there are lines." He raises his brows as if expecting me to agree with him.

Ted is the last person to talk about crossing a line, and apparently he gets the picture from my stare, because he steps back, hands up. "Whatever works for you guys. It will be cool to have some friendly faces. Kim and I have been wanting to do something like this, but we tried couples therapy once and it was intimidating. Thought it might be easier to talk through our feelings in a fun setting."

That's exactly what Mia wanted to avoid. What could be

worse than a public discussion of our relationship with her sister and brother-in-law listening in?

A man with a clipboard approaches us. "Have you checked in?" he asks, dividing a look between us.

"Not yet," Ted says. "I'm here with my wife." He waves Kim over, and Mia follows, looking apprehensive. "Ted and Kim Wallace. This is our first time."

The man scans the list. "Ah, here you are." He makes a notation. "And you are?"

"Mia Brady and Gavin Lane." She glances at me nervously. "We weren't originally signed up. I think my friend called to change the booking, but if that's a problem, we can go."

He waves a hand. "Of course it's not a problem. I spoke with Serafina last week. Today is definitely an activity to avoid during pregnancy, but it's a fun one. Grab a water from the cooler while I check everyone else in," he says. "Gonna be a scorcher today."

No kidding. Mia and I are in the hot seat, with no time to get our story straight.

We've been making small talk with the other couples for the past ten minutes, and there's been no polite moment to pull Mia away. Finally, I decide to just go for it. "Could you excuse us," I say, breaking into her conversation with a woman showing pictures of her kids on her phone. "I need to talk to my . . . uh . . . Mia for a minute."

The woman sizes me up, not bothering to hide the fact she thinks there's clearly a reason why an inconsiderate guy like me should be here, but I couldn't care less at this point. Mia and I need to be on the same page so I know how to play this.

"Sorry." Mia makes an apologetic grimace. "We'll be right back." Once we're out of earshot, she says, "Thank you for that. Listen—"

The man we checked in with claps his hands, cutting short

whatever she was about to say. "Gather round, couples, and—"
he looks at us with an indulgent smile "—friends."

Mia and I share a look. Clearly Sera filled him in on our
situation. Or what she assumed to be our situation. My heart
drops. If only Mia hadn't wanted to hide things, we wouldn't
be in this mess. "My name is Chip, and I'll be facilitating today. Let's start with introductions. Keep it simple. Your names,
where you met, and if you feel comfortable, how long you've
been together and your current relationship status."

Given how today is going, it's no surprise he turns to us first.
"Why don't you two lead us off."

"Uh, hi. I'm Gavin." I pause, waiting to follow Mia's cues.

"And I'm Mia," she adds. "We met in college."

There's a beat of silence, like everyone is waiting for us to
elaborate. When we don't, an older woman near us puts a hand
on her heart. "College sweethearts. How darling. I didn't know
your generation was still doing that."

"Actually," I say, out of habit, "we weren't together in college. Just friends."

"Sure." She grins at her husband, who smiles knowingly back.

"No, seriously." I open my mouth to say more, but Mia takes
my hand, squeezing it, and I'm so distracted by the unexpected
touch that I stop.

"We've been friends forever." She's still holding my hand,
our fingers intertwined. "Dating is new." Her smile is sweet and
encouraging, but wobbly. I don't know how to interpret it. Are
we going to be honest or play this up? Maybe that's how she's
spinning this. Her sister knows about the trope tests; Mia must
want to play this off as just another trope we're acting out.

Across from us, Ted bends to whisper in his wife's ear, and
Kim shakes her head. Is she telling him it's a game? I can't decide which is worse, Ted thinking he's in on a secret of ours, or
putting on a show for Mia's family and reducing our relationship to pretend.

But the last time Mia dated a friend, he let her down, and I'm not going to be that guy. I'm here for her, ready to follow her lead, and trust we can sort the rest out later.

A man to the side of me mutters, "Couples therapy for a brand-new relationship? Bold."

"Actually, that brings up a good point," Chip says. "This is not couples therapy, nor am I a licensed therapist." A murmur goes through the crowd and a few confused glances are exchanged. "As stated clearly on our website and promotional materials, our organization merely aims to foster bonds between people in relationships. We facilitate healthy strategies for conflict resolution, but we do not aim to provide solutions to relationship issues, nor do we make any claim to provide counseling. We simply provide a way for couples to deepen their relationship."

He beams, but a few of the couples are whispering, and he clears his throat. "Now that the disclaimer is out of the way, let's finish with introductions so we can jump into the fun part."

As the pair to the right of us introduces themselves, I bend and whisper, "Seems sketchy, but good news for us. No one's going to poke holes in our relationship timeline." I'm doing my best to keep things light, but I want her to tell me this isn't fake. That we're past pretending, and we can be ourselves.

But she just lets out a quiet laugh. "I'm not so sure. Chip has 'awkward moments' written all over him."

I glance at the guy nodding intensely at another couple's first-meeting story. "We can bail."

"I'm not a quitter," she whispers back.

"But your sister is here. That doesn't bother you?" I search her face, looking for any clue.

"She knows." Mia squeezes my hand in reassurance. Does she mean that Kim knows about the trope tests like I suspected, or did she tell her sister about how our relationship has changed? "And I'm not worried about Ted. But if you don't want to go through with it, I get it."

Startled to have the tables turned, I shake my head. "I told you, I'm in this, for as long as you want to keep going."

Mia rises on her toes, lips brushing my cheek, and I have no doubt that's real.

"Though now that you mention it, I can think of better ways to spend the afternoon." I bob my brows suggestively and she grins, bumping my hip.

"Shh, you're going to make me miss the directions."

"Which would be the worst thing."

She turns to me, eyes narrowed but sparkling. "You're a bad influence."

"Yet you've stuck around."

"You're going to get us called out."

"By him?" I gesture toward the mild-mannered man currently demonstrating how to don a life vest with all the enthusiasm of a flight attendant. "Pretty sure that's against therapist code."

"He's not a therapist, remember?"

Technically that should make me feel better, since my relationship with Mia won't be under the scrutiny of a professional. But as I turn back toward the river, eyeing the flotilla of inflatable rafts, a quiver of unease shoots through me.

Therapy session or not, something tells me our relationship is about to be put to the test.

"Remember, there are no winners here," Chip says.

"Then by default, we're all losers," remarks the man next to me, and from the look on Mia's face, bobbing up and down on an inflatable tube, she probably agrees. We're gearing up for what was described as a Truth Relay, and I can't imagine a more terrifying game in our situation.

Chip directed one half of every couple to remain on shore, and the other to wade out to one of the floating rafts tethered in a line between two anchor points. With each honest answer, we're allowed to take a step into the water toward our partner.

If we refuse a question, we go backward. Each couple who completes the challenge receives a voucher for a sunset dinner cruise on Lake Michigan.

I may not be as competitive as Mia, but I can't think of a more romantic date to celebrate being done with faking it. I crack my neck, ready to win. We're going to ace this. We're friends first, and that gives us an edge over everyone here.

Chip calls out the first question. "What's your partner's favorite film genre?"

Easy. "Anything with romance," I answer.

Chip looks to Mia, and she nods enthusiastically. "Go ahead and take a step into the water," he says.

"Question," Ted says, kneeling on the next raft in the row. "How do we know people aren't cheating? They could just go along with whatever answer their partner gives."

Mia sends him an are-you-kidding-me look, but it's her sister, standing by me on shore, who says, "When has Mia chosen anything other than a rom-com for movie night?"

"Hey, I'm not *that* predictable," she says, even though Kim's defending us.

"It's an honor system," Chip says, jumping in. "Remember, the object is to have fun and learn more about your partner. There are no winners or losers because communication is the ultimate win."

Ted looks like he buys that about as much as Mia does. Good. That will make beating their team even more fun.

Chip asks Ted and Kim the same question, and she gets it right by answering, "Documentaries."

"Don't get used to it," Mia taunts her sister, and the woman floating next to her laughs.

Chip sighs like he's already exhausted from dealing with us. Maybe he'll decide to call it early.

The next question is whether our partner would choose to live on a tropical island or snowcapped mountain, and then he asks what's one topic the other person could give a one-hour lecture on with no advance warning.

"The importance of romance novels," Kim calls out before I can.

Mia playfully splashes her, though the water doesn't make it where we're standing, knee-deep. "Thanks for the free point," she says, grinning.

Even though a few people argued over the answers, everyone seems to be having a good time. Chip flips to the next card, and a look of grim determination overtakes his face. Uh-oh.

"Now that we've had fun with the surface-level questions, time to dive a little deeper." He grins at his own pun, and I fight back a groan. I'm getting flashbacks to corny counselors at summer camp and phony trust exercises.

"This round is for both the people on shore and on the rafts. What's your partner's preferred form of conflict resolution?"

One of the women on the shore says, "Can we go back to the softball questions, Chip?"

He chuckles. "Just think back to the last time you two fought. How did you resolve it?"

I can hear the other teams around us murmuring, and one of the other women points at her partner. "Don't you dare say sex, honey," she says, earning a chuckle from everyone.

Wanting to get it over with before all the easy answers are taken, I say, "Talking it out," at the same time as Mia says, "Avoidance."

Ouch. Okay, I know she's playing to win, but there's no need to be so honest. But no one seems to notice, each team calling out answers in a rush to not be the ones on the spot.

When everyone has answered, Chip directs us to all take a step forward. "See? No pressure. No judgment. Today is all about discovery." He flips the card. "Next question is for the people out on the rafts. Answer honestly and your partner gets to advance another step."

"Are these life jackets really necessary?" one of the men standing in the river asks. "The water is barely waist-deep where they're floating."

"Safety first," Chip says. "And speaking of, I'd like you to tell your partner what you need most to feel secure in your relationship."

Mia pulls a face, and I wonder whether she's ever considered the question. I haven't. The others give their answers, which I miss because I'm so focused on hearing her response. What will she say? When the last of the group has given their answer, she seems to sense everyone waiting on her.

"Uh, I dunno." She scratches at her neck, nose wrinkled. "A crystal ball, I guess?" Whatever I was expecting, it wasn't that.

Chip crosses his arms, and even though he says he's not a therapist, I can easily picture him leaning back in a chair, fingers steepled. "Care to elaborate?"

"No." The word is as flat as the calm water, but then Mia cuts her eyes toward Ted, who's watching her. Seeming to take that as a challenge, she rolls her shoulders back. "I'm not sure anything short of knowing the future would make me feel secure in a relationship."

The woman who called us college sweethearts clicks her tongue in sympathy. Meanwhile, my stomach is in knots. What she wants is impossible. There are no guarantees on love.

"Everyone, take two steps toward your partner as a reward for that great show of honesty," Chip calls, and I do, sloshing toward Mia even though her words have widened the distance between us.

"If you could change one thing about your relationship with your partner, what would it be?"

I can't help but mutter, "Really?"

Next to me, Kim shakes her head. "Chip didn't come to play."

"No losers my ass," the man on my left says. "If I answer this honestly, Lisa will have me sleeping on the couch for a week."

"Maybe I'll sit this one out, too. Strength in numbers," I tell him, but our voices must carry over the water because Mia shakes her head, rocking the inner tube.

"Don't you dare duck out on this one, Gavin. I'm not being worst winner."

"Admitting your feelings is the biggest win," Chip says.

"I'll go first," the older woman says, raising her hand. "I wish Glen would stop telling me to be quiet when the game's on. It's our living room, not a library."

"The neighbors complain, Velma. It's common courtesy."

"They're just mad because they're sticks-in-the-mud." Without waiting for Chip's prompting, she takes a big step forward and I fight back a smile, all the while wracking my brain for something equally innocuous.

I don't like how Mia always waits to see what I order before choosing her own, but then complains if mine is better, as if there's a rule that says we can't order the same thing. It drives me nuts how she complains about watching any show without a plot. But I wouldn't change anything about her, not really, because those things are part of her.

Finally, wanting to get things over with, I decide to keep things light. "What I'd change about our relationship is nothing, because we're just starting out."

"Your friendship, then," Chip says. "Anything you'd change about that?"

"Chip's taking no prisoners," I hear someone say, and that's exactly how I feel—trapped.

The day is warm, but I'm starting to get cold. The current tugs at my ankles and despite all my forward progress, I haven't reached Mia. "Well, we've been friends for close to ten years, so I'd say we're doing a pretty good job of it."

"Sixteen years together," says a guy out on the raft to his husband, "but I'd still change how we resolve conflicts. I take too long to see his perspective." His thoughtful answer stands out in stark contrast to flippant ones. Honest and self-aware.

Suddenly I'm tired of walking this tightrope, keeping my feelings in check. "Fine, I'd change how Mia spends too much time looking for the worst-case scenario. It takes all the fun out of the moment."

Judging by the way Ted's eyes widen, it's not the right choice.

"It's called planning ahead," Mia says. "Being prepared."

"Or hedging your bets. You're not willing to commit because you're worried things won't end well."

"Says the man who hasn't decided whether he'll be changing careers and leaving the state."

Her jab hits its mark. "I'm not doing this right now, Mia," I say, gesturing around us at the other couples, who are hanging on our every word.

"Do you two need a moment?" Chip asks, and she shakes her head.

"No, sorry." She attempts a smile, and I instantly regret getting defensive. "I didn't mean to make things weird."

"You're good, sis," Kim calls out, darting an irritated glance my way. Even Ted is glaring at me.

"Well, it was a little weird," one of the guys says. "But it also makes us look better, so . . ." He trails off, earning a few chuckles, but most people seem tense. Mia and I just brought down the vibe in a major way, and all I want is to turn around and head out, but I'm not going to leave her stranded out there.

The inflatable tubes are only a few feet away, close enough that I can see Mia shivering, droplets of water highlighting her goose bumps. I want to make my way over and fix things. But this will never work out if she's holding herself back. I'd give her the world if I could, but I don't have a crystal ball. I know she believes people can fall in love. I'm just starting to wonder if she believes they can stay there.

twenty-eight

Mia

I'm shivering and cold, inside and out, and it's probably even worse for Gavin, standing in waist-deep river water.

He hasn't met my eyes since he called me out, in front of my sister and brother-in-law, of all people. This is the opposite of how I wanted things to go. I thought this would be the perfect time for a grand gesture. Confess my feelings for Gavin in front of a crowd to show him I've let go of my reservations and I'm not afraid of letting the whole world—in this case, a medium-sized group of strangers—know how I feel about him.

Except the moment I saw Ted, I remembered that in real life, declarations of love don't always go as planned. If I confess my feelings, Gavin might tell me he doesn't feel the same. Seeing Ted reminded me of that nauseating feeling of rejection. The kind of rejection that would feel infinitely worse from someone I actually love.

Ted's on a tube next to me, and all I can think about is how much simpler things would've been if we'd never dated. No awkwardness wedged between me and Kim in those early days of their relationship. But I didn't ever love him, and there's no comparison of how I felt when he broke up with me to the feelings surging in my chest at watching things go awry with Gavin. Though I tried to hold back, I know in my bones I've already passed the point of no return with him.

"Last question," Chip says. He's gotten on my nerves since we arrived. Too cheerful. Too blasé about his lack of qualifications. "Either teammate may respond, and once you do so, those standing in the water may join their partner on the tube."

If it weren't for my competitive streak, I would've already jumped off the raft and sloshed my way over to shore. But there's still time to be brave. I write love declarations for a living, after all, and I'm damn good at my job.

Chip checks the set of cards in his hand. "Where do you see yourselves, in relation to one another, one year from now?"

You've got to be kidding me. It feels like he's singling us out after my answer earlier. My answer should be: *Together.* Whether I believe it will come true or not is irrelevant; what matters is that I want to be with Gavin.

But before I can respond, he locks eyes with me and says, "Who knows? I don't have a crystal ball handy."

My heart plummets. He's my teammate, my friend, the man I'm falling in love with, and he's throwing my insecurities back in my face?

Not looking at me, he splashes toward my raft and hops up next to me with a casual show of athleticism to complete the challenge, but I can't fake my way through these emotions any longer. I slide off the tube into the river, sinking into silty mud up to my ankles.

It's humiliating to run away, but tears are already blurring my vision, and I need to get out of here. I move as quickly through the water as possible, which is pretty much sloth pace with the mud tugging at my feet and the current pulling me sideways. I make it to shore and speed up, hurrying toward the parking lot and privacy.

Chip calls out, "Wait, the life vest." I whirl around and he shrugs. "It's company property."

Teeth gritted, I grind the words out. "I'm not stealing the vest, Chip." I walk around the embankment to the mesh bag that stowed the life jackets. With trembling fingers, I unbuckle the top strap.

The sound of sandy gravel crunching lets me know I've been followed. Gavin jogs around the corner, slowing when he catches sight of me. Seaweed clings to his wet shins, his swim trunks bunched and dripping. His hair is windblown, cheeks reddened from the sun. He's a mess. A gorgeous, wonderful, frustrating mess.

"I told you this was a bad idea," he says.

"Maybe this—" I gesture between us "—was the bad idea." It doesn't feel that way, not really. But I'm still reeling from him calling out my insecurities in front of everyone.

He shakes his head. "The problem is you've been doing this halfway. Not being real in front of the people closest to us in case it doesn't work out. Keeping our relationship a secret gave you a reason to hold back."

All I was doing was trying to protect my heart. "Maybe the timing isn't right," I say, unwilling to admit he's right. "I'm working on what could be the biggest book of my career, and you might be moving—"

"All of which we can get through together, like we always have."

"As friends."

"But isn't this better?" He steps closer. "There's nothing holding us back now." His words knock against my greatest fear, like a wrecking ball to dominoes. Nothing held back. All my defenses gone. My heart could get broken, and he wouldn't be there to pick up the pieces.

"This isn't the way friends get a happy ending."

Eyes wide, Gavin runs his hands through his hair, scattering droplets. "That's why you've been blocked, isn't it? Not because you don't see chemistry between Sydney and Victor. But because you don't believe they can have a happy-ever-after."

"They're not us. You know that. My characters are never real people."

"But they're friends. And that's the problem."

I have no choice but to nod. "Yeah. But it's a 'me problem,' not an 'us problem.'"

"Except we're an *us* now, Mia. We're not just friends, and if you truly don't believe we have a future—"

"This is ridiculous. I'm not having this fight with you."

"Then tell me you believe in us."

"There's no one I trust more in this world, Gavin. You know that. But love is different. It's out of our control."

"Actually, I disagree," he says. "I think it's a choice." He's so close I can see his eyelashes are clumped, dark with water. The crystalline droplets on his forehead and cheeks. The anguish and yearning in his deep blue eyes. "But it's a choice that two people have to make together."

I want to choose him, but I'm scared. There are too many unknowns. Fingers trembling, I yank at the straps of the life jacket. "Waste of time," I mutter in frustration.

"Considering you tipped us at least three times last time we went canoeing at the cabin, I'd say it's a good precaution." His teasing pulls me out of my head, lightens the moment in the way only he can. He undoes the buckles, each click another piece of my armor breaking down. What will happen when there's nothing left? I'm afraid love like this will tear us apart.

"What if we don't work out?" I ask quietly, eyes on his hands working the snaps loose.

"What if we do?"

For a moment, I imagine it, the image deliriously sweet. Gavin and I bumping hips in the kitchen as we fight for who gets the first cup of coffee. Gavin next to me while I'm writing on the couch. Gavin, mine.

The tug on my heart nearly yanks the breath from my lungs. The last buckle falls away, and I lift my eyes to find him staring back with intensity that's oxygen to my soul. I pull in a lungful of longing, but then another vision of the future clouds out my hope. What if we go for it and wind up pushing each other away? What if I never get to be this close to him again? What if he's never mine again, not even a little?

"I need you too much to take the risk."

"And what about me?" His gaze never leaves my face. "What if I want more, and can't settle for less?"

"Don't say that." Tears are stinging, threatening to flow. "We've had that, you can."

"I can't, sweetheart." The endearment feels like too much. Too soon. Too late. "Not anymore."

"But . . ." Feeling strangled, I yank off the wretched life vest. "You promised." There was never any going back. I knew that, and yet I let myself believe. "This isn't us. We're losing each other."

"Only because you're too scared to grab ahold of more." He takes my hands. "I'm right here, asking you to give us a chance. Telling you I want you. But I'm done pretending, and right now, that's all our friendship would be."

"You'll change your mind," I say, gripping his hands tight. "You'll see friendship is better. Safer."

"I don't want safe. I want you."

"I want you, too, but not like this. Not tangled up with risk and ruin."

"Ruin? We're building something, Mia. Not tearing it down. Tell me you don't feel the same." He bends, pressing his forehead to mine.

Dropping his hands, I grip his shoulders, rising to kiss him. The warmth of his mouth against my chilled lips consumes my senses. I could get lost in his strength, his steadiness. The way his breaths turn shaky, like his walls are crumbling, too, and he's letting them fall. Letting me in.

He knows exactly what I need in this moment, but what about tomorrow? Life is a long series of changes, but he's been there all along, every moment, steadfast in the role of friend. I'm not ready to lose that version of us.

I pull away, hand to my lips, holding in the sensation even as my heart closes the door. "It's not too late," I say, begging him to agree. "We can go back to before."

"Maybe you can." He shakes his head, water droplets falling from his honey-brown hair. "But not me."

"You'll change your mind."

"This isn't my mind talking." Frustration is in the firm set of his mouth. "For all your stacks of books on love, I don't think you've ever once followed your heart."

He turns his back on me and walks toward the river, taking a piece of me with him. Proving all this kind of love is good for is tearing people apart.

twenty-nine

Gavin

I forgot about the kittens. The moment I step through my front door, I'm swarmed by meowing balls of fur. Their mom is nowhere to be seen, probably sleeping and dreaming of carefree days before the tomcat knocked her up. I pick up the kitten closest to me, cuddling her against my chest. Pinpricks jab my shin, and I look down to see the tuxedo kitten using his tiny claws to climb up my leg.

"Chill, Juniper." I pry him off gently, his squirmy body slippery in my grasp, and hoist him to my chest, then carry both kittens to the couch and collapse. Cedar runs in from whatever mayhem he was up to and soon all three kittens are crawling around me, taking tiny, tentative steps, whiskers brushing my cheeks.

It's hard to be heartbroken while surrounded by this much cuteness, but then I catch sight of Mia's scrunchie on the arm of the couch and the reality of what I told her hits me like the slam of a door.

I've lost her. Our relationship, our friendship. Gone. All because I asked for more than she could give. The one thing I told myself I'd never do. Look where it's left me. Alone. Well, not counting the kittens who are currently ambling along the top of the couch like a tipsy trio of tightrope walkers.

Juniper pushes his dry nose against my chin, purring. "I bet you're wondering where Mia is, huh?" I promised this wouldn't happen but, in the end, I let her down. I'm no better than all the other boyfriends I've told her were no good for her.

Someone knocks, and for a second, I think maybe it's her. But when I check the Ring cam after sliding my phone out from under a curled-up kitten, I come back to reality with a thud.

"It's open," I call, and Morris comes in, a six-pack from the local brewery in hand.

"Dear lord in heaven, what am I seeing right now?" he asks, setting the bottles down. "Blink twice if you're in danger."

"Shut up." I lay a calming hand on Ash's gray head as Mama Cat slinks into the room. She's still nervous, but starting to follow the little ones' lead and explore. "You're just jealous."

"I am, actually." He sits down on the coffee table and reaches out a tentative hand toward Ash, who sniffs it, then sneezes. Morris pulls back his hand with a grimace. "Did they get all their shots?"

"They're fully vaccinated, no thanks to you."

"I told you," he says. "I'm not cut out for pet ownership."

"We'll see." The kittens have to go somewhere. They're cute now, but my one-bedroom house is not about to become a four-pet household.

"Are you gonna keep guilting me about getting you to take these cats? Because I can take this beer and go drink in my garage while I watch the Giants."

"That's your team?"

"Why would they not be?"

"You're from Reno."

He blinks at me.

"Yeah, okay, that tracks." I let my head fall back. "Why are you here?"

"Because you missed trivia night."

"Shoot. I forgot all about it."

"No shit. Wouldn't have mattered except Riley stood me up since that guy she's been texting finally asked her out."

"What about Carlos?" He's actually good at trivia, and I think he gets tired of playing with scrubs.

"Once he saw it was just me, he jumped ship. Apparently, he didn't trust me to answer anything since I, quote, 'just show up to heckle people.'"

"Do you not?"

"I sure as hell do," he says. "But I can't very well heckle teammates who aren't there."

"So you decided to bother me at home instead?"

He fetches pint glasses from the kitchen. "I came to check in on you and find out what's really going on with Mia." Elbowing the cabinet shut, he says, "First she sleeps over, now you're skipping trivia night. I was expecting to find you here with her, but instead I found—" he makes a vague gesture at me and the kittens "—whatever the hell this is."

Wallowing, but I'm not about to admit it. Instead, I frown at him, which is hard, given the purring kitten on my shoulder.

"Don't get me wrong, she put on a good show." He passes me a beer. "But if I suck at trivia, your weakness is lying."

"Not being able to lie isn't a weakness."

"It is if you're a spy." Can't argue with that. "Or y'know, a dude who wants to keep a secret."

I don't, though. I would shout it from the rooftops if Mia wanted to be with me. Would it suck to hear Scott's *I told you so*? Not at all, if it meant having her. "She's the one who wanted to keep it a secret. She wasn't ready. Won't ever be ready, I don't think."

Morris takes a swig of his beer. "Did she tell you that or did you tell her that?" He wipes his mouth with the back of his hand. "And don't give me that actions-are-louder-than-words bullshit."

"She told me we should go back to being friends." Even though I laid it out there as matter-of-factly as possible, he flinches.

"Well, damn."

I take a big gulp and swallow it down, wishing for something stronger. "Yep."

We drink our way through the six-pack with the buzz of the game in the background. Morris might be a pain sometimes, but he does know when to keep his mouth shut, and tonight, I'm grateful for it.

Mia would normally be the one showing up at my doorstep after a breakup. I think of all the times she told me there was someone better out there for me, not knowing I was hoping that someone was her. That hope is gone now, and even though I knew we couldn't go on the way we were, I wish I could take it back. Come up with another answer. But my last thought before falling asleep is that I don't know how to not love her.

My head is killing me. It's the next evening, and the pounding headache I woke up with hasn't left. Likely a combination of not bothering to hydrate after being in the sun all day, a few beers last night, and no sleep. My heart is aching, too, but I'd rather not dwell on that.

I sneeze. Possibly catching a cold from the river water, too.

Joe frowns at me. "You sure you're up for shortstop?"

I'm not up for anything, but I need the distraction. Figures that today would be the one time they don't put me in the outfield. "Just a little tired."

"From the couples retreat?"

"Mmm-hmm," I answer.

"I get it," he says. "Between the physical challenge and the emotional work, it takes it out of you."

"Yep."

With one last sidelong look, he jogs over to his position at second base.

Between my headache and thoughts of Mia, I miss an easy ground ball and drop a catch that would've stopped a run. I'm getting glares from Joe, and it's one thing to let myself down, but he vouched for me. Then again, he also threw us to the wolves in the form of not-a-therapist Chip. I'm so caught up in my thoughts that I nearly miss tagging a guy trying to steal second.

By the time the inning's done, I wish I'd stayed home, and from the looks of my teammates, so do they. Back in the dugout, I ignore their scowls and take a pull from my water bottle, fingers hooked in the chain-link fence.

Next to me, Joe does the same. "I take it things didn't go well at the retreat?"

"You could've warned me our relationship would be under a microscope."

"That's kind of the point," he says: "Examine things. Find what's working, and what's not."

"The whole thing, turns out."

"Your friendship with Mia is rock-solid."

I drop my water bottle in my bag and turn, sagging against the fence. "Yeah, well, we didn't go in as friends."

He pulls off his sunglasses, brown eyes full of concern. "You were in a fight?"

"We were . . ." I hesitate, because whatever I tell him, Sera will find out, one way or the other. He's no good at keeping secrets, and this isn't something I'd ask him to keep from his wife. But Mia worked so hard to keep it from them so we wouldn't make things awkward. Too late for that. "We were together. We hadn't put a label on things, but I did what you said. I told her I wanted more than friendship, but in the end, that was more than she could give."

"All this went down at the couples retreat?"

"Afterward. Chip's methods sort of pushed us over the edge." I fill him in on what's been happening between Mia and me, ending with the nightmare of the floating raft exercise.

By the time I'm done, he's shaking his head. "I'm sorry, man. We just meant to give you a nudge."

More like a punch in the gut. "You and Sera really liked the program?"

He glances out toward the field. Our team is next at bat, but the others are chatting, too, and no one's made a move to start the inning. "Chip's methods are unconventional, but we learned a lot about each other. This was more of a trial run, though. After the baby comes, we plan to sign up for some actual therapy because the transition can be a strain on the marriage."

Despite my mood, I smile at him. "Look at you, all grown. You're going to make an awesome dad." I expect Joe to grin, but he looks down.

"I don't know. I gave you terrible advice. Isn't that half of what being a father is?"

Shit. "I didn't mean to make it sound like your fault. You gave me a push, but I was the one who wanted more. You were right—we weren't going to be best friends forever."

"Maybe you would've, though. You lasted this long." He leans against the fence next to me, looking as defeated as I feel. "I only encouraged you to speak up because I really thought she'd feel the same. I catch her looking at you sometimes and . . ."

"That's what gets me. She feels something for me, I know she does." The way she kisses me . . . "But she was scared I'd break her heart, and guess what?" I throw up my hands. "I did."

"She broke yours, too," he says. "Don't go shouldering all the blame."

My heart *is* broken, but it's not Mia's fault that she doesn't trust love. Her doubts are hurting her, too. But hearing it wasn't all me helps ease some of the guilt. "See that?" I nudge him. "Coming back in with the dad wisdom."

He shakes me off, but he's smiling. It makes me feel a little better. I don't want things to change between me and him and Sera. Wishful thinking, probably.

"Joe, you're on deck," one of our teammates calls, and he lifts a hand in acknowledgment.

"I know things are rough right now," he says, looking over his shoulder to where the first batter has already struck out. "But please don't let this be the thing that pushes you to move. Even on your worst day, we don't have a hope of winning without you." He grins, and I do my best to smile back.

A few months ago, I would've told him there was no way I'd ever go back to the farm. But as hard as it would be to leave behind all my friends, maybe a fresh start is exactly what I need.

thirty

Mia

It's easy to think I'd never act like one of my flawed main characters, but I had the chance to be brave and instead I let my fears topple our friendship. Even though being together was new, it was enough to show me that things would never be the same. I can shout at the top of my lungs that it was just a failed experiment, that we should be able to slip right back into friendship, but we both know that's a lie.

There's no saving face or laughing it off or predicting it will be a funny story one day to tell at each other's weddings during a toast. I gave Gavin my heart with every kiss and every touch and now there's no going back. It's everything I feared, and the worst part is, I knew this would happen. He said he'd never let me go, no matter what, and then he did.

When I get home, I see a string of we-need-to-talk texts from Kim but none from Gavin. I would normally be dying to debrief with him about Chip's Machiavellian methods. Laugh over the sketchy verbal disclaimer and the ridiculousness of it all. The ache of missing him is raw. I told myself I did what had to be done to save our friendship, but a friend wouldn't have asked Gavin to shut off his heart. A friend would've never gone down this road in the first place.

I text my sister and let her know I made it home okay. She won't settle for that, but I don't have the energy to explain. Instead, I pull out my laptop and try to escape into writing. But this time it's not writer's block that stops me, it's a broken heart. I can't power through, and for once I don't try. I put on my coziest pajamas and open one of my comfort reads, barely absorbing the words on the page until sleep claims me. All day on Monday, I wrestle with a sense of dread as I make another attempt, but by nightfall I'm still spinning my wheels and I decide I've given enough to this project. I close the document, open my email, and tell my editor what I should've months ago. I can't write a book I don't believe in, and it's time to stop trying.

Of course, it's not that easy. The next morning my inbox is filled with a frenzy of emails from my agent, my editor, and my publicist. By midafternoon I've spent hours on the phone, and still I've come to the conclusion that this is the only way. Maybe someone else can get the story right, but I can't.

I should stay off social media, but I get tagged in another video, this one making the case that Sydney and Victor are better off as friends. Normally I'd get the urge to like it out of solidarity with the poster, but today it makes me mad. They deserve all of each other, not less. Gavin deserves all my love, but I'm too scared to give it.

I feel like a failure for passing the responsibility on to someone else, leaving a mess for the show's writers to clean up, but I gave it my all and came up short. A few times, I composed a text to Evie, telling her what I've done. But if I send it, she'll encourage me to go back to the bulletin board and my scene cards. Find a way through. But I've lost my best friend and the last thing I want to do is write my way out. Right now I need someone who will tell me this defeat doesn't define me, even though right now I feel swallowed whole.

Mia: I did a thing.

Sera: You turned in the book early??? Go, Mia!

Mia: The opposite. I told them I can't do it.

Nothing, for two full minutes. Then:

Sera: Can you be here in an hour? I'll send Joe to get us food.

I knew she'd come through. Tomorrow I'll get back to working on the problem—I'll need to make the switch from grappling with Sydney and Victor's future to figuring out my own—but today I need distance from the mess I've made.

Shutting my phone off, I shower, then head out. The drive takes longer than usual because of an accident, so I arrive about half an hour later than expected, but Sera let me know I should let myself in when I arrive because they're setting up the nursery. I find her sitting in the rocking chair surrounded by open boxes and a half-built crib.

"Holy crap." I stop short at the sight of the mess, at odds with the rest of their immaculate house. "Please tell me you haven't been doing this by yourself."

She shakes her head. "Joe started this morning. Then he got stuck and called Gavin."

Hearing his name sends a reflexive jolt of happiness through me before I remember that we're not friends anymore. Might not be friends again, ever. "Gavin's here?" I ask, though he's obviously not. Pretty impossible to hide a six-foot guy in a small room whose only furniture is occupied or in pieces. "Does he know I'm coming?"

With an odd look, she says, "They're on their third trip to Home Depot. Didn't expect it to take this long."

I'm barely listening, mind spinning. "I can't be here right now."

Sera stops rocking. "What's wrong?"

"Gavin and I sort of . . ." How do I tell her we broke up when she's in the dark about what was going on between us? "We were together. And now we're not."

She puts both hands on her cheeks. "Shock, surprise, astonishment, et cetera."

I narrow my eyes at her sarcastic pantomime, and she drops the act. "You knew and let me come over anyway?"

"He played softball with Joe yesterday," she says. "Don't be mad. Neither of those men can keep a secret. It's why I didn't tell Joe the gender of the baby."

Her casual announcement totally distracts me from being upset that Gavin confessed the truth of our relationship, which was probably her plan. "You found out?"

She puts a hand on her belly. "No way I was waiting nine months when we've waited years. But Joe wouldn't be able to keep it to himself. He'd tell all our friends and family, and I don't want them to force names on us or be obnoxious. So I'm keeping it to myself."

I'm impressed by her willpower. "How can you keep a secret that big?"

"Why don't you tell me?" she says. "You've been keeping a pretty big secret of your own."

The hurt in her eyes fills me with guilt. "It was really new. And we—" I swallow against a sudden lump in my throat. "I was worried it would change the dynamic. And then there's the book. There was so much riding on getting it right. Not just for my own career, but the actors', screenwriters', crew's." As I say it, I realize how selfish it sounds. "I wanted to protect what was happening between us by keeping it separate, and telling you and Joe would've opened everything up."

She sighs. "Well, I have a confession of my own. Joe and I have thought for a long time that Gavin might have feelings for you." At my startled expression, she laughs. "Hon, that man has been wrapped around your finger since I've known him. We thought we'd grow old waiting for him to make a move."

"Gavin knows better than anyone how I feel about dating friends."

"Which is why Joe and I intervened. We saw you two being all cutesy at the party and it looked like you finally might be ready for a nudge."

"The couples retreat." Gavin was right about the matchmaking.

She rocks back, smiling. But then her face falls. "Except we didn't know you were already together. It was meant to get you to admit your feelings, not talk yourselves out of them," she says, shaking her head like we're hopeless.

The rumble of the garage opening fills the quiet house, and I look toward the door in horror. "They're back."

"Maybe this is good. When you texted, I thought this could be the perfect opportunity to get you two in the same room together," she says. "Don't you want another chance to talk through things?"

"Trying to talk things out is what got us into this mess in the first place," I hiss. "That and your meddling."

"If you would've told us in the first place, we wouldn't have had to meddle," she says, green eyes sparking with indignation.

"I didn't want to make things awkward for everyone." I raise my brows at the sound of car doors slamming. "Seems like that was the right choice."

"Was it?" she whispers back. "Because holding back with someone you've been close to your whole adult life seems like the mistake to me."

I glower at her, but there's no time for a reply because the guys' voices get louder along with scuffling and grunts. Curiosity gets the better of me, and I poke my head out the door. Gavin is backing into the hallway, struggling to maneuver a long box through the entrance. At the sight of his muscles bunched underneath his tee, triceps bulging, my stomach gives a pleasant twist, before my brain catches up to the fact that things are over between us.

I duck back into the room before he sees me. "What am I supposed to do?"

Sera crosses her arms, but between her perch in the rocker and her baby bump, she hardly looks intimidating. "Have a conversation?"

"About how I told my editor I can't finish the book because I'm an emotional wreck?" It makes me feel so vulnerable. "I might've just tanked my career, and I can't even talk to him about it. He told me no matter what happened, he'd be my friend." My voice hitches at the word. "He lied."

Sera's face melts into sympathy. "Oh, honey, I didn't realize."

A loud thud vibrates the wall, and Joe shouts, "Careful!"

Eyes darting between me and the doorway, Sera says, "Hide." At my blank look, she makes shooing motions. "In the closet, hurry."

It's stuffed with unopened boxes, and I wedge myself between them, half in and half out. There's no way the folding door will close. A thought hits me. "My car," I whisper to Sera. "They must know I'm here."

But it's too late to come out. Joe and Gavin have reached the nursery. He glances over and when our eyes meet, his face lights up in a grin. I smile in response, but then the weirdest thing happens. His whole face shutters, like blinds pulled over a window, and that's when I remember everything's changed. This isn't another of Mia and Gavin's escapades. There's just me, hiding from the person I care most about. It's not silly, it's sad.

He looks away, pivoting to maneuver the rectangular box into an open spot near the wall, and I realize I'll probably never get to see that unguarded smile again.

"It was on sale," Joe says, before Sera can ask. "A dresser."

"We have a dresser."

"But this one is solid oak. The other one is particleboard."

Sera is giving him what can only be described as a wifely look. "I thought you went for a wrench."

He palms the back of his head. "We may have forgotten that."

"Are you kidding me?" They start arguing, and I take the chance to slither out of the closet, but that leaves Gavin and me with nothing to do but stand in awkward silence.

After a moment, he says, "I didn't realize you'd be here."

"Same. I wouldn't have come—"

"It's fine." He heaves an audible sigh. "When I said I didn't want to be friends, I didn't mean we'd have to avoid each other forever."

"What's the alternative?"

He shrugs. A quick, jerky motion, like he's uncomfortable. "Coexist, I guess."

"Right. Simple."

"You do just fine with Ted."

I turn toward him, scowling. "Are you kidding me?"

He shrugs again, not meeting my eyes. "You seem to think I'm just like him."

"Sorry that you don't know what it's like to be related to an ex," I say, temper rising.

"Stop using what happened with him as an excuse when we both know the truth is you're never going to trust anyone enough to fall in love because life isn't one of your carefully scripted romance novels."

There's an audible gasp, and we both turn to find Joe and Sera gaping at us. Joe's mouth is open, and Sera's brows are nearly touching her hairline. This is the first time they've heard us fight. One of the few times we've fought, period. It feels all wrong.

Goose bumps break out on my skin, but inside I'm burn-
ing up, and I wonder distantly if I'm about to faint. But since
this isn't one of my precious books, as Gavin pointed out, no
well-timed swoon overtakes me. "I have the right to protect my
heart," I tell him, unable to let it go.

"And I have the right not to go along with a charade," he
says. "I can't shut off my feelings and go back to being friends
just because it's easier for you."

"Then you never should've kissed me in the first place."

"You're right. I shouldn't have." He crosses to the door, and
a moment later, his truck engine rumbles to life, punctuating
the absolute silence in the nursery.

I can't bear to look at my friends. "I didn't mean to bring
our mess here. Stress can't be good for the baby."

Sera waves a hand. "Please. I binged an entire season of *The
Real Housewives* the other day. But, Mia," she says, and licks
her lips, "you do realize that's the first time I've seen you two
fight."

"We argue." Never so intensely. I've always felt that I could
be honest around him, and bottling things up has me feeling
like a simmering pot.

"Maybe." She looks doubtful. "But not like that. It's like we
weren't even here."

My shame grows. I've managed to mess up so much today. "I'm sorry. I never would've come if I knew he was here."
Where would I have gone, though? To Kim's, maybe. But the
thought of not being able to see two of my closest friends when
I'm hurting because I might run into Gavin . . .

"You're not understanding," she says. "Whatever is going on
with you two, it doesn't look like it's over."

Joe nods, still looking stunned. "Believe me when I say, that
man has feelings for you."

"Serious ones," Sera adds.

"He thinks he does, but it's all just a product of circumstance." I tell them about the trope tests. No point in holding back now that all hell's broken loose.

When I finish, they share the kind of look that seems to be reserved for married couples. "So you're saying his feelings aren't real?" Sera asks. "Just the result of a bunch of romantic situations you put yourselves in?"

"Like sitting around in your home office, visiting a run-down escape room, and doing yard work?" Joe says.

"Superromantic," Sera adds.

I let out a frustrated huff. "You weren't there, okay? It wasn't about where we were or what we were doing, it was about—"

"Who you were with?" He punctuates his words with a romance hero–worthy smirk. "Admit it. You could've done those things with a hundred other men and never once caught feelings."

Sera jumps in to back him up. "You've gone on how many dates to fancy restaurants, and concerts . . . Didn't one of your boyfriends rent out a wing of the art museum for your birthday?"

"It was his friend's gallery, but yeah."

"And in all of those romantic settings, did you ever once fall in love?" She knows the answer. "Where are those men? All I see is you, standing there, claiming you think you feel something for Gavin because of a few of the least romantic scenarios I've ever heard of."

I open my mouth. Close it. Unable to argue that point, I try another tack. "Let's say you're right, and our feelings have nothing to do with the experiments. It doesn't change the fact that friendship is a guarantee. Love is the gamble."

"You've never lost a friend?" she asks. "What about Martha?"

"We can't count Martha." An old coworker of mine. "She was an outlier."

"She was a toxic, jealous human. But she was also your friend for three years. And now she's not."

"But what about Stewart? We would still be friends if we hadn't dated," I say, remembering how terrible it felt to lose one of my first friends in the publishing world.

"No you wouldn't, because he was a possessive, presumptuous weirdo," she says. "All relationships are gambles. Are romantic relationships more risky since there's a deeper level of emotion and entanglement involved? Maybe. Or maybe for people who are deeply compatible, interested in a lifetime of love, they're just as likely to last forever as a friendship."

With a glance at his wife, Joe says, "True love, real love, won't turn your life upside down. It will make your life make sense."

Isn't that what I was thinking about Gavin's potential move? That if we were together, things would fall into place?

But I have evidence to the contrary. "I've tried dating friends. One of them is now my brother-in-law."

"Ted wasn't the guy for you," Sera says. "But his and your sister's marriage is going strong all these years later. Think of it this way." She settles her hands on her small belly, fingers laced. "You can't be the main character in every story. Just your own."

I think back to the night I met Gavin, moments after Ted told me he was in love with my sister. It was the end of our brief romance. But for Ted and Kim, that night was the moment he started to fight for his happy-ever-after—finally getting up the courage to tell me he was in love with her.

Maybe I shouldn't be looking at that night as the end of my story with Ted, but the start of mine and Gavin's. Not a sad ending, but a meet-cute. The beginning of our love story. What if that breakup wasn't a lesson in how to guard my heart, but how to open it up to the right person?

thirty-one

Gavin

The long-overdue drive out to the tree farm gives me too much time to think. I replay the argument with Mia at Joe and Sera's. Is this how it's going to be between us? Bitter and tense?

I promised I wouldn't do this to us, but what was always enough feels like crumbs after what we shared. I can't put my feelings back in the box, and what's awful is I don't even want to. Loving her hurts, but it also feels like freedom after denying my feelings for so long. Like I can finally think clearly because I'm not wasting energy lying to myself.

The front yard is full of people, but my nephews spot me before anyone else does and I treat them each to a spin on the tire swing, grateful for the chance to get my bearings. The hostas circling the base of the tree look healthy, their variegated leaves full and glossy, a fresh coat of mulch around them.

I'm surprised Dad found the time. Then again, maybe it was Scott. My brother walks up, two plates in hand. "See you've found the boys," he says. "Who were supposed to be eating." He fixes them with a look.

"No one else is yet," Paxton says.

"That's because all that's done are hot dogs." He holds up the full plates. "Which you love."

"You'd better listen to your dad." I take hold of the tire to slow it. "I'll push you on the swing afterward."

After a few more protests, they clamber down, taking the plates of baked beans and hot dogs from Scott, who calls after them, "Don't drop them. Two hands!" To me, he says, "Might want to wait a couple hours to make good on that swing promise. Last night they came out after dessert and Brett threw up from the spinning."

I check the ground reflexively and Scott chuckles. "Birds probably got to it."

"Parenthood has changed you, man." This is a guy who used to make me do all the worst chores, and now he's talking about puke like it's nothing.

"In more ways than one," he says. "I think spending the summer here with the boys just gets me nostalgic. I shouldn't have told you to take this on, but it hit me that with Dad retiring, they wouldn't be spending lazy days swimming at the lake or eating ice cream on the porch."

"I've thought of all those things, too." And it hasn't helped my decision one bit.

"But I owe you an apology," he says, catching my attention. "Mia, too. I was so sure she was your reason for staying. And then I caught you two, holding hands, when all along you said there was nothing going on. But I talked to Amber, and she asked why I thought I had the right to judge your reasons." He shoves his hands in his pockets, thin arms tanned under the freckles.

"She told me that whether it was Mia, or yourself, you want to stay. That's all I need to know," he says. "And she was right. I thought you should be the one to quit your job, leave your friends behind, sell your house . . . All to keep this place in the family just because you happen to like trees more than I do." He lets out a laugh that startles the group near us, and I watch him, speechless. "Seriously, how messed up is that?"

"Pretty messed up," I agree, smirking, and he narrows his eyes. There's the cranky brother I know and love. "Besides, I like more than trees. Don't get me started on shrubs, perennials—"

"Yeah, yeah. You got Dad's green thumb, we all know."

Realization dawns. "You're jealous."

"How could I not be? You two were always so close. But Dad and I've talked a lot recently. You should . . ." He trails off. "Sorry, no more advice."

"Talk to him? I'm going to." Looking out past the house, I take in the rows of saplings and spruce trees. "But I get what you were saying earlier, about not wanting to say goodbye to this place for good," I admit. "That's part of why I've put off coming out here. There's so much good here, and I knew if I came back, I'd do the same as you. Start thinking of our wheelbarrow races and riding in the tractor instead of invoices and sales calls."

"Not the sales calls." Scott hangs his head in disgust. "Remember how Dad used to make us wear ties even though we were on the phone. Said, 'Dress professional . . .'"

"'Act professional,'" I finish, repeating the phrase Dad drilled into us during our high school years. "From a man who showed up to work every day in a flannel shirt."

"Yeah, but he wanted us to learn every part of the business."

"Worked out well for me. I have a hand in most things at Hill and Dale." I bump him with my shoulder. "Not like you, planning to work remotely in your pajamas once both kids start school."

"Hey, I'll dress halfway professionally." He flips a nonexistent collar. "Like a mullet, business up top, party on the bottom."

"What are we talking about, boys?" Amber walks up, holding a beer. Her straight black hair is pulled into a low ponytail, and she looks relaxed in jean shorts and a tank top.

"How lucky we are to have a dad who believed in being well rounded," I say, sharing a knowing look with my brother. "Speaking of, I better find him before he finds out how long I've been here without saying hello. Mom, too. Can we catch up later, Amber?"

"Absolutely. I think you owe me some news," she says, a twinkle in her dark eyes that has my gut twisting. She's talking about me and Mia, except there is no Mia and me. Not anymore.

But I promise to find her after I make the rounds, then head off in search of Dad. This would be a lot easier with Mia by my side.

Dad is busy flipping burgers and Mom isn't outside anymore, so I head in through the back door. The windows are open, a gentle breeze stirring the curtains. Passing through the hall, I find her filling a vase at the sink.

"Gavin," she says, giving me a one-armed squeeze, her rose perfume familiar and comforting. "I'm glad you came. Scott says you haven't been out much this summer. Makes me feel a little better that you haven't paid me a visit."

"There's been a lot going on." The same reason I'd given my dad for not visiting, but this time it feels true because I did want to see her. But I've avoided coming here because I didn't want to get into the truth of why I moved away. Isn't that what I did with Mia, too? Buried my feelings instead of facing the reality that I'm in love with someone who might not ever love me back?

"Does that have anything to do with why Mia's not here?" She sets the vase on the counter next to a bunch of hollyhocks laid out on a dish towel.

"I don't always bring her."

"Don't you?" Mom's ash-gray hair falls along her cheek, concealing her face, but I'd bet she's wearing the carefully innocent look she perfected during my childhood to get me to confess to my misdeeds. "Could you hand me those shears so I can get these in water? Or better yet, you do it while I make us coffee."

I pick up the pruning shears and set to snipping the stems. "Scott told you."

"He did, but I told him we'd better wait and hear it from you." She dumps out the morning's leftover coffee with a grumble. Dad doesn't mind stale coffee, but I'm with Mom on that one.

The screen door bangs open and Dad steps inside with a foil-wrapped tray, saving me from answering. "Thought I'd find you two in here," he says. I take the tray from him, and he gives me a hug, tall and lean in the flannel he wears year-round, sleeves rolled in concession to the summer heat. "Missed you, Gavin."

"You, too," I say, surprising myself. I haven't had much chance to miss him over the years. "Been too long."

"Yeah?" he asks, a smile tugging at his suntanned cheeks. "You've been busy, though." The twinkle in his blue eyes is as obvious as Mom's hints.

Guess I'll have to get it over with. "I know what Scott told you, but Mia and I aren't together."

Dad's face falls so fast it's like a cartoon. Mia would have a better way to describe it, but all I can think is how it looks like he'll have to pick his jaw up off the floor. "Well, okay," he says, blinking. "Scott must've got it wrong."

"Nope. We were, for a short time." I keep it brief, feeling like the wind has been knocked out of me. "Turns out it was a mistake."

"Better off friends?" Mom prompts.

But Dad shakes his head, watching me. "I don't think so. You're in love with her, aren't you?"

If he'd asked me any other roundabout way, I could've denied it. But it's so unexpected I answer him honestly. "Yeah." The word lingers in the quiet kitchen, conversation and laughter flowing in through the open windows. I put a flower in the vase, not knowing what to do with my hands. "She's not in love with me, though."

"How do you know?" Dad, again.

"Because I told her how I felt, and she said she wasn't ready." I keep my head down, focusing on arranging the long-stemmed flowers.

"You told her you loved her?" Mom, this time. She shoots a quelling look at Dad when he starts to answer for me.

I start to nod, then think back. Did I? "She wanted to go back to being just friends and I told her I couldn't because my feelings were bigger than that. I think that's pretty clear."

He shakes his head. "Nothing is obvious in relationships. You might think it is, but unless you've said it once, twice—" he shoots a glance at my mom "—a thousand times, you can't take for granted she heard it. And I think *I love you* is something worth saying."

"I wasn't about to toss out the word *love* like a Hail Mary," I say. "I'm not putting that on her. Not when she's made her choice already."

"A choice without all the facts." Dad removes the foil from the pan of burgers and breaks off a bite, offering it to me.

I take it; maybe it will settle the nerves this conversation has stirred up. "As much as I love you two giving me relationship advice, I didn't come here to talk about that." Another unspoken look passes between my parents that I can't quite interpret, so I keep going. "You know I love it here, Dad. But after Scott left and the . . ."

I glance at Mom, feeling guilty, but she says, "Our divorce?"

I nod. "After that, I felt stuck in the middle. Not by you," I tell my mom quietly, wondering if I ever should've brought this up. "But, Dad, I know you needed help here. And I was happy to give it, but sometimes it felt . . . heavy." Queasy with nerves, I lean against the counter.

But Dad doesn't look hurt or upset. He rubs a hand over

his graying hair, a gesture I recognize as my own. "I put a lot of weight on your shoulders," he says. "Trust me, I know. I should've realized sooner, especially with you not wanting to work with me. But I always thought it was rebellion or something." He looks at me and grins. "Ridiculous, since you never even missed curfew. Scott's more rebellious than you are, and that's not saying much."

"I missed curfew once." I smile, the tightness in my chest easing a notch.

"To drive your friend home when he got a flat," my dad says, shaking his head. "The point is, I looked to you for the cause of it, when I should've been looking at myself. I spent so long thinking about what I'd lost when your mom left that I didn't look at what I had."

I dart a look at my mother, but she's listening with a small smile on her face, and my dad continues. "I leaned on you for support, but I never appreciated you. Not as a son, or a friend." He shoves his sleeves up. "Didn't realize until I got a few friends of my own who talked some sense into me that things between us had been one-sided for a long time. I expected you to come out here for visits and never once stopped by your place. I knew next to nothing about what you did for fun, or the life you've made in Illinois. I'd stopped asking questions, and when you stopped coming around, instead of reaching out, I got bitter."

"That's when he got the smoker," my mom chimes in.

He laughs, a hoarse chuckle. "That's when I started smoking meat, yeah. Sounds silly, but it was a hobby. And I started looking for tips, found an online group for people new to it. Turns out several of them live close by."

I feel like maybe I should warn him about the dangers of sharing personal information with strangers online, but he's moved on. "I made friends, is what I'm saying. Do you know how long it had been since I had friends?" He points at me. "Don't answer that."

I grin. "So you don't need me anymore?" I hadn't been wrong. He'd stopped relying on me, just like I wanted, but it makes me feel hollow somehow.

He shakes his head. "You're my son. I'll always need you in my life. But I don't want you to feel like you need to hold me up. I'm not that old yet," he says, and grins. "What I want to do is get to know you."

"That's why you're moving to Colorado?" The sarcastic reply has me feeling like a snippy teenager and I half expect Dad to call me out on it, but while Mom gives me a sharp look, he just shakes his head.

"I'm moving out there for now, but I'm not sure where I'll end up. I'm retiring because I realized there's a lot I haven't had time to do. One of those things is visit you. Haven't even seen your house yet. And you and Scott are always going to baseball games. That sounds fun. I haven't made it to a game since your high school days."

"Fun?" I can't believe this. "You're retiring because you want to have fun?"

"Why else?"

"I dunno. Duty, I thought. He said you wanted to be near the grandkids."

"You think I spend time with Pax and Brett because I have to?" His brow wrinkles like he can't believe what he's hearing. "I happen to like my grandchildren, son. And Scott. And you," he adds. "I've just done a measly job of showing it."

"Not always," I tell him. He's been a great dad in so many ways, and I don't want him selling himself short. "I have so many great memories here. With both of you." I smile at them. "But I've made my own home. That's the real reason why I don't want to move back and run the business. I love the life I've built, and I don't want to leave it behind." My throat gets tight. Mia used to be a part of that life. Am I really willing to give her up just because she'll never love me back?

"Good," my dad says, catching me off guard. He grins at Mom. "Because we're counting on the money from the sale of this place to retire."

"We?" I turn to her. She teaches college classes as well as her role in managing the company. "You're retiring, too?"

But she shakes her head. "Not from teaching, but I won't miss having to split my time."

This is a lot to process, and I realize in avoiding discussing my feelings, I've missed out on a lot of their lives, too. A thought strikes me. "Not moving to Denver, are you?"

A pause. "What?" She laughs. "No. But, honey, I know you say you're happy, and that there's no future for you and Mia, but I can't help but think of how she's been a constant presence in your life. Has that really changed overnight?"

So much did change for us this summer, and while for me it had been a long time coming, it was something Mia had been avoiding for years. "She made up her mind and gave me an ultimatum. Friendship or nothing. I don't want nothing, but I've tried for years to pretend I'm not in love with her, and I'm not sure I can anymore, or that I even want to."

The coffeepot beeps, and Mom pours some for herself. "Then don't give up without giving it your all. Take your father's advice. Tell her you love her. It's the one thing left unspoken between you two."

It is, isn't it? We talk about what makes us happy and gets us mad, about our families and our dreams and what's disappointed us. But in all of that, I never said three words that could change everything. Will it make a difference? I don't know. But I have to try.

I can't let Mia go without telling her I'm in love with her. Try to show her one last time that we're not losing anything being together. We have everything to gain.

thirty-two

Mia

I wander out to breakfast the next morning after spending the night tossing and turning in Joe and Sera's guest room and open my laptop. Wincing at the flood of emails, I take a bracing sip of coffee, and one catches my eye. Adjusting my glasses, I lean forward, squinting at the screen.

"Oh my gosh." I grab Sera's arm as she sits down with a plate of toast covered in peanut butter and honey. "Jayla and Rob want to meet on a video chat." We're going to see each other at the season three premiere in just over a week. But apparently this can't wait. Did they already get notified I'm not writing the book? A whole new terrifying possibility opens up: They're exiting the show and I'm about to get blamed for it.

Sera takes a bite of toast. "Who?"

"Jayla Lewis and Robert Cho." I enunciate the actors' names slowly. "They want to talk to me about the book."

Understanding lights her eyes, and she drops the toast onto the plate with a clatter. "Mia, this might be the best day of my life."

"Hearing me get chewed out by A-list actors?"

"They might guilt you, but they're so nice—" She cuts off when I glare. "Sorry, but this is a big moment for me. Movie stars are about to get a glimpse of my house." Pushing back from the table, she yells, "Joe, get the vacuum!"

Two hours later, the living room is spotless, and Sera forced me to change out of my leggings and T-shirt into one of her dresses. It's about four inches too long, but no one will see the bottom anyway. She's also had me switch seats exactly six times, trying to decide which wall will provide the best backdrop. The last time I talked with the actors on a video chat about the script, I was wearing a hoodie in my office, but one thing about Sera is she's always going to be extra.

The time comes, and I take a deep breath. The past two hours have been a distraction, but of all the people I'm worried about disappointing, they're the top two. I expect to see them calling in from two locations, but to my surprise, they're sitting on a couch together in a sunny room somewhere. Los Angeles, probably.

Out of sight of the camera, Sera is fanning herself and Joe is muttering that she needs to breathe. If I didn't know better, I'd say they were practicing for labor. I try not to let their nerves rub off on me, but it starts to sink in that this is a really big deal.

Rob waves, cheek creasing in a dimple. "Mia, hi. Tell me my agent has it wrong."

Jayla gives him a playful shove. "We were going to be understanding, remember?" She smiles at me. Her locs are swept up in an elaborate updo, her eyelids highlighted with shimmery gold eyeshadow. She looks like she just came from a photoshoot, and I take a second to be grateful Sera made me look presentable. "We received word that you're not writing the book, but we're hoping lines got crossed, because we are so excited to bring your story to life."

"Our story," Rob says, and she gives him another warning look. "What?"

Jayla turns to face me. "Listen, I know you never planned for our characters to get their own book, but it was the best news when we got word you'd write it."

"It wasn't that I didn't want them to." The earnest way they're looking at me makes me want to tell them the whole story. And honestly, what do I have to lose? "This isn't public knowledge, but Victor and Sydney were the main characters in the first book I ever tried to write, back before I got published."

Jayla's perfectly shaped brows arch in surprise. "Seriously?"

"I was in college, and I'd always had a soft spot for the friends-to-lovers trope. But then I got dumped, by a former friend."

Rob frowns in sympathy and, man, I can see why his fandom goes so hard.

Blinking to regain my composure, I say, "It soured me on the friends-to-lovers trope. And along the way, other life experiences bore that out. I decided Sydney and Victor would be happier as friends."

"Sydney maybe," he says. "But no way would Victor be okay with that."

"What do you mean?"

"Victor's been gone for Sydney since day one."

That's not how I wrote it the first time around, but it does align with what I discovered as I went back through the books, analyzing things from Victor's perspective instead of Sydney's. I can't believe Rob saw it, too.

Jayla is nodding. "Sydney is just too stuck on her idea of what love looks like to see it. But we figured that you'd be able to get them both out of their own heads. No easy feat, we know." They share another look, and that's when I realize how close they are on the couch. Almost as if they're cuddling.

"Are you two . . ." I stop myself, because I'm 90 percent certain asking celebrities if they're dating is the number one intrusive question.

But Rob bites his lip and nods. "We're together, yeah. You're actually one of the first to know, so keep it under wraps, okay?"

I don't dare look at Sera, but out of the corner of my eye, I see Joe hand her a glass of water. I could go for a glass of something stronger, though maybe that wouldn't be the best idea since I already feel dizzy from the surreal situation. "But I thought you were just friends."

"We were," Jayla says. "But I realized my feelings were deeper than friendship."

"And I told her I fell in love with her at our first table read."

She rolls her eyes indulgently. "Love at first sight is not a thing."

"Agree to disagree," he says, nestling closer, the sleeve of his somehow-expensive-looking white T-shirt bunching as he threads their hands together. "But the point is, we're excited to give Sydney and Victor the happy-ever-after they deserve. And we want you to write it."

"No offense to the show's writers," Jayla adds. "But this story is yours to tell. And from what I'm hearing, you need to do it for yourself, too."

I hesitate, expecting the usual twist of nerves, but all I feel is anticipation. Optimism. A desire to tell them *yes, I'll do it*, not because I have to, but because this is a once-in-a-lifetime chance to fix what went wrong for two characters who deserve a full dose of happiness, and I want to take it.

So I promise to give it one more try, already getting nerves from all the apologies I'll have to make, but ready to get back to the book. Jayla says she can't wait to see me at the season premiere, and after a few more minutes of surprisingly chill small talk, we end the call.

I close my laptop just to be safe and find Sera looking shell-shocked.

"Rob and Jayla are a couple. And we're the first to know."

A slow grin spreads across her face. "Once the news gets out, I'm about to become insufferable."

I laugh but I'm still trying to wrap my head around it. He liked her from day one? That strikes a chord, and I realize why. It's the pattern I've been seeing during this rewrite. Victor didn't fall in love with Sydney over the course of this book. He fell for her years ago, when they were trying to keep the peace between their friends, the rival bookstore owners.

His love continued to grow during book two, the second-chance romance between his cover-model college roommate and the one who got away. And when Sydney's editor friend was squaring off with the director of marketing at their publisher, Victor was on the sidelines wondering if she would ever see him as more than a friend. Then she came up with the idea of method acting and gave him the hope he'd been craving for years.

The solution was in front of me all along, but I couldn't get inside my characters' heads because I've been too stuck in my own. Jayla and Rob have been playing these roles for three seasons, and their insight woke me up to what I've been missing: Victor loves Sydney for who she is, not because of role-playing smoke and mirrors. He's not faking it, it's not new, and she can trust his commitment because she trusts him.

I stand up, grabbing my laptop.

"Where are you going?" Joe asks.

"To finish this book." And then, I'm going to tell Gavin he was right. Friendship alone isn't enough. Not anymore.

thirty-three

Mia

Much as I'm yearning to see Gavin, I decide to wait to talk to him until after he gets back from Wisconsin. I stand by what I told him about not wanting to affect his decision about his future. He deserves space to make his choice.

But I've already decided—whatever he chooses, I want him. I love him, and if he loves me back, we'll make it work, just like we have for nearly a decade of friendship.

Focusing on work is hard, but with just over a week to finish the book, I block out distractions the best I can. Now that I know the way forward, I lean hard on my routine, using my years of consistent writing practice to power through, writing around the clock in a creative haze that feels like clarity. Even though I haven't let myself dwell on the possibility, the truth is that I might not get a second chance with Gavin, but I can do right by Sydney and Victor. Then I plan to fight for the future I want in my own life.

Instead of shying away from my feelings, I let the emotions pour out of my characters. Until now, they haven't been honest with themselves or each other. On page, they stop holding back and freely give what I wasn't ready to. They embrace the unknown future because they know they're each other's surety.

The days pass in a haze of coffee and short sleeps and words, so many words. It's like the faucet's been left on and the sink is overflowing and instead of bothering to shut it off, I dive into the flood. When I finally come up for air, I realize almost a week has passed. I make myself eat a handful of raw veggies to supplement the random food I've been eating and text Kim and Sera so they don't drop by to check on me. Water the monstera and gardenia and then get a good night's sleep. The next day I read through the book in one sitting, and not only do I love it, I'm proud of it. I shake out my wrists, take a deep breath, and send the manuscript to my editor.

The book is finished, again, and this time it ends with them trusting in their love. There will be revisions ahead, ways to make the story better, but the heart of their journey is written, and it's good and strong and beautiful. However things work out—whether the studio takes my version or not—I've done my best. I've written a happy-ever-after worthy of Sydney and Victor, and now I need to focus on my own.

That starts with revisiting an old wound to make things right. Time for the conversation that I should've had with my sister nearly ten years ago when I found out she reciprocated Ted's feelings. I was so focused on not standing in her way that I pushed down my hurt instead of dealing with it. So here we are, facing each other over giant Italian beef sandwiches, the first hot food I've had all week.

While we waited to place our order at the counter, we stuck to small talk. I was dying to tell her about Rob and Jayla, but not here. This is my first time being in on a celebrity secret and I'm not about to risk being the one to leak it.

She gave me a big celebratory hug for turning in the manuscript, and I listened to her frustration over glitches in a new portal the school uses to communicate with parents. But now that we're seated in a red-upholstered corner booth, she's obviously done settling for anything less than a full recounting of what's going on with me.

Ignoring her food, which is never a good sign, she asks, "How are things with you and Gavin?"

"Right now, there is no me and Gavin." I take a steadying breath. "He thought we were putting on a show for you. My fault, since I'm the one who said I wanted to keep things a secret. I never got the chance to tell him that I didn't plan to act in front of you, and he had no idea what was real and what wasn't."

"Why didn't you tell him before we got started?"

I spin my fork on the table, searching for the right words. "I thought he understood that I had explained the real situation to you. And I was working up to a declaration. But seeing you and Ted reminded me of the stakes. How there was no guarantee he'd return my feelings. He could end up with someone else, and I'd have to stand by and be happy for him."

"That's how you feel? That you have to pretend to be happy for me?" Her voice falters, and my stomach twists.

"For a while, yes," I answer honestly. "It felt like having to watch you have something I'd never experience."

"Mia—"

I put up my hand. I'll hear her out, but I have to say this first so she understands. "I don't have to pretend to be supportive anymore. Not for years. But at first, I was hurt." I take a drink of the water I chose over my usual chocolate malt, not trusting myself to stomach a rich milkshake.

"I kept it to myself because I didn't want to stand in your way. But I didn't realize burying that hurt gave it the chance to sink its roots into my heart. Roots of doubt about love and trust. It made me scared to give my whole heart away." I pull off a piece of the crusty roll, crumbling it to bits between my fingertips. "That's how I made it through breakups. Even though it hurt, it was never heartbreak."

My sister's brown eyes are soft with concern, and I fear I'll hurt her by saying this is why I've held back for so long. But I have to trust she'll understand. I need her support more than ever if I'm going to make a go of things with Gavin.

"I want you to know that this isn't about you and Ted," I say. "It's about what I've internalized. And I realized recently, looking at it from your perspective, you probably had it worse. I can laugh about the irony because I was never in love with him. But you are, and knowing he dated me first, even for a little while, was probably awful."

She gasps out a choked laugh. "You have no idea."

My heart goes out to her. "I didn't, because I've never had feelings that big. But I get it now. If Gavin dated you before me, I would be so jealous. Yet you comforted me and let me know that our sisterhood was your priority."

The next part will be hard to say. Confessing aloud will make my feelings for Gavin real. Feelings that might end in heartbreak, because I can't hold anything back with him, even though I tried.

"I've never let myself consider dating Gavin because I care about him so much," I tell her. "I knew going beyond friendship could be catastrophic because I wouldn't be able to say it didn't matter when it ended. And I couldn't bear being a stepping stone to his happy-ever-after."

"Oh, Mia." Kim scoots around to my side of the booth, wrapping me in a hug. "You're no one's stepping stone." She pulls away. "Ted never should've dated you, feeling how he did, but he wasn't the only one in the wrong. If I would've told you how I felt instead of bottling it up . . ."

"Then I never would've dated him in the first place," I say, agreeing. "But you were looking out for me, too, by hiding your feelings. And believe me, I've long since gotten over it. The root is what needed weeding. I thought that I had to keep my feelings to myself so your relationship with Ted wouldn't come between us, but that wasn't giving either of us enough credit."

"I don't ever want you to hold back your feelings to spare mine. We can work through things together, but only if we're honest." She hugs me again, an awkward jumble of elbows and arms that reminds me of how she used to give me piggyback rides when we were kids. "I felt like I was on eggshells sometimes," she says. "But bringing it up felt cruel to you. And to myself, if I'm honest. I don't love thinking about you two ever being together, even though I know it was so long ago. But I played a part in it, too. I was so willing to accept your explanation that you hadn't felt anything for him, but how could you not have? You were friends. I should've tried harder to make sure you were okay."

One more tight hug, then she pulls away, expression as stern as when she used to babysit me and took the charge seriously. "I know you said you've started to untangle what you've internalized for this, but I would be heartbroken to hear you'd let this keep you from Gavin. He loves you, I'm sure of it."

I've never doubted his love, but I'm afraid I pushed it to the breaking point. "I love him, too. So much." Saying it aloud is a mix of nerves and wonder, but mostly relief. "I just hope it's not too late. How's he going to trust me after I rejected him?"

She picks up her milkshake and offers it to me like medicine. "From what you said, you were trying to protect your heart."

"But it doesn't need protecting from him."

She smiles. "Bingo."

My next stop is a visit to Evie. She's at her day job in the admin building, but I bring her an iced green tea from our favorite café and apologize for not catching her up on all the events of the past few weeks sooner.

"I've been thinking about something Gavin said during the trope tests," I tell her, when she asks how I got to this place of certainty. "How I purposely seek out guys who aren't my type. And I realized it was because I wanted to keep some of my love in reserve. I was scared to love anyone as much as I love him."

Leaning back in her desk chair, she frowns. "You've been trying to find someone you love *less* than him?"

"Not consciously, but yeah." Sounds wild to think about. How could I have not known how much more was waiting for us? "That's when I realized he's always been the one for me. I just have to be brave enough to love him with my whole heart."

"You're plenty brave," she says.

"I basically told the man I love that he should stop loving me."

"Okay, yes." She taps her highlighter against the edge of the desk. "But you finished the book. All along, you said you couldn't write it because you didn't see a way for them to stay together, but I also think you were scared of sharing a story so close to you. Which I get." She knows better than anyone the vulnerability of sending a book out into the world. "But you did it anyway. For yourself, but also to do right by people you care about. You're braver than you think. Own it."

"You're saying I should go big?" A grand gesture leaves no room for holding back.

"Do it. Make Sydney and Victor proud."

Sydney and Victor. The idealistic, hopeful parts of myself. I'm ready to start believing again.

I've written my fair share of fictional grand gestures, but in real life there are constraints like scheduled flights and press appearances, not to mention contending with the terrifying possibility that this might be the last time you see the person you're madly in love with.

Now that I've realized I'm in love with Gavin, I'm desperate to tell him in a way that matches the magnitude of my feelings. Normally I'd be spending the days before the premiere in full glam mode—hair, mani-pedi, a facial. An appointment with the stylist I treated myself to after landing on a worst-dressed list at my first Hollywood event.

But this time around my top priority isn't finding the perfect braiding hair or shade of gel polish. I'm in the stationery store, scanning the shelves. This time it's not procrastination or feeding my notebook habit. Gavin is due back from Wisconsin tomorrow, the day I fly to Los Angeles. A narrow window for a grand gesture, and I barely slept last night arranging the details.

This is the last step, and I want to get it right. A few other customers are in the shop, but no one pays me any attention as I flip through the cards.

Amari walks up in an ink-stained apron, a pen tucked behind her ear. "What are you shopping for today?"

"I need your help with a grand gesture."

Her entire face lights up with a wide smile. "You're kidding." When I shake my head, she says, "Wait, literal or figurative? Like, are we talking for a character or . . ."

"For real." I'm counting on her discretion, but I'm also willing to risk the internet finding out I put it all on the line for Gavin. "I'm in love with my best friend."

I figured this would be boring compared to a potential celeb couple, but she squeals. "Like Sydney and Victor?"

For once, I don't bristle at the comparison. "Exactly. Except in this case, there's no happy-ever-after guaranteed."

She clutches clasped hands to her chest. "Even more romantic. Whoever this is for, I hope they deserve it."

"He deserves everything, because he's given me all of himself."

Her eyes lose the starry look and her lips tug to the side. "That line could use some work. But I'm sure you'll get it together when you write it."

Nothing like being humbled by a fan. "Actually, I have," I tell her, pulling a slip of paper out of my pocket. "Could I put in a rush order for custom calligraphy? I need an invitation."

"It would be my absolute pleasure. Any chance I could get a mention in the acknowledgments of your next book?"

"You have a deal." I just hope typing her name won't be a reminder of the first time I wrote a grand gesture that failed.

thirty-four

Gavin

Nothing prepared me for the stress of trying to plan a grand gesture for a woman who wrote the book—*books*—on how to win back the person you love. Mia's characters have done everything from standard groveling to lying their way into VIP sections patrolled by grouchy bouncers, and I'll never be able to measure up to professing my love from outer space or while climbing a sheer cliff.

But her books have taught me that a grand gesture needs to be personal, envisioned with the person you love at the forefront of your mind. I force myself to stop worrying about what the heroes in the pages of her novels would do, and focus on Mia.

I've loved her for nearly a decade. Loved being quizzed by her on note cards for my college exams. Loved watching her graduate with honors and later shift careers entirely to even more success. Loved spending rainy days watching movies with her. Loved listening to her theories on why cold pizza is the devil's handiwork. Loved how she always knew the right thing to say, even if I didn't want to hear it. But it wasn't until this summer that I realized I'm deeply in love with her.

I believe we can have the kind of lasting love she writes about, the kind of love that surpasses friendship and dives head-long into passion. I can't help feeling that we've been moving toward this all along. Toward each other. At least, I hope so.

I stayed the weekend with my family, but by the time Monday rolled around, I couldn't wait any longer to get started on my plan to win Mia back. When they heard what I had in mind, Scott and Amber even left the boys with Dad and drove out to pitch in for a couple days. Funny how supportive family can be if you open up to them. But this is a big job and I practically begged my friends to help me pull this off before Mia gets back from LA. Faye told me to take as much time as I need, teasing that if Mia forgives me, she plans to ask her to name a character after her.

We're at the community lot where the cats were found, working on a project that I hope will show how much I care about her. Morris took some convincing to spend extra hours volunteering, and he looks up from where he's planting a row of rosebushes. "Dude, these will never fill out in time."

"It's the thought that counts?" I didn't mean it as a question, but everything is up in the air right now. I don't know if it matters that I already planned to do this. Can a grand gesture be the same as a gesture of friendship? All I know is I think Mia will love it. Whether it's enough to make her forgive me is another story.

"Positive thoughts, Gavin." Riley clasps me on the shoulder. "You've gotta go big when you screw up."

Joe pulls a petunia from a seedling tray. "Yep, the apology has to be equal to the screwup," he says. "Marriage has taught me that."

"Well, in that case, I've got months of groveling ahead."

"Sure do," he agrees.

"At least," Riley adds.

"You've just met and already ganging up on me?"

"Us?" Joe says. "Never."

"Little bit." Riley pinches her index finger and thumb together. "Just enough to make sure you don't chicken out."

No chance of that. The only worry is what happens when I go through with this. I jam my shovel into the dirt and turn over a fresh patch of soil. Good thing I've got a few days to get everything in order.

I raise my head, swiping my gloved hand across my brow, and do a double take at the man who's making his way toward us over the grassy field. *Ted?*

"Someone you know?" Riley sits back on her heels, shading her eyes.

What's he doing here? The only thing I can think of is an accident, something wrong with Mia or . . . I'm jogging over before I've even formed a coherent thought, fear hurrying my steps. I reach him and ask, "What's wrong?"

"Nothing." He puts a hand on my shoulder. "Everything's good. But you're a hard guy to track down. Didn't answer your phone, and I stopped by your house, called your work." I pat my pockets for my phone but come up empty. Must've left it in the truck. "They said you've been spending a lot of time here." He looks past me and gives the others a wave. "Hey."

Impatient, I tug on his shirtsleeve. "Ted. Why are you here?"

He smiles, and I get the sense he's enjoying having the upper hand. That eases my mind—he'd never play games if Mia was hurt. But it's also infuriating. "I have a message for you. Kim was supposed to bring it, but her meetings ran long, so here I am." His face goes blank. "Whoops, left it in the car. Hang on." He jogs back toward the road.

I turn toward my friends with what I'm sure is a WTF expression plastered on my face.

Riley shades her eyes, squinting in the direction he left. "He's, uh, coming back. With balloons."

I look back and sure enough, he's rushing toward us with

a bunch of confetti-filled balloons. He holds out an envelope and I take it, the paper thick and expensive-feeling. My name is written on the front with gold lettering.

Unable to contain my curiosity, I flip it over and break the wax seal, but not before noticing it's stamped with Mia's initials. My stomach turns over. She wouldn't go to all this trouble for bad news. But she might be trying to convince me to return to friendship. With shaking hands, I slide out the card stock inside and scan the embossed note.

Gavin,

Will you be my date to the season premiere?
I have a lot to tell you, starting with I'm sorry, and ending with I don't want to go through life without you. I'm not scared to tell you (actually, that's a lie, I'm terrified, but I'm doing it anyway) that you mean the most to me. I don't want to just be your friend anymore (though that's a big honor). I want to be the person you wake up to every morning, the one you tell all your secrets (even if you tell Joe right afterward).
I understand now why you can't be my friend, and I don't want to be yours, either. I want to be your girlfriend, if you'll have me.

P.S. I almost forgot the details. Enclosed is a first-class ticket to LAX, and if you want to fly out and spend the whole time in the hotel and eat room service and never see me, that's okay, too. But I really want a chance to tell the world I'm in love with my best friend, so if you're up for it, I put you on the list as my plus-one for the premiere.

I can't help but smile at how she included the logistics. Of course she'd leave nothing to chance.

Ted clears his throat, and I look up to find he's been reading over my shoulder. "There's a boarding pass in there for you," he says. "She wanted you to know it's no strings attached. You can go and just tour Hollywood if you want."

As if I'd waste my time doing that when Mia is right there. But I can't imagine her being okay with Ted delivering this message, of all people. "Does she know you're here?"

He makes a face as if to say, *Obviously*.

My heart starts beating faster. Ted's the last person Mia would want to be vulnerable in front of. Their relationship has come a long way, and she gives him way more credit than I ever would, but I know she's still holding on to the humiliation of baring her soul to him right before he chose her sister instead. If she's willing to let Ted deliver this message, balloons and all . . .

"But you said Kim was supposed to deliver this. Does she know it's you instead?"

"Of course she does." He glances over his shoulder, then looks back quickly, shoves his hands in his pockets.

I cock my head, eyes narrowed. "Ted," I say carefully. "Is Mia in the car?"

He winces, stubbled chin puckering. "Don't tell her I told you, okay?"

I'm already running when he calls out, "You'd better be saying yes!"

I reach the car and bend down to peer through the open passenger window. Mia's seat is fully reclined to stay out of sight, and I have a flashback to her drowsing next to me the morning we volunteered together. Today she's in sweatpants and an oversize T-shirt that reads COFFEE FIRST, LAST, AND ALWAYS. That's the Mia I know and love.

Her eyes meet mine and she scrambles upright, fighting against the seat belt. "What are you doing here?"

I lean my arms on the window, relishing the sight of her, disheveled and gorgeous. "Accepting your invitation."

"Did Ted tell you I was in here?"

"Nah. I guessed." Ted deserves a break.

"He insisted on the balloons."

"That tracks," I say, and smile. Shifting onto one elbow, I squint over my shoulder at the others, who are watching us with zero shame. They've closed the gate on the project, and I need at least another few days to finish it, but I'm tired of waiting for the right moment. "This was supposed to be a surprise, but do you have a few minutes to spare before your flight?"

Mia lights up, eyes bright at the prospect of a surprise. "Technically I have three hours. You know how I feel about getting to the airport early."

I laugh and pull open the door. The moment she steps out, I wrap her in a tight hug. "I'm sorry. I went back on my word. I said we could be friends, and—"

She pulls away, just enough to look at me. "I can't. Or maybe I could, with a lot of practice. But I don't want to. I want all of you, and I want to give you all of myself. No more holding back."

Her eyes search mine, glowing and warm. Hopeful, not that frightened look from the last time we spoke. "What I'm trying to say is that I'm in love with you. I didn't plan to tell you until we were in LA, if you came, that is," she says. "And you don't have to say it back—"

"Oh, but I want to." I'm bursting with the need to tell her how I feel. "I'm in love with you, Mia. Romantically, physically, emotionally, wholeheartedly. I love every part of you." I kiss her then, and her hand grasps my shirt, keeping me close.

When we break apart, she says, "That was a really great line."

"I wrote it down." My arms are still around her. I can't bring myself to let go. "It took so many tries, even though it was only a couple of sentences. How you do that for hundreds of pages, book after book, I'll never understand. I think I'm better with showing than telling."

Taking her hand, I lead her toward the garden, heart in my throat, pulse pounding in the spot where our palms meet.

thirty-five

Mia

Gavin's hand is in mine, rough with dirt from working in the soil, warm from the sun, and I never want to let go.

He's leading me toward a tall chain-link construction fence lined with black fabric that wasn't here before. We're at the other vacant lot the crew was cleaning up, the one with the shed where Morris found the kittens. But the shed is gone, or at least not visible, since the fence makes it impossible to see what's inside most of the lot.

I don't understand why they're working here when cleanup finished already, or why Joe's standing beside Riley and Morris, in gardening gloves and a neon long-sleeve tee looking at home among the crew. They're all gathered outside the gate, clearly trying to play it cool, but Riley's toothy grin would be a dead giveaway even if Gavin hadn't already told me to expect a surprise.

Ted's holding the ridiculous balloons, and I'm sure even without seeing our linked hands, everyone here knows we're a couple. But my worries about passing the point of no return have vanished. This feels like how it was meant to be all along. Gavin and me, in love.

We reach the group, and he says, "Thought I'd have more time to finish this before I showed you."

"Didn't stop him from guilting us into helping him work on it," Morris says, and Riley elbows him. "What? I just don't want him to take all the credit."

"Mia helped out at the other lot," she says. "During Community Give-back weekend we cleared out all the bushes."

"Had the blisters to prove it," I agree, raising my hand to show them, though it's already healed.

Gavin squeezes my shoulder. "I still feel awful about your soft writer hands."

"Soft?" I fake a scowl. "Let's see you churn out ten thousand words in a day while on deadline. Calluses or not, these hands get the job done."

"They do," he agrees. And it might be my imagination, but I swear there's a wicked twinkle in his eye. "Soft but mighty." He drops his voice. "Not a bad thing to be vulnerable sometimes," he says against my ear, and the barest caress of his lips sends tingles up my spine.

"Quit flirting and show her already," Riley says, and this time, Morris nudges her.

"It's all about timing," he says. "Let the man have his moment."

"On that note," Joe says, "we'll leave you to it." He takes off his gloves and tucks them in his back pocket. Passing by, he pauses, voice pitched low so the others won't hear. "Sera's expecting an update on the happy couple after the premiere."

I laugh, knowing he's not talking about me and Gavin.

Ted follows, and I offer a quick smile of gratitude. He grins back. "Guess you found another ride to the airport?" I look up at Gavin to confirm and he dips his chin in a nod.

"She did. Thanks, man." He and Ted are always civil, but

there's a new undercurrent of respect in Gavin's voice that warms my heart.

The others head out, too, Riley shushing Morris's complaint about doing all that work only to miss the big reveal. When they're gone, I heave a sigh of relief. I love Gavin and I don't care who knows, but I'm grateful for this moment to ourselves.

"Close your eyes." He turns so he's standing directly in front of me. "Or better yet, can I borrow this?" He points at the scarf I've tied around my curls.

"What if I promise to not peek?"

"You cheat at every game."

I don't bother to deny it. "I'll look a mess if I take it off now."

He shakes his head. "You don't have to, but you look beautiful, always."

Cheeks warm, I unwind it and hand him the length of cloth.

"Not how I imagined this going," he says, winding the scarf around my eyes. "But maybe even better." He comes around behind me and the scarf pulls tighter, a light pressure against the back of my head. "This okay?" he asks, breath warm against my neck, and my whole body lights up with sensation.

I start to nod, then swallow. "Yes."

His hand settles on my shoulder, fingertips sliding along the seam of my shirt. Lips press against my neck, and I melt back against him, steady, like he's always been, but now he's mine.

Another kiss, this one to the sensitive spot just behind my ear. "We'll have to remember this," he says, and I don't know if he's talking about the blindfold or the moment we reconciled, but I breathe out my answer.

"Yes."

Then his presence at my back is gone and he takes my shaky hands in his. I keep my eyes pinched shut as promised but picture him in front of me, tall and sturdy, a joyful, cautious grin lighting up his blue eyes. Tugging gently, he leads me forward, step by small step. "Almost there," he says. "Stay here."

I wobble with uncertainty as he lets go. The creak of hinges reaches my ears, followed by the hiss of grass scraped by the metal gate, then he's back.

"No peeking."

"I'm not." But impatience tinges my words, and he chuckles.

"It's killing you not to."

"And you're loving it," I grumble, but he puts a gentle hand on my shoulder, stopping me.

"We're here." I fight the urge to tug off the blindfold, rewarded when he does it for me, loosening the knot with a gentle tug until the fabric slips free.

I'm startled to find we're standing in the middle of a garden.

"Don't be too harsh," he says. "It's a work in progress."

I know a thing or two about those, but it doesn't look like the early stages of a project. An arched entry swoops overhead, painted letters in bold hues proclaiming FIFTH STREET COMMUNITY GARDEN LIBRARY, and below, ALL ARE WELCOME.

The overgrown lot I pass by on my coffee-shop commute is now a beautiful garden with wrought iron benches placed under freshly planted trees along the paved paths. Flowering bushes frame the boundary, with a sprawling fountain made out of river rocks as the focal point.

"Gavin, it's gorgeous." A clear-front cabinet near the entrance catches my eye, and I walk over, peering inside at shelves lined with books. Some have well-loved covers, the colors faded, spines creased. Others look brand-new. I look around and see several more enclosed shelves along the path.

Overcome, I turn and find Gavin standing with hands in his pockets, bashful. "How long have you been planning this?"

"Thinking of it?" He bites his lip. "A long time. You helped me fall in love with reading, and I wanted to honor that by making a space where the community could gather and enjoy books."

"So you've had this in the works for a while." Legs feeling

wobbly, I sit on a nearby bench and take it all in, unable to believe what he's done in just a few days.

He palms his neck, looking shy. "Yes, long before I realized I was in love with you. But I think a part of me has always known."

If I had to craft the perfect declaration of love, and I do, many times over, I couldn't have come up with anything so perfect. But I don't need to create this grand gesture, because Gavin already has, for me. I hold his words in my heart. Let them sink in and take root.

He comes closer and sits next to me. "I wanted to believe that what we had was just friendship. But with you, it's both. I can't separate how much I love spending time with you from how much I want to kiss you. Hold you. Make you mine. Once upon a time, my dad told me to never marry my best friend, but I never expected my best friend would be you."

And that's when I know with absolute certainty that I don't want to settle for just okay. I want to be with the man who's loved me in every season. Who's always been a midnight text away.

Unable to bear even the smallest space between us, I scoot closer to him, awed by the beauty around us, the unrealized potential he brought to life. "I thought I needed to know how things would end to fall in love, but it turns out all I needed was to be on the journey with you."

I'm surprised to feel so at ease confessing my feelings, but then again, I've never felt the need to censor myself around Gavin. Turning to him, I say, "I love you, Gavin, and I'm ridiculously happy every moment I'm with you."

"Except when we're telling the characters in rom-coms to just kiss already."

"You're right," I tell him. "That's downright blissful."

He laughs and presses a kiss to my forehead. "I love you, Mia."

"As a friend?" I can't resist teasing, but his expression turns solemn, full of love and promise.

"As everything."

epilogue

Mia

The hammock sways as Gavin pivots the laptop to face me. Leaves rustle overhead, butterflies flitting between fragrant blossoms by the new greenhouse he put up this spring. "All you have to do is fire up the number generator." After years of hearing me complain about the chore of naming characters, he finally suggested I make a list and choose one at random.

My arm is wedged beneath his, so I press my cheek against his shoulder. "You do the honors." Obligingly, he navigates to the browser and inputs a number range of one to forty-three but doesn't click the button.

"I can't be the one to do it," he says. "Don't want to be responsible."

"Oof, fine." I leverage myself up, the woven rope of the hammock digging into my elbow as I tap the button and watch the spinning circle that's about to decide the name of my next hero. "Twenty-five." Falling back, I cover my eyes with my arm. "Please don't let it be Legolas." The elf's name was Gavin's sole, entirely unhelpful contribution to the list.

"If it's Legolas, you're using it. That's the deal."

"My publisher would veto."

"Okay, but in draft zero, it's Legolas or nothing."

I peek from under my arm. "Is it actually Legolas?"

Gavin shoots me a grin. "Nah. It's Toby."

"As in Tobias?" I squint up at the wisps of clouds in the afternoon sky, trying to remember putting that one on the list.

"As in you have your hero." He shifts the laptop to my outstretched legs, the plastic warm against my bare thighs where my cotton dress has gotten bunched. "Go forth and do your magic."

Toby. Tobias. I roll the name around in my mind, trying it out. Stalling. But Gavin is already clambering out of the hammock. He never reads over my shoulder, unlike the rest of my friends with whom I have to slam the laptop shut the moment they enter the room. Then again, he's not just a friend. Not anymore.

He's halfway to the house, walking along the tidy brick path between hydrangeas and rosebushes, when I call out, "How old is Toby?"

"Thirty-three," he answers without turning around. "No kids, two parrots."

"Parrots?"

He does turn then, walking backward. "To keep each other company. They live a long time."

"Don't be getting any ideas," I warn him. "What would the cats do?" We didn't keep them all, but we couldn't let Mama Cat go after all she'd been through, and Cedar had sunk his tiny kitten claws into our hearts from the start. Morris pushed past his fear of screwing up pet ownership and adopted Ash, who now has her own social media account, and Sera surprised us by taking Juniper home to keep her company while on bed rest. Their daughter is infatuated with him.

I don't catch Gavin's reply because I've already slipped on my noise-canceling headphones. A new book is always a mix of excitement and intimidation, but now I'm writing with the

knowledge that I'm not weaving fairy tales, I'm writing possibilities.

Hours later, I reach the end of a chapter and glance away
from the screen to find Gavin watering the patch of daylilies
by the shed. He's dressed to go out, and twilight paints him in
smudges of purple and blue. When did the sun set?

Taking off my headphones, the soothing sound of falling
water reaches my ears, the orange flowers swaying under the
near-invisible spray from the garden hose. "How long have you
been out here?"

"Not long. I just got off the phone with Mom and Dad. He
surprised her with concert tickets." His parents have reconciled,
though they aren't remarried. According to his mom, they're
taking things slow this time around, but seeing them date is the
cutest thing ever. "You were really caught up." He stoops to
turn off the tap. "Nice to see you writing instead of struggling
with names."

"You're taking credit for the success of randomness?"

He comes over and I tip my chin up for a kiss. "If you
think I'd ever take credit for your success, then you're not seeing clearly."

As if to prove his point, he removes my glasses, the earpiece
catching on one of my braids. Gently, he reaches behind my
ear and frees them. He wipes the lenses clean on the hem of
his shirt, then, with a satisfied hum, puts them on himself. The
black frames that are Book Nerd Basic on me look outright
dashing on him, especially with his crisp button-down.

"You're awfully dressed up." Though *awful* isn't how I'd describe him. His cheeks are pink, freshly shaved, hair gelled into
a neat style that likely won't last through the opening credits of
the season-four watch party Riley has planned.

"Not every day I get to attend a premiere." He came with
me a couple years ago, right after we finally got together, but I
brought my sister and Ted to the premiere of this season, so this

will be Gavin's first glimpse of Sydney and Victor as a couple, on-screen, that is. "Better hurry or we'll be late."

Passing him the laptop, I climb out of the hammock. "Would that be so terrible?" I never let on to anyone else, but Gavin knows how uncomfortable I feel to watch my books play out on-screen. Despite the actors' talent and the nuance brought out by the adaptation, I haven't gotten used to it.

He tucks the laptop under his arm, draping my headphones over his wrist, and not for the first time, I notice his strong forearms. Now those are the stuff of romance novel legend.

"Pretty sure Riley plans to use the fact that *The* Mia Brady is attending her watch party as social media bragging rights for life, so she might not be too happy if we skipped it." Gavin slips his free arm around my shoulder. "But I heard she's making book-themed snacks."

"Now that I can get behind." We stroll toward the house, walking hip to hip, absurdly close yet in sync, and if I had a pen, the moment would make a damn good metaphor, but I'm learning to soak up life and not hoard each moment, knowing inspiration comes when I let go.

An hour later, we're standing on the threshold of Riley's place, hand in hand. Gavin tugs me up against him after he rings the bell, and I rise on tiptoe to kiss his cheek, just as the door opens. Morris groans and shuts it in our faces.

We're both laughing when the door opens again, and this time it's Riley. Without hesitation, she waves us in. "Sorry Morris is a prude."

"Am not," he hollers from the kitchen. "I just don't need further evidence of how happy everyone else is when I'm about to be subjected to hours of on-screen romantic bliss."

"His date is a no-show," Riley explains, leading us through to the patio, where she's arranged a table of snacks and drinks. A projector screen is set up in the yard, blankets spread over the grass. As much as I love the glitz of Hollywood premieres, this is much more my scene.

"It's beautiful out here, thank you." The night is perfect. Warm, with stars twinkling overhead.

"Thank *you* for not giving up on the book," she says, pouring two glasses of wine. I reach for one, but she picks both up, clutching them against her chest. "Nuh-uh, these are mine. I'm going to need both to get through watching Robert cheat on me."

I chuckle as she goes and sets them on a low picnic table near the screen. Despite Gavin's worries over us being late, there's no one else here yet. After getting our own drinks, I lead him to the blanket farthest from the screen. Riley puts on the season trailer to test the projector, and I grab a pillow and wrap it around my ears, eyes squeezed shut. "I know I said I could do this," I say, probably speaking too loudly. "But I can't, it's too much."

Gavin gently peels the pillow away from one ear. "Would it help if I played the role of Victor?" He lowers his voice into a deeper register. "Sydney, you've got to get into character. We need—"

I let go of the pillow and shove it at his chest instead. "What have I told you about quoting my books?"

Shifting into his normal voice, he says, "We could go home if you want. But, Mia, look," he says, nudging me. I lift my eyes to the screen, but he shakes his head, gently turning my chin so I'm looking at the house, where a group of Riley's friends are coming out onto the patio.

Huddled by the snacks, they're focused on the screen, nudging each other when Victor whispers in Sydney's ear. "They're here because of you. It's okay to be proud of yourself. I couldn't be prouder."

He kisses my jaw, and my eyes drift shut. The next kiss parts my lips, and it's not a novel-ending, happy-ever-after kiss. It's a here-and-now, trust-in-us kind of kiss.

We break apart when the preview ends, plunging the yard into silence. A clap goes up from the new arrivals, and it hits me that this is what I worked for. This is why I never gave up. Because stories like this give people hope and happiness.

I wrote and rewrote until Sydney realized that letting down her defenses didn't leave her open to loss. It opened her up to love. I wrote my heart out so Jayla and Rob could get the spotlight they deserved. For the fans who've been with me since day one to get the story they craved. To hold up my end of the bargain for everyone who works on my books and the show's cast and crew. To prove to myself I have the power to write my own happy ending.

Morris comes over, plate stacked high with food. He's watching Riley with open interest. She's posing for a selfie with Robert's face on the title screen, angling her body to conveniently block Jayla. "She does know they're engaged, right?" Without waiting for our answer, he sets his plate on a blanket and strides over, beckoning for the phone to take the picture for her.

Gavin chuckles. "Guess it's not the worst thing his date didn't show."

"I think they'd be a good match."

"But, Mia, they're friends," he says, in a tone that insinuates, *the horror.*

I elbow him. "People can change their minds, you know. I came up with that theory when I was twenty-one."

"I'm just glad you're so open-minded it only took nearly a decade to revisit your conclusion," Gavin says, mischief sparkling in his eyes. Then he pulls me close and brushes his lips against my cheek. "I wish I'd known how to tell you how I felt back then."

I've wondered if he has regrets. It would be understandable, knowing he had feelings for me and kept them bottled up. But I'm grateful for our years of friendship, just as grateful as I am for this new phase in our relationship. I'm not sure I could love him as deeply as I do now without first learning how to love him without reservations.

"I wish I hadn't let worries of how we'd end up cloud things at the beginning," I say, searching his expressive blue eyes. "But I can't regret a single moment of our friendship."

"Regret?" His face clouds over, and he rests his hand on mine. "I don't regret a minute we spent together. All I'm saying is I wouldn't mind a few more kisses to look back on."

"Kisses, huh?" I thread my arms around his neck, fully aware we're on a lawn full of people, but no longer afraid they'll see just how hard I've fallen for the man I swore I'd never date. "Guess we'll have to make up for lost time."

"Nothing's ever been lost between us. I'm just glad we found our way to this."

"What a line." Morris's voice comes from above, and I look up to find him standing over us, hand pressed to his heart. "Mia, you'd better watch your back. This dude is coming for your job. The poetry." He staggers back, like he's swooning, and I laugh.

"Always room for more voices in romance," I say.

Gavin grins, his teeth a flash of white in the darkness. "Think I'll stick to cheering you on from the sidelines. But if you ever need a new assistant . . ." He pauses for dramatic effect. "I am *not* the man for the job."

With a laugh, I shake my head. "Workplace romance, fish-out-of-water . . . We don't need those tropes. Give me friends-to-lovers any day."

"Next you're going to be getting matching friendship brace-lets," Morris says with mock disgust, and Gavin gives him the middle finger, but his eyes never leave mine.

"I wouldn't mind getting matching jewelry someday," he says, his smile turning into something private and sincere. He lowers his hand to capture mine. "Not that we need to talk about it now."

I lock my fingers with his. "We talk about everything, Gavin. Why would our future be any different?" That's when I realize I haven't lost my best friend, I've just found a new way to love him.

acknowledgments

In case the dedication didn't make it obvious, happy endings are my absolute favorite. Don't let anyone tell you books that end happily aren't worthwhile, meaningful, or valid. The truth is, they're all of those things, and joy is worth celebrating.

Thank you to my agent, Rachel Brooks, for your encouragement and commitment to getting my books out into the world. To my editor, Errin Toma—your enthusiasm for this project meant so much. To the entire team at Canary Street Press, thank you for helping make this book a reality.

Huge thanks to my husband. I couldn't have found the time to finish Mia and Gavin's story without your support. I'm so grateful to my writing friends who continue to uplift me on this publishing journey. Deepest gratitude to readers, and to all the booksellers and librarians who have spread the word about my books—thank you.